BURNED

Spread-eagled, she lay atop a reflective sheet of metal. All around, an elaborate arrangement of mirrors and lenses had concentrated the sun's rays on her. With a small sigh, Mikani knelt next to the body and ran his hands over her, not quite touching.

There is no anger, here. Strange. Mikani smelled the girl's fear, feeling her agony in phantom shivers and pain. Terror, shards of emotional memories screamed against the very stone. But of the killer . . . the mirrors and lenses were clear. Empty, as if they'd known no human touch.

And yet, there is purpose . . .

He saw her struggle, as aftershocks of terror rather than visual images: the taste of blood from a bitten tongue, the pain of constraints against wrists and ankles, harsh stone against the girl's back, and the sickening scent of the charnel house her body became. *That would be so much simpler—to see, rather than feel.* Shivering, he turned away. Already, his head pounded in protest, and from a detached place in his mind, he knew that when he came down, he'd pay dearly.

BRONZE GODS

A. A. Aguirre

ACE BOOKS, NEW YORK

THE BERKLEY PUBLISHING GROUP
Published by the Penguin Group
Penguin Group (USA) Inc.
375 Hudson Street, New York, New York 10014, USA

USA | Canada | UK | Ireland | Australia | New Zealand | India | South Africa | China

Penguin Books Ltd., Registered Offices: 80 Strand, London WC2R 0RL, England
For more information about the Penguin Group, visit penguin.com.

BRONZE GODS

An Ace Book / published by arrangement with the authors

Copyright © 2013 by A. A. Aguirre.

Ace Books are published by The Berkley Publishing Group.
ACE and the "A" design are trademarks of Penguin Group (USA) Inc.

For information, address: The Berkley Publishing Group,
a division of Penguin Group (USA) Inc.,
375 Hudson Street, New York, New York 10014.

ISBN: 978-0-425-25819-4

PUBLISHING HISTORY
Ace mass-market edition / May 2013

PRINTED IN THE UNITED STATES OF AMERICA

10 9 8 7 6 5 4 3 2 1

Cover illustration by Cliff Nielsen.
Cover photograph © iStockphoto/Thinkstock.
Cover design by Judith Lagerman.
Interior text design by Kristin del Rosario.

For our beloved children,
who put up with us while we wrote this

Acknowledgments

First, Andres and I would like to thank each other. When I asked him who he wanted to mention in the acknowledgments, he said, "*You*, woman. I love you." Obviously, I feel the same. I'm glad I could help make his dreams come true, as he's been doing that for me for years. Other married couples have said they didn't think their marriage could survive a similar collaboration. Ours did, and, if anything, it's stronger. We created this together; it's forever, and *Bronze Gods* came out beautiful in the end.

Along the way, a number of people contributed to polishing this diamond. See, we wrote the first draft ten years ago, and since then, this book has changed faces more than Mystique; it's been rewritten more than eight times, and when we were on deadline, we penned two-thirds new material to make it live up to Anne Sowards's high standards. So that's where we'll begin.

Anne loved the world and the characters, but the plot was problematic, and she made us perform. We feared revisions might defeat us, but ultimately we got the job done, and we're so proud of this book. So thanks to her for being a demanding taskmaster. *Bronze Gods* is infinitely better for her input.

I suppose now it's time for the usual suspects. Thanks to our friends and family for understanding why we had no time while we were working on this. Thanks to the Loop That Shall Not Be Named for being there when my sanity was imperiled. I bow to Cliff Nielsen for a gorgeous, perfect cover and give gratitude to the whole Penguin team. Thanks to Enrique for always listening to Andres and being awesome. Kudos to the Schwagers, who are the best copy editors ever. Many, many thanks to Tricia Sullivan, an amazing writer, who read our book and helped us whip the timeline into shape so Anne didn't kill us. Much love to Laura Bradford for being a wonderful agent, and who doesn't know it but will soon be asked to sell our epic sea monster story. (Not really.)

Heartfelt thanks, finally, to all readers who take a chance on this book. And us.

Turning and turning in the widening gyre
The falcon cannot hear the falconer;
Things fall apart; the centre cannot hold;
Mere anarchy is loosed upon the world,
The blood-dimmed tide is loosed, and everywhere
The ceremony of innocence is drowned;
The best lack all conviction, while the worst
Are full of passionate intensity.

—W. B. YEATS

PROLOGUE

Long ago, ten princes lived across the waters and through the mists in a land called Hy Breasil. They governed the wild, fey folk who dwelled in that place, where every rock, tree, blade of grass, ripple of water, and whisper of the wind contained powerful magic. The Ferishers were terrible and immortal, but they were few. Yet even in those small numbers, they divided amongst themselves into two Courts.

The Summer Court embraced all those bright and beautiful while Winter plotted against them in briars and darkness. Into their eternal struggle came the barbarians: the bearded folk from another world—a sweeping, enormous one—outside the safe confines of Hy Breasil. In that land, ships went missing from time to time, their cargoes and crews simply vanished, no wreckage found. And so the conquerors came to Ferisher lands with their relentless drive, cold iron, and incomprehensible ways. With them, they brought mortal bloodlines.

After the long and bitter Iron War, both sides hovered at the brink of annihilation. The bearded ones bred quickly; they had numbers while the Ferishers had magic. Auberon, the most powerful of the princes, chose the loveliest of the human flotsam to keep the peace. His siblings followed suit. Those treaty-born marriages created a lasting peace and a new people. Thus the first ten great Houses were founded, though some failed to withstand the test of time.

THAT COURSE CREATED a schism in the Ferishers. Some felt it was better to fade and leave the physical world than to defile pure bloodlines. The two Courts fell into disarray, and eventually, eons later, only a handful could claim more than a flicker of fey blood. Hy Breasil changed forever, and the centuries marched on.

ONLY THE WIND knows what happens next . . .

CHAPTER 1

WAKING HAD NEVER BEEN EASY FOR JANUS MIKANI; WHERE others merely dreamt, he was seduced. His Ferisher blood brought visions of a different world than the one in which they lived. On rousing, he was left with a lingering headache and a sense of loss. That afternoon was no different as he wound his way through the thinning crowd toward South Ward Station, affectionately dubbed Southie. He paused at the corner to let an omnibus clatter past, blue eyes narrowed and hat braced against the breeze from its passage. Cradling the weathered cane under his arm, he resumed his trip and let his mind wander while force of habit guided his steps.

In his dreams, he was a gray knight, fighting for the honor of an icy, untouchable queen. By night, he wore dark, rumpled suits and fought against an unstoppable tide to control the city's sins. Most members of the Criminal Investigation Division had trouble adapting to sleeping during the daylight hours, but he was, in truth, more at home in the darkness. Sometimes he wondered if his dreams weren't truly glimpses of the world before, before the bearded strangers landed and the Courts splintered during the Iron Wars. Rarely, he'd heard of people dreaming future events, but never of the past.

Ah, well. I was ever backward.

Mikani shunned the steam coaches and hansoms that wound their way through the busier city streets, their rattling din mingling with the invective of pedestrians. The clamor had always seemed particularly out of place among the redbrick homes of South Ward; their tall, peaked roofs and simple lines had, for him, always evoked a time before steam and steel ruled supreme. A hansom chugged hard, then puffed out a cloud of tawny, bitter smoke and shuddered to a halt. Cursing roundly, the driver got out to check the boiler and ember sphere assembly, which drove all steam engines. The Houses kept close the secrets of binding fire elementals into the devices; other than what he'd once learned to keep an engine running smoothly, Mikani cared little for the hidden details. He moved past the driver and down the worn stone steps of the station.

Unlike most, he preferred the underground, likely from a combination of the comfort he'd always derived from dark places and his voyeuristic tendencies. After work, he sometimes surrendered to sleep as he rode the rails home, cocooned in the fading darkness until the rising din of the packed cars drove him out to find his way to his quiet cottage on the weathered cobblestone street, half-asleep and lost to the lure of dreams. It was a dangerous habit—an idiosyncrasy that would earn him an appointment with the headquarters mental examiner, should anyone report him. The demands of life as a Criminal Investigation Division inspector had wrecked more than one man's mind; Mikani would claim it was the work that kept him half-sane.

His reflections were less grim half an hour later when he emerged from the fading warmth of a half-empty car and stepped onto the scuffed marble floor of Central Station's main platform. The still air was redolent with oil and the scent of humanity. Wending his way through milling knots of people waiting for their trains and past columns whose carved reliefs he'd long since memorized, Mikani spotted a slender figure across the platform.

Celeste Ritsuko took the same car to headquarters each night, and she sat in the same seat. She wore her shiny raven hair parted on the left and bobbed neatly at chin level, and Mikani sometimes teased her that she used a slide rule to measure it. She used peach lip rouge to protect her mouth from the elements and nothing more in the way of adornment. She'd told Mikani that paint was a waste of time, better spent on other things.

Looking at her, it's hard to believe she keeps a knife in her boot.

As she did every evening, she checked her attaché case and credentials. Her glance wandered over him from across the platform, and she pursed her lips in faint disapproval. But he reveled in his slept-in chic and resisted her efforts to improve him. Wearing a faint smile, she crossed to his side.

As they went up the stairs and into the cool night, he said, "The darker it gets, the prettier she looks."

He gestured at the somber, baroque tower housing CID Headquarters, looming high above the neoclassic buildings and palazzi at the near edge of the park. HQ at Central was a relatively desirable assignment, second only to the Temple Constabulary Office. Other wards had higher crime rates, worse felons, and token law enforcement.

"Mmm." When Ritsuko took that particular tone, she was already obsessing about work. The solitary trait they shared was the tendency to be consumed by the tragedies that filled their nights. They just dealt with it differently.

"Mind if we stop for a drink?" he asked.

Ritsuko checked her timepiece. "It's fine. I'd hate for Electra to go a day without your pretty face."

Mikani laughed. "True. It would be criminal."

He had been buying his coffee from Electra for years. His favorite waitress was no delicate flower; her dark hair flowed to the small of her sturdy back. She had strong features, a sharp nose, and a determined chin, which probably contributed to her outcast state. As a daughter of the Summer Clan, wanderers who mysteriously appeared on the isles a scant century ago, she wasn't supposed to settle—to serve drinks or read cards in the same places year after year. But Electra did as she pleased, part of the reason he liked her. With such incredible power through their control over the shipping and transportation industry, the Summer Clan could easily force her to comply with their edicts, but so far, they'd let her sow her wild oats. Mikani was sure the patriarchs imagined she would get rebellion out of her system and return to the fold in due time.

"I'm glad I stayed late," the waitress said to him in greeting. "You're a mess."

"Espresso," he ordered, grinning. "You know how I like it. But then you know that I'm always a mess, too."

She fetched his drink, her brow furrowed. "A *different* mess. All red, black, and violet, frayed about the edges. That means bad things are headed your way."

Beside him, Ritsuko made a scoffing noise. Mikani didn't bother to read Electra, as she made her living from dire pronouncements. Half a dozen people would panic at such news. He wasn't one of them as he'd seen her trick forty silver crescents from a mark, only to have some mundane tragedy revealed.

He shook his head. "No reading today, thanks."

"Tomorrow," Electra predicted.

Laughing, he took his drink in the ceramic cup she trusted him to return, one of the benefits of being a favored customer. He turned to Ritsuko, who said, "So tell me what you did last night."

Mikani knew his romantic history fascinated his partner in a horrific sort of way. "Went home to an unmade bed and a note. Jane's gone to visit her brother. Or so she claimed. I doubt I'll ever hear her complain about my job again, though."

He'd been first to bring his relationships into casual conversation; it had since become a ritual of closure. Over the years, his partner had met a few of his women, and Mikani remained friends with a scant handful. The disappointment never lasted for more than a week or two.

Awkward silence reigned between them for a few seconds. Then Ritsuko touched him on the shoulder. All around them, tradesmen and heirs, dilettantes and nouveau riche made their way to and from their gorgeous homes, their days finished with the encroachment of evening. Mikani paid them no mind.

"Surprise. I have a story, too. Warren moved out last week."

He arched his brows at that bit of news. The memory of Jane's angry eyes receded as he glanced over at his partner. "Warren?" They drifted apart as they rounded different sides of a gaggle of bodyguards and sycophants holding some noble scion in their midst. When they resumed their side-by-side position, he continued. "I'm sorry to hear that." Even in sympathy, he couldn't

.

call her by her given name. "I thought nothing could come between the two of you."

She watched a hansom rumble past before she answered, her steps matching his. "You were right. God forbid I ever say it again, but you were right. You know, all the times you said we were just using each other?" She sighed and juggled her bag unnecessarily. A telling cue, because Ritsuko did not fidget. "We just looked at each other over dinner one night and knew. That it was pointless."

Mikani nodded. "I'm glad the two of you realized that in time. Now you can go and find someone worthwhile to build a future with. Someone completely unlike me." He winked and touched the tip of his hat to her as he turned to HQ's massive front doors.

"I feel guilty," she said.

He paused midstep and angled a penetrating look at her. "Why?"

"Because I denied my grandfather's dying wish . . . to see me settled with a respectable man. I followed my heart. And it led me to this." Her almond-shaped brown eyes conveyed rueful sorrow. "I'm a ruined woman, unmarriageable by contract now, and for what gain?"

"I know it's traditional for you to . . ." He trailed off, unsure how to best express the custom of choosing a mate from a buffet of dossiers compiled by the bride's family.

"It's the only way to safeguard our heritage and cultural identity," she said.

But he could tell she was only parroting her grandfather; and her regret came from disappointing the old man in his last days. "For what gain? Freedom. If you'd accepted one of the choices your grandfather offered, you'd be bound for life, no matter how you felt."

"True. The flat is emptier now than I realized it would be." Her tone was almost soft, or the closest Ritsuko ever came to it. She appeared to realize her mistake at once and increased her pace. "Nearly time to start the madness."

"That it is." He stood at the top of the steps, looking up the elaborately carved stone of the building's facade, toward recessed windows and decorative motifs in dark granite, darker than the smoke-attenuated night sky. "So. You don't want me to hunt him down like a dog?"

Mikani enjoyed her startled expression. The little grin he tried to hide said it all; her glare spoke volumes on his sense of humor. Together, they entered the cathedral-like CID Headquarters, weathered gargoyles and carved Furies watching their passage.

As with any old, refurbished building, the fixtures were past their prime, and the gas lamps flickered at odd moments, throwing shadows that wavered with lives of their own. The dingy green tiles showed wear from the countless feet that had tramped up and down the aisles, being led to holding cells, shipped to the penal farms and exile . . . or if they were fortunate, bonded into the custody of someone willing to take responsibility for their misdeeds.

At night, a light crew worked in their department—Criminal Investigation Division, Park Ward—comprised of Mikani, his partner, Inspector Celeste Ritsuko, and Anatole, the man who mopped the floors. There were officers with other assignments down the hall, and other city wards and Council divisions, each located in its own hole in the sprawling complex. They all sacrificed their own officers nightly, lest the cogs of the great machine grow cluttered with criminals and the city shudder to a stop.

Night brought a particular madness, as they had quickly learned. All the depravity, mayhem, and deviance that hid itself from the day oozed into the streets like runoff from a sewer. And without fail, much of it landed on Mikani and Ritsuko.

Sometime later, he engrossed himself in piling documents on his desk, arranging them so they wouldn't collapse in disarray too soon. Anatole and Ritsuko's matched disapproval of this pastime only made it more appealing, but over the years, she'd learned to express her discontent with stern looks instead of nagging.

"The moment it falls, I'll start filing them." He did not even need to glance at his partner to know she was glaring at him.

Given the city's tendencies, the silence rarely lasted long. So it was no surprise when a whoosh announced mail from the sorting facility—a system of pneumatic tubes permitted citizens to send messages and small packages back and forth throughout the sprawling city of Dorstaad. More sensitive correspondence was entrusted to a private courier. Ritsuko moved to fetch it, but Mikani already knew the gist. The incident report comprised the beginning of a tale unlikely to have a happy ending. Clumsy with the weariness of boredom, he ambled over to read across Ritsuko's shoulder as sheaves of paper cascaded to the floor.

"We have a missing House scion," she said.

He swore beneath his breath. Offspring of the great Houses tended to be spoiled, rarefied, and persuaded of their own importance. Given the power and wealth attached to their stations, he couldn't entirely blame them, but drawing this case would complicate their lives. Leaving the mess of scattered documents, they hustled toward the lift, a monstrous cage of iron and bronze. Each time it groaned into motion, Mikani thought it might be preparing to tear free from its gears and pulleys to send them plummeting into darkness. But like a crotchety old woman, it did the job, just not without complaint. They alit on the subterranean level, where the sleek steel-and-brass cruisers were parked.

Mikani favored the red one with white-rimmed tires. It also had been equipped with a ceramic condenser by an aspiring engineer, long since gone north—and it could, in theory, be pushed well beyond the posted speed limit for mechanical conveyances within city limits. Anything that required less maintenance was a good thing; and as Mikani saw it, anything that could outrace House roadsters was a great thing. As luck would have it, Big Red was waiting for them, and he claimed the keys from the tyro with a half smile. He'd once minded the CID vehicles, so he knew what it was like to watch other officers jaunt off to their investigations.

MIKANI DROVE LIKE a man possessed, which Ritsuko sometimes thought he was. He wove through the chaotic traffic with hard jerks of the steering wheel and taps of the brakes, the cruiser's rumbling a counterpoint to his murmured imprecations about other drivers and some pedestrians. Certainly, he had issues, but she had long since given up trying to reform him. Mostly, he was a rogue with good intentions.

They had been partners for just over three years. At first, she'd resented being assigned to someone with such unorthodox methods; it was an open secret at HQ that Mikani had been blessed with a unique ability to ferret out information he shouldn't possess, both at crime scenes and about potential suspects. Ritsuko thought that was office gossip until she saw him in action. Unquestionably, his talent was real—and it hurt him. Sometimes she worried about the consequences of using his gift as often as he did, but their closing rate depended as much on his uncanny methods as her own impeccable attention to detail.

Dorstaad was a dark mistress tonight. Clouds hung heavy over the city, threatening rain. Mikani was silent as he navigated the last turn and stopped the cruiser with a muted hiss of venting steam. As she stepped out, the wind felt chill on her bare fingers. Fashion demanded she wear a hat and gloves, but such frippery got in her way during the course of an investigation. Tonight, the air carried a hint of damp inland from the sea, a whisper of salt, as if the wind were kissed with tears.

House Aevar occupied several blocks across city center southwest of the park; their holdings proclaimed their power. They took heritage seriously and liked to glorify themselves, which had to be taken into account during questioning. With a daughter of the house gone missing, these interviews would require tact. Ritsuko flashed her credentials for the security bondsman guarding the gates. His gaze followed her, as if disapproving of a mannish woman who worked for a living and wore split skirts. Mikani ambled in her wake, his lazy manner concealing a vicious streak.

The monolithic walls rose into the night sky. Built to impress, the front doors stood wide and tall; beyond, the atrium within held enough art and luxury to awe any visitor. These details, however carefully arranged to enhance that effect, seemed lost on Mikani as he marched through, striding over the hand-woven carpet with a tap of cane and sharp slap of heel. He paused a moment, his dark blue gaze drifting from one door to another and ignoring the servant signaling the way into the drawing room. Ritsuko hoped he wouldn't cause trouble or offense, both of which were her partner's specialties.

Under ordinary circumstances, they wouldn't even be here. The girl had been gone for a day—not long, perhaps, but sufficient to alarm her family. Murder was their métier, and they only attended on missing persons under two circumstances—if the family was powerful or there was some reason to suspect foul play. In this case, Ritsuko suspected it was both, and Mikani was sensing . . . something. She watched as he canted his head, attending to currents undetectable to an average person.

At last he said, "Come on, then. Let's see if we can get at the truth."

She nodded, leading the way into the interrogation chamber, for no matter how luxuriously it was appointed, she treated the people in it the same as she did those who were confined at the CID. That was to say, she treated all suspects better than most. This space, however, put the drab gray interview room to shame, with its silken carpets, luxurious wall hangings, and the hand-carved table upon which a porcelain-and-gilt tea service perched.

Donning her helpful smile, she extended a hand to the gentleman who was clearly the head of the House. Despite silver at his temples and lines about the eyes, Oleg Aevar still retained considerable charisma. Most of his attention was devoted to a pale woman weeping into a linen handkerchief, but he broke away to greet them.

Aevar clasped her hand. "Officers," he said in such a gracious tone that she found it off-putting.

House scions didn't waste courtesy on underlings unless they had something to hide. She'd been promoted as the first female inspector, and she meant to have that achievement acknowledged, even by Oleg Aevar. No matter his station, she wouldn't permit him to treat her like a coffee girl. Her face reflected none of those thoughts, but she corrected his mode of address.

"I am Inspector Ritsuko, and this is my partner, Mikani. We know this is a troubling time, and please be aware that any questions we ask, which may seem difficult or insensitive, are intended only to help you find your daughter"—her gaze skimmed from wan woman to older man—"and your granddaughter. Shall we get started?"

"By all means," Aevar said.

She sat beside Mikani on a small settee while Aevar claimed one of the damask striped chairs opposite. The other woman held a fine, lace-trimmed handkerchief to her face, daubing at tears that kept trickling. If she wasn't mistaken, Aevar looked a little impatient with his daughter. Ritsuko could almost read his thoughts. *Don't show weakness in front of the help. You're better than this.*

"When did you become aware Miss Aevar had gone missing?" Ritsuko asked.

Aevar exchanged a look with his daughter, then he answered, "Cira never returned home last night."

"Is that unusual behavior?" Some House scions liked to kick over the traces, spend time with unsuitable companions, drink and gamble, before settling into profitable marriages contracted by their families.

The girl's mother spoke for the first time. "Yes. Cira doesn't have a wild bone in her body. She comes home every night by ten of the clock, without fail."

Except last night, Ritsuko thought, glancing at her partner.

Mikani's reading them. She didn't altogether approve, mostly because of the suffering it inflicted on her partner, but there was no denying its effectiveness. Though the CID didn't officially sanction it, the practice wasn't verboten, either. They accepted that some of their officers possessed Ferisher blood, so why not make use of such tricks, glamours, and small magics? Sadly, she had none, just logic and dogged persistence.

"Have you been in contact with her friends and acquaintances?"

Aevar nodded. "I sent word round to all her companions. Nobody has seen her or admits to knowing where she might be."

"I'll need a list of those names," she said. He nodded, then she went on, "Did your granddaughter have any enemies? Anyone you can imagine wishing her ill?"

"Of course not," the girl's mother gasped.

Ritsuko ignored the hint of shock and outrage in the other woman's voice, directing her next query to the man across from her. "What about you, sir?"

A stunned silence followed, which she took for surprise; it had never occurred to Oleg Aevar that his rivals might use his grandchild against him. To his credit, the man gave the question due consideration, before nodding.

"I'll make a list of those who might believe they have reason to harm Cira because of me."

"Thank you. Do you have any information on who saw her

last? Did you find anything in her suite to give you a clue where she might've gone?"

Cira's mother hiccuped out a sob. "No, there's nothing. No trace . . . it's like she's vanished into thin air."

That's impossible. There's always a trail, however faint. But she didn't argue with the distraught woman. "We'd like to see her room now, please."

As Aevar stood, Mikani signaled her with a nod, and she fell into step with him. Some distance behind, they trailed the old man down the hallway. "There's something odd about this." His whispered words were barely above a breath, meant for her ears alone. "I can feel it."

A girl has vanished without a trace. That's not odd enough? As if he heard her thought, Mikani's mouth compressed into a white line. The lack of evidence was enough to drive a person crazy, not that Mikani had that far to go. He worried her with his sixth sense and his hunches. But there was no denying he knew how to read people.

"Verdict?" she whispered.

"They're truly frightened. Aevar's a little angry, too. No deception, though."

At times like this, he was uncanny, and if he said the family had nothing to do with the girl's vanishing act, then she believed him. In silence, they followed Aevar to the elevator cage, Mikani pausing here or there, canting his head in touch with some reality no one else shared.

To distract the patriarch from Mikani's behavior, she fell into step with him, encouraging him to remember happier times, which often provided small clues regarding the victim's life. Hints that when relatives dug after them, resisted being brought to light. By the time the lift stopped, she had a pretty good idea what type of person Cira Aevar had been.

Victim. Had been. Mentally, Ritsuko chastised herself for having formed a conclusion without evidence to support it. But she was not without instincts of her own, or she would never have passed the CID's rigorous qualifying exams to become an inspector. All those instincts told her that Cira Aevar would never be seen alive again.

Aevar could not bear to enter his granddaughter's room, so

he excused himself, leaving the inspectors to conduct their investigation in private. Done in pink, ivory, and gold, the suite confided that it had housed a young girl, one with varied interests and rather sweet taste. At once, Ritsuko paused, letting Mikani pursue his practice of touching and pausing and ambling on, before she began the more scientific aspects.

"Check the window, would you?" Mikani sounded distracted already.

With a faint sigh, she got to work.

CHAPTER 2

MIKANI'S WORLD SHRUNK TO FINGERTIPS AND INSTINCT, BEYOND
sight and smell. Slowly, he drifted through the room, eyes closed
to a slit under an intense frown. Surfaces slid under his fingertips,
the thin kid leather gloves a hindrance he could compensate for
after long practice. With the careful touch of a surgeon, he
started his round. Cira Aevar had left her mark here. Scents of
joy and pain mingled in her pillows; the grit of arguments dusted
desk and bedspread. Brighter than those echoes burned the passion in the sketches littering her drawers and hidden between
pages of heavy books. He flipped through to find that they
showed various articles of clothing: a fetching hat, an elegant
skirt paired with a tailored jacket. From what he knew of fashion,
the designs appeared to be good.

Under the commonplace, however, he caught a glimmer of
something else. Contrasting with Cira's shadow and memory,
recent enough to be barely discerned. The trace tasted odd, nothing he'd ever experienced before. His nose filled with the scent
of copper, not blood, but deeper and sweeter, layered with dust
and a touch of decay. It was not, precisely, the scent of the grave,
but that was as close as he could come; it was wrongness, a presence that no longer belonged to the natural world.

"Someone besides the family has been here." That much, he
gave his partner. The other impression, he'd keep to himself until
he could articulate it. "Keep a sharp eye out."

He blinked, trying to clear his head. The headache would get
worse; better to hurry while he could still see. "Don't think there
was sexual activity, but I'll check the sheets. Something's really
not right."

There was no question that Ritsuko recognized the symptoms
of an impending attack. Her gaze was sharp with concern as she
nodded. "We'll get you back to HQ as soon as possible. I'll be
quick."

He stepped toward the bed, giving his partner space to work
around the desk. The sheets were cool, misted with Cira and
sweat, a whisper of her nightmares, the faintly floral scent of her
dreams. He had the impression the missing girl had enjoyed
gardens and that she sometimes cried herself to sleep. Most
nights, however, she was content enough, a princess in her tower.
The feedback from such glimpses sliced through his skull like
a knife; the pain was instantaneous.

Ritsuko went to her hands and knees, examining the carpet
with a magnifying glass. Mikani knew she would leave no stone
unturned. Through vision gone hazy, he watched her open drawers and search for hidden treasures. Before long, the girl's secrets
lay exposed on the floor in the way of erotic etchings and lingerie,
a handful of crystal bottles that doubtless contained the latest
street drug, and which her family would be shocked to discover.
Or they would pretend, at least.

"What do you make of this?" Brandishing a small case in a
gloved hand, she showed him her find, tapping the greasy streak
on the box.

Mikani straightened from his perusal of a drawing that had
drifted under the bed. His red-rimmed eyes had stopped tearing,
at least; the waves of pain came regularly enough for him to do
his work in fits and starts. "A sewing kit? Odd. She'd have no
reason to mend her own clothing. What's the smudge?"

He was careful not to reach for the case, suffering too much
to risk a wash of what it meant to the girl just yet. Together, the
clothing sketches and the quality needles added up to a significant clue, but he lacked the wherewithal to draw the connection

at the moment. Just as well, Ritsuko excelled at such logical deductions.

"Looks like some kind of makeup. We'll know for sure once we get back to the lab and test it." Ritsuko glanced around, then walked over to the shelves, where several books of memorabilia occupied places of honor.

"Good thinking," he murmured.

He knew his partner sought more casual photos of the girl, not the posed portrait that her family had displayed. Laying hands on an album, she paged through until she found what she was looking for. Tapping it with a fingertip, she showed him the picture. "Plain. She didn't wear paint, did she? I think we're done here."

"We are." Mikani surveyed the room one last time. They had found no sign of forced entry. Windows and locks had not been tampered with; they had found none of the telltale minutiae left behind in a struggle. Moreover, there was no emotional residue hinting at violent distress. "No clothes missing."

He knew Ritsuko would have gathered as much already; he also knew he would forget if he did not reinforce the observations with words. That was the price he paid for the rest. "Let's get this to the lab, then. We'll have the bereaved relatives down tomorrow. See if they remember anything on our ground. Shall we?" He turned an expectant look toward her.

With a nod, she waved him out. He knew she'd smooth things over with the Aevars as a matter of course. It was a pattern they'd fallen into early on; Ritsuko eased his path over the details, and he cut corners so they wasted less time in grunt work.

Before too long, they returned to the cruiser. He wasn't steady enough to drive, so she did. This, too, was part of their routine. He drove out to all their crime scenes, but she manned the wheel on the way back if he used his gifts at all. An ice pick tapped quietly inside his brain, so he missed most of the journey. Blessedly, Ritsuko chose to be silent, knowing that words would only ratchet up the pain. At times he questioned whether the payout was worth the price, but whenever they brought someone home or delivered a killer to the scales of justice, he decided it was, all over again.

He sat in the cruiser while she signed forms with the

requisition officer. At her signal, he slid out. The world reeled, and he was half a shade from dissolving. He set a hand on the steel door as his partner came over, ostensibly to collect her attaché case, but in reality, she offered him an escort. Other officers were used to seeing her on his arm, and sometimes they joked about inappropriate relations, but the truth was, he often wouldn't make it back up to HQ without her steadiness at his side.

The ride in the lift set his stomach to churning, and he fought the building migraine. When Mikani opened his eyes, the room swam with ghosts. Stale memories of despair and guilt, sharp flashes of anger left behind by killers and their captors. The flickering lights felt oily against his skin . . . their spreading coronas indicating he'd soon be incapacitated. He'd opened himself too fully in Cira's room, been profligate with his gift, and now he'd suffer the consequences.

Ritsuko fetched him a drink; he took the glass wordlessly. After the first sip, he closed his eyes. Rubbing the bridge of his nose, he leaned back as far as he could in the uncomfortable chair. This case marked the beginning of a hell of a mess; he just knew it.

Poor girls from the tenements down in Iron Cross might go missing, and nobody would bat an eye. But let some pretty House scion get taken, and the newssheets would be screaming about it first thing in the morning. The City Council then called the commander, who in turn put the boot to their backsides. Sometimes, the divide between privation and privilege rubbed him the wrong way, but he loved his job too much to do anything but complain inside his head.

"How are you feeling?"

"I just need some time. And quiet." And a couple of chemical solutions that would win him a long, impassioned lecture on treating his body like a temple. While Mikani appreciated his partner's concern, he had his own methods of coping.

"Will you be able to get home?"

"If I say no, will you take me there and tuck me in?" It wasn't the first time he'd teased her thus.

The wrinkle on her brow evolved from concern to aggravation. Truth be told, he preferred the latter. "Of course not. I'd just enjoy some advance notice if you mean to get yourself murdered on the underground. I'd like to scout who my new partner might be."

"Your sensibilities never cease to charm me," he said, managing a half smile.

The resurgence of his skewed humor seemed to reassure her. "Oh, shut up."

As Ritsuko eased into her chair, Mikani opened his eyes and gave her a nod in appreciation for the night's work. "Let's file this and get out of here."

"Your turn," she said.

And it was. She only cut him so much slack, after all. Document in hand, he filled in the details on the missing girl; that done, he set the toggles for the index-card press.

A person reduced to numbers and codes, a few comments, to be filed away.

"GO HOME. I'LL drop the evidence off at the lab." It was easy to be kind to Mikani when he looked as if he had been dragged six blocks behind a hansom.

"Thanks. You're the best." Her partner pushed to his feet, somewhat unsteady, but she trusted that if he were seriously incapacitated, he would forgo that dreadful sense of humor long enough to ask for help.

Once she put the forms Mikani had filled out in the correct bins, Ritsuko gathered up her things and headed for the lift. This late, Anatole was probably taking his meal break, so the hall was quiet, eerily so. Flickering gaslight threw ominous shadows on the walls as she stepped out of the bronze cage. The lab was housed in the lower levels of HQ, affectionately called the Dungeon by those who had reason to utilize its services.

Like the rest of the division, Analysis and Laboratory Services struggled with budgetary and payroll issues, so there was only one man in the austere room when she pushed through the doors. With tired gray paint and cold stone walls, the Dungeon earned its name. It was a large, cold room where bodies could be stored without risk of immediate decomposition, and there were four tables overburdened with various types of equipment.

The scientist who had the misfortune to work the witching

shift from midnight to eight in the morning glanced up as she came in. Cyril Higgins was also the youngest member of the team, only four years out of the Academy, where he had studied the latest forensic techniques and could be relied on to run experiments that other lab specialists would refuse for fear of failure or loss of prestige. Ritsuko wished she could've persuaded her grandfather to send her to school there, but he'd said higher education was wasted on a woman; that was a pity since the Academy had opened its doors to female pupils in recent years. *I would've loved to enroll.* The foremost institution of higher learning in Dorstaad offered so many intriguing study options for girls of moderate means, not only business and clerical skills but hard sciences such as engineering and mathematics, as well as softer courses like art and literature for those of a more romantic bent. With a wistful sigh, she put aside thoughts of missed opportunities and focused on the task at hand.

Higgins was a tall man, well over six feet, with the pallor of one who never voluntarily sought the sun; only a splash of freckles saved him from looking ill. His hair was perpetually in disarray though it was an agreeable shade of ginger, complementing bottle-green eyes, shaded by a pair of silver spectacles.

"What can I do for you?" he asked cheerfully.

Ritsuko greeted him with an answering smile, as many inspectors didn't bother to do. They also waited a lot longer for their lab results. She'd learned that she was better off entrusting her requests to Higgins anyway, as the older scientists disapproved of her on principle, and therefore, they dragged their heels on her work, perhaps thinking that if they delayed enough, her cases would become impossible to close, thus causing her to be discharged for incompetence. She walked a constant line, and sometimes the effort to remain in balance was dizzying.

"I need you to analyze this sample, please. See if you can figure out what it is." She slid him the evidence packet, along with a properly annotated request form. "Whenever it's convenient."

By his appreciative look, he rarely received such courtesy. Ritsuko was sure other inspectors couched their requests in the form of demands for immediate information, mostly because she had worked as an assistant in the Dungeon, early in her career, and the men had barked at her as if she were both deaf and mentally defective. There would be less traffic at this hour, but she didn't imagine the late hour offered any improvement in a boor's manners.

"As it happens, I can set aside what I'm working on and tackle this immediately." He offered a conspiratorial grin, inviting her to share this quiet revenge, the only kind people like them ever enjoyed.

"I appreciate that tremendously. Do you need anything, Mr. Higgins? I could fetch you a cup of tea or coffee before I go."

"Tea would be lovely, if you don't mind. One sugar and milk."

"I'll be right back. I remember where the lounge is."

The room where specialists took their rest didn't offer a lot more warmth than the Dungeon, as it was just down the hall. In an attempt at comfort, someone had put down a rug, and there were some armchairs, but mostly it was a dank, depressing room. She put the kettle on the gas cooker and waited for it to whistle, then she found the requested milk and sugar to prepare the cup. In a moment of inspiration, she added a few biscuits to make it a snack as well. All told, it was an endeavor of five minutes, but the delight on Mr. Higgins's face made it obvious it had been time well spent. Ritsuko was not, by nature, a nurturer, but she had found that small kindnesses often delivered excellent results when provided to people who did not generally receive them.

Higgins set the cup and saucer aside to let the tea cool. "If you'd care to wait, there's a simple test I can run to determine basic chemical composition."

"It would be my pleasure." Wistfully, she considered the comfort of her empty bed, but if ten minutes meant a head start on the investigation the following day, it made sense to keep Higgins company.

The scientist had a number of odd mannerisms as he went about his work, but some of them were endearing, such as the way he bounced on the balls of his feet. Sleepy, she made polite conversation, asking about his family as a matter of course, but he seemed to take it as a profound gesture. Higgins paused, one hand flattened on the counter, as some strong emotion stirred in him.

"I . . . That is, thank you. I didn't realize you knew my mother was ill."

Ritsuko hadn't had a clue, but she said, "I hope she is improved?"

"I've taken her to the best physicians, and I do hope for a successful treatment soon."

"You have all my best wishes for a speedy recovery."

Five minutes more of this, and Higgins glanced up from his microscope with an excited air. "It is as I suspected from the aroma and texture. This is a cosmetic, greasepaint. It's much thicker than you'd usually see, though. Perhaps something a theater or a performing troupe might use."

She recalled the sewing kit, the intricate fashionable design sketches. "That's a valuable clue, Mr. Higgins. It gives us an excellent place to begin on the morrow."

"My pleasure."

"Good evening," she said, turning toward the door.

"Miss Ritsuko." The words came in a rush, as if he couldn't believe he was speaking them. "I had heard . . . that you are no longer personally . . . that is to say . . . you might be willing to consider walking out with a new gentleman."

She tried to hide her astonishment. Certainly, she had filed the papers notifying the CID that Warren should no longer be considered her emergency contact, if the worst came to pass in the line of duty, but she never imagined that the gossip mill could churn so quickly. For Higgins to have heard already, people must be talking in all corners. To salve her pride, she pretended not to feel enormous chagrin over the notion of people discussing her private business.

"I'm sorry if I've offended you," Higgins went on, looking fairly desperate. "I shouldn't have said anything. You have my deepest and most profound apologies. I—"

Bronze gods, does the man mean to grovel all night? His green eyes glinted with profound remorse, touched by abject embarrassment. There was something sweet about his desire to maintain her good opinion, however. So she said, "I am often busy with work, but . . . I have Sundays free."

Her hesitation was, unfortunately, perceptible. It reflected her doubt about his intentions. If he sought to capitalize on her alleged loneliness, then he wasn't the man she'd thought him to be. And it would be very disappointing.

"At this juncture, you probably aren't interested in another immediate entanglement," Higgins said with more acuity than she would've given him credit for. "Nor can I afford such with my mother's health weighing on me. But perhaps it wouldn't be unwelcome for us to enjoy a more companionable friendship outside of work?"

He seemed to be warning her that he wasn't looking for a marital alliance. And that was fine with her; the last thing she wanted was a husband, common law or otherwise. Ritsuko didn't think she had to worry about Cyril Higgins breaking her heart. He was polite, friendly, and had excellent manners, plus a touching devotion to his mother. She could do worse for a casual companion.

"I understand. And I agree."

Higgins nodded, relieved. "Perhaps we could share luncheon sometime then?"

"That would be most agreeable."

Cyril Higgins seemed to like her, at least, which was more than could be said of Warren, toward the end. She suspected the only reason he had stayed so long was for fear of admitting to failure and showing he was as fallible as anyone else. He had cared for appearances to the exclusion of practically everything else. People probably whispered in these corridors that she was heartbroken, but in fact, she felt nothing but relief.

"Come visit me again," he invited, smiling.

"I'll certainly do that. Good evening, Mr. Higgins."

Most inspectors would have taken the lift directly to the ground floor and gone home at once. But then, they weren't female, working twice as hard for three-quarters of the same wage. So instead, Ritsuko went back to her desk and filled out a request form, asking for a complete listing of all licensed and operational theaters and performing troupes currently in the city. With a satisfied nod, she dropped the form into the delivery tube, which she then fed to the access slot that led to the pneumatic whoosh of interoffice mail. She had no doubt the document would be tremendous, but with any luck, it would be in her incoming bin by the time she returned to work the next afternoon.

Sometimes it paid to go the extra mile.

CHAPTER 3

THE NEXT AFTERNOON, MIKANI ARRIVED AT HQ EARLY—JUST
in time to start the interviews with the rest of the family. He
strolled past the queue of cousins and House hangers-on, entering
the room with a quizzical smile. Ritsuko was already pouring
tea for the girl's aunt, who was pale and red-eyed. She looked a
good deal like Cira Aevar's mother, he thought, just a bit older
and more worn.

"I'm sorry to put you through this at such a difficult time,"
Ritsuko was saying. "But any insight you have could be crucial
in locating Cira."

He sat beside his partner, cracking his senses like a bottle of
beer, just enough to let a rivulet of emotion trickle into his consciousness. Anna Aevar was distraught, worried about her niece.
Mikani sat silently and gathered impressions while Ritsuko
asked all the pertinent questions. At the end of the session, he
shook his head subtly to indicate the woman wasn't hiding anything. They went on in such fashion for an hour, until Cira's
cousin stepped in.

She was a sly-looking creature with fine brown hair and a
narrow face complete with deep-set eyes. Though she said all

the right things, she exuded a quiet satisfaction, as if Cira's disappearance was no more than her just desserts. Mikani nudged Ritsuko's foot with the tip of his cane to indicate there was something wrong.

His partner broke from the prepared questions, leaning forward to spear the young woman with a stern look. "Miss Aevar, why don't you simply admit that you're hiding something? Your prevarications cannot fool the CID."

The girl's face paled. "There's nothing, I swear."

But sweat beaded on her prominent brow, and Mikani's sense that she had a secret intensified. So he broke protocol and joined the interrogation, thinking she might find him more intimidating. "You do realize that we are at liberty to detain you at our discretion."

"My grandfather would never let that happen," the girl cried.

"Let's call him down here to ask," Ritsuko suggested coldly. "When I tell him that we believe you're concealing key evidence relating to your cousin's disappearance, do you think he'll be inclined to protect you?"

"Cira's always had everything, and she didn't appreciate *any* of it."

Mikani exchanged a look with his partner, wondering if this girl had a hand in her cousin's vanishing act. "Prove your innocence. Tell us what you know."

"I don't know everything," the girl whined. "Only whispers. My mother said Cira was involved in something Grandfather wouldn't approve of, and her mother was covering it up. That's all I know, I swear."

Ritsuko glanced at him for confirmation. At his thoughtful nod, she made a note, and said, "Thank you again, Miss Aevar. You may go."

"We definitely need to interview Cira's mother again," Mikani noted when the girl stepped away. "If the cousin's correct, and Mistress Aevar is hiding something, we need to find out what."

"Let's ask the commander to set it up before we start canvassing theaters."

"Great job on the greasepaint lead," he said, pushing to his feet.

Ritsuko smiled. "It helps when a lab specialist likes you."

They spent the remainder of the evening canvassing, covering three theaters, where nobody had heard of Cira Aevar, though they had, of course, read about the poor girl in the newssheets. Past a certain hour, however, the CID went to a skeleton crew, and they had to spend the wee hours responding to other calls. Yet there was no question that this case would be top priority until they closed it.

The following day was Sunday; normally they took the day off, but with a case this pressing, they had to work straight through. Mikani waited for Ritsuko at the Royale, the next stop on their master list of places where Cira might've come into contact with greasepaint. Age left its mark on the walls of a place, and the theater was among the few structures that had survived the renovations of the previous century. Its dome design and marble columns bespoke classical origin, unaltered over the years.

He lit a slender cigarillo, summoning a thin shroud of sweet smoke to the lobby. As he dragged on the laced tobacco, he glanced about the hall and spotted his partner coming toward him. Nothing about her ever changed. Same charcoal wool tailored suit and split skirt, same polished case. Her hair shone like black silk, and her expression was pleasant, if not delighted. Some people got stuck with lazy partners or surly ones; occasionally other inspectors commiserated with him on being saddled with a woman, but he wouldn't trade her for three men.

"This must be a record," he observed, referring to his earlier arrival.

"I went to HQ first to pick up a few things. I intend to take samples from their makeup kits."

"Speaking of . . . the Old Lady's getting a cosmetic lift." He gestured toward the cans of paint and scaffolds scattered against the velvet-covered walls. "Handymen, stagehands, and carpenters . . . someone just added a few dozen suspects to our list." Despite it all, though, he felt almost cheerful. *If nothing else, it keeps things interesting.* "A convenient coincidence."

There are no coincidences. Someone had told him that once.

Ritsuko glanced from the plush rug, threadbare around the edges, to the faded gilt trim of the moldings. For a moment, she watched two men struggling with the tacks that secured the runner in place. Mikani studied her as she watched them, absently trying to work out if he had ever remained in contact with a female this long before. His partner called him an unrepentant rake, but it was more like he lacked a key piece, preventing him from forming lasting attachments in the customary sense. That lack led to growing anger, frustration, and eventual hatred or resignation from those he tried to share his life with. He was left, as often as not, with a faint befuddlement as to where it had all fallen apart and a growing list of farewell notes. A list from which he hoped, one day, to discern the shape and heft of whatever it was he could not see.

"The place needed it," she said, snapping him from his reverie. "Wonder where the money's coming from. Last I knew, this place was going under. They haven't had a full house in over a year. Not since the accident." She seemed to notice his astonishment, explaining, "Warren was on the board until Leonidas the younger took over. Warren doesn't like him."

"I didn't realize you knew so much about the theater."

She shrugged. "It was Warren's passion, but I absorbed a few things."

"What accident . . . ?"

"Leonidas's parents were killed in a steam-carriage mishap, and he was dreadfully scarred. I've heard he has rooms in the Royale, rarely leaves the premises."

"Dramatic."

Ritsuko showed a gleam of amusement. "I also understand he dons a mask whenever he must deal with the public. How's that for theater?"

"Impressive," Mikani admitted.

Ritsuko gestured toward the auditorium. "Shall we?"

"We should." He shook his head, dismissing the strange sense that he didn't know his partner as well as he'd thought. Odd that he'd never contemplated what her interests might be, outside of work. Teasing her about Warren hadn't fallen under the heading of real life, somehow. "We need to talk to the owner and whoever is putting on this show."

As he tugged open the heavy doors and stepped into the hall, a familiar wrongness pulled at his senses, leaving him vaguely nauseous, but the back-row seats were empty. Echoing silence above spoke of no hidden audience in the box and season seats, either. *That makes sense, if it is a new rehearsal.* Behind him,

Ritsuko commented on the renovations, to which he responded with a noncommittal grunt as he started down the aisle. Upon the stage and all around it, performers stretched and spun.

The black curtain was down in the rear, and the stage lights glowed, making it hard, if not impossible, for anyone up front to note their entrance. *Just as well.* The faint hum of corruption swelled as he neared the front of the theater. Excitement and stress drifted through him, overwhelming more subtle emanations.

The performers didn't notice their arrival; their attention seemed focused on someone offstage. A mellifluous female voice gave detailed instructions as to how the dancers had gone wrong in their last attempt to master her choreography. Mikani listened for a few seconds, filtering impressions and doing his best to ignore the dancers' ebb and flow of emotion, frustration, elation at the simple joy of performance.

Then he stepped forward, clearing his throat. He had credentials in hand, the badge glimmering in reflected light. "Good afternoon, madam. If I might be so bold?"

There was no need to check on Ritsuko. By the time the woman reached them, his partner had ID packet in hand as well. Mikani could always count on her. She'd fought hard to take her place in the force, despite quiet prejudice against female officers.

Now standing in the spotlight, the choreographer peered into the shadows before the stage. She wore a simple black leotard with a long black skirt wrapped around slim hips. Dark brown hair twisted atop her head in a simple chignon, revealing the elegant line of her neck. She had lovely green eyes and a porcelain complexion; it was beyond Mikani *not* to notice such things about a woman even if he had no interest in anything beyond physical assessment. Some women possessed an ageless quality where it became impossible to tell if they were thirty or fifty, and this woman owned it. At first glance, she seemed youthful, but something in her eyes made him rethink the judgment, which also hinted at strong Ferisher blood. He made a mental note to check her background.

He sensed something about this female. Or more accurately, he sensed too much about her: she overflowed with presence, palpable, sharp, and sweet. *Damned if I can put a name to it, though.* It might be nothing more than powerful fey lineage. Those from the most potent bloodlines could create a fascination glamour, but he had no sense of a conscious effort to try to befuddle him—not that it would work. A few particularly gifted felons had tried over the years, and he'd proven more or less immune to it, much to their chagrin.

The woman looked harassed for a moment, then she appeared to realize that she wasn't being interrupted by one of her own. "Of course. That is . . ." The brunette called to the dancers, "That's dinner. Come back in an hour."

En masse, the performers relaxed. A few filed out, presumably to find an eatery close by, while others wandered backstage to claim whatever they'd brought from home. A few people found seats at the edge of the stage and others reclined in the seats, legs stretched out. Soon, the air not only smelled of sweat, sawdust, burning glass, and wet paint, but also of meat and cheese, fresh fruit and bread. Coffee and chocolate added to the mix until the odors all but overwhelmed Mikani. He tamped down his senses, the throbbing at the back of his skull strangely eased by the woman's proximity.

Once the initial rush of movement passed, the choreographer faced them again. "I have an office of sorts, backstage. I sense this discussion would be best conducted in private." With that, she led them up the stairs and across the stage through the wings.

IT'S COMFORTING, RITSUKO thought, *to have an established routine.*

She and Mikani didn't need to confer to know that she'd handle the verbal questioning while he scanned for inconsistencies and overall impressions. She followed the other woman into the back room, overflowing with battered shelving, boxes of costumes and props slated for repair, and a scarred desk. The choreographer perched on the edge of the desk, drowning in papers, which she edged aside with one hand. There was nowhere for them to sit, but it was probably better to keep it formal anyway.

"I suppose introductions are in order. I'm Aurelia Wright, the director and choreographer." That confirmed what Ritsuko had already gleaned.

For once, her partner performed the courtesies himself, not

letting his eyes glaze over just yet. "We apologize for interrupting your rehearsal. I am Inspector Mikani, and this is my partner, Ritsuko."

She stepped forward, taking his cue. "We're following a lead in an ongoing investigation and were wondering if you would be so kind as to answer a few questions?"

Miss Wright replied, "I don't mind. According to the dancers, it was past time for them to have a break."

"Your cooperation is appreciated, I assure you," he said.

Ritsuko opened her notepad, eager to get started, as there was a host of cast and crew left to question. "When did you set up the show?"

"About a month ago," Miss Wright answered.

She made a note. "And who are your backers?"

It was clear the choreographer was turning over the questions mentally. Her frown deepened. "The show has no backers, per se. It's an independent enterprise sponsored by the Royale's owner and myself."

Ritsuko paused, her attention caught. From what Warren had told her, it was common for a group of financiers to be involved with such an endeavor. Whether that anomaly was significant, she couldn't yet say. "That's a substantial investment."

"Are you asking about my financial status?" the choreographer asked.

"You don't have to answer their questions." The words came in a deep, near-strangled growl from the shadows in the doorway.

Shifting, Ritsuko glimpsed a tall figure in a black greatcoat, shrouded even indoors. The man wore the collar up around his face, almost like a highwayman's cowl, and an actual masquerade mask covered the top of his face. In the dimness, his eyes resembled black holes, bottomless and impenetrable. *This must be Leonidas the younger.*

"We'll get to you soon enough," Ritsuko told him. "As I advised Miss Wright, our questions are pursuant to an official investigation, and if you decline to cooperate, a magistrate might construe it as belligerent obstruction of justice."

"By all means, carry on then," the Royale owner said, sounding amused. "I'm only belligerent and obstructive on Tuesdays."

"Don't believe him," Miss Wright put in. "He's always

belligerent and obstructive. Just ask him about replacing the fixtures in the lobby and see for yourself." But her tone was gentle, and Ritsuko saw that she had some affection for the man she teased.

"See if I attempt to protect you again," Leonidas muttered, slipping away as quickly as he had come.

"We'll need to speak to him later," Ritsuko said.

"Good luck finding him. I swear this place was built on a labyrinth. But you were asking about my financials, I believe?"

"I won't need them yet," she answered. "But we do need a list of everyone you've hired in the past six weeks."

"Why?" Ah, she'd reached the point at which Miss Wright could no longer give out information blindly.

"A girl has gone missing," Mikani interjected. He'd stood when Leonidas had entered: he remained standing by the door, leaning heavily on his cane. By his weary expression, the exchange had been taxing . . . and informative. "We believe she may have ties to the theater."

"Oh, of course. I have the work assignments somewhere." In a lithe movement, Miss Wright leaned forward over her leg, sorting the papers on her desk.

Ritsuko nudged her partner, indicating a cosmetic case that sat in the bin of props. After receiving a *go-ahead* nod, she went to work quietly, opening the case and collecting a sample. The case was in full sight, with a clear connection to their investigation; they needed no special dispensation beyond their discretion in pursuing the investigation. But they wouldn't find out what they needed to know for several days, unless she charmed Higgins a bit more. Oddly, she didn't altogether mind the prospect.

"Here." Miss Wright proffered the roster, and Ritsuko took it, skimming the names before surrendering it to her silent partner. "Am I being accused of something?"

"If I thought you guilty, Miss Wright, you would be bound and on your way to HQ." Mikani spoke absently as he perused the list. He hesitated, frowned, and glanced up. "I apologize if I seem brusque, but we *are* pressed for time."

Ritsuko considered hitting him. "I second the apology. Sometimes, Inspector Mikani forgets that citizens greatly ease our way with information they provide."

"Do you know Cira Aevar? She's a House scion who disappeared recently." Mikani flashed the black-and-white image in a heart-shaped frame.   •

Miss Wright shook her head. "The name doesn't ring any bells, and I can say with certainty that she's not part of my cast. It's possible she may have been hired as an assistant by one of the department supervisors, though."

Ritsuko could always tell when Mikani was finished with . . . whatever he did. He rose, paced a few impatient steps in the small room, then patted his pockets for a cigarillo that she wouldn't let him smoke in here anyway. He seemed to realize as much; his hands fell quiet, but his face didn't lose its faint discomfort, like he had one leg caught in a trap.

"We need to ask around, then. Who would have access to your makeup kits? Do you maintain your own, or do you keep them in the theater?" Mikani was nearly out the door, asking over his shoulder.

"Anyone. We'll be using theater facilities, all across the board," Miss Wright said. "Perhaps you're unaware, Inspector, but I've never staged a show. Choreographed, but not staged. So I don't have anything that's my own, besides the script."

"Excellent. We shall start with the interviews, then. There may be more questions later . . . for now, however, we're finished. Thanks for your time."

"I appreciate your assistance, Miss Wright. I wish you much success with the show." Ritsuko stood, shaking hands with the woman before stepping into the wings.

Once they left earshot, she smiled and elbowed him. "You remembered your manners. I'm proud of you."

"A result of your sterling influence, no doubt."

"I can only dream of such grandeur. What did you get from them?"

His dark blue gaze met hers, filled with resigned amusement and pain in equal measure. It was quite unfair that a scoundrel like her partner should enjoy lush, curly-tipped lashes that would've looked too feminine if not for his sizable nose and his stubborn jaw, constantly in need of shaving. By the look of things, it had been three days since he had bothered to make use of his razor.

"She wasn't hiding anything." He motioned toward the nearest knot of people, a dozen dancers watching with suspicious eyes. "So far as I could tell, she's trying to put on a show, and that's all. So if Cira's disappearance is connected with the Royale, she's not a part of it."

"And from her champion?"

Mikani frowned. "He's an odd one. Definitely in pain; though whether it's emotional or physical, I can't be sure. He's surprisingly good at blocking, so I only received trickles from him."

"And that's unusual?"

"Very," he said, sounding troubled. "People only learn to shield if they have something significant to hide."

Ritsuko lifted one shoulder, philosophical. "We'll do it the hard way. Interview them all, one by one, and see if anyone knew her."

"Why don't you take the technical crew? I'll talk to the dancers."

His innocent expression made her laugh despite the weight of the investigation. "Are you sure it's not too great a sacrifice? So many young women, so little time."

"I'll endeavor to bear up under the burden."

"Excellent. When we're finished, I'll meet you down front." So saying, she descended, immersing herself without delay in a sea of men, most wearing bad haircuts, spectacles, or both.

Around them, the rehearsal went on as scheduled, except for those they were questioning. Miss Wright ignored their presence as best she could, opting to focus on the dancing. By the time she'd conducted a dozen interviews, Ritsuko was heartily tired of being propositioned by the crew, as they assumed her presence in the workforce meant she was a woman of loose morals and "game for anything," as one hopeful put it. A stern look and a harsh word quieted most of them down, though she had to show one man her restraints to remind him she was a CID inspector.

The fourteenth person she spoke to finally offered some useful information. This woman was the head of the costuming department, older and painted as if that would disguise her years. Her red lip rouge had smeared onto her teeth, but Ritsuko observed the fluttering grace of her hands as she spoke.

"Oh yes," the woman said. "I know her. I hired her three

weeks ago to help with costumes. Dab hand with a needle and so eager to please. If I gave her two sheets and a length of rope, I do believe she'd try to sew me a ball gown."

So she worked at the Royale. The occasional donation would be acceptable by House standards, but bronze gods forbid she turn her hand to actual work. Pleased with the break in the case, Ritsuko soldiered on. In the end, six people recognized Cira Aevar's photo. They all agreed that she was a quiet girl who seemed to derive pleasure by proxy: watching her costumes onstage. Everyone liked her, no one had seen her in days, and all were concerned about her.

Ritsuko was completing her last interview when Mikani approached. "This is Mr. Gideon. He's managing lights . . . and he says Cira was a costumer on the last show he worked, too."

Helpful revelation, that. At least we know Miss Wright's production wasn't her first foray into the workplace.

"Did you know her well?" Mikani asked.

"I'm afraid not. As I was telling Inspector Ritsuko, she kept to herself. I'm sorry I couldn't be more help."

"Thanks for your time." Ritsuko turned to Mikani, drawing him away from the curious cast and crew. "Did you finish the dancers?"

He arched a sardonic brow. "Must you be so lewd? I'm only a mortal male."

"You are incorrigible." Only Mikani could make her laugh with such an inappropriate remark. Anyone else would receive the icy death stare she had perfected over years of clawing her way up the hierarchy.

"Are you ready to go?" he asked, smiling down at her.

"More than." As they walked out together, she glimpsed a swirl of movement overhead, fabric, perhaps, from the reticent owner. "Why do you suppose Cira went to work in the theater? She didn't need the money."

Somber for once, Mikani replied, "For love. Why else? And I suspect she died for it as well."

CHAPTER 4

THE NIGHT SMELLED OF DAMP WOOD AND DISTANT SMOKE. EAR-
lier that evening, a conversation with Aurelia's mother had
unsettled her enough that instead of seeking her bed afterward,
she'd wandered into the garden maze behind the Acheron Club.
From beyond the stone walls that encircled the property came
sounds of passersby, those with lives less complicated than her
own. There was an inviolable air about Aurelia as she paced;
she'd once been told she resembled a nun at prayer, but the like-
ness was superficial. Aurelia Wright believed only in herself.

After all, when you're sent into exile, you have only yourself.

She certainly couldn't depend on her family. Her beautiful,
cool, remote mother, who didn't understand fear of madness,
probably never had a nightmare. *I wish you would see someone.*
So easy, so predictable that counsel, but, of course, Aurelia was
no longer even permitted within the confines of the main house.
For the crime of working at what she loved, she had been banished from the complex, forbidden to see her relatives or use the
family name. Her mother had broken the rules of exile by arranging that furtive dinner, but Aurelia came away feeling as though
she'd disappointed her mother yet again.

By refusing to see a specialist and declining to come home.

"I don't want to know if there's something wrong with me," she'd protested. "If I'm mad."

Longevity took some people that way. Despite the gift nature had given their bodies, their minds were not equipped to deal with the sheer volume of memories. Years, after a certain time, became burdensome. Aurelia feared to know if her mind had begun to give way beneath the weight, for there was no cure; there were probably other explanations for the occasional bad dream and the sense of foreboding that had plagued her recently. As she wound through the twists and turns of the maze, she wished she could be sure she was imagining the sense that someone was watching her.

Not at the moment, however. Her father's club was safe; the Acheron Club was a private establishment that catered exclusively to gentlemen. Food and service, cards and companionship—it was an escape from their wives, daughters, and responsibilities, where they could smoke and act as if they hadn't a care in the world. It cost more than most men would earn in a year to buy a membership, and the manager, Hargrave, only sold so many new vouchers. It was a way of keeping the riffraff out.

She hadn't wanted to live here initially, but like most of her father's arguments, his reasons were too compelling to ignore. He'd whispered to her of kidnappings and lack of privacy and reminded her that in a normal building, people would notice too much about her and begin to talk. It would attract attention he knew damned well she didn't want. In the end, she caved, though after her official exile, she'd had little choice. His offer of rooms had presented a safe solution to her dilemma, and she did love the maze. The hemlock hedges had offered solace more than once, a place to pace away her cares.

Just then, she had a surfeit of them, between the stumbling show, Leonidas's increasing paranoia, the sense that she was being watched, and pervasive loneliness. Nobody had ever warned her that pursuing her dreams could cost her everything. At least, not until it was too late.

There came a noise nearby, or something less than sound—more an impression. A frisson along her spine whispered that someone else shared her space. Chills rose on her arms, for she'd had that impression more than once, coming home late from the theater. That feeling had never arisen here. She'd told herself it was nothing, an overactive imagination, but it hadn't stopped her from glancing over her shoulders, listening for an echo of a careless footfall, the movement of a shadow that shouldn't exist.

Tonight had been no exception.

Now, apparently, the danger or delusion had followed her home. Heart thudding in her ears, she called out, "Is anyone there?"

"Such a question is often offered. Human nature, I believe." It was a man's voice, soft and sibilant, as if sand slid against silk.

Aurelia shuddered. There was art in his voice, flavored with an accent she found hard to place. Now she recalled myths of mazes, maidens, and the dark creatures to which they were sacrificed. If she possessed a grain of good sense, she would walk back the way she'd come, avoiding the owner of this voice at all costs.

But he couldn't be the silent stalker she had sensed before; otherwise, why announce his presence when he had so successfully eluded detection ere now?

"I was not calling out to God," she said quietly, moving in what she judged to be his general direction. "But to you, whoever you are."

"Alas, I cannot claim a divine aspect. I am but a traveler, come to the end of my journey, perhaps. Such is writ where I cannot read it."

With the slow grace of opiate dreams, the man stepped into sight. Above, the moon hid her face behind a wall of clouds, and the stars were no more than tiny dots of light, seen through a wispy veil. *Not* only *a traveler,* said her quiet self. *Though that is true, as far as he has spoken*. It did not reassure her, for there were many ways to lie, and she was familiar with most of them.

With a long, narrow face, he was not handsome, and something in his bone structure suggested that the veneer of civilization ran thin. Impeccably groomed raven hair and a trimmed goatee softened some of the sharpness though he still possessed shades of the potentate. Tall but not gaunt, the stranger emanated power from the tailored cut of his coat to his manicured hands.

"Either your feet have trod this path before, or you had need of refuge," she returned, concluding her study.

"Either, or," he agreed. Careless and languid, he stopped three paces distant, giving her a smile, ivory against olive skin. "Fortune has smiled upon me that I behold such beauty. And how shall I address you?"

The formality of his manner told Aurelia he was very old indeed, even if his face did not agree with his eyes. An ancient part of her soul thrilled to life, recognizing his fey strength. He might be full Ferisher, the way she felt in his presence. But no, they were gone. Those who had not interbred with the immigrant population had passed from sight and were now lost spirits, unable to touch the world that once belonged to them unless they were called through various rituals.

He drinks the light. Her nerves jangled as if she stood on the edge of a great precipice. *And he speaks in riddles, frosted with flattery.*

"In the dark, I daresay you have little idea whether I might break mirrors with my face. But I will forgive your lapse this once. I am Aurelia."

"I have sharper sight than most. And I should stand by my words against any challenger." His gaze slid from her face as if reluctant.

"I dislike being praised for a merit which was none of my doing." Her smile was a bright, fleeting thing.

"Call me Theron, should you choose to address me. What do you name this place, then?" His attention settled back on her, light as a shadow, and as revealing.

"This is the Acheron Club. Do you realize you're trespassing?"

"Ah." His gaze rested on her still, her pallor reflected back to her in his eyes, and he ignored the question. "Do you often wander this maze, Aurelia?"

She arched a brow. "That answer depends on why you ask me."

"I ask that I might know." Apparently sensing her growing impatience, he added, "If you are here often, you might direct me to the exit."

"You found *me*, easily enough," she murmured, "and moments ago, you boasted excellent sight. Thus, I doubt you need rescuing. But I have no reluctance to play the part since you seem to want it so."

With that, she took his arm and began to walk, negotiating

the first turn. Aurelia was aware she had not answered his question any more than he'd answered hers; such dissembling
annoyed her, but she was not her father's child for nothing; nor
had she come away empty-handed in guile.

"You shall be rewarded for your kindness." He matched her
pace easily. Slow as his movements seemed, each step devoured
distance, her hand resting in the crook of his arm. "Too long
have I spent already wandering, after all." His smile was tinged
with rue.

Aurelia contemplated his words as they walked, paring them
away to the smallest kernels of truth. Thus, in silence, they completed the rest of the turns that carried them beyond the hemlock
hedge. Once they reached the stone path of the garden, Aurelia
paused, looking up into his face, and she gave him an uncharacteristically gentle smile.

"You look most weary," she said. "And having wandered, are
no doubt happy to find yourself home again." The words were
instinct, no more, based on the intuition that familiarity led him
here. "That being so, I offer you the hospitality of the club,
Theron."

"Home. No." As he turned to her, the gaslight danced in his
eyes, granting an infernal aspect. "But I gratefully accept your
invitation."

A few words with Hargrave granted temporary access to the
club. Her companion would not be permitted inside any of the
members-only areas, but even though she had yielded all claims
to the family name, she was still her father's daughter, and it
counted for something here. Perhaps, like Leonidas, she had
grown paranoid, but with courtly manners, she'd led this stranger
into the light in hopes of learning whether he harbored ill intentions. The longer they spoke, the more she could gain a sense of
whether he prevaricated.

You see enemies everywhere, her mother's voice said.

While that might be true, she had managed to survive for
years where other exiles died once they were ousted from the
safety of their nests. Granted, the club provided more security
than most could manage outside a House compound, but she
didn't remain here all the time. And while traveling back and
forth from the theater, there was no doubt she was at risk. *Possibly from someone like this,* she thought, glancing at Theron.

"Are you hungry?" she asked.

"Rather."

She led the way into the public dining room, preferring to discover his reasons for lurking about the maze under the safe observation of multiple witnesses. Aurelia swung open the heavy door. A dearth of windows, wood paneling, and muted lights in brass fixtures encouraged the semblance of privacy. Each table was edged three ways by a wooden screen, and at the center of the room, a stylized stone fountain burbled away, drowning conversations to all but its principals. A brown-and-gold carpet softened their steps as they followed the host to the table. Near a solid wall, the booth she chose was quieter than most, set with a white rose. A few members noted her entrance, but they had been advised by her father not to interact with her.

Treat her as if she's not there.

It was his version of enforcing her exile. Both he and her mother hoped she would change her mind, return to the fold, and resume her rightful place in the natural order. But she'd tasted freedom, so returning to a gilded cage was no longer possible. At first, the silence and ostracism stung, but she'd formed other friendships that weren't reliant on prestige or stature.

"Agreeable," Theron said. "What do you recommend?"

Without glancing at the menu, she signaled the waiter. "For two: spinach salad with the vinaigrette to start. To follow, the lemon herb chicken with asparagus. Turkish coffee to finish." Then she turned to Theron. "Whatever you prefer in the way of wine. The cellar is excellent."

"Chardonnay. I believe Thorgrim still has the best vineyards on the isles."

"I couldn't say. I've long since given up pretensions as to superiority. I only know what I like."

"Then order it."

Smiling, she did.

They made desultory conversation while she attempted to read him, mine his secrets, but he held them close and tight. That indicated a disciplined mind. From the intensity of his gaze, Aurelia rather thought he was taking her measure as well; though for what purpose, she had no idea. Idly, she wondered if Theron had been engaged by her father to pose as a suitor when he was, in fact, a paid minder. There might be some new threat of which she was unaware; from time to time, people sought to use her as leverage in negotiations. Her exile didn't mean he had stopped loving her.

Before she could delicately craft a question, the waiter returned. She glimpsed herself in the raised dome of the silver platter in his hands. Her own face seemed paler than usual beneath the brass fixtures; she was a creature of plain lines and stark hue. Aurelia glanced away, not caring to consider how many years were *not* written in natural passage on her skin. Theron watched with eyes dark as sloe, hooded and slightly foreboding. Possibly, as in the old stories, she should not have invited him in, but she preferred to keep potential enemies close.

The salad was crisp and tangy, the chicken succulent. After the servers arranged the meal before them, artfully displayed on white china, quiet descended on the table. As they ate, the only sounds were the distant fountain and unintelligible murmurs from other tables. And when Aurelia added the cream to her cup, she smiled, providing the signal that she was ready to resume the conversation.

"Now then, why don't you tell me what you were doing in the maze?"

"So direct." His smile gained layers, amusement and something else, a darkness.

"It would be unwise to underestimate me," she said quietly.

"I have no wish to be your enemy, Miss Wright."

"Then what *do* you wish?"

Theron tilted his body toward her, but the move felt calculated, choreographed to make her respond. To her annoyance, it worked. She wanted to lean toward him as well, and she sensed a whisper of glamour trickling from him.

"You won't beguile me into cooperating with whatever you want from me. If this is about my father, I'm no longer privy to his plans or schemes. I have no influence over his decisions in any sphere."

"It's not about your father," Theron said softly.

Aurelia didn't know whether she found that reassuring. "But you concede your presence here tonight was not by chance?"

"Few things truly are. I came for my own ends, but I am delighted to meet you."

"For what reason?" she demanded.

"You are, rather, a legend among some circles." She sensed some prevarication in that reply, but it wasn't entirely false. Maddening. "The girl who gave up her name and became the woman who will not bend? Impressive."

"There are others who've done as much. Why seek me out?" It was like bashing her head against a brick wall.

"Who's to say I have?"

That silenced her a moment as she considered her next question. She felt sure he had an agenda but decided it was unlikely he'd disclose it on a first encounter. Intuition insisted he had a particular aim in mind, but Aurelia hoped she was too wary to permit herself to be used, however strong a man's charisma. And forewarned was forearmed.

"You're not the first person to come in search of some nebulous favor. But you'll gain nothing by associating with me."

"You presume that's not my goal in its entirety."

"Getting to know me?" She laughed. "A thin achievement to be sure."

Theron only smiled, his eyes as dark and unreadable as the night sea.

After he departed, she didn't sleep well, haunted as ever by bad dreams. But for the first time since she could recall, Aurelia did not dream of drowning. Instead, she dreamt of burning and woke gasping for air, checking her flesh to ensure it wasn't charred as it had been in the nightmare.

REHEARSAL WAS A disaster; the dancers were distracted by the ongoing investigation, and she capped the afternoon by arguing with Leonidas. He stormed out in a rage, not that he ever *left* the Royale. She worried about her old friend. His grief over his parents' death had driven him deep inside himself, but now it was twisting him strange. He'd once been an open, friendly man of great personal warmth, but now . . . ? Aurelia wasn't altogether certain what he was becoming.

Finally, she shouted, "Stop! We'll try again tomorrow. I hope you'll all bring more focus and a better frame of mind."

Depressed, she returned to the club, and the sense that someone dogged her footsteps returned in force. The whole way, she kept an eye over one shoulder, and she didn't relax until she stepped inside the foyer to be greeted by Hargrave.

In waning daylight, she passed through to the conservatory to stand before the stained-glass windows, blazing light from the setting sun. Twilight crept up on her, bearing purples as a gift. She gazed down at the city, remote from this vantage, until the sky darkened entirely, and lights glimmered to life like fireflies. The dim glow beyond gave the stained glass an empyreal glow, coronas of crimson and purple.

This room was Aurelia's undisputed domain; her father had warned the other members to stay away, and she appreciated it. Otherwise, her life must be contained within the two rooms she kept above, and there wasn't enough space for what she loved. She stretched and turned on her toes in a pirouette. There was only the distant murmur of the most determined gamblers in another part of the club. Aurelia moved past the sliding stage that pulled from the wall. Dominated by a grand fortepiano, along one wall stood a glass case containing various reed and wind instruments. Her skill with such was mediocre. Though she loved music, she wasn't gifted at its creation.

Flexing her feet, she glanced about, then her gaze settled on the Victrola beneath the stained-glass arch. Dancing always helped when she was in a mood, so she set the needle on the phonograph. The resultant sound was sweet, echoing off the stone for a richer resonance, a layered harmony of lament. Aurelia stretched, then she began.

Toes pointed, arms arched, she flowed into the forms, letting instinct drive her movements: *plie, pirouette, arabesque, fouette, glissade, jete, and again.* She could hear her instructor's accented voice calling out the steps. She melted into the music, tears shimmering in her eyes as she danced.

Sometimes, freedom felt very much like an anchor.

CHAPTER 5

ONLY AN EMERGENCY LIKE THIS ONE WOULD'VE DRIVEN MIKANI to the Mountain District.

His first visit was an exercise in polite hostility; Ritsuko's ancestors had negotiated well in securing a sizable portion of land on the rolling hills of northern Dorstaad. The intervening generations had turned their enclave into a walled community separate from, and barely beholden to, the rest of the city. He had time to admire the clean symmetry of the gardens and flowing fountains while someone deep within decided whether he was worthy of admittance. So after they processed his request, he deliberately trampled through several rock gardens to make up the lost time.

He jogged to her building, attracting curious glances from a few guards and the terrace patrons of a teahouse. Double-checking the address, he glanced up at the sparse lines of the white building before him. Stark, topped with the curving red tiles characteristic of the Mountain but unlike any in the rest of the city. Full-length windows dominated this side of the building, milky glass giving the illusion of paper. Inside, there was no lift, so he raced up four flights, taking the stairs two at a time.

He pounded on the door. "Ritsuko! We need to run."

It took two more tries before he heard movement within. Mikani paced while waiting for her to open up the door. When she finally did, she had on a thin white nightgown with lace at wrists and throat; and her hair looked like a bird's nest. She rubbed her eyes with a decidedly cranky expression.

"What?"

Mikani concealed a smirk. "You may want to put on something a bit less, ah. Lacey. We found a body in Iron Cross. Do you have coffee, by chance? I had to rush out."

Ritsuko bit out a curse that surprised him, as she didn't ordinarily use them. It was impossible to tell whether she was bothered by the rude awakening, the prospect of a corpse on a sunny day, or his unprecedented presence in her domain. Possibly, it was all of the above. With a vague gesture, she beckoned him in.

"Help yourself. I'm sure you can find everything. Let me get dressed."

He stepped in, letting the door slide shut behind him while he cast a quick look around. Clean lines, sparsely furnished. But he could tell where furniture was missing, where prints or frames were gone from the stark walls. Low, dark tables and cushions had been shifted to fill the space or balance the room, which gave no hint of her personality.

As near as he could tell, he was the only spot of grime in the place. *I should get her a plant. I doubt she'd appreciate a pet.* He made his careful way to the kitchen. While he searched for a coffeepot, coffee, and mugs, he hummed. From the back, he heard the movements she made, the splash of water, rustle of clothing. *It's not like taking off that flimsy white thing would take long . . . Ritsuko, naked.* He fumbled the coffeepot as he pictured—

With a silent oath he slammed his hand down on the counter, focusing on the pain instead, then called, "Make sure not to wear anything you'll mind getting dirty."

"Noted." When she emerged, she'd brushed her hair and wet it so it lay smooth. Instead of a gray, tailored suit, she had on black trousers and a supple leather jacket, both more worn than her customary attire. "And ready."

Mikani took in her ensemble with an arched brow. "That

is . . . different." He managed to hide the grin by lifting the coffee mug. *I do think this is the first time we look like we belong together. Mostly.*

When they got back to the cruiser, Mikani revved up the engine from humming idle and eased into heavy traffic. The ubiquitous hansoms chugged along, mingling with overladen steam buses, colorful Summer Clan wagons, and ever-present messengers on their cycles. Ritsuko's mingled irascibility and frustration kept him company during the ride across town. Mikani slowed when they reached the hulking maze of dark structures and brass pipes that housed the primary industrial complex for the city. Factories joined to one another by walkways and tubes until they seemed part of a colossal machine beast that lay across several square miles at the city's southeast edge; the main road into the complex gaped like a dark maw with dim gas lamps glittering along its throat.

The ward officers' signal beacon flashed up ahead. He tapped Ritsuko's arm and nodded toward the blue-tinged lantern as he steered the vehicle toward the site, a quarter mile away along the dark passage. After he parked the cruiser, they rode a cargo lift to the top of the building where a maintenance crew had found the body.

Against the clanking of iron and brass, Mikani had to shout to make sure Ritsuko heard him. "She was burned to death. Preliminary sweeps are still under way . . . they didn't want to touch anything until we got here." He was already pulling on his gloves as they stepped out onto the windswept roof.

Only the tic in her cheek revealed she was moved by the information, and her dark eyes were as flat as lager-bottle glass as they walked. Mechanically, she flashed her credentials to the uniforms milling about the area, then she paused about five yards from the site itself. "Mikani." She sounded hesitant. "Are you going to read the scene?"

"If you can think of a better time and place, let me know." Corroded exhaust pipes and slow-turning fans dotted the rooftop. A fine layer of oily dust completed the sense of quiet despair that had started seeping into Mikani's head the moment they had driven into the metal-and-stone warren. Around the body, red rope cordoned off the area, and two constables stood about fifty feet away, as if they wanted to distance themselves.

The rest awaited the result of their inspection near the elevator or conducted searches throughout the buildings below, which made the charred remains seem more forsaken. Spread-eagled, she lay atop a reflective sheet of metal. All around, an elaborate arrangement of mirrors and lenses had concentrated the sun's rays on her. With a small sigh, Mikani knelt next to the body and ran his hands over her, not quite touching the heat-withered remains.

There is no anger, here. Strange. Mikani smelled the girl's fear, feeling her agony in phantom shivers and pain. Terror, shards of emotional memories screamed against the very stone. But of the killer . . . the mirrors and lenses were clear. Empty, as if they'd known no human touch, or the very fire they'd summoned had swept away all traces of their owner. Even the residue of decay and rot had been eradicated around her body; it lingered as a pervasive and faint trail of corruption leading from the stairs and to the apparatus's periphery before fading.

And yet, there is purpose. He planned all this, abducted her, then killed her slowly and painfully.

Though no positive ID had been made, Mikani already knew it was Cira that they'd found. He recognized her fading echo from the pretty pink-and-gold bedroom she'd left behind.

He saw her struggle, as aftershocks of terror rather than visual images: the taste of blood from a bitten tongue, the pain of constraints against wrists and ankles, harsh stone against the girl's back, and the sickening scent of the charnel house her body became. *That would be so much simpler—to see, rather than feel.* Shivering, he turned away. Already, his head pounded in protest, and from a detached place in his mind, he knew that when he came down, he'd pay dearly.

"I'll take over," Ritsuko said at last.

Mikani started: he had been too lost in Cira's death to hear his partner approach. He nodded curtly, watching her summon a junior officer.

"How's your shorthand?" Ritsuko asked.

"Excellent, ma'am." The young man pulled a pen out of his pocket as if to prove his eagerness.

He felt ancient compared to the kid with the notepad.

His partner said, "Then take dictation for me."

She opened her kit and produced a magnifying glass. As

Ritsuko crawled over the ground, she spoke. "The mirrors and lenses were pounded into the ground by hand. No trace of drill work. Our killer possesses exceptional strength." Next she examined the apparatus more closely. "This is set in a complex geometric pattern. From the precision, I gather that the suspect has an advanced knowledge of mathematics, Academy level. Check at the registrar's office."

She paused at the edge of the metal plate, and Mikani stumbled over to take a closer look at what she'd found—an ashy substance. After delving into her case, she scraped a sample into an evidence packet, then she collected a spare.

"Just in case?" Mikani asked.

She ducked her head, sheepish. "Of course."

Her thoroughness amused him, but in a good way. The fact that she could make him smile through the pounding in his skull? Felt like a minor miracle. He stumbled toward the wall and eased down. A quiet sigh escaped as he lifted his face toward the sun. Though it was a bright enough day, the warmth didn't penetrate.

Watching her label the samples, Mikani dug for a handkerchief to blot the blood off his upper lip. When he pushed his gift too hard, it felt like his brain tried to expand with his senses until it hit bone, and he got terrible nosebleeds. As if she could read his mind, Ritsuko handed him a crisp cotton square, saving him the trouble.

"What do you think?" He gestured vaguely at the murder machine.

"Geometric pattern, but I don't know what it means. I also found an organic compound, but we won't know what it is until the lab gets back to us," she said. "Rest. I'm going to question the workers."

"Thanks."

It could've been ten minutes or half an hour before she came back. And she didn't look excited, so no phenomenal break in the case. However, she did seem thoughtful. Puzzled, even.

"What?"

Ritsuko came over to kneel beside him, pitching her voice so nobody else could hear her. "I don't understand how this contraption could burn someone to death, just harnessing the sun. It would take a long time, wouldn't it?"

"Probably. There are workers day and night . . . there

should've been a witness. And someone would've interrupted him before the process was complete."

"And that's the thing. I talked to the maintenance crew. Checked their work log. There's a record with date, time, and initials, each time someone accesses the roof. Security reasons."

"And?"

"There was a four-hour window, Mikani. To make this happen, start to finish. Now you tell me how that's possible."

"A cover-up involving the factories? Probably not. Most of the owners would rather kill each other than cooperate." He held up a hand, resting his head on the wall and closing his eyes for a moment. "All right. Give me a minute here." Mikani chewed his bottom lip to distract him from the throbbing of his skull. "Maybe the body was placed here? It would still take some work to assemble this . . . thing, and bring it up without someone's noticing, but far less so than keeping her murder quiet."

"So let's ask Dr. Byfeld. I believe he's finishing up with his analysis." She glanced down, then added, "Let me get him. I'll be right back."

As he watched, she rounded up the doctor and herded him toward where Mikani sat, leaning on the wall. It was good of her not to draw attention to his problem though the constables probably thought he was drunk or lazy. Better they should think that than realize the truth.

Dr. Byfeld was a short, round man with a tonsure of patchy brown hair. He had a nervous habit of peering down his nose at people while pursing his mouth, and it gave him a rather rabbity air. But he was also incredibly observant, so perhaps the squinting served some purpose. As they approached, Ritsuko was saying, "I hope you can shed some light on the machine and the state of the remains."

The doctor tilted his head back, the better to make sure Mikani caught his disapproving glare, then cleared his throat. "I cannot tell you much about that . . . thing . . ." He gestured with a vague wave toward the device. "But the body suffered extensive injuries from a source of high heat. It was concentrated here"— he tapped at Mikani's forehead with his pen—"and it spread until it consumed her. The burn marks are clearly radial and gradual. The pattern of the molten tissue seems to indicate that liquefaction occurred on-site."

Mikani grunted and pushed himself upright, forcing the doctor to step back. "She was . . . burned, here. Did she die here?"

"Oh, yes, yes. There are evident signs of struggle after the process started—"

"Thank you, Doctor." Mikani clapped the smaller man on the shoulder to disguise the stumble as he pushed past him and toward the lift.

Rather than force him to answer questions from the others, his partner put on her sternest expression and strode over to a nearby knot of officers, demanding attention in a tone that made them cluster about her. "I want this area cordoned off until further notice. Nobody touches a single bolt on that device until I give the order. Is that clear?"

"Yes, ma'am!"

The collective terror of the uniformed constabulary gave Mikani a chance to shuffle out unnoticed. He made it to the vehicle, but barely. Things were spinning, so he crawled into the passenger side and lay for a second with his face on the seat. A minute later, he hauled himself upright. By the time his partner joined him, he was sitting with his head tilted back, her handkerchief sealed against his mouth. He didn't open his eyes when she slid into the driver's seat.

"So we have a lengthy murder on the roof. No conspiracy by the factory owners, no death off-site, and a noisy construction project. You have to admit, this is unusual."

She sighed. "It's also impossible. The available time simply *does not* allow for any of it."

"And yet, these are the facts. Therefore, we're dreaming, we're crazy, or the impossible happened. And in my dreams, we're—" He started over. "So, follow my crazy. If it can't happen, then there may be . . . magic, involved."

Magic was rare among the general populace and heavily regulated for obvious reasons, but there was a small minority who resented how power had been stolen from the natives, centuries ago. Like most fringe groups, they had little actual agency, and, generally, they were too poor to afford the licensing fees, so they hid from authorities and worked small glamours in private. This crime, however, felt much bigger to Mikani, far beyond their scope. So he needed help figuring out who could do something like this.

But he had to be careful how he approached it. This angle
would get them both pulled off the case so fast, their careers
would never recover. They'd be lucky to work directing traffic
in the park thereafter; and if the newssheets got wind of it,
Mikani could imagine the colorful headline: MYSTICAL MUR-
DERER USES MAGIC TO INCINERATE HIS VICTIMS! The magistrates
would love that.

"Magic," she repeated. "Well . . . it exists."

He looked up, the handkerchief falling from his mouth, and
gave her a newly appraising look. "Indeed. This is far past even
my level of strange, though. But I know someone who could lend
a hand. If she's willing."

"Why am I not surprised?" she asked, starting the cruiser.

"Because I'm too wrecked to be my usual, unpredictable, and
infuriating self. Now, unless you have some painkillers in your
bag, I'd appreciate if we could make an unofficial stop, Ritsuko.
I'd normally wait until I got home, but . . ."

"Whatever you need, Mikani." It was the gentlest thing she'd
ever said to him. "Just tell me where to turn."

AS THEY DROVE, Ritsuko noticed few pedestrians, but the noise
was constant: shouted conversations and threats, children playing
in hidden spaces beyond the patchwork walls. And underlying
the noise, the constant thrum and metallic clang of machinery.
Gaslights hung in shards, disrepair creeping from the industrial
area toward the rest of the city. Tenements had sprung up around
the monolithic factories at the center, encroaching on the streets,
so Ritsuko needed to focus on her driving to avoid the shanties.
The thoroughfare was choked with crates and barrels, but no
refuse; the hordes of scroungers wasted nothing, even in Iron
Cross. Their finds would be traded in various rag-and-bone shops
all over the city.

"You'll be turning left on Tenth. Then go straight until we
get to the Ribbon . . . but are you sure I'm not keeping you? I can
get a hansom." His tone made it clear that he preferred not to
drink alone.

*What am I doing? A bagful of evidence that needs to be
tagged . . .*

Even as she thought it, she answered, "I'll stay, Mikani."

With a sideways glance, she drove on, negotiating turns at his direction until she reached their destination. When she saw the place, Ritsuko concealed her misgiving as she secured her kit behind the seat, then waited for Mikani to alight.

The building appeared vacant, all the upper windows sealed. Ritsuko took a closer look, however, and saw movement beneath the tightly fitted blinds of the sublevel. *Wouldn't you know it? Mikani drinks in a dungeon.* External steps carried them down to the entrance, a peeling door that had been painted red at some point. Inside, the pub was a jungle of dim lights, tangy smoke, and pocked tables. As she stepped in, her eyes teared up, and she turned to make sure Mikani was behind her.

Mikani slipped past to signal the bartender, then led Ritsuko toward the far end of the room. He guided her to a ripped leather stool near the back. As Mikani sat, he rested his head against the wall. The relaxation of his pose marked the place as somewhere he felt safe, unlikely as it seemed to her.

"What'll you have?" the barman asked.

She answered, "Gundarson's Stout. In the bottle, please."

He glanced over in surprise, a half smile curving his mouth. "Never would've guessed that about you. I'll have the usual."

A few moments later, the barkeep delivered her bottle, plus a surprisingly clean glass brimming with dark beer. At a nod from Mikani, he also relinquished a pair of pills before returning to the other side of the counter. Like her partner, she needed something to blunt the memory of a girl reduced to human cinders—and despite its seediness, she saw what brought Mikani here. The place possessed an accepting anonymity.

Whoever you are, whatever your sin, be welcome among us. And drink. So she lifted her bottle and did so, sighing as the ale went down smooth.

Mikani grimaced as he swallowed his pills. *Bad-tasting medicine that smells like apples.* Oh, bronze gods, he was downing Dreamers. After taking them, some people went catatonic; others had incredibly vivid visions. One could never predict the results, which was why she disapproved. CID command wasn't delighted about its agents being compromised either, as it could wreck a trial. Instinct warred with duty; it was her obligation to report his use of a recreational chemical during work. Exhaling,

Ritsuko pretended she didn't recognize the tablets . . . and chose friendship above regulations.

But she had one concern. "Will those impede your ability to do your job?"

"Less than this headache. Or bleeding all over the reports."

She remembered one occasion where he'd stared off into space for an hour after a particularly strong response to the pills. But if he said he was up to the mark, she had to believe him. As long as he wasn't hallucinating, it likely meant they hadn't hit him hard.

And Mikani self-medicates enough to be licensed as a chemist.

"Fair enough."

He took a deep breath and a long drink of beer, foam staining his upper lip when he set the glass down. "You did great up there, partner." He hesitated a moment. "And thanks for keeping them off me."

"All in a day's work." Sighing, she lifted her bottle and gulped half of it. When she set it down, she couldn't read the expression on Mikani's face.

He shook his head and cracked a thin smile as he took another drink, gestured at her with the sloshing glass. "You go well beyond duty for me, Ritsuko. I know it. And . . . appreciate it."

At first, she didn't know how to respond. He seemed quite serious; for once, the customary levity was absent. The stout was working through her system, making her feel warm, easy, and so it made sense to explain, "People talk about both of us. For different reasons. But I'll be damned if I ever let them get at you. Not if I can stop it."

"Same for you, partner. Just ask Shelton and Cutler—" His brows shot up, as if concerned by what he'd almost said, and he took another drink to cover the confusion.

"Ask them what?"

Mikani propped his chin in his hand, tipping his head to the side, his eyes gone dreamy. "They said some things . . . and maybe your name came up, so I had to pound some sense into them. Didn't want them making trouble for you and Warren."

"That's why they had medical leave?" She'd heard, of course, but she didn't know why. Five weeks ago, Mikani had taken some time off as well, but she hadn't realized the two events were connected.

"I'm the only one who gets to make trouble for you, Ritsuko."

"I should probably be mad, but . . . thank you. For caring enough to do that for me." She smiled at him and finished the Gundarson's in another long swallow.

He drained his own beer with a deep pull, before saying, "Anything for you, partner. You're always there when I need you, and that means the world to me."

Warmth spread from the tips of her toes all the way to the top of her head. With anyone else, at a moment like this, she'd be thinking about the curve of his bottom lip or how his whiskers might prickle if she leaned a little closer. Before she knew it, her hand was moving, brushing against his jaw to find out. He leaned into her touch, smiling faintly as he caught her gaze. His skin was hot, the scruff prickling against her palm, and she slid her hand farther back into his hair, because she knew his head ached after a bad night. She pressed her fingertips to a few key points in slow, soothing circles.

"How's that? Better?"

His lashes drifted shut as he dipped his head forward. When he opened his eyes, their noses were nearly touching. "Much."

Her breath caught. She noticed flecks of gray in his dark blue eyes, framed by long lashes. His brows were thick, not that she could ever remember noticing that before, and they had a quizzical arch. And his mouth . . . well, his mouth was right there. She could feel his breath on her lips, and she wondered how he kissed, what that would be like. The warmth became heat, followed swiftly by absolute confusion. Her heart pounded like mad, and a tremor worked up from her knees to her hands. It was all she could do to ease back, hoping the insanity didn't show in her face.

That . . . what was *that?*

Gundarson's, she decided. *And not enough sleep. And . . . we've never been unattached at the same time. There was always Warren, or one of his girls . . .*

"Barkeep!" she called, praying for a steady tone. "Another round."

"Just one," Mikani muttered, looking flushed. "For the road. We still have business at HQ."

CHAPTER 6

THE MORNING AFTER WAS ALWAYS AWKWARD. THANKFULLY, Mikani had only shared a few drinks with Ritsuko, nothing irrevocable. He was too used to such vices, so his head felt fine. He couldn't remember the last time he'd suffered a hangover. He quickened his step, anxious to be about his errand.

River Park dominated the center of Dorstaad. It was the spot of the original settlement, over a thousand years before; remnants of the old stone walls dotted the three square miles of lightly wooded land. It was one of the few places in Dorstaad where the sun shone down unimpeded by acrid smoke or the shadow of tall buildings. Mikani swung his walking stick to warn other pedestrians to get out of his way; he considered springing the hidden blade to prod them along, but that might be lack of coffee. His path carried him past the café where Electra worked, and the smell enticed him to stop.

"Mikani," Electra called. She was busy with other customers, but the smile was just for him. "Keeping out of trouble?"

He grinned. "Almost never."

"The usual?"

He nodded.

"Coming up." She studied him, head to toe, and shook her head. "Things have gotten worse, haven't they?"

It was a good guess, possibly based more on his expression than his alleged aura. But given his own talents, Electra's power might be real, too. "Unfortunately."

"Are you sure you won't let me read your cards? Maybe I can help."

"I don't have time today." Mikani flashed a smile. "But I might be back."

He drained his cup and returned it to Electra before heading down ash-lined Strand Avenue as it followed the river's curve. Mikani took his time, as the smell of running water and growing things eased the churning of his mind. He mulled the case with the possible complication of magic, this errand in search of help, and the recent awkwardness with Ritsuko. Though two drinks was nothing to him, his partner had seemed to feel the effects long after the pills and the liquor wore off for Mikani.

After the odd moment at the bar, they hadn't talked much, going over interviews and statements, filing and storing what they had so far. Anatole must have sensed something amiss: he'd stayed well away from the duty room. Mundane tasks had blurred into one long stretch of tedium; by midnight, things returned to normal, with a tacit agreement to concentrate on the case—and at that point, they were exhausted. They'd headed out to get some sleep.

Though not much. Not with the Council bearing down. It won't be long before we do something stupid if we don't get some real rest.

How long's it been? Sometimes, he kept in touch with women who left him, but most often, they preferred a clean break. It was rare that he found himself needing to ask a favor from a former lover, but with the pressure from above, he reckoned he had to use all the resources at his command.

Saskia wouldn't be amused to be described as an asset.

He hurried the last few blocks to an unassuming, brightly painted building crammed between two far-more-imposing structures. A stylized, human-headed-owl sign proclaimed it to be the main offices of Siren Trading. He rapped on the frame sharply with his walking stick.

A woman opened the door. Nearly Mikani's height, she was

light where he was dark: braided blond hair to the waist, dressed in a flowing cream dress cut to classical lines. Pale green eyes met his, and she smiled.

"Janus." He could not help the smile back: she'd always had that effect on him. Her gaze slid over his shoulder, and back. "You're not here to arrest me, then."

Oh, hells and Winter, she remembers.

"Not this time, Saskia."

"You usually keep your promises. I'm disappointed." She turned back toward the building, and he followed, closing the door behind him. All around them, clerks and secretaries waved papers, filed documents, and carried on in an intense hubbub that she ignored as she led him to her office upstairs. Her bare feet made no sound on the worn wood: she'd grown up on her family's ship and claimed shoes were only good for slipping on wet timbers.

He slouched in an old, overstuffed chair while she walked around the carved oak desk, folding herself into the chair to look at him expectantly.

"I'm sorry to drop in like this. I need your help—"

"I'm well, thanks for asking, Janus. It has, indeed, been a long time. Two years? The concern's prospering, as you can see."

He ran a hand through his hair, abashed. "My apologies. I trust you—"

She interrupted him by tossing a crumpled piece of paper at his head. "Stop being horrid." She let out a long sigh as she leaned closer, over her desk. "It really is good to see you, you know."

"And I truly am sorry it's been so long." He offered a conciliatory smile, resting his elbows on his knees. "I'll do my best to make it up to you. But first, I need your help."

She frowned, studying him for a long moment. He returned her silent gaze. *Come, Saskia, you know I wouldn't have come to you if I had another choice. Not like this.* The silence stretched for a full minute before she leaned back, letting out a long, soft breath. "I sense that you're going to ask a . . . complicated favor." She poured two glasses of whiskey, sliding one toward him.

"It could result in official disapproval, should my superiors find out." She made a soft, amused sound. They both were well aware of her disdain for authority—House or Council. He sipped, watching her as the burn spread down his tongue and throat. "And it will involve a trip to Iron Cross."

Her eyes narrowed; local factory owners, who preferred to keep suppliers under their thumbs, saw her and the other Free Traders as a necessary evil. Over the years, she had struggled to build up her business, and she wouldn't look kindly on any endeavor that could threaten her life's work. Even if it came with the appealing prospect of putting him in her debt.

"Tell me the rest."

"It also means using your gifts." He turned away when the liquid in her glass spattered as she slammed it on the desk.

Saskia glared. Her fists were white-knuckled on the desktop, all color drained from her face. Her bottom lip trembled, as she finally whispered, "Janus Mikani, how dare you ask me that, after what happened?"

He stood and leaned on his walking stick, blue eyes steady. "Only you can help me. I trust you and . . . and I need you. We're trying to catch a killer." He held a hand up as she tried to dismiss his argument. "This monster killed a girl, who hadn't done a damned thing wrong. Help me."

"You . . . you're a selfish, arrogant . . . idiot. Why me?" She sounded as weary as he felt.

"Because this has the smell of sorcery, Saskia. It reeks of it, and I need you to tell me that I'm crazy for thinking it."

"Oh, Janus. You're all kinds of crazy, but your instincts are usually sound." She finished her glass in a long gulp. "But I still don't see why I should help you."

"Old times aren't compelling enough?"

She gave him a look. "You know me better than that."

"What do you need, then?" Mikani didn't have the kind of money that would tempt Saskia into helping out. He waited for her reply, wondering how bad it would be.

"I could use a hand with some craggers."

"Bastards," he muttered.

Though he didn't deal with their ilk, they were a nasty, solitary lot who prowled the bluffs of the Winter Isle. They must be hitting Saskia's ships. How *he* could help, Mikani had no idea, but it wasn't as if he could turn away her aid should he secure it.

"I'll give you the details later. Let's go before I change my mind."

"Then put some shoes on, grab a shawl, milady. Let me offer you an excursion to Iron Cross." He offered his arm.

"Fool," she muttered as she stepped around the desk. "You always took me to the worst places."

MIKANI LIT A cigarillo. He drew deeply, savoring the burn. He wasn't used to inactivity, but Saskia had been adamant that he stay out of the way. So it required all his self-control to keep from pacing, peering over her shoulder, and generally making a nuisance of himself.

The ward constables waited downstairs, keeping the scene clear for him and his consultant. At some point, they'd covered the device with a tarp, but otherwise, it remained undisturbed so far; a team from Headquarters was due to disassemble, study, and catalog it, but they were waiting for approval. Once it came, Mikani suspected the whole thing would be sold off as scrap metal before the week's end.

Saskia walked a circle around the machine, her eyes half-closed as she whispered a soft incantation. Her right hand drew graceful patterns in the air; she carried intricate henna traceries all over her forearm, which shimmered and shifted when she flexed her fingers. Every few steps she paused and jingled the bells of the charm bracelet on her left wrist. They had been at it for an hour; dusk was fast approaching.

Mikani watched her through the curls of smoke, frowning. *I shouldn't have dragged her into this. I can still taste Cira's death; gods know what she's getting from that thing while actively digging around.*

"Janus." Her voice was tight; she stood very still, looking down at her feet. He tossed the cigarillo and stepped closer. "No, don't." She licked her lips, and he tensed. "Tell me . . . what do you feel?"

He hesitated, then closed his eyes and stopped trying to block the echoes all around him. Even from ten feet away, he could sense that something had changed. "There's something . . . pushing me away. No, I feel like I shouldn't be here. It's . . . subtle."

"It was present when she . . . when he killed her. The effect would have kept everyone away." She canted her head and slowly stretched her arm toward the device once more before pulling it away quickly.

"Saskia." When she'd lifted her arm, he had felt a sudden chill. He took a step closer before she shook her head and warned him off with a look.

"No, I'm well enough. I guess you felt that, too." She retraced her steps carefully. "This machine feels as if there's a . . . hole. It's a deep, cold pit, as if something grabbed a piece of the world and yanked it out. It's frightening." She completed the circle and stepped away from the machine, rubbing her arms.

He draped the shawl over her and took her hands: she was deathly cold. "It's magic, then."

"It's twisted and wrong, Janus. Be careful. Whoever did this is dangerous and probably mad." She glanced over her shoulder. "No sane person *would*."

"I owe you, Saskia. I'm sorry I put you through this." He squeezed her fingers.

She nodded. "You do. And I'll collect, soon. You can start by getting me away from here, though."

Their lives had just gotten much more complicated.

RITSUKO DIDN'T REQUISITION a car since she was working on her own this morning; splitting up meant they could cover more ground, investigate leads more efficiently, and the tube took her where she needed to be. Her head throbbed faintly, a combination of a light hangover and lack of sleep. She envied how her partner could shake off the aftereffects, but she wasn't used to drinking.

Hurrying along the sideway, she made mental notes as she went. *I need to question all the professors in both mathematics and engineering. They might shed some light on the design of the murder machine.*

A well-kept redbrick building occupied the corner of Academe and Sixth Street, where she crossed. Someone had planted flowers in the window boxes; the fragrance was profuse, permeating the whole block. Ahead lay the quad, an open green where the students lazed around in the sun. Some young men had a ball they were kicking around, while girls in pretty frocks cheered them on. She skirted well away from the game, heading for the registrar's office.

Inside, there was a couple arguing and a bored woman behind a desk, dealing with a queue of students. Ritsuko flashed her badge, and said, "I'm looking for the dean."

"His office is in the next building." The clerk gave directions, looking both nervous and intrigued.

She imagined it wouldn't be long before the woman found an excuse to tell a colleague that the CID had arrived. Her heels clicked briskly against the pavement as she hurried from the building and into the next, a gracious structure with creamy white columns out front. Within, the first floor was divided into offices, with the dean residing in the last and largest one. In the antechamber, a comely redhead was shuffling some papers, doing her best to look as if she hadn't been hired for her features.

She smiled as Ritsuko approached. "May I help you?"

"I need to speak with the dean, please." Again, she showed her credentials.

"Oh. Right away." The girl hurried to warn her boss, but Ritsuko followed too closely to allow any private conversation.

"Sir, I need your cooperation." Pointedly, she stared at the assistant until she returned to her desk, then Ritsuko stepped into the office and closed the door.

The dean was an elderly gentleman with a crop of close-cut white hair. He was thin and stooped in the way of men who had spent long years hunched over a desk. Lines on his face said he had little Ferisher blood, or that he was incredibly old, but his gray eyes seemed sharp beneath the wild caterpillars of his brows.

"Yes, miss, what is it?" A gruff tone, but not recalcitrant.

"I'm Inspector Ritsuko with the CID. I'm working a case, and I need to consult with your engineering department. I don't need to ask your leave, but I thought the instructors might be more forthcoming if they knew this endeavor carried your blessing."

"May I see your identification please?"

"I showed your assistant before she showed me in." But Ritsuko got her ID packet out, nonetheless.

The old man laughed. "I daresay you could've shown her a

napkin with ink spilled on it, and her reaction would've been the same."

She raised a brow. "If you think so poorly of her acumen, why did you hire her?"

"I'm an old man. I have few pleasures left, and one of them is looking at pretty girls."

She smiled at that, for he reminded her of her grandfather: acerbic but amusing. "I understand. Will you send word to your instructors for me?"

"Unless it's confidential, I'd prefer to know what this is about."

"A girl was murdered," she said quietly. "And her killer built this horrific apparatus to do the deed. I thought, perhaps, your engineering and mathematics teachers might know which students have the technical skill to create such a thing."

His gray eyes were shrewd. "And you'll take the measure of the professors, who won't be on their guards, as they'll believe you're searching for a student?"

"Sir, I've told you all I can. Will you help me in this?" He was a clever old devil.

"Absolutely. If there is a madman among my students or staff, I wish to see the blackguard brought to justice. I'll have Miss Winters carry a message at once. Will you have tea while we wait for her to return?"

"That would be lovely."

Ritsuko used his facilities and prepared the tray once the assistant had gone. The dean watched with narrowed gaze, looking pensive. When she returned to the maroon upholstered chair before the window, he said, "You have some skill in that."

"Yes, I did my share of fetching tea and coffee in the beginning at the CID."

"You speak as if you've been working there for years."

"Ten," she said proudly. "I spent three years as a clerk. Then I talked my way in into a lab position. Another four years there while I studied the field manuals, memorized procedures, and spent my free time practicing."

"Practicing what?" the dean asked, lifting his cup.

"Everything I needed to work as an inspector."

A smile creased his face. "When did your receive your promotion?"

"Just over three years ago."

"It is most gratifying to see hard work rewarded. You know that it was only eight years past that we started accepting female students at the Academy?"

"I am aware. Most forward-thinking of you, sir."

"Can't imagine why some of these girls want to work when they're pretty enough to marry, but you know what they say, changing times and all."

Their cups were drained by the time the red-haired assistant returned. "Some of the instructors complained, but I've carried the memo to both departments."

"Good, Miss Winters. You may go."

Once the door shut behind the other woman, Ritsuko stood. "I wonder if I could request a final favor of you, sir."

"Nothing ventured," he said.

"Could you request the registrar to search your records and collect a list of those who have graduated with applicable courses of study?"

"That will be quite an undertaking. For how many years?

She considered, then answered, "Fifteen should be sufficient, I think. I can't imagine a man of a certain age constructing such a contraption."

"A man my age, you mean?" He rose, offering a polite half bow, then assured her, "You should have no trouble, and *if* you do, deliver the scallywag to me. Trust that I shall deal with him harshly."

"Or I could arrest him."

A laugh escaped him, quite deep and merry. "So you could. I suppose the days are past when a woman needs a man to be gallant."

"*Need* is, perhaps, the wrong word, but it's always charming. Thank you for the tea." She shook his hand and strode out.

The assistant provided her with a hastily drawn map of the campus, showing where the mathematics and engineering departments were located. Both were situated away from administration, a fair walk across patches of grass that grew between sprawling buildings. Each discipline reflected a different design, so that made it simpler to tell the study areas apart.

That probably helps new students.

It made her job easier, too. She went to the mathematics department first, where she interviewed five professors; a sixth was absent. None of them seemed like a good bet for creating such a monstrous device, and though she lacked Mikani's uncanny sense for such things, her intuition was decent. The last instructor made a list of students who were also taking engineering courses.

"Thanks for your time," she said, moving on.

It was noisier in the engineering lab, less time spent with pen and paper, more time devoted to practical applications. She had to search hard for the professors, who were getting their hands dirty along with their pupils. In exasperation, she waited for the class to end, then she snagged a beanpole of a teacher.

He pulled off his safety glasses and eyed her with faint annoyance. "Yes, yes, I got the memorandum from the dean. I'll answer your questions. Follow me."

His office was quieter, but cramped compared to the dean's. Books and schematics overflowed his shelves, tumbling down to a cluttered desk, littered with the remnants of lunch. Ritsuko tried not to show her disdain, but she must've done so because his lip curled.

"I imagine your digs are much nicer down at the CID."

Cleaner, anyway. She didn't answer aloud, however, no point in antagonizing a potential resource. Instead, she began with her customary inquiries, running down the list, and his answers were much as expected, until she asked, "Do you know anyone capable of building such a thing?"

"What do you mean, capable?"

"Having the necessary aptitude, knowledge, and even . . . potential desire." Her tone was grave, as she knew how serious an accusation it would be.

"Give me your list," the professor said. He skimmed it, then took up his pen and drew two stars. "I'm not saying either of those boys is guilty, but neither is quite right. They don't work well with others. They're quiet. Odd."

"And they're both taking engineering and mathematics," she said softly. "Thank you for your time. Are the other instructors around?"

"You won't find anyone smarter than me to provide information," the man said.

"Perhaps that's true, but it's my job to be thorough." With that, she turned and went in search of his colleagues.

None of them cared to speculate on their students' state of mind, but one of them, Mr. Hollis, seemed excessively nervous. Finally, she asked him, "Why are you tapping, sir? Do you have a prior engagement?"

"No," he stuttered. "It's simply that this is very unnerving. I've never been questioned by the CID before."

That could be it, she supposed. But she put him in a mental list, along with the two boys the other professor had singled out. At least this junket had given her lots of leads to pursue. That might keep them on the case, provided no more bodies surfaced.

Somehow, she didn't think they'd be so lucky.

CHAPTER 7

FAR OUT TO SEA, DARK CLOUDS ROIL, HEAVY SWELLS BREAKING FAR BELOW against a beach of boulders and gravel; a cold wind brings hints of the storm's fury. Ships bob on the towering whitecaps in the distance, there but not there, shadows of things to come. As the veil between the worlds thins, stretches . . . and breaks with a boom of thunder, the clouds open and rain falls, icy cold needles driven by the mounting gale.

The fleet vanishes. Lightning crashes.

A great wail rises from Clíona, who guards the strait; her call vibrates from the seafloor, shaking through sinew and bone, a pitiless, piercing alarm to the Summer and Winter Courts. The ocean splits, disgorging a massive wave, and on its crest surge the missing ships. Some have broken masts, and bearded men list on the decks, hair sodden with salt. Belowdecks, children are weeping below the raucous call of circling seabirds. The gulls dive, again and again, seeking in the storm-dark water.

Bodies float upon the sea; this crossing is not made without cost.

The once-mighty vessels limp toward the shore while arguments rage. Oarsmen have been washed away. Supplies are

*missing. Families weep and search for the lost. Eventually, four
ships run aground, and exhausted wayfarers tumble to the
sands, desperate, bewildered.*

"What is this place?" a man asks in a harsh, guttural tongue.

*"It doesn't resemble our world. Ālfheimr, perhaps? Or
Valhalla."*

*A woman pales, clinging to the hand of a weeping child. "Are
we dead, then?"*

*The leader strides forward, his eyes reflecting a fierce and
indomitable spirit despite a bruised face and bleeding shoulder.
"Wherever we may be, we shall prevail."*

MIKANI STIRRED, THE movement of the underground vibrating
up through the soles of his shoes. He still smelled the brine and
the cold wind on his cheeks. This dream reminded him strongly
of the legends he'd heard of how humans first came to the fey
isles; and it seemed so real. His hand closed on a man's wrist—
the chieftain in the dream, he'd thought—but real world and
fantasy were overlapping. Today, not a thousand years ago, someone was rummaging in his pocket without any particular skill,
and he cried out at Mikani's iron clasp.

The first kick on his shin shattered any lingering doubt.

Coming fully awake, Mikani twisted and pulled the pickpocket's arm, yanking the other man against the wooden side of
the train carriage. His first blow shattered the thief's collarbone;
Mikani followed with an elbow to the throat. He didn't hold back,
wasn't known for mercy. Officers of the Guard were left to pursue
their own training for self-defense: Mikani's chosen trainers had
been the sailors and mercenaries he'd managed to provoke
throughout the bars and dives of Dorstaad and beyond.

When he saw that the thief wasn't resisting, he slammed the
other man against the carriage door and pinned him there with
a forearm pressed to his chest. The train slowed with a screech
of brakes and a hiss of venting steam; Mikani unlatched the door,
dragging the thief out behind him. A small group of tradesmen
scattered out of his way.

*Bastard's lucky I didn't draw the blade from my walking stick
and skewer him in my sleep.*

He let out a long breath as his heartbeat slowed. When he realized how frightened the passengers on the platform looked, he dug out his bronze badge of office and held it up. "I'm Inspector Mikani. This chap is a pickpocket who had a bit of a stumble and nearly fell off the train in his haste to get away. I'd appreciate it if one of you fine citizens would summon one of the ward officers."

He straightened his jacket, tugging at the torn lapel and shoulder seam. He offered them his best semblance of a friendly smile as they scattered in search of a constable, casting a few final, quick glances at the thief cowering against the wall. He rubbed the gritty feeling from his eyes. The lingering scent of the sea remained, as did the chill in his bones. *I'm having those dreams more often. And it's getting harder to wake up from them. Maybe I should take a couple of days after we get this mess wrapped up.*

Eventually, constables showed up to take charge of the pickpocket. *Well, that was inopportune. Damn it. I think I lost my hat.*

It was lucky that South's Officer of the Watch was an old acquaintance from his days walking the beat, so the formalities were brief before they carted the thief off to a quick hearing before his final processing, but logging the incident for the record delayed him further. Reporting at Headquarters in a torn and dirty suit would be more trouble than he was willing to endure. The paperwork for showing up to work garbed in a manner unbefitting an inspector was one of the few regulations the commander was happy to enforce, probably because it involved a fine. So that meant he had to go home and change.

Ritsuko won't be happy I'm making her wait.

An hour later, Mikani disembarked at South Ward Station, not far from his house. A young hawker with a sheaf of newssheets thrust one in his hand and wouldn't take no for an answer. He ran alongside Mikani until he dropped a few coppers in the boy's hand. On the front page, there was a long article about the grisly murder in Iron Cross. He skimmed it and sighed.

Damned gutter press. At least they didn't print Miss Aevar's name.

He hurried through the early foot traffic dotting the cobbled roads that ran parallel to the Summer Highway, a mile or so to the east—he could make out the faraway whistles of the trains and heavy steam coaches that carried traffic and passengers from Dorstaad to far-flung towns and villages throughout the Summer Isle. Hy Breasil was made up of a number of smaller islands, but Summer and Winter were the largest.

He stepped out of the way of a couple of bondswomen headed for the local market, then quickened his pace. Mikani ducked out of the alley across from his cottage, keeping his head down and shoulders up for the final dash across the street before his neighbors could add this tidbit to the growing volume of rumors about him that had accrued over the years.

Sometimes, when there are no more roads to follow, we must make our own trail. His father had taught him that. *And sometimes, the best way to solve a problem is to hit it repeatedly and see if it breaks.* His first Officer of the Watch had taught him that; he'd then demonstrated the precept by beating a confession out of the smuggler responsible for most contraband leaving Rivermouth Docks.

He slipped into the cottage. Just inside stood a coatrack draped with miscellaneous rumpled jackets. Atop it, he would've perched his favorite bowler; Mikani experienced a fresh, fleeting twinge of regret for the loss of that hat. Leaning against the door, he let out a sigh and afforded himself the luxury of a half minute's rest. Without wanting to, he remembered how Ritsuko's hand felt in his hair, that spun-glass moment where she'd been close enough to kiss, the scent of camellias warmed on her skin.

No more of this. I have a job to do.

With a muttered curse, he headed to the bathroom, tugged his tie loose, and shrugged out of his ragged coat. Most men would've left the walking stick at the entrance, but he kept it close, as it was all that remained of his father. After hanging the cane on a sconce, he grabbed a towel.

Twenty minutes later, he'd sluiced off sweat and grime; next he dug through his armoire for a clean shirt. His hair was a sodden and tangled mess, dripping onto his shoulders, plastering the thin cotton undershirt to his back. He murmured an oath when he heard the knock on the door.

                              *   *   *

WHEN MIKANI FAILED to report for duty at HQ and the incident
report hit Ritsuko's desk about his scuffle in the underground,
she'd come looking for him. *Hope he's not trying to walk off
broken ribs again.* Her partner had a habit of trying to self-treat
injuries that required stitches, bone-setting, or a visit to the
apothecary. One of these days, he might appear in the office with
a gash in his head, dripping blood.

She pounded harder on the front door.

If he's passed out in there, too stubborn to seek help—

But no. From within, Ritsuko heard movement, then a muffled
curse. A few seconds later, Mikani unfastened the dead bolt and
opened the door. Clean trousers clung to his hips, as he hadn't
dried off properly. Beads of water slipped down his tan skin,
tangling in dark chest hair. He was more muscular than she
would've imagined, not thin as Warren had been, and he looked
incredibly strong. His biceps flexed as he beckoned with an impatient gesture, and for a few seconds, she forgot why she was here.

"Come in," he muttered.

Ritsuko stepped through, smoothing her skirt. Partner or not,
entering his home felt oddly intimate. *We've had drinks. Now,
I'm coming into his house while he stumbles around half-
dressed . . . oh, bronze gods, turn my grandfather's eyes from
me. He wouldn't approve of this.*

Of course, he hadn't supported her decision to work for the
CID either. It wasn't womanly. He'd wanted her to marry and
give him great-grandchildren instead. He hadn't liked Warren,
or appreciated their choice to handfast instead of a legal binding,
a local custom, not a cultural one. When he was still alive, her
grandfather had shown her various dossiers on good men from
marriageable Mountain District families, descended from uni-
versity students who had washed up like other immigrants. The
students had claimed to come from the Kingdom of the Rising
Sun; she didn't know precisely where that was, but she guessed
the other side of the veil, past the dreaming sea.

"You were late." He'd hate the idea that she'd come out of
concern, so Ritsuko wrapped the truth in faint annoyance. If he
pondered the explanation, he'd realize it was a long way just to

round up an irresponsible partner, but fortunately, he was only half paying attention as he rushed to dress.

She glanced around the receiving room, noting the dark wood shelves dominating the far wall. They were filled with books and odd knickknacks—a wine bottle holding a candle, a broken toy horse. He had a collection of small crucifixes and tokens of various gods scattered over the writing desk crammed into a corner, facing a window overlooking a small herb garden. An overstuffed chair sat alone in the center of the room, facing the fireplace: half a dozen books lay open, upside down, or stacked around the seat. What wall space was not covered by the shelves was covered in prints and framed sketches. The space felt cozy if a little crowded; it was chaotic and unkempt.

Just like him. I wager Mikani spends his time here when he's home.

"I ran into a bit of trouble on the train," he called from deeper in the house. "Duty before everything, all that."

"I heard," she murmured, low enough that he wouldn't catch it.

Ritsuko followed his voice, peeking into a well-appointed kitchen: polished brass pots and pans gleamed from hooks on the wall. Yielding to curiosity, she stepped into the kitchen. Herbs were drying over the windows, alongside onions and garlic strands. The room smelled faintly of bread, baked a few days ago. Ritsuko shook her head as she stepped out of the uncharacteristic island of order.

This . . . is surprising.

She never would've guessed Mikani could boil water, let alone bake. He didn't give the impression of being particularly domesticated. In fact, he was more like a dire wolf, especially if you woke him up. Or that was the word from some constables who'd handled the paperwork for the altercation that sent him to tidy up and made her worry that he was injured worse than he'd let on to the other officers.

"You're an exemplar. I'm certain that the people of South Ward feel safer with you guarding them, even in your sleep." Ritsuko let a trace of mild chastisement creep into her tone. There was a guilty silence from the bedroom, and she smiled. She crossed her arms, remaining on the threshold of the entryway to his private rooms. "A lesser woman might point out that she'd warned you repeatedly about dozing on trains."

"Which is why I'm grateful to have a *great* one as my partner." Mikani emerged, straightening his tie and tugging at his jacket enough to rumple it. He flashed a cocky grin as he finger combed his shaggy hair and reclaimed his cane. "I'd offer you tea, but that would delay us further. And I don't drink tea. So there's that."

After executing a half bow, he turned, brushing her hip as he stepped into the foyer; in that same moment, she shifted to let him by. That sudden contact, accompanied by an unexpected frisson of . . . something, surprised her into stillness. Mikani paused as well. She jerked away, a clumsy withdrawal, while he danced backward. In the confusion, he knocked a wall clock down but caught it with quick hands.

This is . . . decidedly odd.

"After you." He cradled the clock, grinning sheepishly.

Ritsuko cleared her throat as she led the way to the foyer. "It's a lovely house."

Yes, definitely time to step outside.

"Thanks."

"I'll be in the cruiser. You can drive. You're better with the evening traffic anyway." She wondered what he made of her staccato delivery and the heat in her cheeks as she strode out the front door.

I knew there was a reason we never socialized outside the office.

"It's a matter of making sure they're more scared of you than everyone else on the road." At the cruiser, he took the keys from her, their fingertips brushing for a moment. Mikani made his way around Big Red, unlocking the door and holding it open . . . before looking up, seemingly startled at his own gesture.

"Did you take a knock to the head?" she asked, truly wondering if he had.

Mikani had never opened a door for her that she could recall. Some women might be put off by this apparent lack of manners, but she interpreted it otherwise. To her, it meant he considered her capable of doing it herself, and that, well, that was everything.

"In the last few years? Repeatedly."

She slid into the cruiser, half fearing he meant to hold her elbow and ask if she needed a lap rug. A teasing Mikani she could handle, but a solicitous one? It made her fear that she'd contracted a fatal illness, and he didn't know how to break the bad news.

He shook his head, then shut the door before making his way around to the driver's side, to sit quiet as the engine warmed up to running speed. To her mind, the silence felt layered, as if he had a secret he couldn't share. And that was . . . strange. In the past, he'd had no qualms about telling her too much—more than she wanted to know, in fact—about past liaisons. Then he teased her about prudishness and her inability to relax. It felt as though something had shifted, and she wasn't certain the change improved matters.

Mikani drove like a man possessed; which was to say, like his old self. But when they pulled up to the theater, he wove around the block and into the alley rather than parking at the front entrance. After easing the engine to a low, idling hum, he tapped his fingertips on the steering wheel for a moment.

"We're still waiting for the laboratory results?"

"Mr. Higgins did confirm that the greasepaint we found on Cira's sewing kit matched what I took from the case here." She sighed, staring at the Royale. "But it will be several days more on the ash. He received a reprimand for willfully ignoring the assignment priority list. That will teach me to employ my wiles in the line of duty."

"I assure you, that only makes your wiles more enticing." He gave her a cryptic smile and slipped out of the cruiser, moving toward the back doors to the theater.

Fighting a blush, Ritsuko followed. That *sounded* almost flirtatious. It wasn't out of character for him to tease, but not in a way that showed any awareness of her femininity. As she walked, she rubbed the grit out of her eyes; the scant sleep she'd snatched didn't feel like enough, and it left her with a residual headache, made more trying by her partner's enigmatic behavior.

"Right now, our only clue leads us here, and thus, to the Royale's owner." Mikani pushed the door open and led the way inside.

Silently, Ritsuko agreed. Between the greasepaint and the

crew's knowing Miss Aevar, they really needed to talk to Leonidas.

A startled woman with a mop looked up at their passing; Mikani flashed her a smile and tugged his forelock. Then he headed into the dark theater corridors, tilting his head this way and that, as if sniffing out a trail. The silence was complete, unlike the first time they called and interrupted rehearsal. Trickles of sunlight filtered through cracks beneath doors, swathing the great room in shadows that seethed with movement. A faint scent of burning glass lingered, along with an astringent aroma, probably from the charwoman's bucket. She had no idea what they were searching for, as there was nobody here to question.

Except the reclusive owner . . .

Mikani paused at each junction and door, tapping his fingertips against the wall and hinges. After a few moments of the silent search, he stopped at a nondescript door, easily missed in the half-lit corridor, then opened it.

"You think he's our man?" Ritsuko asked.

"Maybe. The usual motives could apply."

"Sex or money," she guessed, trailing him through the doorway. "With Cira, both are possible. He might have recognized her and demanded money for his silence. How else do you explain all the renovations?"

Mikani said, "So, a blackmail scheme? Then he killed her when she threatened to charge him with the crime . . . possible. She's also a pretty young thing. Perhaps she found his reclusive nature fascinating."

"But the charm would pall after a while." They had always done this, filled in the blanks for each other. Despite outward appearances, their thoughts often marched along the same lines. "So perhaps—"

"He murdered her rather than let her leave him."

"A terrible devotion," she said softly. "But what about that bizarre apparatus?"

"A puzzle indeed."

"Leonidas *did* appear troubled," she conceded.

"And there's the matter of the secret he's hiding."

She nodded. "So it can't hurt to ask him some questions. We should have done so the other day, but I couldn't find him. And I *did* look."

"I know, Ritsuko." Distracted in his reassurance, he was examining a blank wall.

Mikani knocked on it lightly, listening with a satisfied smirk before pressing on one side, then the other. She had seen that expression before, usually right before he did something that would get them in trouble should they be caught at it. Over the years, she'd learned to ignore minor infractions in favor of results. *Like the Dreamers.* She knew he used them occasionally, but never on duty. *That must've been some headache. Wonder how often he takes them.*

And then . . . then there was the Moment.

Which never happened.

Heaving a sigh, she followed him down the staircase revealed when the panel popped open. No wonder she hadn't been able to find Leonidas; Miss Wright hadn't been exaggerating when she said the theater was built on a labyrinth. There was no light down below, just an endless darkness, that of no stars, no breath; it whispered of the grave and of small, creeping things with too many legs and claws that skittered across damp stone.

"Perhaps we ought to get a lamp," she said.

"He might see us coming, then. And that would ruin the surprise."

With a resigned glare at the back of his head, she dogged his heels, then she smothered a gasp of surprise when his warm fingers wrapped around hers. It was probably to lead her, or ensure she didn't get lost. But it felt profoundly affectionate for him to serve as her only tie to the living world in this sea of shadows.

They descended for eternal moments, the soft rasp of leather on stone the only sound other than their breathing. Then the darkness gradually lightened: she glimpsed his outline before her, growing darker as the passage below grew lighter. He squeezed her hand lightly before releasing it, casually swinging his walking stick over his shoulder and turning enough not to block her view when they reached the bottom of the stairs.

At irregular intervals along the wall, gaslight flickered in smoky glass sconces. Ritsuko could tell these tunnels were very old; the mortar had crumbled in places, so that crevices puffed out stale air from somewhere deeper in the earth. The stone itself was dry and clean but dark with age. She found no signs of vermin or the creatures she had feared while they descended that endless staircase. Mikani cocked his head, visibly drawn, and he moved off down the hall at a quickened pace, clever enough to keep his cane off the stone floor. She tried to step lightly, not allowing her boots to click, as Leonidas doubtless knew this warren like the back of his hand and could slip away if he heard them coming. As if he shared her fear, Mikani led her through breakneck turns, winding left and right, seemingly at random, but she was sure he'd sensed their target.

Up ahead, the dimness kindled with a faint glow that grew brighter, the closer they got. At last, they reached a chamber memorable only in its despair. The amenities might've been chosen by an ascetic seeking to do penance: a simple bed and a pile of books. A lavish velvet throw draped across the thin mattress comprised the only concession to comfort, but that was practicality as well, for as they'd gone down, the temperature dropped as well. Leonidas was sprawled against the headboard, reading, when they stepped in.

"Good evening, Mr. Leonidas. I'm Inspector Mikani, this is my partner, Ritsuko . . . and we have a few questions for you."

The theater owner glanced up from his book, a weighty tome entitled *Cults of Winter*. The mass of scars that twisted his mouth into a grimace made his blossoming rage impressive to behold. "How in the blazing hells did you get in here?"

Ritsuko produced her notebook, and said politely, "We have a number of questions . . . somehow, you eluded an interview last time. It won't take long."

"You enter my private quarters uninvited, and you expect me to cooperate?" The Royale's owner fumbled with cloak and mask, desperate to conceal his disfigurement. Only once he was covered did he look at Ritsuko directly, his eyes shaded. "Is there some reason you couldn't make an appointment?"

"You've given us no reason to imagine you would keep it," Mikani said coldly. "If a man hides in a burrow like an animal, one must presume he is guilty of *something*."

She caught an unmistakable flinch and saw the moment when pain edged toward anger. If Mikani continued in this vein, Leonidas would become overtly hostile. So she said quickly, "If this isn't a good time, sir, please direct us when to return."

Beside her, Mikani huffed out an impatient breath. He

preferred to charge at problems head-on, but sometimes it was best to use a more tactical approach. She noted that Leonidas didn't care to dignify their inquiry with a moment of his time; and he was ferociously angry at the invasion of his privacy. It would require some finesse not to get banned from the theater entirely.

So she added, "Please, sir. We can't cross you off our list until you've answered our questions." That angle sometimes worked; people wanted the matter done and buried. Some criminals thought they were so much cleverer than the people paid to catch them.

Finally, Leonidas bit out, "Day after tomorrow, six in the evening."

"We'll show ourselves out." Mikani set a brisk pace, retracing their steps. "Did you see how angry he was?"

She sighed. "Yes, but people who come from money expect to be handled with kid gloves. Tact's . . . not your greatest strength. Did you *learn* something, at least?"

"One thing. You . . . disappeared when he was close by. That means, somehow, he erases the emotional echoes I normally pick up . . . but which were gone entirely from the device that killed our victim."

"You're saying he felt . . . dead? Empty? Like the machine."

"Precisely. There's . . . too much about him that doesn't track. We should keep digging to see what surfaces."

CHAPTER 8

"I WILL HAVE THEIR BADGES," LEONIDAS SNARLED.

Since he was in the main part of the theater, he wore his full black regalia. It seemed excessive to Aurelia, as other men had been scarred without resorting to such measures. But she suspected his behavior was his method of dealing with heavy guilt for surviving where his parents had not. Possibly, he was also this vain, as before the accident, he had been a handsome man. There was no doubt that he'd suffered, however; burns were incredibly painful and slow to heal even with the aid of magic.

"You disappeared without permitting them to interview you the first time. Did you think they'd just let it go?" Aurelia puffed out a sigh, rubbing the bridge of her nose between thumb and forefinger.

Her genuine concern seemed to penetrate his anger. "I'm sorry. I just . . . they came upon me unaware. I wasn't . . . ready for visitors."

"Why don't you simply tell them?" It wasn't such a shameful thing, nor as uncommon as Leo wished to believe.

A low growl escaped him. "That I'm paying one of the dancers for companionship?"

"She can verify that you've been here, all night long, for the past month. And I can vouch for your days. Which means you've nothing to do with any missing girl."

"No, it only means I'm a monster."

Aurelia gave him an exasperated stare, wishing he would dispense with the affectation of cowl and mask, at least in her presence. But he wouldn't during the day. They had been friends for a long time, and he'd stood by her after she made the decision to step outside the parameters of her life as a House scion. So she was trying to help him now; unfortunately, he was stubborn and difficult.

"Other men keep mistresses."

"Because they choose to, not because they can't attract women on their own."

"You don't know you can't," she pointed out. "You haven't tried."

"Enough of this. I'm *not* going to the CID."

"So your pride is more important than clearing yourself of a crime?" She shook her head. "If you don't come forward with the information, Leo, I will. I thought the show was a good idea . . . that you'd rejoin the world a bit, but so far—"

"I've let you down."

"Stop already. Please. I have to get back to rehearsal now."

For a little while, she lost herself in the music, watching the dancers execute their steps with more precision today. It had been long enough for them to forget the excitement of the CID visit, and they were performing beautifully. Now and then, she corrected someone's form or demonstrated the proper step. The drills continued for two more hours, and by the end, she was as tired as her troupe. Such tireless preparation would be rewarded with the first standing ovation and when the newssheets printed what a phenomenal production she'd staged.

"Much better today," she called. "That's all."

One dancer lingered—Elaine Day, who would creep downstairs to find Leonidas once the others left. Aurelia raised a brow, knowing the girl harbored the wrong ideas about the long-standing friendship between Leonidas and her. "What's troubling you?"

"I was just thinking. Shouldn't I play a larger role in the finale?"

Really, Leo? This one? She didn't begrudge him the companionship, but it seemed to Aurelia he could've done better, chosen a less grasping female to share his bed. Outwardly, she didn't give any sign of her thoughts.

"On what grounds? Your skills are adequate, not exceptional. Not star material."

"That's not what Leonidas says," the girl said nastily.

A few other performers hovered, drinking in the conflict. She had to nip this in the bud. "He isn't the director of this show, either. If you can't play your part as requested, I'll find someone who can. Do you understand, Miss Day?"

"I understand perfectly." Her mutinous expression said she believed Aurelia was jealous of her youth, beauty, talent, and her relationship with Leonidas.

"Then you shouldn't keep your patron waiting."

Once the girl flounced away, presumably to seek out Leo and fill his ears with venom, Aurelia muttered, "I wouldn't mind if *she* fell down a dark hole."

"That was unpleasant." A man stepped out of the wings, a member of the technical crew, she thought.

She'd seen him before; he was tall and slender, with dusky skin and dark hair, not handsome, but he worked hard. Come to think of it, he was always the last to leave, always tidying up and putting things away. *Mr. Gideon,* she remembered. *Lighting.*

In silence, they negotiated the wings, passing through grotesque shadows thrown by milliner's dummies half-costumed for the show, metal stage hooks and dangling pulleys, sandbags and piles of newspaper from forgotten reviews.

In parting, she said, "One of the hazards of the business. Have a good evening."

"I'm leaving as well." He fell into step with her as they moved toward the exit, and she wondered with a touch of cynicism what favor he meant to ask.

Perhaps he thinks he's wasted behind the scenes, a natural performer. Or his dear auntie is ill, and he needs time off to tend her . . .

Waiting for Mr. Gideon to frame his request, Aurelia stepped into the cool night air. Though it was still warm during the day, the long summer was wending its way to an end. To her surprise, the tech turned the other way, going about his business. With a philosophical shrug, she strode down the alley until he disappeared from sight. She felt pleasantly surprised at being wrong.

The shortcut navigated, Aurelia emerged on a main thoroughfare, five blocks from the underground. Tonight, she didn't sense the presence that had hunted her for the past months. *Perhaps it was your imagination. Or madness.* With effort, she set aside her worries. It was a lovely night, and after she returned to the club to change, she meant to lose herself at a Summer Clan revel. In a pretty dress and a colorful mask, she could pretend to be someone else for a while.

But first, an errand. Feeling vaguely guilty, she stopped at the post office and sent an anonymous message to the CID. *Ask Elaine Day what she knows about Leonidas.* Her friend would be furious, but better his pride took a hit than the CID wasted days investigating him to no avail. Surely, that would be counterproductive.

As she stepped out of the building, the clouds broke, drenching her in sheets of rain. She'd be washed away before reaching the station at this rate. Her budget would stretch to a hansom, so she ran, hailing one with both arms. Gaslight shimmered in the puddles, and as she ran, her feet left patterns wavering in their wake. The carriage stopped with a metallic screech; the driver gestured for her to climb in.

She did.

To her astonishment, the carriage was occupied. Theron pulled her inside, dry and elegant in black evening wear. After he spoke the club's address, the vehicle shuddered into motion. She herself was breathless, cold, and a trifle worried. This wasn't like their initial encounter. It was too premeditated, too private.

"Am I being abducted?" she asked.

"Do you wish to be?" He didn't await a reply. "It would be odd of me to kidnap you by transporting you to your residence."

"True. How do you know that's where I was going?" She listened to him with all her senses, including the one that registered deception.

"Weren't you?"

Fleetingly, Aurelia wondered if he ever lost his icy detachment. "I wish you'd cease this game. You have some purpose in mind, so it would be to our mutual advantage if you would stop trying to beguile me. I'm not susceptible to such tricks, no matter how skilled you are with them."

He laughed quietly, seeming amused. "You appear to reckon me some master seducer. I assure you, I've spent the last century in seclusion, quietly working on various botanical projects."

Truth. No doubt, shades, or prevarications. She stared at him, bewildered. "Are you some blandishment of my father's, meant to tempt me back to House life?"

Dark eyes peered at her, incredulous. "Do I appear as one who could be . . . purchased, like a sweet?"

His dismay is real. Her frustration mounted.

"And yet," he went on. "I'm flattered that you think me charming enough to enjoy a measure of success in that role. Perhaps I was merely passing and saw you stranded in the rain."

False.

"You were *not*," she said with conviction.

His brows went up. "You know this? Fascinating. As I told you the other night, I'd like to make your acquaintance, Aurelia Wright."

Truth. Perhaps nobody put him up to it.

"Are you an aficionado of my work?"

"You're very gifted." That wasn't what she'd asked, but the words rang true.

She was tired of asking the wrong questions. "I wish I knew what you want."

"The same thing as other men, I expect." The small bulb in the coach flickered, casting long shadows. His gaze lingered on her face, but whatever he saw remained unspoken. "You seem determined to read me, as you would a beloved book. What, then, intrigues you so? Or do you treat all thus?"

"Most are easily read, apparent to those with an eye for such things."

"There is truth in that." He sounded almost weary. "And yet, most of those writings are not worth the time to read them. There is something you cannot see in me, though. Or such I gather."

"True enough," she said, studying the deep of his eyes. Something more than darkness hid there. He possessed some secret agenda, involving her, but she had no idea what it might be.

"When you learn something, do not shout it for the world to

hear. At least, not if you intend to unearth aught else." He touched her cheek with cool fingertips. "And I am not one to be read, I think. My secrets are best left alone."

"And I would find that a tragedy."

"Tragedies are some of the more memorable tales. But if it pleases you to interpret whatsoever glyphs you can within me, so be it." His gesture was baffling. "The attentions of a young woman are never to be scorned."

Sometimes he spoke like an old man, as if inside, he had silver hair and wrinkled skin. He carried the weight of more years than her father, if such a thing were possible. It made her uneasy, even as he lured her with his half-truths and demon-dark eyes.

The hansom stopped before she realized they'd traveled so far. "I think you're past being flattered by a woman's interest. And your silence on the questions I pose offers its own answer."

"Perhaps."

Declining his aid, she alit onto wet pavement. The rain had abated, and everything shimmered. "Will you walk? I won't be able to sleep so early. I love nights when the moon hangs like a ripe yellow apple in the sky."

He paid the driver and joined her. "Luna. She's a fickle lady. As are all ladies, in my experience."

"You must have been frequently disappointed to feel so."

"Disappointment is not something I feel oft, and when I do, the remedy's rapidly undertaken." His tone was almost curt. "Or have you something particular in mind?"

"Only the pleasure of your company."

It was impossible to determine what he wanted. Possibly, he hoped to win her affections and thus ensure an alliance with her family. Safely wed and removed from undesirable associates, it was possible for a House scion to climb back into society's good graces. Her return to respectability would endear Theron to her father, guaranteeing the Architect's support in whatever scheme he had in mind, but there was only one way to be sure of his intentions. Therefore, she'd keep the man close until she puzzled them out.

Aurelia plucked a branch of evergreen and drew deep of its scent. This man's secrets would be wooed from him in quiet moments; she could not read him if he was unwilling. Or take what he would not give.

He spoke after a long silence. "No one has asked that of me in a long time." Beside her, he was dark upon dark, olive skin hued to shadows broken only by the jet of his eyes.

"I am sorry to hear that." In that moment, Aurelia felt very gentle toward him.

It didn't matter what his agenda was; she didn't think he meant to harm her. More likely, he had some plan to *use* her, and she was accustomed to that. Being the Architect's only living child had its drawbacks.

As a small girl, she'd had no notion of his power or importance. She simply ran to him with scraped knees or for a sweet. That changed the day a maid mustered up the courage to ask, "Did your father truly close the Veil? There will be no more crossings?"

Aurelia had no idea what that meant, so she'd gone to her father to pose the same question. He'd gazed down at her, explained the world beyond Hy Breasil, then offered a simple, somber nod. Everything changed that day.

Theron was saying, "No need. Had I required company, it could have been arranged, but I found other matters more crucial." He gazed into her face, traced its lines in a complex look. "Come."

It cannot, actually. Sincerity is one thing that cannot be bought. His reply struck her as strangely sad, as he did not see any incongruity in it. Unlike Leonidas, he apparently didn't see any shame in paying for companionship. But then, Theron was an appealing male, not a disfigured one. So perhaps therein lay the difference; if he cared to bother, Theron could woo and win a woman whereas Leonidas feared discovering that the damage to his face rendered him unlovable for all time.

"The view from this place . . . it is truly worth the trouble to find it." He guided her, easily as if under the noon sun, through the narrow passages, fragrant with life. "You are curious to me, Aurelia. In more ways than one." Within a few heartbeats, though, they left the maze, stepping into star-filled night.

"Curious, in that I wish to know things? Or curious, in that I make you wonder about me?"

Before them, the city sprawled, glittering like a strand of gems. Arches and buttresses; spires and towers; lights, shadows, and darkness mixing, struggling, and merging. "Both, perhaps. Does it matter?"

His eyes were lost in the world below them. He drank it in; he embraced it. She saw the hunger in his eyes and in the set of his mouth. He made no effort to conceal it.

"It matters," she said quietly. "You matter." To her surprise, Aurelia found it was true. And the honesty rang in her low voice, unmistakable in its music.

They had only met twice, so he *shouldn't*. But even if his persona had been created tailor-made to intrigue her, well. It was working. She wasn't ready to fall into his arms, but she wanted to spend more time with him. His secrets and his quiet intensity drew her.

"Does it? Do I? I would know why." His eyes torn from the metropolis below, the hunger took a long moment to fade. "What is it *you* seek, then, Aurelia? In truth?"

Turning from the city that lay like a penitent on its knees before them, Aurelia met his obsidian eyes, reflecting starlight. "What I seek, I have." Prevarication wasn't one of her principal gifts, but she'd learned it at her father's knee. Rubbing her hands along silk-clad forearms, she gazed at the cityscape. "What is it you see when you stare out?"

"I see people. Souls. Potential, blood rushing from countless hearts; I see streams and rivers of possibility. And you?" His tone was near enough a whisper that she had to lean closer to hear him.

Ah. Now that *is truth.* And it told her more than he realized; he no longer saw the individual lives or the stories they represented. He was too old, and it was a wonder he hadn't gone mad. He must be ancient beyond reckoning if he claimed only one name, no ties to House or kin.

"I see all the stories being told at once, right now."

"Stories." He frowned as if she were a mythic creature crawled from some tapestry. "A different manner of looking at it. Would you hear said stories?"

"I would know them all, yes." Aurelia bent, then stood, a pebble in her palm. Softly rounded, as if it might have once lain in the bed of the sea. "Imagine," she murmured, "what we could learn from this if it could speak? Where it lived, what it saw. And how it came to be here."

"Perhaps. And yet, who is to know what a stone holds important?" There was no mockery in his tone, however. "But who is

to say that what we hold important . . . is important?" He allowed
a purring chuckle. "What would you hear from the stone?"

Puzzled, Aurelia knit her brows together, closing long fingers
over the pebble. It was, as it happened, quartz. "Naught but truth,
as you must know by now."

"Truth. Such a thing to value. You are a strange one, Aurelia.
The stories below, then, you would have their truth? And mine,
as well?" Humor twined through his voice.

"Such things come in their own time." Yielding to the impulse
to make a connection, Aurelia brushed the knuckles of her free
hand against his cheekbone, hardly more than a shimmer of
warmth. "So then, it would be my turn to ask a question of you,
having answered all yours. What is it you see when you look
at me?"

"A woman who has seen enough mysteries to wish for more.
Too much, perhaps, for her own good. That said, will you considering dining at my villa, Aurelia? Knowing it may not be in
your best interests."

I know, she thought. *Oh, Theron, I should not be so intrigued
by you.*

"Yes," she said softly.

As Aurelia knew, women had ever been drawn to dangerous
men who whispered in the dark.

CHAPTER 9

THE MORNING AFTER MIKANI CORNERED LEONIDAS AT THE
theater, he tackled the unenviable necessity of asking Saskia for
additional help. He made his way along Strand Avenue though
this time he didn't stop for coffee or to chat with Electra. Siren
Trading bustled with service people rushing in and out. He
skirted past them and waited until Saskia noticed his arrival.

"Twice in as many days, after two years. Are you trying to
tell me something?"

He offered a teasing smile. "I've seen how prosperous the
concern is. You're quite the catch these days."

Saskia nodded. "Indeed I am. But I collect you didn't come
entirely for the pleasure of my company."

"You know me too well," he said.

"Let's hear it. Do I get to add another mark to the debt
between us?"

"I hope not. You were pretty shaken the other day, but I
wanted to ask—do you have any idea who could've done something like that?"

"Nobody I know would." She broke eye contact quickly.

She only does that when she's telling me half-truths.

So he prompted, "Then who would?"

"I hate it when you do that." Her rueful expression spoke volumes, but her eyes hinted she was reluctant to divulge whatever she knew.

"I'll cook dinner for you some night next week," he promised.

Mikani saw when she weakened. Women were always charmed that he knew his way around a kitchen. They took it as a sign of impending domestication when the truth was, he preferred not to starve, and takeaway grew tiresome.

"Only if you make your special ragout."

"Deal. But if I'm called away—"

"You have to answer. I understand." There was a quiet sorrow in her eyes; she was one who had professed to love him before the demands of his job and the invisible wall between them grew too much for her to scale on a daily basis.

"That much hasn't changed."

"Be careful. These are dangerous people. And I'll be expecting a note about dinner, Janus."

She scrawled an address on expensive stationery. At the moment, there were two junior clerks waiting with documents in hand, presumably for Saskia's perusal. She gestured them into her office to wait, but Mikani feared if he lingered, she might decide to come along.

"Soon," he promised.

He left without looking back, had been doing so for as long as he could remember. Mikani strode the five blocks to the nearest station, the paper safely in his pocket. The underground carried him to Iron Cross; there he had to switch to a ramshackle old train that would take him beyond the borders of the city proper. Mikani had rarely traveled beyond the end of the line, but the address he sought lay among the saltwater tenements that clustered along the cliff's edge on the other side of the bay. Here, the buildings were no more than worn scrap wood with tin roofs, hammered together with hope and rusted nails. The windows were rough-cut, covered in skins, and the smell combined all the worst aspects of the sea and unwashed humanity. It was a fierce enough stench to bring tears to his eyes, but if people could manage to live here, he could tolerate the smell for an hour or so.

There were no numbers on the houses, but Saskia had added some landmarks and descriptives to help him find the place. In

Dorstaad proper, this would be considered a warehouse. But Mikani saw no goods as he poked his head inside; instead, it was more of a longhouse, a larger structure where citizens gathered to talk, out of the wind, away from the sharp bite of the sea. It was cool today, but not cold; winter had yet to unleash its fangs, so the fire pit in the center of the room was unlit. People lounged on rough-hewn furniture while others practiced a knife-fighting technique Mikani identified as unique to some of the northern Summer Clan. In the back corner, a young man in a harlequin's vest was unmistakably casting a glamour. The air glimmered silver around him, sharp and bright to Mikani's enhanced senses. He wondered what effect the boy was trying to invoke.

Conversation halted.

Mikani had been the cynosure of unfriendly eyes before, but this was the first time he believed everyone present was weighing the odds of successfully disposing of his corpse. Impressions of shock and rage bombarded him. *It usually takes more than this for me to enrage a room so fully.* Before anyone could react, he flashed his credentials. *Hopefully, that will give them pause.*

"I'm Inspector Mikani . . . and I'm looking for a magical expert."

That seemed to free everyone from their shocked stillness. A titter ran through the room, then someone called, "Yer mum thinks I'm both magical *and* expert."

He ignored that. "Perhaps I should've led with the fact that I'm investigating a murder. I'll make it worthwhile for anyone who speaks with me."

"Who got it?" a woman called out.

"A young girl." He omitted mentioning that she came from one of the great Houses, feeling pretty sure that would make it impossible to get any information.

"I'll talk to you." It was the boy in the vest, who had been casting.

He had lank dark hair, and as he strode before the windows, Mikani saw that he was younger than he'd initially estimated, no more than thirteen and gaunt to the point of emaciation. But he carried a faint shimmer, as if he had magic in his skin. The others turned away, appearing to return to their business, but Mikani sensed that they were listening to every word.

He didn't insist that he needed an older expert; sometimes

street rats knew surprising things, a lifetime of being overlooked and sneaking into places they shouldn't be. Instead, he explained the apparatus that had killed the girl and produced sketches. Succinctly, he summarized the circumstances and how there hadn't been sufficient time for Miss Aevar to die, at least not without paranormal intervention.

Mikani ended by asking, "Do you have any idea what the lenses are or how the killer used magic to murder her?"

"First, we'll be talking bits, crescents, and talons, yer investigorship. Or if you prefer, I also accept notes. The more *I* get, the more you'll get."

Mikani wasn't sure whether the boy knew anything of value, so he put five silver crescents in his palm. "Is that enough for an answer?"

The coins disappeared. "Just one. And the machine sounds like a siphon."

If Ritsuko were here, she'd be scratching notes, determined not to miss a single word. Mikani cracked his senses wider and let them drift; the amount of raw power in this room was *staggering*. Any one of these people could easily be a killer, and their living conditions were such that he could almost understand if they were driven to it. The boy before him felt like a shard of ice, frozen sharp, and tight with hatred. Not of Mikani, precisely, but for the whole world order.

"What's a siphon?" He knew what the word meant in a general sense, but not in this context.

The boy opened his palm, and Mikani sighed as he paid five more crescents. "Sometimes people want power they don't possess. There are ways to steal it."

Hm. So magic can be transferred? He made a mental note to talk to Saskia; though if she'd had any insights about the device, surely she would've shared them.

"Have you ever seen anything like this before?"

"Oh no. You couldn't pay me enough to answer that." Which was a frustrating and fascinating answer.

"Do you fear reprisal? I must remind you, this is an official CID investigation. If you fail to share knowledge that could lead to the arrest of the perpetrator, that constitutes obstruction."

The boy held out his thin wrists, eyes mocking. "You want

to lock me up, yer inspectorship? Have at it. At least then I'd get fed regular."

It was impossible to threaten someone for whom gaol represented a step up the social ladder. "What else can you tell me?"

"Were there any conductors present?" The boy answered with a question.

"*Metal* is a conductor. Can you direct me to someone partial to such creations? Or at least theorize a purpose for the contraption, the reason she died like that."

"My life wouldn't be worth a copper if I aimed you at my fellows. As to the other, if I had to guess? He killed her to steal what power she possessed. But for some reason, he couldn't absorb it directly."

"Are you sure you can't—"

"Forget it. That's all you're getting out of me." The boy finally yielded to the silent demand all around him that he stop cooperating with the authorities. He turned and bounded out a nearby window, limber as a half-starved cat as he went over the sill, the stained leather shade flapping behind him.

In that moment, the mood turned.

An older man with bent shoulders stepped out of the mob. He gestured and spat an unintelligible sound. Mikani's chest went tight, and the bitter hint became an overwhelming, nauseating taste that made him want to throw up. He felt something cocoon him, a sticky and vaguely slimy sensation on his skin. *Bronze gods, what's he done? No.* Then, just as suddenly, the feeling vanished. He panted for breath, covered in a thin sheen of sweat, and glared at the old man.

"That was a *lesson*. The Houses gobble every hint of the old ways up and pretend they're keeping people safe by hoarding the power, but it's still out here, still among even the lowest of us." The man's eyes burned black, so dark that the pupil and iris overlapped, just holes that fell endlessly into his head.

"You've made your point," Mikani croaked. His throat felt raw; his skin tingled.

"Have I? You tell me how it's fair that the Houses control everything. The mirrors, the ember spheres . . . all the elementals and all free trade. The rest of us are left scrambling for scraps from the high table."

"I don't quite see how this relates to my line of inquiry. I'm just trying to discover who killed a young girl in a quite horrific way. And why." He was cool, not intimidated by the way the ragged men drew closer. He'd faced worse odds . . . and the anticipation of trouble was already rushing through his veins, better than whiskey or Dreamers. *Granted, either of those would likely make what's coming a lot less painful.*

"Why?" The old man offered a dry laugh. "Those who possess power are always in danger of having it stolen."

"I think it's time you moved along," another man said.

"If I don't? Are you going to glamour me again?"

"No magic," the old man ordered. "Otherwise, do as you will."

Their collective rage and resentment blistered his skin, and five men encircled him. Mikani no longer felt sure his badge and official status would be enough to protect him. He wondered if they were hiding the killer, covering for him. There was no telling what they imagined they'd gain by offing a House scion, but maybe they saw it as the opening salvo of a slow-building class war.

"Your shiny badge don't mean nothing here." A tall, thin man spat at Mikani's feet.

They didn't wait for a reply; they all came at him at once, and he answered with a sweep of his walking stick. So long as they didn't bespell him, he'd fight at these odds—and not report them for the magical infractions he'd observed, much to his partner's chagrin if she ever found out. But Ritsuko had surprised him with her willingness to overlook the Dreamers; maybe she'd understand this, too. His cane connected with a ferocious thwack, and blood spattered from the man's busted lip.

It's such fun, after all.

MIKANI HAD BEEN gone most of the day. Bronze gods, she hoped he was staying out of trouble. He had a propensity for stirring the pot when left to his own devices . . . and that had been happening more of late. They were running leads separately to cover more ground, but also because . . . well.

Best not to think of the pub . . . or the Moment.

It just seemed best to get some space between them, in addition to being more efficient. He had an angle on the magical connection to follow, which had left Ritsuko following up on Academy leads. None of the interviews had produced anything concrete though she'd frightened one of the students badly enough to confess to several unrelated misdemeanors. Now she was wrapping up their paperwork—and she'd noticed how often her partner skipped out on the busywork, but since she didn't have any gifts to augment her flare for organization, she figured it was fair that she did the lion's share of the filing. Such tasks suited her nature anyway; she liked putting everything in order.

With a faint sigh, she reviewed the latest report. It took days for the lab to determine anything, but they thought the ash she'd found at the murder scene had an herbal origin. She couldn't make any sense of that. Who bound a woman to a giant metal slab and cooked her with lenses and sprinkled herbs around the perimeter? The case had no precedent. After her interviews, she'd gone through many old files and found nothing similar.

Mikani's consultant had confirmed—the reason the murder seemed so clean and impossible? Magic. *That's all I need.* To make matters worse, House Aevar was leaning on the City Council for a fast arrest. They didn't care about the truth; they might even prefer a scapegoat. Ritsuko didn't operate that way. More than most, she had to be sure of her facts because they would be called into question simply because she was a woman. Some officers would deal only with Mikani, and when they did acknowledge her, they acted as if she were obligated to run their errands.

At last she tidied her desk and tried to slip from the office, but as she headed toward the lift, the gruff tones of the commander stopped her. "Ritsuko, I'd like a word."

Damn. And I was nearly gone for the night.

The commander had taken to working late because he didn't want to deal with the constant interruptions during the day. Messengers had been in and out of his office all week long—from the high Houses, the Council, and even the Ward Representative Assembly. They all wanted to know the same thing: *How could this happen? Who would dare assail so many centuries of unquestioned superiority?* Thugs and commoners fell into low company and came to bad ends. Not lovely, innocent House scions.

"Yes, sir," she said, altering course.

The old man looked tired tonight. He peered at her over his desk, over the edge of wire spectacles. Commander Gunwood was deceptively bookish, but his mild exterior hid the heart of a lion. "You know I took a great risk in appointing you to the CID."

She nodded. Every other city branch had refused her anything but a spot in the clerical pool. They thought she was only suited to taking notes and fetching tea. From the first, she'd fought for every inch she gained; it had required five separate recommendations before they agreed to let her to do lab work. Getting herself accepted as a field agent had required even more determination. She laced her hands together, hoping she wasn't about to be demoted.

"But you turned out to be one of my best officers," the commander went on. "I'm not sorry I backed you."

"However," she prompted.

"If you and Mikani don't resolve this soon, I'll have to pull you off the case."

Her teeth clenched. He didn't need to explain. She knew why. The brass would be telling him there was no way a man, saddled with an incompetent female partner, could be expected to crack a case like this. Why not slide it to one of the other teams? A decision like that would mar her record.

"I understand." Ritsuko worked to keep her features blank and expressionless. "We suspect the Aevar murder may be connected to the Royale, so we've been watching." Trying to read his expression, she hastened on. "But that's not the only angle we're pursuing. I have a list of Academy students with the skill to build such a device, and I spoke to some of them today. I'll also be checking the emporiums for purchase records. It's only a matter of time until I run this monster to ground."

See how thorough I am? For obvious reasons, she didn't mention the magic angle. Her status felt shaky enough already.

"I pray you're right," Gunwood said tiredly. "Go home, Ritsuko. Get some sleep. You're no use to me if you're dead on your feet."

"Yes, sir."

Pressure tightened her chest as she turned away; the coat over her arm felt heavier than usual. She suspected she'd just glimpsed the end of her career. Oh, they wouldn't fire her; they were too proud of what she represented. So they'd just shuffle her off to desk work while pretending she still possessed the full confidence of the CID. That way, whenever suffragettes picketed the building, they could trot her out and explain that they did, in fact, give proper consideration to all female candidates but only chose the best.

That was her. So why couldn't she get a handle on this thing? Nobody had seen anything. Nobody *knew* anything. It was as if a great, dark shadow had scooped Cira Aevar up. They didn't even know whether she'd been taken from her home, or on the streets, from the theater, or somewhere in between. But there were no hungry ghosts haunting the city. Someone made of flesh and blood had affixed her to that infernal apparatus, though for what purpose she could not even begin to guess.

Her mood was glum as she rode down on the puffing lift. But to her surprise, she found someone waiting for her in the lobby. Security hadn't permitted him past the first checkpoint, so he sat on one of the benches, staring at the red-veined marble floor. When his head came up, she recognized Mr. Gideon at once.

"If you'd explained to Tolliver that you needed to speak with me regarding an investigation, he would've notified me of your arrival."

The stagehand pushed to his feet, twisting his hat in his hands. "I remembered after you left . . . but I wasn't sure if it was important. I thought I should tell you—"

"Yes, of course. Any information might prove unexpectedly valuable."

"There was an actor who paid attention to Cira. He teased her, flirted with her. I recall thinking he was a bit old for her. She couldn't have been more than twenty."

Nineteen, she corrected silently, then produced her notepad. "Do you know his name?"

"Toombs. Gregory Toombs."

"Can you give me a description?"

"He's nearly forty, I think. Dark-haired. Women seem to find him irresistible."

"So Cira favored his attentions?" She watched him. His reaction would tell her a great deal, whether he'd known the girl better than he claimed.

"I'm not sure."

"Did he come on strong?"

Mr. Gideon considered. "To a girl half his age? Yes, I believe so."

"Do you have any idea where we can find him?" This was the final question and the most important one.

"No," he said. "That's the odd thing. I haven't seen him since Cira disappeared."

Could this be the lead they'd been waiting for? Perhaps the actor had wanted to turn Cira into some form of macabre art. Perhaps her death was, in itself, theater. Ritsuko was already mentally making plans to circulate a picture of Toombs.

A happy shiver worked its way through her; her career might not be over after all. This was another piece of the puzzle, and she believed the solution must lie in hard work, logical thinking, and methodical investigation. So instead of going home, she went back upstairs to search the files on Greg Toombs. Fortunately, it wasn't so late that the Records department would be closed.

The commander arched both brows when he saw her stride into the duty room. "You're not very good at following orders, Ritsuko."

"New lead. A man from the Royale came down with a tip regarding Miss Aevar and an actor. I suspect he didn't want his colleagues to see him as an informer."

"Understandable," Gunwood admitted. "Very well, you're clear to pursue this, but promise me you'll rest sometime soon."

"I will." *As soon as we catch this maniac.* "After I check with Records."

After filling out the form, she took it downstairs personally, hoping the clerk would be kind enough to get into the archives immediately. The woman on duty looked tired and overworked, much as Ritsuko felt. Further complicating matters, she had a backlog of document requests all over her desk. Most male inspectors would respond to this by barking; Ritsuko took another tack.

"I worked in this department for years. Why don't you let me help you get caught up? Unless the filing system has changed. I don't want to make more work for you."

The other woman stared up at her with exhausted eyes, pale

in the gaslight; she looked queasy as well. "Why would you do that for me?"

There was no point in pretending altruism. "Because I'll get what I need sooner."

A smile creased the clerk's wan face. "The system hasn't changed. Come on back."

CHAPTER 10

THE DAY WAS WELL ADVANCED BY THE TIME MIKANI ROLLED out of bed.

Damned be. No point in going to HQ at this hour. Which was just as well. The case had run him ragged, giving him no chance to tend to the little civilities of life. After a quick bath to soothe the bruises from the fight at the warehouse, he got his walking stick, inspected it for damage, then unsheathed the blade to oil and clean it. He propped it against the desk and saw some unanswered letters from his sisters, so he took the chance to reply.

That done, he went into the kitchen to make the week's bread. While it was baking, he went to the mirror station to post his sisters' letters and sent a quick message to let his partner know he'd see her at the theater for the 6 P.M. interview they'd scheduled with Leonidas the other night.

Later, Mikani met his partner down by the stage at the Royale. Rehearsal was in full swing; though the dancers weren't in costume, they seemed to have mastered more of their routines. There was less yelling from Miss Wright, at any rate. He glanced around in search of their quarry. Leonidas was a riddle he meant to solve; this time, neither good manners nor procedure would get in the way of figuring out why the Royale owner felt like so much nothing. As Ritsuko had said, just like the machine.

Mikani tilted his head and listened for the absence that marked Leonidas. Like a hound after his prey, it took him only a moment to trace the eddying lack of trail of the owner, heading somewhere backstage. "This way." With a brief glance to Ritsuko, he headed in, smiling absently at those he gently shouldered past. "He's in the office, I think. Wright's with him." The flare of the choreographer deepened Leonidas's shadow, rendering it more tangible.

He led the way, as they'd visited once before, and found the two waiting. Ritsuko greeted them politely with a handshake while he stood back and tried to read the prevailing mood. The owner's interference made the whole room fuzzy; his partner barely registered, between Wright and Leonidas. But he could tell the choreographer was nervous, her mood flickering.

"Mr. Leonidas. Thank you for granting us this interview."

"Unless I craved more invasions to my privacy, I had little choice but to comply. Aurelia made it clear you won't simply go away."

"Speaking of which." Ritsuko turned to Miss Wright. "While I appreciate your desire to support your friend, I'm afraid you must go about your business. This shouldn't take long."

It was the nicest method of saying *go away* that Mikani had ever heard.

He waited for Miss Wright to give Leonidas one last long look and leave, before turning to the theater owner. "Miss Aevar worked as an assistant in the costume department. Were you two acquainted?"

"I knew her by sight. To the best of my recollection, we never spoke. She seemed shy." Leonidas gestured, indicating his forbidding appearance. "I'm not one to put young women at their ease, either."

"Then you had no dealings with her outside the theater, and don't know her circle of acquaintances?" Mikani frowned, listening for any shift in the man's emotional barrier.

"No, I told you I never spoke to her. I certainly didn't pay attention to her friends." He sounded terse, annoyed even, but due to the mask, it was impossible to verify via facial expression.

Ritsuko had her notebook out and was checking facts they'd gathered over days of exhaustive interviews. In a quiet, neutral tone, she read them off. "Cira Aevar went missing eight days ago. The head costume designer is the last person to report seeing her alive. She left this theater and was never seen again. Her body was found four days ago." At that point, she glanced up to ask, "Where were you the night Miss Aevar disappeared?"

Leonidas turned his attention to Ritsuko. "I was here." He raised an arm, almost hitting the wall in the small office. Junk teetered on overflowing shelves, threatening to topple. "I'm always here. I don't have much call to leave these days." He sounded pained by the admission.

"Is there anyone who can corroborate your claim?" Ritsuko asked.

Mikani added, "During the day, I imagine you're hard to miss, but once everyone leaves . . . ? We've been down to your domain. There may be hidden exits that would make it quite easy to slip in and out."

Leonidas leaned closer, his eyes narrowed. "There are no hidden exits, Inspectors. No secret bolt-holes or tunnels out of this place—" He stopped and took a deep breath, lowering his voice to a conversational tone. "I sealed the theater months ago. I value my privacy far too much to give carte blanche to thieves. Feel free to search the place, top to bottom. And if you get lost, I *might* send help."

Mikani started to respond to that challenge, but a scream rang out from the theater beyond. Leonidas flung open the door, and they ran into the wings. The scene was chaotic, but he assimilated it in a glance: an overturned lamp, smoke writhing in the air, and flames licking at the stage curtains. Dancers flew around in various stages of panic and preparedness, some fetching water, others screaming. The fire raced upward. If it reached the ceiling, the timbers would burn.

"Let's get these people out, Ritsuko," He need not have worried; his partner was already directing stagehands and dancers to help or flee. "Come, Mr. Leonidas, we should lend a hand." Mikani paused, looking back over his shoulder at the theater owner gazing at the flames, still as a statue. "Gods and spirits, let's move!"

He grabbed the man's arm, then he fought the urge to recoil as a roiling wave of fear and pain washed over him as soon as he touched Leonidas. It was an all-consuming roar, far louder than the screams around them. Mikani felt his face blistering, peeling away, the lick of fire against his chest. And stronger than the burning curtains and scorching wood, the taste of burned flesh choked him. He stumbled with surprise and shock, letting go of Leonidas. He gasped for breath, nauseated by the onslaught, so that he dropped his hands onto his knees.

Overhead, the burning curtain charred into strips, and through blurred vision, he saw that part of it was about to drop on them. It took all of his strength when he dove at Leonidas, and Mikani used weight and momentum to drive the other man out of the way. They hit the ground hard; impact seemed to wake him up, whether it was the hit or the pain, Mikani couldn't say. Leonidas scrambled away from the flames, away from the smoldering fabric, on his hands and knees. Mikani helped him up, then shoved him toward the safe portion of the hall.

Later, he'd consider what this meant. For now, he joined his partner in fighting the fire. They tore down the heavy draperies, which collapsed with a shower of sparks and ash onto the stage. Quick-thinking stagehands sliced open the sandbags used as counterweights for the curtains, using the coarse sand and gravel to help smother the flames. As Mikani bent to pick up a cumbersome sack, he felt a wash of cold air, smelling strongly of the sea, against his cheek. Confused, he glanced up to see one of the dancers kneeling near the edge of the stage, murmuring under her breath.

The wash of air spread past them, swirling around the flames. Damping them, with a whisper reminiscent of the ocean. When she caught him staring at her, she started, her face going pale as milk. Her eyes were huge, fear of reprisal shining clearly. The flames flared, and he gave her a nod; she recovered and resumed her chant, tears rolling down her cheeks. Mikani turned away to empty the last of the sand. The next time he checked, the girl had fled.

Ritsuko joined him, lifting her fingers as if she could touch what she sensed in the air. Within the theater, it still felt clean and damp as high tide. Between the quiet invocation and the application of sand and hard effort, the fire was out. He glimpsed Leonidas collapsed in a seat toward the back of the hall, safe enough, but the man appeared utterly wrecked.

"Did she just . . ." Ritsuko trailed off, seeming unable to finish the question.

Mikani hesitated. "She helped put out the fire. We all did. We should get medals. Or drinks. I'd settle for the latter . . . We should check on our person of interest, don't you think?" He nodded toward Leonidas.

Though he had complete faith in his partner, the girl had risked her own safety—and her liberty—for everyone else. Plausible deniability was best when there was even a hint of magic. Better for all concerned if Ritsuko only suspected.

Wiping at the soot and ash caked over his face, Mikani led the way back toward the theater owner. "Mr. Leonidas . . . ?" He stopped three feet away, tentatively reading the man. The barrier was slowly coalescing once more, raw pain and fear withdrawing into the shell. Mikani was debating touching him once more, when the man looked up. "I believe everyone's safe. Do you need a physician, sir?"

"No. Thank you for your . . . intervention." The man's voice was rusty, as if he'd been screaming for hours. "What I'd most like is to be left alone, if that could be arranged. Is there anything further, Inspectors?"

His partner shook her head. "I believe we have everything we need. I apologize again for our intrusion the other evening . . . and we do appreciate your cooperation."

TEN MINUTES LATER, Ritsuko joined Mikani in the foyer. She'd washed up as best she could in the lavatory, removing the worst of the soot from face and hands though there was nothing she could do about the smoke damage to her gray suit. Fortunately, it didn't show as badly as it would on some shades. By her partner's expression, she could see he had something weighty on his mind.

So as she approached, she said, "Tell me."

Mikani shook his head, as if weighing his words. "When the fire started, I finally got a reading off Leonidas. It was as if a dam had broken. The man was terrified, Ritsuko. I . . ." He ran fingers through his hair. "His parents died in an accident? The one that left him scarred?"

"Yes?" she prompted.

"He's in constant pain. I suspect I can't feel anything from him because he's trying to block the anguish even from himself. And he would no more go near a fire on purpose than I'd get married."

"So he's not the one. But you said that his emptiness felt familiar, it was like the machine. So does that mean the killer's in pain, like Leonidas? He's been injured somehow?" That would make him easier to track down. "But . . . a weak or recuperating man wouldn't be able to assemble such a contraption without help, would he?"

"I wouldn't call Leonidas weak. But it's worth looking into." Mikani glanced around the theater, traces of smoke still lingering in the air making his eyes water. "I do think you're right; Leonidas is not our man. But we do have that tip to look into before we head out, assuming we can find Elaine Day."

Yes, the anonymous note.

She was still turning the new theory over in her mind. "Maybe it's not necessarily physical pain. Would an emotional wound or heartbreak do it? A sudden loss that might've triggered . . ." She couldn't find the words to describe what the monster had done.

Mikani canted his head for her to follow. "He might blame the Aevars for his tragedy, yes. And that would lead him to make them pay through their daughter. It must have been something unbearable, to have snapped his mind. Let's find the choreographer; she should be able to point us toward the right girl."

Miss Wright was near the foot of the stage, consoling the dancers who hadn't fled in a panic. One girl sat with Leonidas at the back of the theater, and they were talking in low, impassioned tones. Ritsuko read reticence in the man's body language, insistence on the part of the dancer, who was a pretty girl with fair hair and large eyes; at this distance, it was impossible to judge the color.

"I'm sorry to bother you, as I know it's been a dreadful day, but I wondered if you could point me in Elaine Day's direction." Ritsuko didn't mention the anonymous note they'd received, but the other woman froze for a moment, a telling response.

"Yes, yes, of course. She's actually talking to Leo right now."

Interesting.

Ritsuko spun to study them, taking new interest in the couple. "I see. Thank you."

Leonidas stood, stepping before the slender girl protectively as they approached. "I believe we're done here, Inspectors." Elaine peered at Ritsuko from behind the man's shoulder. "I need to see to my theater, get all this cleaned up."

Mikani smiled, and Ritsuko saw that it wasn't his usual sardonic look. "Feel free, Mr. Leonidas. We'll take care of Miss Day. We'd like a word, if you'll come with us, miss."

The theater owner shook his head, shielding the girl with his body. "Miss Day needs her rest—" Just then, the dancer stepped around Leonidas, tilting her chin up. "It's fine, Mr. Leonidas. I—I think it may be for the best."

Ritsuko had a feeling there was a reason Leonidas didn't want them talking to the girl, but given what Mikani had said earlier, she suspected it wasn't related to the murder. Still, they couldn't proceed without giving due diligence to all suspects. Once they could cross Leonidas off the list for good, it would give them more time to pursue other leads, like the names she'd gotten from the Academy and the tip from Mr. Gideon about the actor, Gregory Toombs.

"This way," she said to Miss Day.

She headed for the foyer, where it was bright and clean. No doors for privacy, but the remaining cast and crew were with Miss Wright anyway. Ritsuko imagined that the air backstage would be thick and choked with smoke, making it impossible to breathe, let alone question someone. There were red padded benches where they could sit, so she led the way to a small grouping to the right of the ticket office, where she invited the dancer to take a seat, then she asked Mikani with a silent raised brow who would take the lead here.

Her partner nodded once and moved aside, likely to get a better feel for Miss Day's reaction. *Business as usual, then. I ask the questions, and he weighs the emotional context.* She took a seat beside the girl, whose expression wavered between excitement at the attention and nerves over being singled out. Everyone had been questioned once; no other dancers had received a second interview.

So she's probably wondering what this means.

"We received a note, advising us to ask about your relationship with Mr. Leonidas. So why don't you tell me how well you know him?"

The girl's eyes went wide, the color draining entirely from her cheeks before she blushed hot. Licking her lips nervously, she glanced away. "I—I know Mr. Leonidas from the theater, of course; he's never been anything but generous and kind to me." Mikani caught his partner's eye and shook his head slightly with a bemused smirk. "He appreciates my talent, see, and he knows that I'll be his star."

"Please don't waste my time, Miss Day. Do you think I'm untrained in spotting deception?" If the girl didn't crack, Ritsuko's next salvo would be an offer to take her down to HQ for an extended interrogation.

Miss Day drew up to her full height and tried to rise. "I *think* you better not take that tone with me!" Mikani stepped up; Ritsuko placed a hand on the girl's wrist. And Leonidas's voice rang out.

"Inspectors! Let her—please, let her be." He stepped forward, and Elaine stumbled toward him. He wrapped an arm around the girl's shoulders as she pressed her face to his chest. "Miss Day . . . Elaine . . . and I are . . . Our relationship . . ." He stopped, seemingly torn between his evident concern for the girl and his need for secrecy. "Miss Day is . . . my companion." Elaine actually started at that, gazing up at him with an unreadable expression. "We've spent a great deal of time together of late, but I prefer not to make things difficult for her with the rest of the cast. Or anyone else."

"Does that include your nights?" Ritsuko asked, trying to be delicate.

Miss Day answered at once, probably seeing she had Leonidas's approval to divulge that much. Whatever else could be said of her, she was apparently loyal. "Yes."

Mikani angled his head, the way he looked when he was sensing . . . something. "You weren't there when we visited a few nights past. Where were you?"

"Fetching supper."

Ritsuko asked in their silent way, *Is that what you're getting, too?*

Mikani rubbed the bridge of his nose and inclined his head

slightly when he caught Ritsuko's glance. So they were telling the truth. She could also tell by his expression that he was reaching the limit on what he could safely read, though he'd never call a halt on his own. Yet in a few moments more, he would be bleeding.

"Just one more question, then," she said, glancing between Leonidas and the dancer. "Miss Day, what's the longest you've ever been away in the evenings?"

She was nearly sure it wasn't Leonidas, but it was a necessary question. The dancer looked thoughtful, and since she didn't reply at once, Ritsuko believed she was truly searching her memory.

"Four hours, perhaps. I went to a party."

"And when was this?" Mikani asked.

"Two months ago."

Too long for their timetable. *It's definitely not Leonidas.* Therefore, it was time to pursue other avenues, other connections. Fortunately, they had leads. Dread clotted in her throat when she imagined how the commander would react to the news that they were still chasing down endless angles instead of narrowing the search to one likely suspect.

It's a good thing I did a little filing. I may be back there soon enough.

CHAPTER 11

MIKANI HAD BEEN RETRACING CIRA AEVAR'S STEPS FOR THE
last two days, leaving Ritsuko to run the Toombs angle. He knew
she believed he was just trying to avoid going down into the
labyrinthine corridors of the Records department, buried deep
under the Courts of Law and CID Headquarters. She wasn't
altogether wrong about that, but his reasons weren't entirely
selfish.

He'd tracked Cira to the Gilded Avenue underground station;
the stationmaster remembered her as a regular. She was hard to
miss, carrying bright bundles of costumes to and from the theater. Several panhandlers confirmed that she passed them several
times a week, dropping a coin here and there and making time
to listen to them play or applaud their acts.

The one thing that no one could recall was which train she'd
ridden.

He should have found it sooner.

Cira Aevar always bought a ticket to the end of the line down
in Summer's Gate. There were three teams of inspectors and
constables checking the records and questioning possible witnesses along the four stations between the Royale and Summer's

Gate. They assumed she could have gotten on and off anywhere between the two points to hide her activities from her family. But Cira was sheltered, and she'd been living out her fantasy through an act of rebellion from the traditional life her status demanded. So she'd wanted her colleagues to accept her as one of them, and that meant taking the underground. It was a clever trick, designed to stave off any questions about her background.

Only she'd never actually ridden. When Mikani had asked the lone street musician playing along the north access to the underground, he remembered her heading *out* of the station. She'd crossed to the opposite platform and slipped out on the far side of Crown Avenue, a wide and busy urban highway that traditionally divided the Houses' demesnes from the rest of the city.

And that'd be why no one remembers what train she rode.

He'd recalled the other teams and set them to work through the cobbled streets bordering the Houses' citadels, staying close to Crown Avenue. Today, the streets and plazas closer to the park were crawling with House retainers; if she'd gone that way, someone would've spotted her. As House Aevar's holdings dominated the west side, he headed east.

For half an hour, Mikani walked without direction. He wandered into the Lee; the narrow strip of apartments, boardinghouses, bars, and cafés gave House scions a place to play at being grown-up and free while remaining within their parents' sphere. Students at the Academy, some distance to the east, mingled with others in full social revolt . . . and the occasional House noble reliving glory days.

Then he spotted the discreet boardinghouse on the corner, a half mile north of the Royale. *Cira needed a place to slip into her other life, and she wouldn't do it in a station lavatory.* As he drew closer, he detected the faintest echo of her, nearly gone now. In another day, it would've been lost, drowned by time and too many other bodies.

Mikani crossed the street in a rush. A black-and-gold hansom nearly clipped his foot, and he knocked over a courier streaking down the street on his cycle. Leaving the kid swearing at him, Mikani stumbled to the steps leading up to the blue wooden door. He reached for his gloves instinctively—then hesitated. The trail was cold as death, and the everyday pollution would make Cira that much harder to track. Right now, he only had that faint echo.

Besides, there was an easier way. He knocked on the door, reaching for the sepia photo he kept with him at all times as a reminder. "CID, madam. Do you know this girl?"

The woman studied the picture, then nodded. "Very nice tenant. Quiet."

Mikani made a noncommittal sound and followed the landlady, Miss Frasizka, whose name was written on her postbox, up the narrow stairs. The smell of cabbage and lilacs permeated the faded wallpaper. Whispers of the other tenants, as they peeked through peepholes or narrowly cracked doors, nudged the edge of his hearing. She probably meant to take him to her flat for the interview, but that wasn't what he was after.

"She pays on time, every month," Miss Frasizka was saying. "She's a good girl, that one. Never makes trouble."

"I regret to inform you, madam, that's no longer the case. Miss Aevar is now at the center of a murder investigation, and I need to search her room." He doubted he'd find anything, but he had to be sure. The commander would have his arse if he and Ritsuko didn't come up with something soon.

"Oh. Oh no. That poor girl." The woman reeled against the wall, her face the color of chalk.

Mikani wished Ritsuko was here, as she was better at dealing with these situations. Unfortunately, he had to handle this one. "Your assistance could mean the difference between a killer getting away with murder and justice for Miss Aevar."

"Aevar," she repeated.

He could tell she recognized the name and was pondering just how much trouble could drop on her head if she didn't offer full cooperation. "I want to help you, but first, if you could show me your ID?"

A wise precaution. He flashed his credentials, and she nodded.

"Good, good." The landlady unlocked the narrow door leading to the attic stairs and waved him up. Mikani turned sideways against the wall to pass the woman, who was half his height but his match for brawn. "You go up and take a look. I hope you find something helpful."

Mikani glanced around as he reached the top of the stairs. Cira had rented the entire attic. Swathes of fabric crisscrossed the sloped ceiling; dressmaker dummies crowded the far wall in various states of undress. Tights, hose, and shirts covered the scant furniture. A seamstress's table and an articulated wood-and-brass mannequin dominated the center of the room. He crossed the space, slipped on his gloves, and headed for the armoire in the corner.

Within, he found the fine silks and wool of a House scion, with the Aevar crest emblazoned on a traveling cloak and short coat. More rummaging unearthed a handbag, high-heeled ankle boots, and a scarf. This was the everyday garb of the daughter of a noble House. Mikani frowned. *The everyday garb . . . those boots are* not *made for walking. But she didn't ride the train back home every night.*

He headed back down then and dug in his coat for his cigarillos. As he stepped onto the street, he lit up and drew deeply. The messenger he had knocked over was waiting for him, a tight ball of anger and righteous indignation.

"You blind, mate? Knockin' over honest folks, all—" Mikani held up two silver coins, and the courier shut up.

"Inspector Mikani, CID. I apologize for disrupting your route, citizen." He inclined his head to the kid, who was surprised into an awkward tip of his riding hat and goggles in return. "In return, I'd like to engage your services to carry a note to CID Headquarters, down in the Courts of Law."

Mikani dug out his scarcely used notepad and scrawled a quick note for Gunwood to send a laboratory team to the boardinghouse. He passed note and coins to the boy, who dashed off with a reckless abandon that Mikani appreciated. With a rueful shake of the head, he turned back to his search for any sign of where Miss Aevar might've begun her double life.

Hansoms and buses dotted the avenue, bicycles, tricycles, and steam cars adding to the flow of traffic as the city awakened. Businessmen in dark suits and expensive silk vests, sporting good derby hats, hurried to work, while bondsmen scuffed their feet, reluctant in their tasks. They, too, wore hats, but they were made of cheap materials and had simple flat brims, separating them from the free men.

Not here. Too busy.

Mikani rubbed the rough scruff on his cheek and peered into the nearest alley. Narrow but uncluttered, it provided access to the street behind the boardinghouse and a small, neglected park. It was also dark enough to offer the illusion of secrecy to a young girl who didn't want to be spotted. He headed into the alley, letting his fingertips brush the walls. Emotion flooded him.

Countless minutes later, Mikani rocked on the balls of his feet, finding himself squatting at the mouth of the alley with blood dripping from his upper lip. His eyes burned, bruised from the friction of his fists as he tried to rub away the pain. Taking a shuddering breath, he straightened.

His rumpled suit rubbed at the nape of his neck and sat wrong on aching shoulders. With a slow roll of his head and a loud pop of stretching tendons, he wiped his face. He'd felt Cira; she'd been up and down the alley often enough to leave traces of her presence in sunlight and the giddy excitement of going against her family's wishes. She'd been happy here, the slight melancholy of her return home overshadowed by the joy of her journeys toward the Royale.

But more than that, he'd caught a whisper of the same faint presence as in her room. Someone had been following her, someone who could sneak into a fortified House undetected. Perhaps it had been a member of the household, tracking Cira across the city. *Maybe her grandfather was not as clueless as we thought.* If Aevar had stuck a tracker on the girl, they might have more information than they were sharing. If not . . .

If not, we have a hell of an infiltrator, a traitor, or a ghost. Mikani sniffed, wiping at his bloody nose and squinting against the growing light. When he heard the distinctive low rumble and whistles of a CID cruiser approaching, he grimaced and patted his coat in search of his darkened glasses. Heading back to the boardinghouse, he slipped them on and lit a fresh cigarillo. His head was pounding, his vision was blurry, and his mood was foul. He couldn't wait to talk to Aevar again.

SUNDAY WAS SUPPOSED to be Ritsuko's free day. No thoughts of the job.

Under normal circumstances, she took the day off happily. With a case like this one, however, she couldn't afford more than a few free hours. So after she met Mr. Higgins for lunch in the park, she went straight back to work. She'd managed to get all

the files on the actor, Gregory Toombs. On paper, he was a solid
suspect. Though he hadn't been on the list she received at the
Academy, he had an engineering background. He'd taken some
courses; had worked for two years in a clockwork firm that spe-
cialized in the gimbaled telescopes used on sailing ships. Then
he abruptly switched his focus to theater, so that gave him a
plausible skill set for building the murder machine. So far she
didn't have a motive, but she hadn't located the man, either. Since
his last production closed down, nobody had seen Toombs.

The CID had sent notices to all train stations and the docks,
containing a description of the actor and a warning to deny him
passage out of the city as a possible suspect in an open investigation. All mirror stations and post-service offices throughout
Dorstaad and the nearest settlements received the same notifica-
tion. Some associate of Mikani's had agreed to do the same for
the less official ships within the Free Trader guilds. As a result
of those combined efforts, Toombs was, in theory, trapped inside
the city. And without access to most official services or forms
of employment, his choice of hiding spots was slim: the tenements, the docks, or with friends or family.

While Ritsuko had no idea who Toombs called a boon companion, she did have an address for his parents, provided they
hadn't vanished. *That would just be too strange.* She pulled her
coat on, collected her things, and headed out. It was a chilly day,
with the earlier sun clouding over to hint at rain; it was always
damp when the weather cooled, sad after long days of endless
light. Today, however, it fit her mood. Ritsuko didn't murmur
her usual apology as she navigated the crowd. She didn't want
to interrupt these people and give them cause to worry about
their son.

But that's my job.

Toombs's parents lived in a small building off a small street
near the Bayside Market. The area had once been prosperous,
before the Houses had abandoned the eastern wards to move
closer to the park or into outlying, self-contained fortresses. With
their leaving, their money had stopped trickling in, and entire
neighborhoods lost their shine. Ritsuko checked the faded bronze
plaque against her notes and headed up the stairs.

The smell of various casseroles drifted from several apartments along the long passage. Hints of sweet spices and stew

mingled as early suppers were prepared, the sounds of children playing in the building's courtyard loud in the quiet Sunday afternoon. She rapped on the door, waited as someone shuffled to the door.

A woman in her early sixties opened it, her eyes dark but encircled with deeper shadows. Her short white hair looked as if she hadn't combed it today, disheveled by careless fingers. Her look turned suspicious when she took in the badge Ritsuko held. She started to slam the door, but Ritsuko stopped it with a firm palm.

"I need a few moments of your time."

Mrs. Toombs sighed. "This is about Gregory, isn't it?"

"Yes, I'm looking for your son. He might be able to aid in an ongoing investigation." Mrs. Toombs looked dubious as she tried halfheartedly to push the door shut again. "It's important. Do you know where I can find him?"

Mrs. Toombs sighed and released the door. "You may as well come in. Don't want the Drusses knowing more of our business than they need to. Our next-door neighbors. Busybodies, the lot of them," she added as she headed into the cluttered confines of her small apartment. An elderly gentleman—Mr. Toombs senior, Ritsuko surmised—slept in an overstuffed chair near a window. "Don't mind him. He'll be more trouble than help, I'd reckon." The woman headed into the kitchen. "Tea?"

"That's very kind, but no thank you." The décor led her to imagine that there was no money left in the budget for pretty things. That usually meant there was little food to spare as well, so she wouldn't ask the woman to prepare a snack she didn't really want.

Ritsuko sat on a worn blue settee, preparing pen and paper. The other woman seemed alarmed by this, as if that made the visit more official. "What are you writing?"

"I just want to make sure I get all the facts right. I wonder if you could tell me a little about your son, first. His likes, dislikes, hobbies, what he was like as a child, that sort of thing."

Mrs. Toombs glanced at Ritsuko's notepad, then at her sleeping husband. "Gregory is a good boy, you understand, miss." She fidgeted as she spoke. "We were so proud when he joined the Academy, we were; his father always worked the docks, see. But our Gregory, well, he had a chance of making something of himself. So bright, my Gregory." Mrs. Toombs smiled, her gaze far away. "So clever, fixing watches and all those complicated devices that they gave him for his classes. Such wonderfully adept hands, such a clever, clever boy. If he hadn't fallen in with that crowd—" She looked up, bit her lip. Then she shrugged, soldiering on. "Oh, but I suppose you know, or you wouldn't be here looking for him, would you?"

As Mrs. Toombs grew more agitated, her voice rose, until Ritsuko feared her husband might do more than stir and snore in his nest. "What crowd?"

"It's those theater folk, I tell you! They were the ones that led him astray with their harlots, their drinking and gambling."

Ritsuko had already known Toombs was connected to the Royale though he hadn't been seen there lately. But the gambling and the devices? That was new information, solid gold, but she concealed her excitement beneath a professional mien.

"How much money did Gregory owe?" she asked, taking a guess. "And to whom?"

The other woman sighed, her hands trembling in her lap until she had to clasp them. "I'm not sure, but . . . I'm afraid it was a lot. The last time he was here, he wasn't himself. I'd never seen him so . . . To be honest, miss, I feared you'd come to tell me they found his body."

Hm. Would a desperate man kill a young girl for money? Toombs seemed like an unlikely assassin, but one could never be sure how far another person would go when his back was to the wall. *Maybe,* she decided, *to save his own life.* She had no idea what Cira Aevar had done to earn such enmity, but perhaps it was political, a blow against one of the ruling Houses.

She shook her head. "I'm just trying to find him so I can ask some questions. It's possible he could be in danger, so any information would help."

"If I knew where he was hiding, I'd tell you. Maybe you can protect him from those thugs who beat him up."

"Do you have any idea who they worked for?"

"No . . . but I bet Mrs. Drusse would. She spies on everyone." A scowl drew her pale brows together.

Thugs always have a boss. And that's probably who holds the marker on Toombs's debts. Ritsuko stifled a sigh. *Two more people I need to talk to.* This case was like a worm; the minute she thought she'd narrowed it down, it split in two more directions. *I'll talk to the neighbor on my way out.*

"Before I go, do you have anything that your son might've built, one of those lovely gadgets you mentioned earlier?"

Mrs. Toombs perked up. With a huge smile, she stood and walked to the mantel, nodding enthusiastically. "Oh, goodness, yes. Why here, he dropped this off the last time we saw him. It's nice, don't you think? It shines like the sun proper when the light hits it just right." She turned to Ritsuko, beaming with pride as she tapped a finger against the small device.

It looked like an intricately carved hemisphere at first. When Mrs. Toombs touched it, though, it slid open with the tinkling of little gears and levers. It blossomed like a polished brass flower; Ritsuko had to agree it looked lovely. *Oh, bronze gods. It also looks familiar.* When the mirrored surfaces clicked into their final positions, Gregory Toombs's parting gift to his parents was also a miniature replica of the murder machine.

CHAPTER 12

BUTTERFLIES FLUTTERED IN AURELIA'S STOMACH. AT LENGTH she rifled through her closet to locate a dream of a dress, all gossamer silk and deceptive lace. It was a misleading blend of bridal innocence, whereas any society matron could elaborate on how inappropriate such a choice was for Aurelia Wright. Deciding it was perfect, she slid into it.

Pearly powder and lipstick completed the picture. She paused in the doorway of her flat before steeling her nerve and locking the door. Outside, she found the hansom waiting as he'd promised, and she clambered into it, settling for a fair ride.

Through gray privacy screens, she watched the city come to life for the night. Softening the old facades, a gentle ocean breeze soothed the day's heat. The dark stone seemed warm in the approaching twilight; columns and patterns of lights previewed the stars yet to appear. They drove along the park to Main before turning toward the city center. House scions and pedestrians were starting to appear as the night shift of vendors and hawkers came to their posts. Bondsmen slouched along the streets, in no hurry to complete their work, as most of them were working off prison sentences. For the most part, it was an efficient system, putting criminals to work instead of incarcerating them. The worst offenders were banished outside the city and eventually made their way to outlaw settlements in the far west.

They left the city limits, passing through the northern gate, cleared land giving way to sparse brush, then forest, as the road wound up a gentle slope. Cleaning the window with her palm, she saw how the silver crescent moon draped the heavy woods in a curtain of ethereal light, and in the distance, she glimpsed her destination: white marble and red tiled roof amid primeval forest. She had been riding nearly two hours by that time, which placed his home on the slopes of the foothills. Outside Dorstaad, the Summer Clan owned the roads, but they didn't bother her.

Soon, the vehicle hissed to a stop in front of the house, and Aurelia disembarked. The air was sweet with oleander, honeysuckle, wild strawberries, and mowed grass, all borne by a soft wind. All around her, the night sang quietly, noises unfamiliar to her. Aurelia had rarely left the city, and even when she traveled, she tended to visit other metropolitan locales. When she tried to pay the driver, he flashed her a cocky grin and followed the circular drive behind the lodge.

"Theron has style," she said aloud.

For a long moment, she simply stood, listening to the crickets and frogs, the whirring wings of insects she'd never heard. The rustle of bats and crackle of nocturnal creatures in the undergrowth nearby stirred Aurelia from her appreciative trance. Certain beasts she preferred to encounter only from afar. In motion once more, her heels clicked against the stones as she crossed to the door, lifting the knocker on a deep breath.

As brass met brass, the opening of the door softened the sharp sound. Before her stood a man of middle height and nondescript features. He was average in every way, but his smile was friendly, a complement to his uniform. The servant beckoned her in.

No coat to surrender, she waited only a moment before the chamberlain led her into the white marble atrium, austere in line and adornment. Only the play of reflections broke the initially sterile impression. As they passed through the far doors, however, that perception was soon dispelled. Tiled in elaborate patterns, the open walkway surrounded a garden. White pillars held lights, the frosty shimmer of the globes the only concession given to modernization that she had seen so far, and they served to frame what must be the pride of the villa. The style was different from what she saw in the city, probably the influence of some early settlers during one crossing or another.

Blooms of all shades flourished against a lush background of plant life. Trees and bushes Aurelia was certain she'd seen nowhere else fought for space against the central fountain. The weather was different from the city as well, and from the tingle on her skin, magic must go into maintaining this unseasonal warmth. A soft spray misting about the fountain, the liquid sound of splashing water reached her as she stood, gazing around. Amazed, she would have continued to do so if the steward had not gestured.

Stirring, Aurelia glimpsed a table beyond the fountain, and upon it, twin candles flickered like captive fireflies. With a parting smile, she picked her way across the courtyard, her heart thundering in her ears. *He's wearing white linen.* Aurelia felt strangely startled, as she'd never seen him in anything but dark suits.

Apparently on his home ground, he unbent a bit, and as she stopped beside the table, set with china, crystal, and white roses, her sense of the surreal intensified. All about her, the courtyard gleamed with the shimmering lights, shadows beyond. It was a perfect foil, his darkness contrasting with the white silk and linen he wore. She took a deep breath, rich with exotic fragrance, and waited for him to speak.

"Good evening, Aurelia. Come . . . sit." His eyes lingered on her face, on the way her dress clung and fell. "You look lovely."

"Thank you."

"Wine?" He lifted the bottle as he spoke, something that drank the light and kissed it with color.

"Please," she murmured, extending her hand for the glass. "It's beautiful out here. I'm surprised you ever come into the city."

"I have not, in many years." Theron poured for her, then himself. "I have all I need, and only rare circumstances bring me forth. The peace keeps me here."

So that makes me . . . a rare circumstance? Or did he meet me by chance on the way to deal with some business at the club? She hadn't given up on winkling out his secrets, but his attraction had other layers as well now.

"You never told me why you came to the club that night."

He smiled. "I did not."

I'll keep trying.

Aurelia lifted her glass and tasted the wine. "The quiet here unnerves me. I've been so long surrounded by humanity that I've grown accustomed to its noises. Omnibuses and the chug of carriages . . . sometimes, I open my window and just listen. The city seems to breathe, as if it were a creature with a heartbeat, and a mind of its own."

"She is. A living thing, that is. Untamed, untapped, no matter what some might think. But be that as it may, I cannot bear living within it."

Her father, the Architect, pulled many strings in Dorstaad. She had no such ambitions, which created some of the conflict. Her sire wanted someone to take over his empire, once he was no longer fit to run it. And she'd only ever wanted to dance. *Poor little rich girl,* she thought with silent self-mockery. But her father had been generous in the end, leaving her an independence that kept her from abject poverty, and he'd provided rooms at the club, too. More than many would've done, given her complete defiance. She had not seen him or spoken to him—or to anyone in the family but her mother—in almost forty years.

"The city affects some people that way," she said.

"So I have noticed. Others, it drives to madness, it would seem."

She wondered if he'd noticed something about her, if the age decay she feared had grown perceptible to others. To cover her concern, she sipped at her wine.

Theron indicated the romantic table for two. "Shall we eat?"

They started with cheese and fruit, both commonplace and rarities brought from the north in the Winter Isle, followed by salmon and bread. Simple fare prepared with delicate care and accompanied by sauces sweet and sharp. By the time she tasted everything, she felt satiated, a little dreamy from the wine. With a dark and slivered glance, he caught her licking her fingers, and she offered a guilty grin.

"That was wonderful," she said.

He nodded. Folding the napkin, time and again, he finally deposited it on the table, neatly squared. "It's been a long time since I cooked for anyone else."

Astonishment registered first, melting into pleasure. "Thank you. No one's ever cooked for me who was not paid to do so."

"It's an old habit. To trust none with my meals."

"Is that because you have enemies who wish you ill?" She could easily picture him engaged in labyrinthine intrigues that resulted in an adversary poisoning his soup.

"Doesn't everyone? Some people make insipid foes, as they can't be bothered to take action. They content themselves with wishing ill rather than working toward it."

"You sound as if you admire the schemers."

"Do I?" His habit of answering with a question made it impossible to read him. There was no statement in an inquiry; therefore, her senses quivered with confusion.

That might also be because of the moonlit garden and the man currently offering his hand. Helping her to her feet, Theron slipped her hand into the crook of his arm, warm and muscular beneath the well-worn linen. She felt honored that he had discarded formality, showing her a more private version of himself. There might be calculation in the gesture, but it was effective nonetheless.

With the euphoric glow of the wine, Aurelia felt oddly content inside his private paradise. Her heels clicked in a cadence that complemented the other nocturnal noise, the song of their passage. Tropical hints reached her, clearly not native to the isle, but somehow, he coaxed their cooperation on an alien shore. The magical resonance she'd sensed earlier echoed stronger here, convincing her such a place wasn't natural. Tipping her head back as they walked, she breathed the perfumed air, bougainvillea and climbing roses, jasmine and orchids that twined about the trees.

"You must be very old," she said quietly.

"That is . . . offensive." He was smiling.

"Is it?

You're not the only one who can do that.

"Among those like us, perhaps not. What are you asking, Aurelia?"

"How do you create such a place?"

He glanced around, inhaling the perfumed air. "It's lovely, isn't it? My greatest and most enduring work. What would you say if I told you that once, our ancestors had the ability to

command the land itself? Those with the most power could re-
arrange the world to suit their tastes and whims?"

"That sounds like legends of the old Courts."

"Some of them, my dear Aurelia, are true."

He believes what he's saying. It's not a lie. Shock reverberated
through her, but she managed not to reveal it. "Are you claiming
to be a pureblood?"

Bronze gods, he'd be thousands of years old, and assuredly,
not even a little human. His mind would be utterly alien, his
goals incomprehensible. She should flee, presented with this as
even a remote possibility. Provided that she believed him. It
seemed a worthy gambit, a move guaranteed to fascinate her.

"I'm not claiming anything. I'm merely entertaining a beautiful woman."

"You're so clever. Or maddening. I haven't decided which yet."

"Can't I be both? Maddeningly clever, perhaps."

She gazed up at him, furrowing her brow. "Your lineage aside,
do you allege you possess the capacity to shape this patch of
ground to your will? And mark me, I'll have a plain yes or no from
you, or we are finished, now and forever."

"An ultimatum already?" He inclined his head then, sweeping
a gesture to indicate the lush beauty around them. "Yes, Aurelia.
This garden grows to please me because I will it so and because
I tend it."

Truth.

He went on, "My power wanes outside these walls, however,
and I prefer to remain where I'm at my strongest."

"Will you ever tell me what drew you out?"

"In time. When I know you well enough to trust that you'll
believe me."

That sounded as if he had a tale, and Aurelia had never been
able to resist one. "Very well. I can be patient. I'll bide my time."

She leaned over to bury her nose in a pale flower with darkness at its center. Like a rose, it bore thorns, but it also had delicately flared petals, and the most luxurious scent she'd ever
experienced. "I've never seen this one before. What is it?"

"The Sangreal. She took some time." His tone was soft, fond,
even.

Theron stepped closer, running a fingertip along the bloom
as one might caress a lover. He released the silken petal with

quiet reluctance, and everything about the touch and his manner told her this flower mattered to him. It might even be the key to his heart, should he possess such a thing.

"You created it? It doesn't smell entirely like a rose . . ." Aurelia trailed off, thinking. "Almost a cross with jasmine or honeysuckle. Or both."

"Both. I needed to strengthen the fragrance." He stood, looking at the bush. "This was my last strain." He swept his arm in a gesture that encompassed the entire garden. "But far from my only attempt. Half these came from my hand."

"They're not all magical?" she teased. "Impossible flowers sprung from nowhere?"

"No. Some came from decades of dedication, and they could grow in any hothouse, given proper conditions and care."

"That's incredible. You have a gift." Longingly, her gaze lingered on the Sangreal, then she turned. "I won't interrogate you more tonight though I don't promise to stop trying to learn what you want from me."

The garden parted before them, relinquishing them to an open space at its heart. There, the stars glittered, and the crescent moon shone brighter than Aurelia had ever seen. Reflections danced in the fountain, formed from stones and overgrown with moss. Rising well past eye level, a lily pond inhabited by gold and silver fish surrounded it. Next to it stood a small gazebo built in the same unfamiliar style as the rest of his home: elegant curved arches and filigree, topped with a tapering half dome.

With a ghost of a smile lingering, he guided her toward the structure. At the entrance, Aurelia stopped, one foot on the step. The magic was heady, dizzying, and the vista offered a beauty so pure as to hurt the heart. A fierce ache welled up until she didn't know where to look, wanting to absorb everything at once.

"Here is the soul of this place," she whispered, tipping her head up.

"So it is." He met her gaze, the small line between his brows bespeaking uncertainty. For a blown-glass moment, they gazed at one another. Then he shifted; at some unseen signal from him, music wafted through the tangle of plants around them. "Would you dance, Aurelia?" His words blended with the music, his offered hands dark against the ivory of his shirt.

Her breath hitched. Some of her confusion manifested in the

lopsided smile she gave him, but she put her hands in his with enough conviction to offset it.

"I'd love to," she said, low.

When he led her into the gazebo, she felt as if they had withdrawn from the world into a quiet place where only the two of them existed. She waited for his lead.

He sought her eyes, and whatever he saw made him smile. Then he led her into what might have passed for a waltz if they were elsewhere and dancing to a different melody. As the music flowed, it called for a closer hold; the slow slide and brush of hip and arm as they spun in languid motions.

She followed, anticipating his turns an instant before he made them. As they circled the floor, her head fell back. The world whirled over his shoulder, less from motion or wine; she was quite simply drunk with *him*. Inhaling deeply through her nose, Aurelia devoured him with a look while the rest of her arched and yielded, twisted and spun in steps so fleeting that she lost the thread of them, her body entirely given to his guidance.

They moved together with a single will, all but merged, until the music peaked and drifted into silence. Holding her close after a last turn, he gazed down at her, his smile long gone, replaced with hunger. Aurelia trembled, her breath coming fast, and for an infinite moment, she met his look. Her short nails curled into the nape of his neck.

If this place is his creation, if his power is strongest here, how do I know this is truly what I want?

She had no qualms about choosing a lover, but it must be her own decision. The knives of desire in her belly swelled into a red-hot poker as she tore herself away.

"I have to go. But thank you. It was a lovely evening."

Disappointment warred with shock in his expression. *He didn't expect me to resist. What* does *he have in mind for me, I wonder?* The attempt to fuddle her with a strong glamour only made him more interesting to her; nobody had so persistently attempted to draw her into his schemes for the longest time.

"I'll call the coach for you. But understand that this isn't the end for us, Aurelia."

"No," she said, smiling. "It's only the beginning. Chase me if you like. Perhaps, if you remain interesting, I'll even let you catch me."

CHAPTER 13

THE NEXT MORNING, MIKANI MET RITSUKO IN THE FOYER OF the CID building. He had been so eager to see her that he forgot to stop for his usual coffee. *Hope Electra doesn't think I'm dead.* They both started talking at once, until she held up a hand, demanding silence. That was so unlike her that he actually quieted.

"Mine's better, I promise. Come with me."

Bemused, he followed her down to the evidence room, where she asked the clerk to produce item 157. The man complied with laconic efficiency, and Ritsuko handed him a clockwork device. *It's . . . What is this?* After a rudimentary examination while she bounced on her toes like a child, he turned to her, astonishment warring with mild outrage.

"You should've located me yesterday, Ritsuko."

Her smile faltered. "But . . . you were following another lead; and then it was time to go home. I logged it."

"If I'd found this, I wouldn't have rested until you knew about it."

"I just . . . I was only thinking about getting it here before Toombs's mother changed her mind and decided I needed to fill out forms in triplicate. I was afraid she'd get rid of it if I hesitated and she realized just how crucial it was and the severity of the related crime."

"I understand. But you still should've come looking for me."

"I'm sorry," she said. No excuses. He could tell by her expression that she felt awful, but there was something else, too.

Though he didn't often do this to his partner, he let slip enough to read her, echoes and impressions. He saw the moment where they spun in an awkward dance in his hallway, the night they spent drinking, when she had her hands in his hair. *That's why? She was afraid of intruding on my off-duty hours, afraid it would be unwelcome?*

"I'm *truly* sorry."

Now that he understood, he decided to move on. *Best not to make her explain further.* "I can understand why you thought I needed a rest. It's been grueling."

Ritsuko nodded and turned to the clerk. "I'm taking this upstairs to show to Commander Gunwood."

The man pushed a form toward her. "Fill this out, please, and sign the ledger."

Mikani's partner did so, then she beckoned for him to follow, as he was still holding the device. Mikani was glad that at least she hadn't presented evidence without him. It should be a team effort when they told their boss they'd narrowed it down to one likely suspect, and they'd need the whole city to tighten the net, use all available resources to restrict Toombs's movements. From this point, it shouldn't be long.

As soon as they stepped into the duty room, Commander Gunwood bellowed, "Mikani! Ritsuko! My office. Now."

It was early enough that there were other officers on shift, some at their desks, others preparing to head out to follow their own leads. All of them mumbled an encouraging word as they passed. Mikani pressed his partner's shoulder gently with a free hand, then strolled into the old man's office. His attitude was sure to draw ire, as it always did. He liked it better that way because he *really* didn't like it when anyone went after Ritsuko. It had started when they'd first met, and he had gleaned in her what most others failed to see: spirit, courage, and a drive to do the right thing. In their three years together, the urge to defend her had deepened even as it grew fiercer. It felt like a waking beast, full of protective rage, and he couldn't always control it.

"You're looking well," he said, knowing that would make things worse. The old man was rumpled, cranky, exhausted, and in all ways aggravated.

"You think this is funny, Mikani?"

Gunwood didn't invite them to take a seat. To be called on the carpet properly, you had to stand like a child before the headmaster, waiting to feel the crack of the birch rod. Ritsuko was very still and quiet beside him; and her fear was so thick he could taste it, a sour, acrid note coating his tongue. Not fear of physical harm, more insubstantial. Based on what he knew of her, he guessed she was afraid of losing the job she loved.

"One dead girl. One *very* powerful House." Gunwood slammed a fist onto his desk to emphasize his displeasure. "I expected you two to have this mess cleaned up five days ago. Care to explain what's taking so long?"

Mikani was about to make a joke that would probably get him suspended, when Ritsuko said, "There is no justification, sir. But we do have some compelling new evidence if you'll indulge me for a moment."

"Just one."

She nodded at Mikani, indicating he should demonstrate the device. Gunwood was already growling, "I don't have time for toys"—when Ritsuko produced a sketch of the crime scene. Wordlessly, she laid it on the commander's desk beside the model.

"It's a match," the old man said.

Ritsuko inclined her head. "Precisely. Built by Gregory Toombs, once an engineering student, now an actor, and he's known to have taken an interest in the victim."

"What are you doing to hunt this maniac down?"

"Everything," Mikani answered. "Or rather, we would be if we weren't having this charming interlude with you."

Gunwood narrowed his eyes. "One of these days, someone will shoot you, and you won't be wearing the right vest."

"Please don't kill my partner, sir. Though he can be difficult, I'm used to him . . . and it would be a bother to train someone new."

Though her tone was light, his earlier reading lingered between them. Her true feelings washed over him, an astonishing amount of pain at the idea of harm coming to him. Mikani didn't know what to do with that truth, so he pocketed it to be digested later. But he aimed a quiet look at Ritsuko, thinking he'd gladly cut out a few hearts on her behalf as well.

"Since you didn't arrive empty-handed, I'll skip the rest of the lecture. You know how crucial it is that we locate this monster." Gunwood sighed, looking more weary than irate. "If you don't, it'll be your career *and* mine. Oleg Aevar has been leaning on my superiors, asking for all our heads on a pike if we don't deliver. You have forty-eight hours to bring me a suspect in chains."

"It's hard to move forward when we file our requests and you sit on them," Mikani muttered.

That still grated. They'd sent in the proper paperwork days before and heard nothing from the commander. He hated the fact that the great Houses could avoid inconvenience to the point that they were almost untouchable. It was no wonder the impoverished, persecuted magicians and sorcerers were looking for a solution. Sometimes, he wanted one himself.

"About that," Gunwood said. "Miss Aevar's mother has returned to the city, and she's willing to speak with you."

He hadn't expected that. The woman had seemed broken the night they'd taken the report of Miss Aevar's disappearance. Apparently the mother had a core of strength not readily apparent. In the great Houses, if there were no sons, the daughter's husband took on the family name to keep the line going. Mikani presumed Cira's father was deceased or gone, as there had been no mention of him.

"Her father doesn't know," Ritsuko guessed.

"Indeed. So you will be meeting Valerie Aevar at a café in the Temple District." He provided the name and directions, then leaned forward and gave them a narrow-eyed look. "You are not to distress her in any way. If she returns to her father with so much as a stubbed toe, I will hold the pair of you accountable. Understood?" Mikani led the way down, still grumbling about special privileges, but they did snag his favorite cruiser.

I'll take that *as a good omen.*

* * *

BEHIND THEM, RITSUKO heard two inspectors cursing because
they were too late. Her partner answered with a smirk and a
salute as they slid in. When they jolted into motion, she realized
it was Shelton and Cutler, the ones Mikani had beaten up on her
behalf, and more than likely the ones who had asked to take over
their case.

No rivalry there.

"You know where we're going?" she asked.

He nodded. "I'll get us there."

"I have a lab report," she said, digging into her attaché case.
"I stopped by on my way up today." Thinking about the tech,
Mr. Higgins, made her smile. She'd enjoyed their luncheon the
other day, more than she'd expected.

The tech was proving to be rather delightful, with a quiet,
dry sense of humor. Her heart was in no danger, but he made her
laugh, and she hoped she offered a little respite from the pain of
his mother's illness. It was nice to have someone who acted as
if your company was infinitely desirable. Her grandfather would
never have approved, of course, but she didn't qualify for a pres-
tigious marriage anymore. So she might as well seek happiness
over dynastic contribution.

"Anything helpful?"

"They identified the herbs I found at the crime scene."

"Well?" he prompted, cutting her a look as he wove around
a hansom, the engine building up to a rumbling hum as they
accelerated.

"Acanthus and hyacinth."

"What does that mean? How does it help us?"

She exhaled in a sigh. "I have no idea. Maybe it will mean
something to Cira's mother. If it doesn't, I'll do some research
when we go back to headquarters. And perhaps you can ask
Saskia? It may be related to the magical angle, though only Mr.
Toombs could say what he's trying to accomplish."

Mikani's jaw clenched. "I want that bastard."

She agreed completely.

There wasn't a whole lot to say after that, so they rode in
silence to the café. It was a clear evening, stars visible through
the pale veil of steam thrown by passing vehicles. Her partner

turned off Crown Avenue and into the Temple District, parking
below one of the ubiquitous bronze statues. The bronze idols to
several dozen gods adorned the plazas that connected the temples, shrines, and chapels that gave the area its name.

Valerie Aevar was already waiting. The time in the country
had done her good; she no longer looked breakable. Instead,
Ritsuko read a particular determination in the woman's eyes.
Since her daughter's body had been found, she no longer had
hope; instead, she burned with the need for justice, and it had
hardened her.

Mrs. Aevar rose as they approached, indicating chairs opposite as if she were the hostess of a party. Even as Ritsuko smiled
at the other woman's manner, she took the indicated seat. It went
without saying that she'd take the lead, and Mikani would do his
thing. At this point, they didn't need to discuss how they would
proceed with a witness.

"Mrs. Aevar, it was kind of you to break from mourning to
answer our questions." She offered a smile.

"I will not say it is good to see you," the other woman replied.
"But I want you to find out who did this, and if there's any way
for me to help, well, I shall."

Mikani signaled for coffee while she framed her first query.
Her partner stirred, and she glanced over at him. "Something
wrong?"

He was frowning. "No. I just feel like I'm cheating on
Electra."

"Don't fret, you can flirt with her another day." Ritsuko
addressed her next words to the other woman. "We've discovered
that your daughter was working at the Royale as a seamstress.
Did you know?"

Guilt clouded Mrs. Aevar's gaze. "I did. Of course I did. At
first, I thought she had a lover, so I had her followed. When I
saw what she was doing . . . it seemed harmless, and it made her
so happy. After we talked about it, I started sending a coach for
her at the boardinghouse where she made the costumes."

"But her grandfather had no idea."

Mrs. Aevar shook her head. "He wouldn't have approved.
Proper ladies do *not* work."

"I can tell you blame yourself for what happened." Mikani
spoke for the first time, eyes closed, and his fingers playing along

the edge of the coffee cup. "You shouldn't. You wanted your daughter to be happy, and you took precautions to keep her safe. It would've been impossible to do more."

Unexpectedly sensitive.

The other woman gave a long, shuddering breath. "Thank you, Inspector. It gives me some comfort to be exonerated even if I cannot yet forgive myself."

"Was there anyone in her life? A man she held in fond regard?"

"I'm not certain. The last few weeks, Cira began to act differently. Not secretive, precisely, but she had a glow about her. When I asked, she would grow flustered and decline to speak of it."

Toombs, she thought. A silent glance exchanged with Mikani said he was thinking the same thing. They needed to find him.

"So there was a guard with her, most times," Mikani said thoughtfully.

Mrs. Aevar inclined her head. "After I learned Cira had been . . ." Her voice trailed away, then she went on, "I fired him."

"Would you happen to know where we could find him?" Ritsuko got out her notepad.

She fought anger; if the woman had told the truth that first night, the trail wouldn't be so cold. But she'd been in denial, still hoping her daughter would come home. She might even have had the guard looking on his own, wanting to resolve the matter quietly if Miss Aevar had run off with an inappropriate man. Once hope died, the need to keep secrets faded, too.

"I have the address he gave me when I retained his services." Delving in her bag, she withdrew a card and passed it across the table.

It was good quality, cottony paper, printed with plain black ink, and it suggested a man of superior taste and a no-nonsense nature. OLIVER DINWIDDIE, PRIVATE SECURITY. One final question, then, before she let Valerie Aevar go.

"Do hyacinth and acanthus mean anything to you?"

The woman raised an elegantly shaped brow. "Should they? They're plants, I think, but otherwise . . ."

"Thank you for your time," Mikani murmured.

Ritsuko realized she hadn't touched her coffee, as they stood. On the way to the cruiser, she said, "What did you get from her?"

He waited until they were both in the vehicle to answer. "She's holding herself together with a thread, guilt's eating her up. She thinks if she hadn't kept Cira's secret, the girl would still be alive. And for all I know, that's true."

"Harsh." But it brought home how one choice could change everything. With a faint sigh, she passed him the card so he could visualize the address. "Are you well?"

His shoulders lifted in a shrug. "It wasn't pleasant, but it was far better than some crime scenes."

"Your head—"

"I said I'm fine." *Leave it,* his tone demanded.

"Then let's go talk to Oliver Dinwiddie."

Twenty minutes later, they were banging on his flat door. No answer. Mikani wore a queer, frozen look. Though she had no Ferisher blood, Ritsuko could sense something in the air as well, not quite a smell, but almost. Her skin crawled. She didn't want to, but she tried the handle. The door was locked.

"Use the jimmy," Mikani said. "We have reason to believe civilian life is at risk."

She'd only deployed the thing one other time—to save an elderly woman who couldn't get to the door. What awaited them inside here might be much worse. Ritsuko got the device out of her bag and set it between the door and the frame. It popped the door like the lid off a tin of beans, and the coppery tang of blood wafted toward them.

Footsteps sounded then, a silvery shatter of glass. "Mikani, there's a runner."

"I'm on it," he called, already pounding down the steps toward the back alley.

A low gurgle from within the flat made her quicken her step. Using protocols that had become second nature, she secured the scene and found Dinwiddie on the floor beside his bed. Blood pooled dark beneath his body. She knelt, knowing it was too late for a med-wagon to save him. To her surprise, his eyelids fluttered open. Impending death dulled his sight, leaving the irises filmy. He clutched her forearm.

"It was him," he rasped. "The man from the theater . . ."

"Toombs?"

"Too—" With a shudder, Dinwiddie died.

She searched the flat before Mikani strode in, more disheveled than usual. "Did you get him?"

"I saw him from the back," he answered. "But no. The bastard ran down an alley, went over a fence, and by the time I hit the other side, he was long gone."

"Could it have been Toombs?"

Mikani gave an angry shrug. "General height is right, I think, but it's tough to be certain when someone's running. He did have dark hair."

"So does Toombs. Dinwiddie said, 'It was him, the man from the theater,' just before he died."

"Sounds like confirmation to me," Mikani said.

She fought down dread and nausea. "Between this and the model we found at his parents' apartment, maybe Gunwood won't kill us when we get back to HQ."

Her partner seemed none too sure. "We were *this* close . . . and he got away. Somehow, I don't think the commander will be too pleased with us."

CHAPTER 14

AS IT TURNED OUT, MIKANI WAS RIGHT. *I WISH I WASN'T, THOUGH.* His ears were still ringing from the peal the old man read over them once they reported in. Ritsuko looked as if she had been repeatedly kicked in the stomach—and he *hated* that expression on her. It made his fists curl though there wasn't anything he could do about it.

"You two are done, do you hear me?" Gunwood snarled.

Before the old man could continue the tirade, Shelton stuck his head in the office. "I hate to interrupt when Mikani's getting what he deserves, but there's an urgent message from Dispatch."

Never thought I'd be glad to see you, *bastard.* He glared at the weasel who had said such filthy things about Ritsuko until the thin man took a step back. At the moment, he wanted to pound Shelton all over again. His partner, Cutler, was nowhere to be found; he tended not to face Mikani if he could help it.

That suspension was entirely worth it.

"Let's hear it," Gunwood demanded.

"There's been suspicious activity down in Landing Point. Some nosy neighbor, complaining about the construction noise, thinks we should check it out." Then Shelton asked the commander, "Why don't you let Cutler and me handle this? Isn't it time to turn this case over to some real inspectors? This office is taking a real trouncing in public opinion because of the general incompetence of the fieldwork so far." Shelton's gaze flicked over Ritsuko, silently indicting her for the failure.

Mikani lazily popped the knuckles on his right hand. The other man shut up.

He could tell that Gunwood didn't like Shelton any more than he did, but the old man was also pretty furious; he rapped the desk, contemplating. "Ritsuko, Mikani. You may as well go out there, get a preliminary picture of what we're dealing with. But I'm *not* finished with the two of you."

Excellent. Something to look forward to. He had the self-control not to say it aloud. So Gunwood sent them back out, his scowl promising dire things on their return. Half an hour driving delivered them to the bay. *It doesn't always reek like this, surely.* He stole a furtive glance at his partner, interviewing residents some distance away. Then he turned back to the street, frowning.

Around them, ancient buildings dominated the skyline. Four to six stories high, the blocky structures were dwarfed by an abandoned House enclave. Far beyond them, the jagged skyline of the city center glittered. Behind them, Landing Point docks stretched deep into the bay, masts and smokestacks swaying like a floating, man-made forest on the slow currents. The creak of timber and groans of metal carried far over the water. Mikani grimaced as a warm breath of wind eddied the effluvium of the place.

There's fear here. And distrust. And they're not used to it; this is the smell of sheep that know a wolf is near. And the whole damned thing is giving me a headache.

Down the block, men slouched against a wall, taking turns glancing their way. No one seemed happy, and the young men with Ritsuko were no exception. They wore sullen defiance in the same way as territorial colors, but he sensed something more, a seething rage. The muffled sounds of broadcasts rippled through the area—warnings of some kind. *That doesn't bode well.* With a quiet sigh, Mikani turned back to the structure; a makeshift mezzanine joined the two buildings, erected in relatively recent times.

A uniformed officer strode up to them. "Inspectors, I think we may have a problem brewing. When we first found the body, a junior agent mentioned—"

"This will have to wait. Ready, Ritsuko?" Without turning around, Mikani cast the question over his shoulder. Something about the structure made him even more nauseous than the rich currents of rice, fish, and sweat all around him.

With a nod, Ritsuko detached herself from the group of youths who spoke little or no English. Her facility for languages was one of the reasons she'd been assigned to him initially; he had a hard time remembering things. It was the CID's policy to pair agents who complemented each other, at least on paper.

"It's showtime. Got your magic kit?"

"Minus the garlic necklaces. Stuff gives me stomach cramps . . . think I might be allergic." Mikani led the way down toward the water. Along the shore, the darkness was as absolute as the stench. A far more real and cloying aroma, drifting from somewhere ahead, subdued the smell of fear.

For the first time in three years, Mikani drew his sidearm, seeking comfort in its weight. With his other hand, he raised his lantern, sending the light swaying. There were recent drag marks across the soft ground: scrapes, divots of churned earth where someone had dragged and pushed something big along the riverbank.

Despite the mild temperature, Ritsuko shivered beside him, her own weapon in hand. The silence bore the heaviness of graves, row upon row of stone, rooted in the ground beyond wind or time. His soft-soled shoes scraped as he followed the stopgap corridor; he passed through the maw into open air yet oddly, the atmosphere grew only more viscous. Decaying wood floors; green shoots that had pushed their way to the surface and from the dry summer and salt water lay in desiccated yellow tentacles. The sweetness of the air, more sickly than any flower, stung his senses.

They made their way on the creaking, protesting timbers to the farthest end of the building, though that word only loosely applied to such a structure; the stilts on which it teetered were half-rotten. With narrowed eyes, he skimmed the perimeter, turning slowly. Various primitive insignia marked the place as ritual ground, and at the far side, some sort of carpentry project

seemed to be taking place. *Bricks, neatly stacked . . . and mortared? Scaffolding . . .* With a growing frown, he moved closer.
At ten paces, he stopped dead, utterly motionless for a moment.
Ritsuko's face glowed pale in the lantern he swung her way,
though she seemed otherwise in check.

"Think you better step this way, partner. We have a customer."

"What did you—" She didn't need to finish the question, once
the light touched the scaffolding.

It was an open webwork of wood and steel in the vague outline
of an inverted pyramid. Suspended in the center was a tall, copper
cylinder. Mikani could guess what the shape was, but he knew
he'd have to get closer. As he spoke, he moved. "Call the constable
on duty. Have him call for a team and seal the place off."

He would lay money on the table that Ritsuko was already
taking care of it, but the words helped him focus as he approached.
Mikani wished, idly, for a cigarillo to help with the smell. He did
not grimace, though, as he reached the construct. The framework
had been painstakingly crafted, each joint and beam buffed so
that it shone in the green-tinged light. *The damned thing is familiar. Definitely the work of the same maniac.*

Mikani turned his full attention to the reddish cylinder. Thick
ropes wrapped around the tube and connected it to the heavy
timber supports. A glass lens gleamed at the top. *Toombs must
have ground the thing. There's no store that carries giant lenses,
as far as I know . . . although, if he had them made on order, we
might have one hell of a break.* Mikani doubted the man had
been that stupid, however, as he'd eluded capture for this long
with the whole city searching for him.

He carefully clambered on the wooden supports and started
to pry the lens loose, twisting and tugging it until it gave way. He
slid the heavy glass lens away and down, letting it clatter with a
loud and lingering ring on the wooden floor. He could see a figure
inside the copper tube, filled to the brim with stagnant water.

She'd been bound at wrists and ankles to hooks bolted to the
inner walls. The body was only slightly decomposed, her features
still recognizable past the leather gag tightly bound to her face.
Bronze gods, Electra.

Mikani remembered the greetings they'd exchanged over the
years, and this last time, she'd seemed truly troubled, offering

to read his cards. *If I'd let her, would things be different?* He had been on his way to talk to Saskia, no time for an acquaintance. His whole body clenched in futile regret. *I'm so sorry, Summer Girl.* This time, using his gift felt both awful and inevitable, knowledge he had to have but didn't want.

She was terrified when she died . . . that's not just rigor mortis, and it was slow enough that she knew what was happening. As Mikani ran the tips of his fingers along the slick metal, he heard the faint echo of her final moments. *Terror and anger; an echoing plea of Why?* With a muttered oath, he withdrew his hand and stepped away.

"Better get the boys in here." His voice sounded strained.

There was no trace of the killer, again. As if whoever had done it was a clockwork man or so detached as to be inhuman. Sometimes he wondered if Ritsuko had some trace of a gift because, as the ache intensified, she crossed to his side and set a hand on his shoulder. The touch felt good, and Mikani fought the alien urge to turn into her arms. He couldn't remember the last time he'd asked comfort of anyone.

"What's wrong?" she asked softly.

He swallowed hard, and into the silence, he said, "I knew her." *I failed her.*

RITSUKO FROZE. *IF one of Mikani's women is inside that tube . . .*

She started establishing his alibi before she even realized what she was doing. "From where?"

Mikani slapped the side of the cylinder. "It's Electra. From the café. I saw her . . . a week or so ago?" He stepped away, pacing a tight pattern. "She was trying to make her own way, proving a point to her father."

She experienced a surge of relief. Someone he saw casually, bought coffee from, that would require a lot less explaining than someone he knew . . . intimately. It was bad enough he had any acquaintance with the victim at all. Gunwood, she imagined, would not be delighted with this development.

He faced her, drawing a deep breath. She hadn't seen him this upset before; he seemed on the verge of racing off to hunt Toombs like a dog. The fury she saw in him alarmed her, as it might prove difficult to restrain. She ran her hand from his shoulder down his back. *Like I'm trying to tame him.* Then, consciously, because she remembered how it affected him at the bar, she smoothed her palm back up and cupped his nape.

"Anything I can do?"

He tensed against her fingers, trembling for a long moment as he seemed to slowly and painfully gather himself. When he finally spoke, his voice sounded almost normal. "Make sure I don't kill him when we catch him." He smiled wryly. "I'd rather that he suffers for a while, first."

"I won't let you throw your life away. Don't think you'd fare well on the penal farms anyway. Too many familiar faces." Before she could decide what to add, pounding footsteps made her turn.

Ritsuko dropped her hand from Mikani as the officer raced up to them. "I'm sorry to interrupt, Inspectors, but, well, that girl's not going anywhere, and the docks are—"

A loud crash from the street beyond drowned out the rest of the constable's sentence. Mikani glanced at Ritsuko before heading to the exit. The tumult of a growing mob grew louder as they raced back the way they'd come. Breaking glass was unmistakable, followed by the rush of running feet.

They arrived to a rolling roar and a sea of bodies packed in the narrow alleys. The crowd charged the thin line of uniformed men doing their best to hold them back; a few of the younger officers looked terrified. What made Ritsuko nervous, though, was the burgeoning anger in some of the veteran constables.

They'll start pushing back soon, and it'll spiral out of control.

Mikani followed her gaze and seemed to glean what she was thinking. He squeezed her arm. "See if you can get our people to cool off. I'll try and defuse it from the other side." He nodded toward a vocal knot of men near the center of the line. They were all garbed in the bright and eclectic style of the Summer Clan, the eldest among them an obvious leader. Maybe even a patriarch, to judge from the way his men held both constables and mob away from him. "Hope I don't have to promise your hand in marriage to pacify them." Before she could answer, he pushed his way toward the center of the crowd.

"What's your name, Officer?" She used her most stentorian

tone on the broad-shouldered man in his early forties. His cap
was askew as he brandished his club at the crowd lunging toward
the do-not-cross line.

"Clemmens, ma'am. I think we might need to contact the
Council. I don't know if we have the manpower to contain this."
His voice was barely audible between the smashing of windows
and the mad growling of the mob.

"Have you sent someone to the nearest mirror station?"

"Not yet. There's nobody in charge, no orders—"

"Free somebody up, send him to notify Dispatch that we need
reinforcements as fast as they can send them, or we might lose
this sector for days."

"Yes, ma'am."

A constable nearby called out and pointed to the crowd. One
of the younger men tried to leave the line before Ritsuko stopped
him with a barked command; it was dangerous to send armed
constables into a furious throng. She looked over, trying to spot
what had caught their attention.

Her partner had made some headway. The crowd parted for
a short distance around him—when one of the bravos stood his
ground and confronted Mikani with an inaudible challenge, her
partner snarled, then lashed out. Most went down with a single
blow, but occasionally Mikani came up against someone big
enough to take the hit, then strike back. The men nearest surged
and cheered, before pulling back when her partner invariably,
stubbornly, pulled to his feet and waded in deeper. His lip was
split, and he took an elbow to the back as he shoved past. She
noticed that he wasn't using a weapon, though, just bare fists.

"What's he doing?" she muttered. "He'll get killed."

She hadn't been talking to Clemmens, but the officer tracked
Mikani's movements with his gaze, then said, "Looks like he's
earning the right to speak with the patriarch."

"By getting knocked arse over teakettle?"

Clemmens shrugged. "It's their way. I've worked the Landing
Point a long time. You pick up a few things."

All around the perimeter, Summer Clan tribesmen shoved,
shouting invective to the officers holding the line with trun-
cheons out and shoulders braced. Though she'd never used it,
Ritsuko got out her club, just in case. She hefted it, offering a
warning glare at a dark-eyed, wild-haired man who got too close.

Inwardly, her stomach churned with terror. This situation was a pile of kindling with a tinderbox on top, just waiting for the proper spark.

"Why are they so angry?" a constable asked Clemmens. "She's just one girl."

Ritsuko leaned in, as she wanted to know, too.

"See the tall, white-haired man over there? Inspector Mikani's nearly to him now." As Clemmens spoke, her partner came up against a towering wall of a man with a chest as broad as an ox, hands like anvils. He had a hard, scarred face, and he wore a multitude of necklaces around his neck, charms and tokens, trophies, perhaps. Her throat tightened, and in reflex, she moved toward Mikani. *He's not fighting that brute alone.*

But Clemmens grabbed her arm. "If you help him, you'll ruin everything."

"Better I should let him be beaten to death?"

Ritsuko hardly noticed when someone shoved her from behind. She was too busy watching the prizefight. The Summer Clan giant might be strong as a great oak, but he wasn't quick. Mikani danced around to the side, rabbiting blows into the man's ribs. He ducked a couple of hard, slow swings, but the third one clipped her partner in the temple. Mikani shook like a wet dog, then went back in, his face bloody, his blue eyes ferocious with determination. The match went on for at least five minutes, while the rioters grew more violent. A glass smashed to the ground at Ritsuko's feet, the shards nicking the wool of her split skirt.

"Don't hurt him," she shouted to the enormous tribesman. "I'll marry you!"

Somehow, he heard over the roar of the crowd; and it was such a ridiculous, inappropriate thing for her to say that it stole his focus for a few seconds.

Mikani took full advantage with a fierce hit to the man's chin, and he fell. Beside her, Clemmens guffawed. "That wasn't completely fair, but the headman's bodyguards didn't give him a clean run, either."

Standing beside the tall, regal-looking elder with his dark, weathered skin and golden ropes around his neck, Mikani beckoned. Ritsuko didn't wait for Clemmens to approve her movement; she just pushed forward, and, to her surprise, the crowd parted. Nobody touched her. There was an odd stillness, like the eye of the storm. Farther out along the docks and warehouses, the madness still raged, but here? Watchful silence, as if one wrong move could alter everything. Mikani took her arm as she reached him, a pointed claim. The Summer Clan leader's dark gaze ran up and down her body, but it wasn't a lascivious look, more an assessing, speculative one.

"That was a tricky strategy," the patriarch finally said. "I don't believe your champion would've beaten mine, otherwise."

Is he? My champion? The words sounded oddly right. But she knew enough about Summer Clan culture not to speak. *Best to let Mikani handle this.*

Mikani gave a lazy smile through split lips. His right eye was swollen to the point that she could see only a thread of blue between the tangle of his sweat-stained locks. "I have bruises from where your men took some underhanded shots."

The Summer Clan leader etched an ironic bow. "I am Luca Bihár, Patriarch of the Summer Clan. And my people are angry. As am I."

"For good reason," Mikani said.

"Tell me, Inspector, why was this monster permitted to murder my niece? You've had sufficient time to catch him."

His niece. Burning hell. Ritsuko hoped her partner didn't mention they'd almost caught him . . . and let him get away. But she suspected even if they had apprehended Toombs at Dinwiddie's apartment, it still would've been too late for Electra. *No consolation there.*

"I swear to you we'll get him," Mikani said grimly.

"That's not good enough. I want a blood vow from you both. In exchange, I will calm my people, save your grim city. But there will be *no trade*, no caravans, no food or supplies in or out of Dorstaad until you keep your word." His face was hard as bronze, his eyes obsidian.

There could be no negotiation, only agreement. In Bihár's ebon gaze, she saw a glimpse of the whole city burning.

"It's a fair trade," Mikani agreed.

In reply, the patriarch barked at his underling, who produced a knife. Before she hardly knew what had happened, she had a slice on her palm and she'd promised to catch a killer. That was her job, but it gained new weight when repeating the words beneath Bihár's pitiless gaze. Then the Summer Clan chieftain gestured to his cohort, speaking in a guttural tongue, what she presumed to be orders to get the mob to stand down.

"Don't break this promise," the patriarch warned. "Or perhaps I'll make you keep what you pledged before. Rudo"—he nudged the groggy giant on the ground—"would enjoy a bride. For a time."

Bronze gods. As dread washed over her, Ritsuko curled her fingers against her injured palm, feeling the blood drip through.

CHAPTER 15

SHUTTING DOWN A RIOT DIDN'T HAPPEN INSTANTLY. IT TOOK hours of argument and negotiation, all of which tried Mikani's patience. Ritsuko didn't appear to be her usual serene self, either. A few paces distant, she was exchanging heated words with a uniformed officer whose name he didn't know. The side of his face throbbed, and he had a number of sore spots up and down his side, but it had been worth it.

The Summer Clan were withdrawing.

Carrying the headman's orders, Bihár's people scattered in groups, slipping into alleys and boarded wagons parked nearby. Even so, there was a lot of muttering, a few scuffles, and the occasional pissing contest that the CID forces broke up before things escalated. Mikani knew there would be trouble when they got back to HQ, but possibly it could be softened by the fact that he and Ritsuko had been instrumental in keeping the peace.

When the Summer Clan reached the edge of Landing Point District, constables trailing to ensure they returned to their caravans, Mikani let out a long groan and sat on the curb, cradling his head in both hands. *Gods and spirits, that's going to leave a mark. Or ten.* He was starting to suspect he'd cracked a couple of ribs, again.

"Don't worry," he muttered when Ritsuko bent down. "Much as I believe you'd be too much for Rudo to handle, I promise that I'll smuggle you away on a ship before you have to attend that particular wedding."

"That's not funny. You could've been killed . . . and this could've ended with half the city in flames."

Mikani didn't need to read Ritsuko to sense her frustration and fear, mingled with the warmer caress of relief. "I'm hard to kill. Like a weed, but more charming."

"You're ridiculous," she muttered. "I would probably do better with Rudo."

"He's not your type. Too sensitive. A would-be musician, from the way he tried to play a symphony on my ribs."

He stood with a barely muffled groan of pain, rolling his shoulders with some effort and glancing around. At the least, the beating had helped assuage the guilt he felt over Electra's death, momentarily eclipsing heartache with aching bones. "We need the good doctor here as soon as possible." *I need Electra out of that thing and with her family at once, too. Not just for their sake, either.* "Let's see if he can get anything useful out of this damned machine, then I'll gladly tear the thing apart myself."

Dr. Byfeld and his team arrived a half hour later, along with a dozen constables fresh from HQ to help secure the area. Mikani stayed on the periphery while Ritsuko and the doctor worked, pacing a broad circle around them and trying to block the lingering echoes of the girl's death from his conscious mind. Ritsuko was methodical, as ever, though she kept directing gimlet stares that he caught from the corner of his good eye. She took thorough notes and prevented the others from bothering him, which he appreciated. As he watched, she took more samples, as there was ash circling the site, just like the other killing. If Mikani had to guess, he'd predict the lab would find it to be herbal—acanthus and hyacinth—like before. He wondered why the design had changed; this was a death by drowning instead of fire.

What's the purpose? But I suppose if I could work that out, I'd be as mad as the murderer.

He looked up when Ritsuko nodded his way. The doctor was gathering his team and tools, all evidence collected. Mikani went

to the device, shouldering his way past the two constables struggling to open the thing. "Get me a cruiser, and a sheet."

They responded with gratifying alacrity. *I could get used to
that.* Mikani fumbled with the ropes holding the top of the cylinder in place before tearing them loose with a hard jerk. He
slowly laid the cylinder down, the scummy water spilling over
him, and reached inside. He freed her as gently as he could from
the restraints, taking Electra's body in his arms. He could've
asked for a stretcher to make the going easier, but he wanted to
carry her. A constable dashed up with the requested sheet, drap-
ing Electra to preserve her dignity.

Mikani signaled Ritsuko, watching from nearby. "Let's get
her home."

She stood to the side so he could pass with his melancholy
burden. The way felt endless as he marched out of that forsaken
place, conscious of the creaking beneath his feet and the weight
in his shaky arms. The day had definitely taken a toll, more than
he'd admit to Ritsuko. She expected a laugh and a quick retort,
but keeping up that facade might do him in before the evening
ended.

Out on the street, Landing Point was scarred in the uncertain
light: shop windows hanging in jagged glass teeth, charred
patches on various buildings from where lit bottles had been
smashed. It was a miracle Dorstaad wasn't burning; *nobody* pursued a vendetta like the Summer Clan, not even the great Houses.
Mikani didn't know if he'd done the wisest thing by agreeing to
the blood vow. His palm throbbed a question. But he did know
there wasn't a better alternative.

When the patriarch and his bodyguards strode from the corner where they'd been keeping watch, Mikani paused. Bihár
inclined his head before resuming his slow progress toward them.
Their eyes met as Mikani handed Electra's body into the older
man's care.

"We'll find him."

"See that you do, Inspector." His voice was hoarse, grief
throbbing in sharp pulses—and Mikani wasn't trying to read
him. The emotion was just too strong to be blocked.

"I'm sorry for your loss," Ritsuko said softly.

They were only words—and from a woman as well—but

Bihár acknowledged them in the spirit they were intended. Then he turned with his honor guard and led the procession down to a wagon decorated in high mourning. They would carry her out of the city, and for a moment, Mikani felt like offering to accompany them out of respect. It took Ritsuko's touch to his shoulder to remind him that the best way to honor her was to keep their vow.

Your time's running out, Toombs. And when we catch you, maybe we'll introduce you to her family before taking you in.

"Let's head in, partner."

"Want me to drive?"

He handed her the keys with an unsteady hand. "You need the practice."

"Obviously. I still can't take it up on two wheels." She skirted the remaining spectators, those ghouls who fed on tragedy, and led the way back to the cruiser, which had sustained some damage during the riot. Nothing that rendered it inoperable, just dents and scrapes.

The ride back to HQ passed in a blur; he had too much on his mind, too many aches and pains to maintain a conversation. By the time they got in the lift, he needed some chemical relief. Oddly, the CID building seemed so quiet by comparison to the docks, eerily so, even though there were still normal noises, the usual number of officers going about their routines. Mikani would rather start a trash fire than do his paperwork, tonight of all nights.

He paused at his desk, toying with the idea of writing the report and heading out for a drink or six. *Not the best use of time, though. We need to get Toombs pinned down, and only Gunwood can help with that.* But he had a quicker, quieter solution. While his partner was busy, he dug into his jacket pocket, produced a pair of Dreamers. This time, he downed them in one swallow. Chewing made them dissolve faster, but it was important not to fill the air with the scent of apples; Gunwood was angry enough without adding this to the list of complaints.

Then Mikani beckoned Ritsuko with a weary gesture. "Let's go make his evening, shall we?" Navigating the duty room required some care as he was compensating for the loss of depth perception from his swollen eye. He rapped the doorframe before barging in. "Commander. We ran into some trouble."

"I'd say that's an understatement, wouldn't you?" It was obviously a rhetorical question, as Gunwood didn't wait for a response. "I gave you two this case with the full confidence you'd wrap things up before it turned into a big circus. But today, instead of a killer in custody, we have a second body, and the Summer Clan means to starve us to death. To say nothing of the riot!"

"Sir," Ritsuko began, but the old man held up a peremptory hand.

"No. Earlier, I said forty-eight hours, but that was before . . . well. Circumstances are entirely different now. You're off this case, effective immediately. I'm turning it over to Shelton and Cutler, and I pray *they* achieve better results."

"What?" Until that point, Mikani was only half paying attention, braced for the usual round of recriminations and maybe a writ. "You can't do that. We're closing in, Gunwood! Give us a day, some men, and we'll have the bastard. You can't just yank us off the case for those two idiots."

"The word came down from Council," the commander said. "It's out of my hands, so I'm ordering you both, go home. Take a few days off. You haven't had a decent night's sleep in weeks. I'm sure by the time you report in, Shelton and Cutler will have Toombs in custody."

Mikani slammed his fist on the commander's desk. "You'll be lucky if they don't drag in the first beggar they stumble over just to call it a night!"

Gunwood stood, bellowing to match Mikani's volume. "And you'll be lucky if the Council doesn't ship you off to Cliffside to guard the sheep!"

"Sheep are smarter than those two!" He was just getting warmed up; he had a host of things to say about Shelton and Cutler, most of them four-lettered.

"Very well, sir," Ritsuko interjected. "Two days off."

Though someone who didn't know her well might think that was a level tone, Mikani could tell she was about to explode, too. Her jaw was clenched tight, and she wrapped her fingers around his forearm. She didn't offer a polite farewell as she dragged Mikani toward the door; he suspected it was beyond her.

Gunwood snapped, "A week, no pay, after the crack about the sheep! Just get him out of here."

* * *

In retrospect, Ritsuko wasn't sure how it happened. But at HQ, it had made perfect sense to go back to Mikani's place, for two reasons. One—she was afraid of what he'd do, left unsupervised, after the day he'd had, and two—somebody had to look at his injuries. The chances were slim to none that she could persuade him to see a doctor, particularly in this mood. So an hour after the blowup in Gunwood's office, she was rummaging in Mikani's bathroom for basic first-aid supplies.

She filled a basin with warm water, located some towels and antiseptic. This wasn't her usual purview, but it was better than going home to an empty flat.

His cottage, in all areas but the kitchen, had a cheerfully careless atmosphere. Things remained wherever he dropped them, and she fought the urge to tidy up. He was sprawled in the armchair before the window, staring moodily out at the dark sky. It was a breathtaking view, though more rustic than she would've imagined. Not that she'd ever spent any time wondering where Mikani lived.

"I think I'm ready," she said, after assembling the supplies on a nearby table.

"We can't let the trail go cold." He sat up with evident effort and gave her medical preparations a dubious look. "I'll be fine. Just need some rest. And maybe some ice. And a drink to go with that ice."

She folded her arms. "Have you *ever* known me to lose an argument once I made up my mind?"

He frowned and met her gaze. "I figured this would be more a matter of your agreeing with me than an argument, really."

"This isn't about the case. It's about *your face*. Which is quite bad enough already."

His undamaged eyebrow shot up. "What the hells is wrong with my face?"

"Nothing, provided you let me attend to it. Otherwise . . ." She trailed off, wondering if he was really that vain.

He opened his mouth and shut it again. Sullenly, he touched the swelling and cuts along his jaw and cheek. "Fine, fine. If it'll stop your fretting."

"You're doing me a tremendous service." Ritsuko dipped the cloth in warm water and blotted away the blood on each wound, her touch gentle.

Then she cupped his chin, leaning close to inspect the damage. The split over his cheekbone likely needed stitches, but she didn't imagine he'd heed her advice, difficult man. So she opened the antiseptic and folded a clean linen square. "This might sting."

"I swear, you're enjoying this."

"Yes, I've always wanted to have you at my mercy."

He flinched at the first burn of antiseptic on open wounds. "I knew you had nefarious designs on my virtue, Ritsuko, from the first night they threw us together."

His tone was lighter, teasing, and that was a relief. Mikani in a rage was impressive, but fairly hard to handle. But his words made her heart give an unruly kick . . . because they weren't as far off the mark as he imagined. She offered what she hoped was an inscrutable smile.

"No, it wasn't the first night. I've only had designs for a little while."

Let him make of that what he would.

She opened the pot of salve, which was supposed to minimize soreness, swelling, and bruising, at least according to the bold-printed claims on the side. Ritsuko bent her head, sniffed; it wasn't disagreeable, just green-smelling, as if from a mixture of herbs. At least it lacked the raw medicinal stink of the astringent.

Mikani was watching her with a puzzled expression, as if trying to untangle her last comment. "Why, Ritsuko. If I'd known you wanted to rub ointments on me, I might have promised you in marriage to some lout long ago."

"Don't be absurd. You'd go mad five minutes after the groom carried me off."

He looked away, murmuring. "So would he, I'd wager."

"Only in the most delightful ways." She wanted to laugh when his chin jerked up, as her attempt to distract him was apparently working rather well.

Ritsuko dipped into the pot with her fingertips, then bent so she could see the worst of the damage. With delicate strokes, she painted the area, feathering across his cut brow and around to his cheekbone. Then she smoothed lower, his jaw, his swollen mouth. With a gentle thumb, she grazed his lower lip, though making sure not to get the salve where he could taste it.

"How's that?"

He looked up at her, blue eyes dark in the gaslight. "Better," he admitted. "So, we should—" He tried to shift back, and winced.

"Shirt off. You can do it, or I will."

"Gods, woman, you're so demanding. I'm *fine*." He did, however, unbutton his shirt, his bruised knuckles making the process awkward and somewhat unsteady.

"I prefer to think of myself as thorough." She slipped the linen from his shoulders so it pooled on the chair behind.

This wasn't the first time she'd seen his bare chest, but it had even more impact this time. Perhaps it was because it was dark, the lamp throwing interesting shadows on his skin, or it might just be because she was about to touch him. Different than a cheek or a jaw, or a wrist, different, even, than the soft underside of his lip. Her pulse skittered, and she hoped her reaction wasn't noticeable.

Ritsuko slicked her fingers with the salve and knelt beside him, perched on her heels to better see his side, which was mottled with bruises. *No time like the present.* Afraid of hurting him, her fingers danced in butterfly strokes down his rib cage, barely grazing his warm skin. But each touch felt like a lick of heat swirling up her palms to her wrists until her elbows actually tingled. He shifted, shoulders tense and head tilted forward. He laced his fingers together when he rested his elbows on his knees, turning to let her get to the darkening bruises on his back and sides.

"I'm sorry I got you into this mess." Stark sincerity rang in his tone.

"I'm not the one who looks like he got run over by a hansom. I've done all I can, though you may want to see a physician as well."

She went into the kitchen then, poured him a drink; and the lull gave her a chance to recover her equilibrium. *I should probably leave soon.* He seemed quieter, less likely to do something rash. When she returned, she carried a glass of whiskey in one hand and ice in the other, wrapped in a towel.

"Here. Your two fondest desires."

He took the towel and pressed it gingerly to the side of his face. Then he reached for the glass, his fingers brushing hers, not quite taking it from her hand. "What, are you going to just leave me half-dressed and helpless, then?"

She couldn't decide if that was a tease, an opening, or an invitation. It had been a hell of a day, and what she really wanted was to curl up against his legs and close her eyes for a few seconds. Some fingers in her hair would be lovely, too. But such contact rarely stopped in innocence. Soft touches would lead to more, provided he was feeling this way, too. It was possible he was just too beat-up to recognize anything but pain.

The moment stretched on, until she decided on a response. "Of course not. Just tell me what you need."

He squeezed her fingers lightly. "Stay awhile."

A long sigh eased out of her, release of the day's tensions and failures, then for once, she followed her impulses and folded to the floor beside his chair, facing the night beyond the window. She leaned against his legs, just a little, and ached because the closeness felt that good. It seemed like ages since she'd slept. Tilting her head back, she offered Mikani the whiskey again.

He smiled at her and took the glass. After he set the tumbler on the windowsill, his hand drifted down to settle on her shoulder.

CHAPTER 16

AURELIA HAD LIED TO THERON WHEN SHE CLAIMED SHE MIGHT
let him catch her.

In fact, the converse was true. Even after years in exile, she
was still the Architect's daughter, unable to walk away from
intrigue. His mystery demanded a solution. So after a surrepti-
tious visit to a seedy shop sandwiched between Chen the tattooist
and Sad Sue's pharmaceutical emporium, she had the means to
discover Theron's true agenda. Her own skills weren't up to
spying on such a powerful man; hence the nondescript charm
hanging around her neck. It wasn't the same as invisibility,
more . . . misdirection, channeling her blood's power to a new
purpose. People's attention slid away from her, registering her
as part of the environment. In this part of town, she supposed
she looked like a beggar.

The southern wards had long since abandoned hope of recap-
turing the prosperity that once lined the streets in figurative gold.
The warehouses and industrial sprawl of Iron Cross formed a
stark skyline to the east, defying the spires and glimmering lights
of the Central District, invisible but for their reflected glow on
the clouds from this distance. Leaving the eternal bustle of the

Summer's Gate District, she wandered into a maze of tenements. It had been thus for as long as she could remember; only the old Craven District farther north along the eastern shore of the bay rivaled the Patchwork in decrepitude. The stench was horrific; pollutants from nearby Iron Cross, rotten wood and garbage, as well as the lingering smell of unwashed bodies.

No hansoms operated here, so she walked the last mile, careful not to draw too near her prey. She slipped through the darkness behind Theron. The cut of his suit and his gold watch fob marked him as a target, but a whisper of glamour sent lesser predators scurrying away. His power made the air tingle as she followed, raising the hair on her forearms. Nobody paid her any attention; she was just another impoverished waif.

Aurelia watched as he stood gazing at a wreck of a building, two walls tipping drunkenly inward. His expression revealed distaste, a hint of anger, perhaps; the reading of people wasn't her forte. Moment of introspection set aside, he pushed through the front door; she waited to a count of ten, then followed. Limelights cast sharp shadows and painful glare on the open area within, spotlighting guards, who didn't stir as Aurelia hovered in the doorway. Theron ignored them, making his way to the rear staircase.

A towering figure stood at its base, bristling with blades. Theron said, "Tell Erebos I'm here." The sentry's eyes widened before he scurried upstairs.

I knew he was a dark horse, but this . . . this is worse than I suspected. She wondered if Theron was some lord of the underworld, responsible for all manner of criminal enterprise. If so, he might have an ominous purpose in mind for her. His courtship could conceal all kinds of dire intent. She'd expected the usual political machinations, a desire for her father's support or access to the Architect's pipeline to new technologies.

Not this.

Once the footsteps quieted overhead, she slipped up the stairs. A woman with more innate caution would have turned and run by now, but it wasn't caution that led her to surrender her family name and forge a life outside her House. She had chosen Wright, many years ago, as it implied one who crafts, as she had done her own path. *But once, once I was an Olrik. And we do not flee the field before battle is joined.* Her family was better known for cunning than bravery, laying traps for the unwary, and there was nothing so effective as foreknowledge.

The stairs ended in a metal platform, beyond which lay an office. If there had been guards, Theron must've sent them away. She stilled in the shadows, watching, listening. Theron stood before a pretentiously sized desk with a squalid man, and a slattern cowered in the far corner. The smaller man pushed himself out of his chair, making an effort to restore order to his hair. There was inherent grime about him that no scrubbing could scour away. Dun hair, sallow skin, and murky eyes could not be enlivened by any number of bright garments or well-tailored coats.

"Theron. It has been too long."

That's a lie. Seldom had her truth-sense rung so hard, vibrating like a bell. She felt certain that this man would be happier if Theron's head parted company with his body.

"Not long enough for you to change, Erebos. Sit. Then we'll talk."

"What about?" The fellow looked as if he might wet his pants.

"I'm searching for . . . someone special. You know exactly what I'm looking for." Theron leaned across the desk with a menacing air, and Aurelia fought a shiver. "And you hear what goes on in the streets."

"You give me too much credit. I have ears to the ground, but . . . one soul in a city this size? That's impossible." Fear laced the man's tone, edging toward visceral terror.

Aurelia couldn't sort the nuances, whether it was Theron the man feared or the object of his search. She had no doubt that Erebos knew precisely who Theron's quarry was, and he believed the man to be a ruthless killer.

Her throat felt so dry, it hurt to swallow. *Please don't let the charm wear off.* Some measure of self-preservation kicked in then, and she backed toward the edge of the landing, toward some stacked crates and barrels.

"You will *not* disappoint me. I'll turn your warehouse into a killing floor if you cross me. See you again soon." The words were loud enough to reach her though she couldn't hear Erebos's reply.

Theron glided past her, but he froze on the stairs, his head snapping up. Muted noise came from buildings all around. She had no words for what happened next, but his face went hard and predatory, a wolf offered a chance to hunt. He loped down the steps, his anticipation so fierce she could taste it in the night air. Her heart pounded like a kettledrum as she left the warehouse, a few moments later. Aurelia had no intention of continuing after what she'd seen—she was sufficiently scared—but the scene playing out wouldn't permit her to escape.

Two shadows slipped into the street from the alley beyond, keeping to the walls and piles of debris. Clad in black, they bore no lights and were geared for death. She saw the faint glimmer of starlight on blades and the barrels of their guns and nearly called out a warning, but if she did, the magic of the charm would be broken. She didn't know him well enough to risk her own life, particularly when she thought he might pose a danger. Two more men slithered down, clad and armed as their companions, from a roof to the left.

If I see them, surely he senses them. Theron appeared oblivious, tinkering with his gold watch. *They can't credit that he's so unwary. Erebos must have warned them.*

In the wavering darkness, Aurelia rubbed her eyes, doubting her vision. Tendrils slid along his fingers, edging them in talons sharp enough to slice the first assassin's throat. He lashed out with lightning speed. Ignoring the dying man's feeble clutch, he forced him to his knees, black blood pooling at their feet as he faced the others.

No. That's . . . old magic. Aurelia had only heard legends of such things, Ferisher princes with such power. *He has the ability to shape his garden to his will,* a small, sly voice reminded her. And terror clutched her until she went light-headed.

"You were careless." He curled his claws as he flashed a predator's smile, giving the body a little shake. The corpse made a wet sound as it hit the ground. "Never again."

Two others rushed him, and Theron dodged a bullet in the motion. Spinning, he tore out another man's larynx, the blood dripping hot through his fingers.

One of Theron's enemies landed a blow; the knife skimmed his ribs, and in response, he split the man from throat to groin. The noise he made wasn't human; it sounded like sirens, rising and falling beneath a drowning rain. Aurelia crammed a fist into

her mouth to stifle her horrified gasp; and only pure self-control
kept her quiet and still. She *knew* if he caught her, she would end
up as another body on the ground, later a pale and bloated corpse
floating on the waves.

Theron ducked as another fired. Lead slammed into the wall
behind him. Another four shots hit the cobbles behind and beside
him, a mark of the marksman's panic, Aurelia suspected. Theron
rolled to his feet, both hands embedded in the third man's torso.
He rent his flesh before discarding the gibbering assailant to his
final moments of agony. She had never been so frightened in her
life, muscles locked, her breathing light and quick.

The last attacker backed against the wall, trembling. With
hands dripping the blood of the others, Theron approached. Took
the gun. The man shuddered when warm, slick claws touched
his flesh, closing his eyes. She couldn't look away as Theron
grasped the survivor's chin between dripping talons.

"Erebos hired you to kill me."

"Yes." A whimpered admission.

Truth. But why? To protect whomever Theron was hunting?
After what she'd seen, she had no doubt that Theron's prey would
meet a brutal end. Before, she'd seen him as an entertainment,
a way to stave off ennui, but now . . . *You've stumbled into such
deep waters.* The irony was, her father had predicted exactly
this, years ago, during one of his endless lectures about her
headstrong ways.

"As I thought."

The man's dying scream woke sleeping dogs six blocks away.
Covered in dried blood and dirt, Theron moved in leaps and
bounds befitting beast better than man. Reaching the warehouse
wall, he tensed and jumped. Razor fingers dug into crumbling
mortar. With a hiss, he started climbing. Talons slipped into
stone with a soft whisper, withdrew with the rustling fall of
mortar dust.

Aurelia fled, then.

She couldn't follow him on such a monstrous climb; nor did
she have any desire to. Her knees felt too weak to support her;
and without the charm, it was certain she'd have been robbed
and murdered before she stumbled the mile out of the Patchwork's maze and into more hospitable environs. Tremors rocked

her from head to toe, and her thoughts felt scattered like a deck of cards flung to the winds.

I just saw four men, murdered. I ought to . . . report it. Shouldn't I? Given they had been hired to do harm, they probably hadn't been *good* men, but it was still wrong to kill them. The lights seemed too bright after the shadows between the derelict buildings, the alleys heaped with refuse. It was so noisy, too, with hansoms and people rushing by, laughter ringing out with a tinny echo.

She reeled, nausea rising until she doubled over. Aurelia caught herself on a lamppost, leaning her brow against the cool metal. Pedestrians strolled past, not seeing her distress, ignoring it, in fact. *Why isn't anyone asking if I'm well? Why . . . ?*

The charm. Of course. With unsteady fingers, she reached up to pull it over her head, but before she succeeded, someone stumbled into her, slamming her chest into the metal post.

"Filthy street peddlers," the man muttered, giving her another shove.

She was already shaky, and her heel slipped off the curb. Aurelia reeled backward, too stunned to attempt to break her own fall. A chugging steam carriage rushed straight for her; she scrambled on hands and knees, but she was dizzy, disoriented again, then strong hands locked on her arms, hauling her out of the street and back to the safety of the sidewalk. The carriage thundered by; and she squeezed her eyes shut. *Two more seconds. Just two. And I wouldn't be standing here.*

"Thank you," she managed, after a few seconds.

The man who had saved her looked familiar. "Are you well? That brute *shoved* you, practically under the wheels of the coach."

At that moment, it was beyond Aurelia's ability to lie. "I'm better than I would've been, if you hadn't come along. It's been a . . . difficult night, all around."

"I'm sorry to hear that, Miss Wright. Can I escort you somewhere?"

When he spoke her name, she placed him—Mr. Gideon— employed by her production as a technician.

She managed a polite smile. "If I wouldn't be imposing, would you mind walking me to the Royale?"

Leo would know what to do, surely. That was, if he believed her wild tale of old magic, savage transformations, brutal murder, and near death. Though she'd experienced the events herself, Aurelia still found everything hard to credit. It sounded like a story written to terrify small children.

"Not at all. Though I think, perhaps, we ought to take a hansom, if you wouldn't be too unsettled after your near accident. It's a long way."

Startled, Aurelia took stock of the streets and her surroundings, then realized he was right. It was over four miles to the theater, and she didn't feel up to walking. "I'd appreciate if you hailed a coach, but you needn't accompany me. I'll be fine."

"If you're certain." Doubtless, Mr. Gideon had plans in the area, for which he was already late because he didn't argue the necessity of riding with her.

Efficiently, he flagged down a hansom, gave the driver her destination, and bundled her into it. Then he tipped his hat and stepped back as the carriage clattered off. Aurelia was halfway to the Royale before she touched the charm at her throat. With a faint frown, she pulled the necklace over her head to examine it. The glass was cracked, so possibly she'd broken it when she fell, or when the ruffian pushed her into the lamppost.

"If so," she said aloud, "then I'm lucky to be alive."

If the charm had been working, Mr. Gideon wouldn't have noticed her predicament. By this time, the worst of the queasiness had passed, leaving her exhausted. Her knees were watery as she climbed out of the carriage to pay the driver. She gave him a generous tip and trudged the last few feet to the Royale, then fumbled in her bag for the key to the side door. The shadows were deep and long, and she had that awful, creepy feeling again, as if someone was watching her.

Theron? What if it's been him, all along? What if he's hunting me, along with that other "special person"? The idea was terrifying and twisted, if he'd been following her for months, making her wonder whether she was going mad, only to step into her life while playing these dreadful games. Her heart was pounding like crazy by the time she got the key into the lock and dashed into the building.

It was late, so there were no rehearsals, just a dark and unnerving theater; Leo didn't pay for lights he wasn't using. To

combat her sudden, irrational terror, she focused on what she
knew existed in the impenetrable shadows. Aurelia moved out
of the wings onto the stage. Though she couldn't make out the
details, the dais on which she stood possessed a pagoda-like roof
and columns at each end. To the untutored eye, they might look
like marble in the daylight, but Aurelia knew it was green oak,
cunningly finished until footlights completed the illusion. As
her eyes adjusted, she caught glimpses that suggested motion
from the velvet drapes to the catwalk overhead.

*It's the wind and your imagination. There's no one here but
Leo . . . and possibly Elaine. Find him.*

Downstairs and through the hidden door, her footsteps rang
loud and quick in the silent halls. Fortunately, she knew the turns
down to his secret room and could navigate them in the dark.
Farther in, there were lamps lit, as Elaine wouldn't come into
the subterranean gloom Leo truly craved, some manifestation
of his guilt, Aurelia suspected. Any other day, she might even
tease him about it, trying to get him to smile.

Not tonight.

Once she could see properly, she broke into a run, not even
trying to disguise her desperation. Others might see a wounded
man, a broken one, but Leonidas had always represented safety,
ever since she turned her back on the Olrik legacy. That much
hadn't changed. She burst into his room without knocking, even
knowing they might be engaged in behavior best not interrupted.
Fortunately, it was only dinner, and Elaine gaped at her, a chicken
leg halfway to her mouth.

Leo sprang to his feet, his masked gaze sweeping her in a
lightning assessment. "Auri? Are you well?"

"No," she said shakily.

For the first time, she realized her palms were bleeding, that
she'd torn the fabric of her skirt, and there were smears of red
there, too. Bronze gods only knew what she'd gotten on her
clothing during the walk into and out of the Patchwork District.
Her whole body hurt from the fall, and she was frightened as
she'd never been in her life, as if there were no safe place left to
hide.

"Elaine, go home. Take your meal if you like." Leo dismissed
his mistress with a casual gesture, one that would cost him later
in baubles or jewelry.

The dancer departed with a glare and a flounce, then Leo gathered Aurelia close. Though he wasn't the charming man she'd known before, he was still strong and comforting. His arms felt like the only haven she could trust. She squeezed her eyes shut.

"Tell me when you're ready. I'm here."

Belatedly, she remembered a long-ago conversation with her father. She had often wished for another gift, one less painful, because people lied *all* the time; it was as natural as breathing. Her father, so distant and dispassionate, had said it was because nobody could bear complete truth. Possibly, he had been right, because she'd been happier not knowing how dangerous Theron truly was. It had been better when she'd considered their exchanges a simple game, not a mortal struggle where the stakes were life and death.

Sometimes, the lie is safer.

CHAPTER 17

THE SUMMER LADY LAUGHED, AND HER PEOPLE CELEBRATED WITH HER: another cycle had come and gone, and the Courts met once more to renew their treaties of peace and restate their declarations of ancient war. The gathered hosts raised their faces to the rain and danced, screamed their defiance to their brothers and sisters.

Across the headland, Winter cheered—the banners of a dozen powerful families waved and whipped in greeting, their cries mingling with the wind. They surged toward one another, then, a slow and steady pace to the beat of the hammering rain and screaming thunderclaps. Splashing and calling challenges as the distance shortened; nobles on steeds. Behind them came towering, lumbering creatures of rock and moss. Translucent sylphs wove through the spray, forms of mist and swirling droplets.

In trying to circle around the Host of Winter, a small hobgoblin troop spotted the strangers moving in the hills. Calls of wonder and alarm spread like wildfire. The whole procession went to the cliffs, trolls carrying sprites alongside skittering shadow forms. They gathered, Summer Court mingling with Winter, old feuds and vows forgotten as they watched the

*bearded invaders march on their revels. The invaders looked
up, weathered faces squinting against the storm. Raising dread
iron blades, they roared a challenge to the figures on the cliffs.*

"There will be war," said the Summer Lady.

"So be it," the Winter Lord replied.

MIKANI JOLTED AWAKE, the midmorning light falling into his
eyes like shards of ice. For a moment, he couldn't hear for his
own heartbeat, couldn't remember what day it was or what was
real. These visions came at irregular, inconvenient times; he had
no idea what they meant. At some point, perhaps when he wasn't
so sore, he'd investigate.

He ground the palms of his hands against burning eyes and
rolled out of bed with a groan. His ribs ached, the multitude of
cuts burned, even with the dressings and salves Ritsuko had
applied the night before. He braced his side, feeling out the edges
of the bandages, and smiled faintly. *Gods and spirits, what's
wrong with me?* He never allowed anyone to tend to him. Even
after he was stabbed by some mercenaries over a card game,
he'd holed up on his own until he could walk again. No doctor.
He'd stitched the wound himself, bore the scar to this day.

I trust her. Like no one before.

He shook his head and rose, swaying slightly. Ritsuko had
gone home last night, shortly after midnight, despite his protests
that she was welcome to his sofa. The mystery of how his partner
had wriggled so far under his skin had to wait, as hell would
freeze before he let a mere suspension keep him from investigating two murders, currently left to Shelton and Cutler.

*If that pair could solve the case of the missing pastry, I'd be
entirely astonished.*

Long practice let him shower and dress quickly, so, walking
stick in hand, he headed toward Electra's midtown address within
half an hour. Each step hurt. He considered stopping to purchase
some Dreamers, but after a moment's consideration, he chose
the pain. Guilt kept him clean and sober, out of respect for her
memory. Elsewhere, the Summer Clan would be mourning with
strong drink, dancing, and endless stories. In that vein, Mikani
could only *remember* her; the last time he'd been to Electra's
flat, it was a warm night, no clouds.

"You don't have to see me home," Electra had said. "I take the underground at this hour all the time."

"It's my fault it took you so long to close up. I'll be a gentleman for once."

She'd flashed him a mischievous look. "No nonsense. My uncle would kill you."

Mikani had laughed. But as promised, he'd taken her home and left her politely at the front door. He had genuinely liked Electra. Possibly Bihár had sensed as much when he accepted the blood vow. He was so lost in the memory that he didn't realize his feet had carried him to the café until he was standing under the bright awning. He swore under his breath and nearly turned away. Since he passed it every day on the way to headquarters, he had to deal with the new reality sooner or later.

Inside, a new girl was tending shop, very young, in tight braids and with a woolen shawl wrapped around her shoulders. "Good morning, sir. What will you have? We have biscuits, fresh made. And, there's fruit."

"I'll just—"

"Also, the teas are lovely. And fresh brewed. You could use a mint tea, I'm thinking."

"No, I don't—"

"Herbal tea? With some toast—"

Mikani slammed his hand on the counter, bringing the girl up short. "Coffee. Black. Unsweetened. Thank you."

As she scurried away, he swore under his breath. *That didn't go well.* Some might appreciate her well-intended suggestions, but he missed Electra. A few minutes later, the waitress brought a cup overflowing with coffee, but it wasn't strong the way he liked it. This was a weak brew, a possible economy on the part of the owners, but Electra had made it fierce enough to stand a spoon. With a faint sigh, he edged the saucer away untouched and left a few coins before striding out.

Don't know if I'll be back anytime soon.

As if stopping at the café hadn't been depressing enough, he still had to sort Electra's flat. Mikani doubted the family had been there yet; Summer Clan placed little stock on material possessions, and she had been wearing all her tribal tokens when they'd claimed her body. *Still, at least it will give me some peace of mind to ensure that nobody's stolen whatever else she owned.*

It took him half an hour more to find the right door in the warren of apartment buildings, boardinghouses, and family-owned businesses off the Leeward promenade. Her street looked different enough during the day to throw him off. She had never invited him to tea or asked him to visit, but she always seemed happy enough when he arrived for coffee.

A white lie to the landlady about being family—aided by a handful of coins—got him the spare key to Electra's apartment. She lived on the second story; the building itself was clean and well kept, though the walls were thin. Mikani wondered whether her family had ever visited this place, or if she had been cut off when she settled down.

Inside, her flat was small. He pulled on gloves to avoid inadvertently reading some object, noting the small collection of shells gracing the windowsill and battered writing desk, the cheap prints depicting sailing ships and the docks of Dorstaad looking far cleaner than they did in reality. *I spoke to her two or three times a week. Yet I never knew she loved the ocean.*

Mikani peered into the bedroom; it looked as if a cyclone had hit it. He closed the door with reverent care. Elsewhere, scarves and wraparound skirts draped the settee as well as wood chairs in the kitchen. On the table, five cards lay in the shape of a cross, beside a chipped mug. The tea had long since evaporated, leaving dark residue; the cards looked old and worn, well handled. Mikani moved with his gift reined in; even so, the cards called to him. Electra had possessed more than a pretty smile and a gift for telling people what they wanted to hear . . . the dying echoes of magic hummed from her deck.

He slipped a glove off and pressed a fingertip to the center card.

The rush of old impressions was faint, faded. Joy and regret mingled, the faint threads of other emotions ran deep. But it was all her; Electra hadn't allowed anyone else to handle this deck. He concentrated and laid his palm on the cards, doing his best to touch all five.

Her gift sparked his. He could *see* what she'd divined, and the shock stole his breath. Three girls, their features indistinct, joined by a silvery web. Looking closely at them, he sensed the weight of their families like watchful ghosts. Their figures turned as one, falling from the web; cast out or choosing to walk away from the network of filial obligation to walk their own path.

Electra. He recognized the arch of her nose and sharp cheekbones. The cards rang faintly with whispers of Cira Aevar's essence, consistent with traces she'd left in the pink-and-gold bedroom he had read weeks before. Though he didn't know her face as well as Electra's, and the impressions were fuzzy, he'd stake a year's pay that she was the second figure. The third drifted, shifted, and that movement—the very uncertainty of it—made him think she was still alive.

Mikani tried to focus on the last figure, but something blocked him. The more he tried to pin down the fleeting impression, the fainter it became, until his senses flared, slamming him with physical backlash that knocked him into the wall. On top of his existing bruises, the impact stung more than it should have, his ribs protesting in a sharp, red spike.

He struggled to breathe, hugging himself despite the pain; nothing like that had *ever* happened before. Blood trickled from his nose, down his lip, and onto his chest. A jagged band threatened to crush his skull, tightening in rhythm with his hammering heartbeat. He had learned more than he'd bargained for, but he needed a clear head. At the moment, he could barely sit, let alone try and piece together the clues.

Damned be, I need Ritsuko.

WITH A QUIET sigh, Ritsuko stepped into the mirror station. As a public building, it was utilitarian, various kiosks offering multiple courier services, access to the public pneumatic mail, and, of course, the mirror station itself. The bustle of early-afternoon transmissions resulted in a queue, nearly obscuring Mikani from sight. He was slumped on a wrought-iron bench, looking worse for the wear. His bruises had faded a little, turning slightly green, though the scruff on his jaw obscured some of them. *A few more days, and he'll have a proper beard.*

Maybe she ought to feel strange about last night, but it had been . . . companionable. Ritsuko had no regrets. At this point, she was only mildly irritated that he felt entitled to compel her presence by courier. *When we're not even working.* She had been in the midst of packing her things, as the flat she'd occupied with Warren no longer suited. But part of her didn't mind the summons, as it was nice to feel indispensable to *someone*. Even a rogue like Mikani.

She threaded through the crowd toward him. His eyes were closed when she approached, but he recognized her anyway. "Ritsuko."

How does he do *that?* Not for the first time, she wondered what it would be like to have his extra senses, if it was exhausting, exhilarating, or a combination of the two.

"You look like a dog's breakfast," she said.

He scoffed and rose, leaning heavily on his walking stick. The front of his shirt had dark stains. "You always know just what to say to me, partner." He offered her a wry smirk and headed for the street, limping.

"Is this CID business, or did you miss me?"

She followed him out, wondering at the wisdom of pursuing an investigation from which they had been officially discharged. Yet she couldn't let it rest, either. The idea that Shelton and Cutler might accidentally stumble over Toombs, after she and Mikani had done all the real work? Ritsuko clenched her teeth.

"Both. I can't let Shelton and Cutler ruin the case, and I missed your disapproving looks." He glanced over his shoulder with a teasing air.

"It didn't occur to you that I might be busy?" she asked, genuinely curious.

He stopped and turned to her, looking puzzled. "No. Were you?"

"Yes, actually. But I'll always come. I suppose you know that." She sighed, suspecting he might become unbearable at the statement that he possessed such power. "Soon you'll have me fetching your laundry and shopping for hats."

"Now that you mention it, I *do* miss my hat." He ran his fingers through his hair. "But that can wait. And . . . I'd cook for you, so it works out." With that, he set out with renewed purpose.

She didn't recognize this part of Dorstaad. When she was off duty, Ritsuko spent most of her free time within the walls of the Mountain District, safe as her grandfather had wanted. It was no hardship since there were shops, lush parks, and elegant gardens, a respite from the rest of the city. She loved the wonders of the arboretum, with its colossal living houses, trees shaped over long years with art and patience, but it was time to leave the Mountain District. There was a lovely rooming house much closer to HQ; she liked the owner and the tenants. It should be less lonely there.

Mikani led her to an apartment building and hesitated, leaning heavily on his cane, as if he didn't want to enter. "This is Electra's flat. I came to see about her things . . . and found more than I bargained for."

She didn't comment on the unusual impulse; most times, family gathered the deceased's personal effects. But the Summer Clan probably wouldn't take the time, and Mikani likely hated the thought of all Electra's belongings ending up in the rubbish bin or a rag-and-bone shop. He wouldn't thank her for noting his sentimentality, however. So instead, she followed him up the stairs and into the apartment, not understanding why he needed her. At the same time, she sensed he wouldn't have called for no reason; it wasn't like Mikani to ask for help, ever. So whatever this was, it must be vital.

"Where should I start?" Presumably there was some evidence to collect.

She couldn't imagine how they would explain this to Gunwood. More to the point, she didn't care. Mikani stopped at a desk and picked up a few seashells, rattling them in his hand before replacing all but one. "These shells. The prints on the walls. And there is a deck of cards in the kitchen. But really, I need you to help me figure this out."

"You're being more opaque than usual. Figure *what* out?" If he'd truly sent for her just because he didn't care to be alone with the task of disposing of Electra's things, she'd have no choice but to hug him.

"She was a fortune-teller . . . turns out she had a true gift, too. And she did a reading before she died. For herself."

In fits and starts, Mikani described something Ritsuko found hard to picture—mental images from the cards, blowback of power—until she was shaking her head. It wasn't that she disbelieved his account; she'd witnessed his gift many times, but it was eerie to consider Electra helping them catch her killer from beyond the grave. She rubbed her hands up her arms in reflex, fighting a chill.

With some effort, she gathered her thoughts, striving to be

logical. "From what you're telling me, there might be a third victim. Could it be someone she knows?"

"It seems an unlikely coincidence that Cira appeared in her reading, otherwise. Connected to them?" He shook his head. "I don't know."

"Can you tell me anything specific about this third person?" That seemed like a natural question.

"No. When I tried to see her, something stopped me."

She fought the urge to demand to see his back; Mikani was a walking battle scar. "Did it . . . Were you hurt? When you hit the wall."

"Please don't be kind, Ritsuko. At the moment, I don't think I could stand it."

She accepted his words at face value, but the quiet pain in his voice twisted her heart. Her response reflected only professional considerations. "This means something, but it isn't the evidence we need to convince Gunwood to reassign us to the case."

"Then let's look for some."

Ritsuko wished she had brought her evidence kit, but she had her notebook, at least. Maybe there was something in the flat that would help. "I'll start in the bedroom."

She could tell at first glance there had been a struggle. Maybe Mikani flung all his covers and pillows on the floor, but it wasn't normal for most people. To her, it looked as if Electra had been yanked out of bed. The rug was askew, pulled toward the window, and the contents of the bedside table lay scattered on the floor: five coins, a scarf, and a novel, open to some random page.

She opened her notebook, drawing the scene, which let her visualize what might've taken place. In her mind's eye, she saw the girl being hauled from a sound sleep. *She's a fighter. They stagger back against the night table because he didn't expect her to react so quickly. He expected her to be paralyzed with fear, whispering,* I'll do anything, just don't hurt me. *But she fights. The coins hit the floor. Momentum carries them toward the window, his arm's around her throat.*

"But is that how he took her out of here?" she whispered, still sketching.

The front door meant going through the hallway, past other people's flats. *Definitely the window. But he must've incapacitated her first. Otherwise, it would be difficult to get a struggling girl over a sill and down. The roof, not likely.*

"Toombs isn't superhuman."

If there was anything in this room to find, it would likely be between the bed and the window. Ritsuko dropped to her knees, then pressed her chest to the floor, searching. She crawled all the way under the bed and emerged, dusty, on the other side. Though it took ten full minutes, she scoured every inch of the floor. *Nothing.*

Next, just to be thorough, she lifted the pile of covers from the floor and a shiny object pinged against the parquet, rolling to a stop against the wall. Her heart lurched, and she scrambled after it. Dropping to her elbows, she peered at a fairly large silver button with a stag's head imprinted on it, along with some glyphs around the edges. She couldn't read them, but she recognized the shape of Old Ferisher characters.

This definitely didn't belong to Electra.

"Mikani!" she called. "I found something."

She heard him come to the door, his stick sharp against the wood. He was silent for a few seconds. "I've never seen quite this side of you, partner."

Blushing, she pulled upright to perch on her heels, gesturing. "Can you forget my posterior? I know it's difficult, but look." Ritsuko picked up the clue and rose to save her partner the pain of stooping. *His ribs must be on fire.* "What do you make of this?"

His smirk faded when she offered him the button and he took it between two fingers. "It's . . . cold. Dead. It feels just like the devices." He met her gaze with blue eyes gone icy as the winter sea. "It belongs to the killer. Toombs."

CHAPTER 18

THE CROWD IN THE MARKET WAS HARRIED AND SHORT-
tempered—more than usual. Waves of discontent lapped at
Mikani's senses, threatening to crash in uninvited if he didn't
keep a tight lid on his control. *Well, I can hardly blame them.
As soon as the Summer Clan cartel shut down the roads into
the city, the Houses started hoarding. Damned if I can find
paprika for the dinner I promised Saskia.*

He shouldered past a particularly stubborn bondsman
attempting to lay claim to a half dozen apples, the last in the
vendor's basket. *Two days.* It had taken two days for rumors to
spread and panic to seep into the city. Seafood was still plenti-
ful. Even the Summer Clan didn't have enough pull over the
myriad fishing and shipping concerns to lock down the city completely, but they'd stopped all shipping along the roads; no produce or dairy products made it past the blockades. Some staples
grew far enough south that the farming concerns were sending
them along the coast, making the water transport companies
happy.

He checked the price on a pound of rice. *Half again what it
was last week. At this rate, the poor won't be able to eat in a week.*

A knot of bondswomen dressed in pressed uniforms, embroidered with House crests, were fighting over bundles of green onions—and they didn't even look fresh. It hadn't come to blows yet, just sharp words, but the crowd darkened, and the vendors looked worried rather than pleased. *If this gets ugly, they won't make a copper.* He moved deeper into the stalls, troubled, as he listened to snippets of conversation.

"I'm telling you, they're ready to let us starve. I heard the Summer Clan is ambushing caravans trying to get in from the southern farms . . ."

"It's the Council's fault, letting them get away with so much over the years."

"The Houses need to send in the Guards, I say, make them clear the roads."

A few paces on, he spotted a burly merchant who had a House servant pinned against the wall. "If you bastards don't open the storehouses and share what you're hoarding, we'll *take* it!"

Mikani sighed. He'd recognize Olaf's hoarse rasp anywhere; he owned one of the few stands where Mikani could find the spicy peppers he loved. But it appeared the man was more interested in pounding his target than doing business. A crowd gathered; the local constables were nowhere in sight.

Mikani tapped the larger man's shoulder with his stick. "Sir, would you kindly—"

Olaf swung a backhand. Mikani caught his wrist between forearm and stick, and twisted hard enough to bring the man to his knees. "Disperse."

He glared at the men who edged closer, and something in his eyes made them back away. *Might be the bruises, come to think of it.* Half Mikani's face was still black-and-blue from his encounter with Bihár's men. It could also be the fact that the merchant struggled against his iron grip, whimpering in pain. The House bondsman scurried away.

"Now. I'm going to release you. And you *will* walk away. Enough nonsense."

Mikani straightened his coat and resumed his way, leaving Olaf nursing his shoulder and ego, muttering dark imprecations after him. *Gods and spirits. He'll either gouge me or refuse to sell me the nagas now.* His signature dish wouldn't be the same without the bite of those peppers. He altered course, devising a new menu for a dinner that looked increasingly improbable.

He stopped at a produce stand. "Mina—" A gangly youth gazed up at him. "Oh. Beg your pardon, is this not Mina's stall?"

The boy said, "She's not coming in. Not safe, you know. What can I get you?"

Mikani bought the last three decent cabbages, four potatoes. When he stepped away with his paper bag, he glanced around the market. *No girls. Hardly any women, at that.* If they normally worked in the market, they had been replaced by fathers, husbands, and brothers. The few females present worked as House servants or bondswomen, accompanied by conspicuous escorts or older matrons who seemed capable of dealing with anything that came their way.

He shook his head. Usually, he delighted in the open-air farmer's market that let him forget the chaos of his work life. But the mood today was too ugly, too tight. If he lingered much longer, he'd end up with a migraine at the least, and at worst? His bruises wouldn't tolerate worse.

He sighed, cut his trip short, and headed straight for the underground station, debating whether he should attempt an impromptu meal or ask Saskia for a few days' grace on his debt. *When you promise Saskia dinner, you'd best deliver.* But he suspected she'd prefer something more palatable than fried potatoes and boiled cabbage.

When he got back to his cottage, he found an envelope had been slipped beneath his door. After tucking the sack under his arm, he stooped to pick it up, then continued through the sitting room into the kitchen. He dropped the bag unceremoniously on the table and broke the courier's seal. Within, there was a single line on CID stationery in Gunwood's irascible scrawl:

Come back to work. The Summer Clan insists.

Mikani couldn't decide if he was smug or angry; the former because it meant hunting Toombs down like a dog, the latter because they shouldn't have been removed from the case at all. *Damned Shelton and Cutler.* He put the vegetables away and went right back out again.

Half an hour later, he arrived at CID Headquarters. It had only been two days, but he'd missed the purpose of the place. Even the cranky banging of the lift didn't diminish his satisfaction; Mikani couldn't wait to see the look on the old man's face. *I wonder if he prefers salt or pepper on his crow.*

Ritsuko was already in the duty room; she was comparing papers, laid out the width of her normally immaculate desk. She glanced up at his arrival, smiling, and he couldn't remember if her eyes always looked that warm, so happy to see him.

"I see you got the word," she said.

"Let's hope it doesn't mean they need a scapegoat for their latest mess."

"We'll find out soon enough. Gunwood told me he wanted to talk to us as soon as you checked in."

"That sounds familiar. Shall we, partner?"

She rose and preceded him to the commander's office. Her knock was less perfunctory than his tended to be, and she waited for Gunwood to call, "Enter!" before opening the door.

Mikani went in, wondering if the old man would actually apologize. "Did they get lost? Shelton and Cutler, need us to find them?"

He folded his arms and leaned against the far wall, clamping down hard on his anger after that single barb. *All right, must play nice, for a little while. Don't want him shutting us completely out.* With a nod, he acknowledged Ritsuko's daggered look; she was warning him silently not to make things worse, now that they'd been recalled.

He had missed their silent rapport, even when she was trying to keep him from doing something problematic—far more common than he cared to admit. Before meeting Ritsuko, Mikani had never been able to communicate without a word.

Hells and Winter, I usually have enough trouble communicating at all. As Saskia never tired of pointing out.

"Your sarcasm is noted. First, welcome back. I hope you enjoyed those days off. You aren't likely to be sleeping anytime soon." Gunwood flattened his palms on his desk, a muscle ticking in his jaw. "It's come to my attention that *both* of you were stupid enough to swear a blood vow to Luca Bihár." He held up a hand to forestall interruptions. "I expect this sort of thing from you, Mikani, but Ritsuko? What possessed you? Honestly. So for obvious reasons, the Summer Clan won't rest until Miss Bihár's killer is brought to justice, and they're determined the two of you will do it."

Mikani stage-whispered to Ritsuko, "I told you Rudo liked you."

Not the time, she mouthed back.

"This isn't just your careers on the line anymore. Bihár will *kill* you both if you don't get the job done. Officially, I'm supposed to say we'll protect you, but I think you already know that the Summer Clan will find a way." Gunwood sighed, and for the first time, Mikani realized the old man appeared to be *worried* about them, hiding it beneath a facade of anger.

Damn it. Mikani squeezed the bridge of his nose. "Listen, Gun—Commander. It was the only way to stop the riot. We'll find Toombs. Just fill us in on the last couple of days, and we'll hit the ground running."

With a frown, Gunwood relinquished his outrage and reverted to weary professionalism. "We've gotten some reports from the emporiums. Not all of them have responded to our requests to check their records. But one shop looks likely as a point of purchase for the components used in the devices. It's possible the killer may buy from them again. It wouldn't be smart, but . . ." The commander shrugged, indicating he hoped to get lucky.

Mikani nodded. "Where are Cutler and Shelton now?"

The old man smiled. "They're waiting outside the emporium. Just in case."

"Anything more?" Ritsuko asked.

"There was a hotel that responded to our circulated sketch." Gunwood checked his files, then added, "Toombs stayed there a couple of weeks ago."

"Was he alone when he checked in?" Mikani wanted to know. The devices were too big for any one man to move around on his own. If he had accomplices, though . . . three or four men would be easier to spot than just one, surely.

"He was on his own, just a small bag, according to the clerk."

Mikani frowned. "How's he moving the machines then? Even if he could lift them, he couldn't tuck them under an arm and carry them home."

His partner brightened, the unmistakable gleam of an idea in her brown eyes. "Delivery. We'll talk to the shipping concerns. Somebody hauled those supplies for him."

Gunwood bestowed a rare, appreciative smile on them,

though it was tired, too. "You have a place to start hunting. Get out of my office and try not to get killed."

"I wouldn't give you the satisfaction. Sir," he said, heading for the door.

RITSUKO SPOKE A little while longer with Commander Gunwood, smoothing over the ruffled feathers Mikani left with his grand exit. *I've missed him.* Though she had been busy—and she was nearly finished bundling up things to give away, others going in boxes to be conveyed to her new residence when she got a chance—she'd wondered what her partner was doing. Until recently, he hadn't been a part of her life outside work . . . and now she couldn't seem to get him out of her head.

Before she joined Mikani, she summoned a neutral expression; only then did she stride into the duty room and over to her desk. She beckoned. "Let me show you what I've been working on."

"First, let's send a message to the emporium, asking about their shipping policy."

"Good idea." She pulled a pen from the well in her desk slotted to organize such things, wrote the inquiry, then hailed a junior officer to take it to the mail tubes. "We should hear back in a little while."

He bent to examine the work she'd laid out. "Is that how you spent your time off? Collating papers?"

No, I spent it reshaping my life. I don't want to be lonely anymore. I wish to meet new people and find some excitement that isn't job-related.

"Funny. Actually, I've been researching the button."

Mikani arched a brow, looking dubious. "We already know it belongs to Toombs. What else is there to learn?"

"You'd be surprised. I thought since it's obviously expensive, stamped, and engraved, that there might be a record about its manufacturer. If I can figure out who made the button, then I can narrow down what tailors buy from them. This button looks too elegant for a ready-made jacket, don't you think?"

He seemed to catch some of her excitement. "Tailors generally keep good records. They measure their clients, work with them personally—"

"Exactly. There's a chance that we could locate Toombs through this button. It's a slim one, granted. But if he's using another name, he might feel safe giving his current address to the man who makes his coats."

"So this is . . ." He paged through the sheets on her desk. "What? Button designs? Manufacturing records?"

She nodded. "I've been comparing patterns, looking for a match."

"I hate to bear bad news, partner, but what if this button's old? And someone poured it by hand, ages ago?"

Disappointment cascaded through her. Ritsuko had thought of that, of course, but she'd wanted so badly to do something productive that she'd worked rather than think about the suspension, or the growing complexity of her relationship with Mikani. She'd cared to think least of all . . . about anything unrelated to the case. Sometimes the rest of her life just seemed too difficult to deal with. So apart from sorting through cartons and packing them, she'd dedicated her free time to the button.

But she rallied. "Then there might be a record of that, too. Somewhere. There are tomes devoted to all manner of minutiae in the city archive. My grandfather was fond of reading about the historical significance of the ceramic teapot."

Mikani smiled. "You'll have to tell me about that another time. I've a couple of teapots at home that have all sorts of historical significance, I'd wager. Shall we do some research, then?"

She couldn't remember feeling more astonished. "You . . . want to go poke through old books with me?"

"I figured I could charm the information out of librarians, but your idea does have a certain attraction. We can read sweet descriptions of historical buttons to each other and make an evening of it."

Bronze gods, that tone. I've heard him use it on his women. Please don't let me be blushing. I doubt he'd ever let me forget the infamy.

"That's not what I meant. You've teased me endlessly about my affinity for the tedious aspects of our work. Now you admit it's . . . useful?" She fought a smile.

"You've a knack for it. And . . . well, you've shown me that it pays off, sometimes." He scratched the side of his neck. "And I'm tired of running around without you."

Without another word, because she didn't know if she *could* speak, Ritsuko advised the junior officer to forward any replies to the city archive. Perhaps she was wrong, but that had sounded like a convoluted way of saying *I miss you*. These days, Mikani made it difficult to see him as only a lighthearted rogue.

After a ten-minute walk, they arrived at the city archive, a gorgeous stone building that Ritsuko had always loved. Stark white walls towered above them, a clean facade punctuated by three narrow bas-reliefs depicting the history of the Isles from the earliest records to the present day. Every few years, a team of artists carved a new panel, adding it to the frieze. The bronze dome crowning the archives shone in the afternoon light, casting a golden glow on the nearest Council buildings.

This place was the one reason her grandfather ever left the seclusion of the Mountain District. She remembered the joy and anticipation she'd felt before each trip, as if they prepared for a long voyage. He used to pack a flask of tea, a packet of biscuits, and they ate them in the park while paging through their reading material. She'd loved the bustle of the city, the electric mix of so many different faces and skin tones instead of so much homogeneity. As a child, she'd only ever felt free during those outings.

Without understanding why, she told Mikani as much. "When I was a little girl, we came here once a month. Later, my grandfather blamed the archive for my desire to leave the Mountain. He said if he'd never taught me to read and speak the common tongue, I'd have been content in my role."

"I don't think that'd have made much of a difference. You're far too smart to be content in a cage, partner." Here, he hesitated, cutting her a considering look through the tangle of his lashes. In combination with his unshaven jaw and the blue glint of his eyes, she had to strangle a frisson of . . . well. *Stop it.* "So . . . how *did* he end up raising you?"

A personal question. From Mikani.

It was silly, but her heart actually skipped a beat. She wondered if he knew these things about his women, or if there were no questions asked, no answers given.

It was a pleasure to reply, "I was two when they died. There was an epidemic . . . a fever, I'm told. When my parents fell ill, they sent me to my grandfather, who lived on the other side of the district. I . . . never went home."

He stopped and turned toward her, seeming concerned. "I'm sorry."

"I don't even remember them." She dismissed the faint discomfort she read in his furrowed brow, climbing the steps toward the archive. "What about you? You don't talk about your family."

He followed closely. "Boring, really. Mother lives up north, helping my sisters care for their broods. Five and counting, last I heard, between Helena and Daphne. I see them now and then." He was silent for a few seconds. "Dad served the Olriks. House Guard. Went after some pirates out west and didn't come back. I'm half-convinced he found a pretty island girl, and I've a little clan of half siblings running around."

"You have sisters," she said, fascinated. "Are they older, younger? Five nieces and nephews? How many of each?"

She'd never pictured him coming from a large family, never thought about it much at all. If anyone had asked, prior to this, she might've even speculated that he'd sprung fully formed from a bottle of whiskey. The hint of pain when he spoke of his father—well, she thought it best to pretend she didn't see it. Annoy him with the questions instead.

"I told you, boring," he muttered, as they reached the research offices. "Helena's older by a full minute. Or so she claims—"

"You have a twin," she exclaimed, delighted. "Does she look like you?"

He scoffed. "I'm the handsome one."

"I'm sure." She kept her tone neutral, aware his self-opinion didn't need padding.

Ritsuko led the way toward the shelves she had haunted for the last few days. The librarian recognized her and lifted a hand in greeting as she passed. A few patrons did as well, but they only smiled, as she'd come here long before she needed to research a case. This place felt like home.

"And Daphne?" she prompted, as she settled her things on a polished table.

"The baby of the Mikanis, spoiled like her little monsters. Four nieces and a nephew, but only one of them takes after their uncle. Rest of them will grow up to be hardworking, decent artisans and smiths, no doubt."

"You may not be part of a crafting guild, but you're hardworking and decent." The words came out fiercer and more heartfelt than she intended.

He arched a brow. "Why, partner, I'd almost think you approve of my lax ways."

"I may not think everything you do is advisable, but you're a good man." *Time to step away from the sincerity.* So she added, "One nephew? Please tell me his name is Janus. I think I speak for the whole CID when I say, we'd *love* a miniature of tiny Janus in short pants." She laid a finger against her cheek, feigning innocence. "I should write your sister. I bet she'd send me one."

"It's a traditional name, I'll have you know." He started pulling books at random from the nearby shelves. "And, I already have one such at home."

She laughed and fetched the volumes she had been using, then she stopped to ask the librarian for some guidance on texts that dealt with antique buttons. The man seemed surprised, but a few minutes later, he delivered a hefty stack for them to sort through. Serious now, Ritsuko divided up the stack. Mikani eyed his share as if it were a coiled snake about to bite him.

We have our work cut out for us.

They read in silence for over an hour before the courier came.

Mikani took the envelope, cracked it open, and offered a sharp smile. "I hope you aren't too enthralled here because we have something more exciting to do."

CHAPTER 19

THE ALSTON SHIPPING COMPANY WAS A FAMILY CONCERN, PRI-
vately owned and operated. They had offices down by South
Bay docks, not far from the Port Authority, where ships bearing
both goods and passengers required clearance. A brisk breeze
blew in from the sea, carrying tinges of fish and salt, along with
a powerful chill. The long days were coming to an end; night
fell faster as the cold came on, so Mikani quickened his step
accordingly. Businesses tended not to stay open down here after
dark.

The office offered no elegance, just a weathered-brick facade
with sagging peaked roofs. Inside, workers hurried between piled
crates and barrels, maddened by the influx of new business,
likely driven by Summer Clan blockades. While the embargo
was terrible for merchants, it appeared to be good for local transport, as the sea routes were booming, and the docks were overwhelmed with shipments. Mikani led Ritsuko through the maze
of supplies, up an open staircase to the first floor, where the
managers worked. There were three offices; he chose the largest
one. No point in wasting time on underlings.

The door was ajar, saving him the pretense of politeness. He stepped into the well-appointed room: large desk set before a window, a wall full of shelves and cupboards, two chairs, and a table with various documents strewn across it. A fortyish gentleman glanced up from the papers, a frown knitting his brows.

"Can I help you?" By his irritated expression, Mikani guessed the other man felt someone ought to have stopped them before they got this far.

"Mr. Alston?" He smiled and produced his credentials.

"Yes, what do you need?" Alston's tone became less impatient, however, when he registered the significance of the proffered badge.

"A moment of your time. And the full manifest of your shipments for Edgehill Metalworking and Foundry over the last two months if you'd be so kind."

Mr. Alston worked his jaw in a manner that suggested he was already out of patience. "You don't need my personal supervision for this." He scrawled a note on a blank sheet of paper and handed it to Mikani. "Take this to my clerk, two doors down. He can help you find what you're looking for."

"Thank you for your cooperation," Ritsuko said.

"That was too easy," Mikani commented, as they retraced their steps to the smaller office.

In here the carpet was threadbare, the shelves made of unfinished wood, and the man staring at them across the desk wore the thickest glasses Mikani had ever seen. But the clerk perked at the sight of Ritsuko, as if he'd never seen a woman before. He stumbled to his feet, banging against the chair, and came around to offer his hand.

"Here's the real gauntlet," she whispered.

"I beg your pardon?" the clerk said.

Ritsuko offered a smile, then her badge. "Never mind. Mikani, you have the writ from Mr. Alston."

He suppressed a smirk and handed the clerk the note. "Your employer said you could help us with this."

The clerk scanned the document and nodded to the point that it seemed likely his spectacles might fall off. "Let me just get the ledgers."

His eagerness to please resulted in a quick return, at least. The clerk seemed quite proud of the hefty tomes he handed over.

But the records requested were written in a tiny, spidery script in columns that might make Mikani go blind. He gave one of the books to Ritsuko, who arched a brow at him.

"*This* is supposed to be more exciting than the archives?"

He laid claim to the nearest desk in the clerk's office, scanning the entries. Each page was devoted to a separate cargo, row after row of minutiae clearly labeled, weighed, and counted. He shook his head and examined the nearly indecipherable writing for mentions of polished brass mirrors and cylinders of the right dimensions. It took nearly two hours of exhaustive searching, but by the time the clerk packed up his briefcase in an unmistakable cue—the man was no longer so enamored with Ritsuko's mere existence—they had an address.

"This is where they took the matching order," Ritsuko said, standing. She arched her back, then rolled her head side to side, presumably to work out the stiffness. "Thanks for your time," she added to the clerk.

Mikani stretched and jotted down the address. Then something on the ledger caught his eye. "Ritsuko, Toombs's mother mentioned he was deep in debt, yes?"

She nodded. "Something about those theater people with their whoring, gambling, and drinking. She wasn't amused."

"Then how could he afford all this? From the value listed for insurance, seems that the brass and copper components alone cost a small fortune."

Before Ritsuko could reply, the clerk put in, "Sir, I don't mean to trouble you, but I need to lock up."

Mikani took the hint, and they left, heading down the stairs in silence while Ritsuko clearly mulled his question. He could tell she was thinking by the neat furrow between her brows and the way she quirked her mouth to the side, then bit her lip. Outside the shipping offices, it was nearly dark, a sky full of emerging stars.

"Either he borrowed the money for . . . this. Or he has a patron," she offered.

Mikani nodded, thinking it over. "There's one more thing, partner. The manifest listed several other items. He's definitely building another device."

"That tracks with what you sensed at Miss Bihár's flat. The third victim."

He smiled at Ritsuko. "We need to find out if he's alone in this."

"I think we should check out the address where they sent his goods. If he's there, our search is over. If not, perhaps we learn something that will help us find him." She curled one hand into a fist. "I hate that he has the whole city to hide in."

"Look at the bright side. Between the constables, the Free Traders, and the Summer Clan, he's stuck in the city. Hells, he's probably unable to leave whatever hole he's burrowed into for fear someone will spot him and turn him over to Bihár. So let's go smoke him out."

"Did you see that House Aevar has posted a bounty on his head? A thousand talons for his capture, alive or dead." She moved toward the cruiser, parked some distance away.

"Really?" He paused by the vehicle. "You know, that would easily buy us a small place in the far south." He watched her expression change before flashing her a grin. "Kidding. I'd gladly hand him over to Bihár, then to Aevar, for free."

Mikani slid into the driver's seat, and she settled next to him. As he started the vehicle, she said, "Oh, that's not what I was thinking at all."

"Enlighten me."

Her smile was positively mischievous, not a look he'd ever before associated with Ritsuko. "I wasn't sure if you realized you just suggested we move in together."

His eyes widened. "I don't do windows." He gave her a sideways glance, trying to gauge her mood.

"You cook. I'll clean. That seems fair." She wasn't looking at him, her face in profile, so he couldn't be sure if she was teasing. But even if he could see her eyes, he might not be able to tell, as she had a fairly effective poker face when required. *Gods and spirits, is she serious? This is* Ritsuko. *Why am I not more worried?*

"Fishing. Farming a little. Maybe some arts and crafts." He glanced over at her briefly. "We'd drive each other insane in two days. Tops."

She laughed. "Relax, Mikani. I *am* moving, but not into your cottage."

Damned be. Can't decide if I'm relieved or disappointed. What's gotten into me?

"Oh, so you think we need a bigger place? Gods and spirits, woman, at least wait until we have the reward." He turned his attention to the road.

"There is no satisfying me." Her words were spoken lightly, but the tone struck him as a challenge.

It was an hour and a half's drive to their destination, fifteen minutes added for quarrels in the street. Once, Mikani climbed out of the cruiser and broke up a fight. Ten more minutes passed while he argued with the Summer Clan trying to stop traffic inside the city as well. The bravos were all spoiling for a fight, darkly brooding, and it wouldn't take much to provoke one. The House Guards were equally prone to whipping out their weapons, as they must be feeling the pressure from above. Part of him was glad Electra's death hadn't gone unnoticed—that her loss hadn't been swept beneath the rug—but he couldn't let the nomads drive the entire city into chaos as they seemed inclined to do.

When he got in the vehicle, Ritsuko was smiling. "I swear you thrive on this."

"You've heard Gunwood. I live for trouble." He studied the road up ahead, then added, "We're close now."

RARELY HAD RITSUKO traveled beyond the city limits. Her grandfather hadn't liked the countryside, too full of spirits, he said, though she had never sensed anything amiss. Out here, the stars gleamed brighter away from the competing gaslight. But it was also equally quiet, no hansoms, no people going about their lives. There was only the whisper of the wind in the trees and the crunch of the cruiser's wheels against the rocky road leading down to a ramshackle farm that appeared abandoned. She saw no lights anyway.

Mikani parked. "Well, if I intended to build a death machine, this would be the place for it."

"Let's check it out." She swung out of the vehicle and checked her weapon. Usually, it was her credentials, but she suspected the gun would prove more useful.

"He's been here." Mikani looked around, his head tilted. "There's that sense of decay all around. Faint, though." He patted his side pocket, presumably to ensure his revolver was there, then he hefted his walking stick.

"You can tell that, all the way out here?" She shivered, fearing what the decrepit building held in store.

He made his way toward the farmhouse. "You know, when you cook a dish often enough, how the smell just permeates the kitchen for days? It's like that. He did . . . whatever it is he does in here so often that the stench is ingrained in the air now."

"I don't, actually. I rarely cook. But I'll take your word for it."

Ritsuko picked a path across the moonlit yard, drawing her weapon as a precaution. The bantering mood left her, replaced by a fierce determination. At Dinwiddie's flat, they'd stumbled onto Toombs unaware, but that wouldn't happen again. If the maniac was hiding here, perhaps he had a way in and out of the city, avoiding the checkpoints and barricades. It would explain why nobody had caught him yet.

With Mikani's comforting presence at her back, she crossed to the farmhouse door, which was locked. It didn't appear to be particularly well made, however. She gave him some room, gesturing. "Have at it."

He mock-bowed to her, then slammed a kick just below the handle. The inner frame shattered, and he grabbed the door when it swung back. "Easy does it." He led the way into the dark house.

The place smelled musty, hints of mold and mildew that indicated a leak in the roof. There was also a trace of decay, an animal stench, as if something had crawled inside and died. But that was an old scent, not fresh like a newly rotten corpse. Ritsuko hated that she knew the difference. As she went farther into the house, her eyes adjusted to the gloom, so she made out a platter of meat, crawling with maggots.

Mikani peered through the two other doorways. "Living room, in worse shape than the kitchen. A storage cupboard. If he lives here, he's got a thing for squalor. Upstairs?"

"I can hardly wait."

Tension clamped down on her spine as she went up the stairs, watching Mikani's back. He gripped his sidearm, surveying the blind spots before swinging up the rest of the way. From within the walls came scrabbling noises, claws, perhaps, or wings. *Bats? Rats? Both, probably.*

He paused at the top of the stairs. "I'll check left, then right."

"Just search the second bedroom. I've got the other."

Ritsuko didn't think there was anybody home. They hadn't

been quiet in breaking down the door; nor did either of them tread up the stairs like ghosts. Some of her fear scaled back, leaving her more or less clearheaded and prepared to investigate.

He cut her a look, but he didn't argue, merely went along to the bedroom farthest from the stairs. She shoved the door before her open with the heel of her sturdy boot. Within, it was dark, and the smell of decay wafted stronger. *Bronze gods, I don't think it was the meat after all.*

Her heart in her throat, she crept into the room, weapon clenched between both palms. But there was no movement, no sign of life. She skimmed the space in a single glance, taking in the pitiful mounds beneath the tattered blankets. Ritsuko took two more steps to confirm her suspicions.

"Mikani!" She pitched her voice only loud enough to carry. "Two bodies in here."

He was at her side in a heartbeat. "They've been here awhile."

Even in the dim moonlight, she saw how desiccated the skin was, sunken back into their cheeks. The hands curled like claws; their limbs were skeletal. Here and there, she saw places where scavengers, carrion-eaters, had gnawed. It was impossible for her to guess how old these people might've been, but by their presence in the same bed—

"I'm guessing they were a married couple."

Mikani peered at them more closely. "He slit their throats here. The sheets are stiff with old blood. Several cuts; he wasn't quick or merciful."

Hard tremors rocked through her. "What kind of monster *does* this? He treated them like they were animals."

"Let's check the barn, then we can see about putting these people to rest, partner."

Ritsuko couldn't get out of that room fast enough. Though she had been around corpses before, she'd never *found* one. Always, when she arrived, it was with plenty of forewarning, a proper report filed, and that gave her the time to prepare mental defenses. Tonight, she felt awful and shaky; and she couldn't stop counting the dead in her head.

Cira Aevar.

Oliver Dinwiddie.

Electra Bihár.

Now they had two more victims. It made no sense that Toombs only killed young women in the convoluted apparatus. Anyone else, apparently, could be dispatched efficiently, or messily, through whatever expedient means fell to hand. Her breathing sounded unsteady in the quiet. *Bronze gods, I hope Mikani can't tell how scared I am. I'll never hear the end of it.*

Across the yard, the barn loomed. *That must be where he builds the terrible machines.* Feigning bravery she didn't feel, she marched to the weathered door to examine the shiny padlock clamped to it.

Mikani leaned close at her shoulder, checking the mechanism. He drew out his kit, appeared to give the tools within cursory consideration, and put the case away; apparently, he thought finesse would take too long. He tested the iron rings holding the lock to the door. With a nod, he wedged his walking stick between the padlock and door and pulled, hard, tearing the rings from the old wood with a loud crack.

"Sometimes I think you just keep me around for my larcenous skills."

Ritsuko whispered, "That, and your manly thews. But how did you know?"

"Caught you looking at my picks more than once. I don't hear anyone inside."

"Sense anyone?" Ritsuko readied her weapon, hands shaking. She'd only discharged it at practice targets, but Toombs wouldn't get away again.

The reward's dead or alive.

He shook his head. "I can just sense the void. Even you're . . . blurry."

A disquieting thought occurred to her. "But if he's cold, dead, as you've said before, how would you *know*?"

Mikani hesitated. "Honestly? I'm guessing."

"That's comforting." With a wry smile, she eased into the storage building, only to draw up short at an ominous click in the darkness. "Mikani . . . what just happened?"

"Don't move." He sounded deadly serious; he crouched next to her. "There's a metal plate on the floor, trap under it, I think. Given what we know of Toombs, I don't imagine it's anything good, either. So hold *very* still."

"Well," she said quietly. "If this is it, I wouldn't trade a minute

of the past three years. If you don't mind, put flowers on my
grandfather's grave for me, once a year."

"Shut up." Navigating past carefully, he rummaged around
nearby. "You're not leaving me with the paperwork for this."

Her knees trembled. She felt conscious of every breath she
took, every infinitesimal shift. The weight of the gun in her hand
grew with each passing second. Fear made her palms slippery,
but she couldn't wipe them. She didn't dare move.

"Admit it. You'll be lost without me."

He dragged a small crate filled with what sounded like metal
bits toward her. "There really *is* no satisfying you, is there? On
three—"

"You should go. If it goes off during the shift, you'll be
caught, too." She didn't want him risking his life for her; it would
be better knowing Mikani made it out.

He stood, his features a hard mask of barely controlled anger.
"So help me, we both make it out of here or neither. I'm done
debating this with you. Like I said, on three."

In a movement so fast it made her dizzy, he slid the crate onto
the plate and curled an arm around her waist. Mikani yanked
her all the way off her feet as he sprinted out the door. Behind
them, something whirred. And then a thundering concussion
blew them forward, a fusillade of copper shards raining down,
cutting into the open door and chewing at the frame. Ritsuko
landed on her face, and her first reaction was pure surprise. Her
back stung, but . . . *I'm still alive.*

"One two three." Mikani rose to his elbows and looked back
at the barn, ducking as fragments of metal kept falling. "Damned
be. I think most of that mess came from the box of scraps. Guess
you're not as light as I thought, partner."

"Do you *want* me to hit you?" She dropped her face against
her hands and swung like a pendulum between the urge toward
tears and hysterical laughter.

He sniffed. "Women usually threaten to hurt me only *after*
we've moved in together."

"And thus, you bring up cohabitation for the second time
tonight. Ask a third time, Mikani, and I'll show up with my
luggage. It would serve you right." She pushed out a shaky
breath. "Also, thank you for my life."

He pushed to his feet and offered her a hand up. "Least I could do."

Ritsuko actually needed his support, between the dizziness and her sore back. While he might be used to it, she tried not to get injured on a weekly basis. When he pulled her upright, she left her hand in his. "And I'm sorry I argued. I just didn't want anything to happen to you."

He glanced away, then back at her, his expression inscrutable. "Just what do you think would become of me without you?"

"You'd drink a lot. Sing some sad songs." She smiled and freed her hand. "At the risk of sounding addled, I'm afraid we need to go back in there. We didn't have a chance to investigate at all."

Mikani sighed. "Stubborn, single-minded woman. Let me go first this time."

CHAPTER 20

THAT MORNING, AURELIA POSTED A NOTICE AT THE ROYALE that read: REHEARSAL CANCELED, then followed Leo out to a waiting hansom. She hadn't gone home. Instead, she'd spent three days hiding in the theater, and he didn't argue when she asked him to leave the lamp on. Oh, she'd tried to carry on rehearsals as usual, but she was too nervous, too scattered, and each day, she turned the practice over to an assistant. Even sitting below the stage felt like too much exposure. For the first time, she understood how Leo felt about his mask.

As a measure of how strong his friendship was, he stood outside with her on a sunny morning when he hadn't left in months. He handed her into the coach and gave the address. She didn't know if he believed her story, but he said she needed to tell it to the authorities if she felt brave enough. Forty minutes later, she walked through the lobby of CID Headquarters. Aurelia was conscious of the fact that she didn't look like an upstanding member of society. She'd been forced to bathe as Leo did, and to rummage in the costume department for something suitable to wear.

Leo led the way to the lift, ignoring the looks and whispers about his mask. Once inside the clanking monstrosity, he said, "This will be over soon."

"I hope so."

The main room opened up directly from the lift with desks and officers hurrying between them. It was more bustle than she expected, but Leo didn't let her hang back. He towed her toward the nearest constable. The young man was bright-eyed and crisply pressed in his uniform. *He'll never believe me.*

"I need to report four murders," she said.

"Four?" The constable set his teacup on the desk, looking flummoxed.

"Don't you need to write this down?" Leo asked.

"I won't be taking the report for such a serious crime. I'm not an inspector. Let me see who's available to take your statement." He escorted them to a small room with a table and four chairs. "Someone will be with you presently."

There were no windows, and the walls were painted a grim, industrial gray. "Do you suppose this is where they interrogate the criminals?"

Leo pressed her hand. "I imagine he just wasn't familiar with the protocol. He looked rather . . . green."

According to the interminable tick of her pocket watch, it was ten minutes before anyone came. After the door opened, two men stepped through: one was thin, with a sly, narrow face and deep-set eyes; the other had a round belly and had lost most of his hair. The second man should possess a jolly air, but his eyes dispelled that illusion, quiet and hard rather than warm. Neither inspector looked delighted to have caught this task.

"Ma'am. I'm Inspector Shelton," the thin one said.

The portly man offered his hand; his clasp was damp and cool, like a dead fish. "Cutler. I understand you witnessed a disturbing event recently."

Forget what they think. You came forward to tell the truth.

In as concise a manner as possible, she related what she'd seen though she omitted the part about Theron's hands turning into claws. By their impatient expressions, she was straining their credulity with even the edited version of this wild tale. Before she finished, Shelton was drumming his fingertips on the table in a not-so-subtle demand for her to wrap things up.

"Thanks for your civic responsibility, ma'am. The constable you spoke to initially will take your name and address should we have further questions." By his tone, Cutler didn't expect that to happen.

"Are you taking this seriously?" Leo demanded.

Shelton smiled, but it wasn't polite. "It sounds to me like four lowlifes tried to rob the wrong man. No great loss."

And not worth CID resources, Aurelia guessed.

"You didn't see the fight," she said quietly. "He's *dangerous.*"

The two inspectors traded a look, then insulting smiles. "That's all we need."

There was no point in protesting further; feeling ridiculous and faintly ashamed, she stood. *I hid, fearing reprisal, and they think I'm a hysterical female.* Leo had his hands curled into fists, as if he fought the urge to pummel both of them. She set her hand on his arm, rigid as she'd expected.

"It's fine. We tried." But Aurelia had rarely felt so humiliated, so disreputable, as if she were a scorned woman out to make trouble for a man who didn't want her.

If they discover you've had dinner at Theron's villa, they'll believe that's true.

It felt imperative to get out of here, before something worse happened. Leo wrapped his arm around her shoulders, shepherding her toward the door. "Let's go. What incompetent buffoons," he added, before they left earshot.

"Which of my esteemed colleagues are you lambasting?" a familiar voice asked.

When Aurelia turned, she recognized Inspectors Mikani and Ritsuko. The former looked worse for the wear, his face so many colors that it could be a work of art. By contrast, his partner reflected cool elegance though her movements appeared too careful, as if she might have a hidden injury.

Shelton and Cutler stepped out of the room behind them. Mikani nodded, then said to Ritsuko, "I'd have laid odds on that."

Her voice was cool, amused. "You'll bet on how long it takes to wash my hands."

"You'll make these good folks think I'm a degenerate gambler, partner."

The woman made a shooing motion. "I appreciate your keeping Miss Wright and Mr. Leonidas entertained with your

impression of an inspector. Now why don't you go away and let
us work?"

Shelton's face went red. "One of these days, Miss Ritsuko, I
will be very sorry to hear that this job has gotten the best of you."

False. Aurelia's truth-sense told her that Shelton would celebrate if something awful happened to his colleague. She took
a step back, bumping against Leo, whose hands lit on her shoulders, steadying her. Possibly it wasn't fair to drag him into this
when he had so much to deal with already: his bereavement, the
scars, a struggling theater. Or maybe this was exactly what he
needed—a reason to step outside his own problems.

The two pairs of agents stared at each other long and hard,
before Cutler sidled away. "This is a waste of time. You want to
coddle her? Go ahead."

"Miss Wright," Mikani said gently. "I apologize. Those two
aren't smart enough to find their own arses with a map and a
compass."

"Let's go to the lounge," Ritsuko suggested.

Leo nodded. "Better than an interrogation room."

Aurelia registered the silent look the two inspectors exchanged. It consisted of an arched brow, a canted head, and a
moue of Mikani's mouth. If she was interpreting the silent conversation correctly, it went something like this:

Let's not leave them with that *impression of the CID.*

*Agreed. If Leonidas came out of seclusion with her, it must
be important.*

Right. Tea, then. And we'll see.

She wondered if the two realized the extent of their rapport;
such communication took years to develop. But she was too
worried about her own situation to pry into theirs. Five minutes
later, she settled into a fairly comfortable chair with a warm mug.
Leo sat beside her, seeming marginally more comfortable than
he'd been with the other two. These officers had enraged him,
but he'd overlook the prior offense for Aurelia's peace of mind.

"You look shaken," Ritsuko said softly. "Is this related to
Miss Aevar's death?"

Oh. Of course they think that.

"No. At least, I don't believe so." It hadn't occurred to her that
Theron could be connected to the girls who had been murdered.

Yet, he is *a killer . . .* She knew the difference between a man

murdering in cold blood and one acting in self-defense, but he
had been *so* brutal. A civilized man would've subdued his attackers, if he could, then called the authorities. Theron's actions left
her fearing the worst.

Mikani smiled. "Take your time. The longer we sit with you,
the longer I get to put off my paperwork."

His humor helped; and his partner got out a notebook, proving
they didn't think she was making up stories for attention. This
time, she gave her account without the nervous stammering that
led Shelton and Cutler to imagine she was a crackpot. Mikani
and Ritsuko listened with somber expressions; and this time, she
didn't censor the story at all. Leo pressed her arm when she
described Theron's hands changing, growing ferocious talons,
but she wouldn't recant.

It happened. I'm not out of my mind.

"That's quite a story," Mikani said, once she finished.

Hot color washed her cheeks. "I know how it sounds."

Ritsuko studied her with quiet sympathy. "It was dark. Perhaps you saw some knives and thought—"

"No. I've never seen magic like that, nothing so powerful,
but I'm *not* crazy."

"Why were you following him?" Mikani asked.

That was the question the other inspectors hadn't thought to
ask. It also rendered her testimony even shakier. But before she
could respond, Leo cut in, "There are four corpses down in the
Patchwork. What do you mean to do?"

Aurelia held up a hand, indicating her friend should stand
down. "No, it's fine. I wouldn't have told the other two, but
Inspectors Ritsuko and Mikani deserve the truth."

She explained the whole story—Theron's sudden appearance
and romantic overtures, her suspicions about his plans, and how
she'd taken steps to uncover his true agenda. By the time she
finished, the male inspector was studying her as if he couldn't
decide on an appropriate reaction.

Finally, he said, "That was . . . enterprising, but ultimately
unwise."

"I had *no* idea the night would end in so much death," she
snapped.

The female inspector nodded. "Likely you thought you'd catch
him meeting with whoever pointed him in your direction."

Aurelia eased back into her chair, relieved that someone understood. "Precisely; some crony of my father's, perhaps. I thought he might even be behind Theron's courtship."

"He?" Mikani asked.

"My father."

The two traded another weighted look, then Ritsuko said, "You're a House scion?"

"My name is legally Aurelia Wright. I haven't claimed any House affiliation in many years."

"And what about this Theron? Is he a House scion as well?" Mikani inquired.

She shrugged. "I've no idea. I was trying to learn more about him when . . . this happened. I won't be pursuing his acquaintance further, I assure you."

"I understand," Ritsuko said. "We'll send officers to check the morgue. If four bodies have turned up, as you claim, then we'll pick Mr. Theron up."

Mikani added, "But if I'm honest, it's your word against his. He could claim *you* killed them, and that's how you knew of the murders."

Terror clenched her stomach into a knot. "Oh, bronze gods. Will he know that I reported him?"

"Don't worry." Ritsuko patted her hand gently. "It's our policy to keep such matters confidential."

Aurelia pushed out a hard breath, the cup and saucer clattering in her lap. "If there's nothing further, I'd like to go home."

Both inspectors stood, but Mikani spoke. "You've given us ample information. We'll handle it from here."

She nodded and shook both their hands, then Leo escorted her from the building. "They seemed to take it more seriously at least."

"Thanks for coming with me."

He put a protective arm around her shoulders, more like her old friend than he had been since before the accident. Aurelia had thought that man lost forever, drowned in bitterness and loss. "As if I'd let you go through it alone. I'll see you to your apartment."

"You don't have to—"

"Auri," he said in a tone that brooked no refusal.

A tiny part was glad to see this Leo back. So she didn't argue. "Very well."

* * *

LATER, AFTER A bath, she felt much better. Leo had arranged
with Hargrave for a meal. The covered platters arrived just after
she stepped out of the bedroom, dressed in a clean, simple shirt-
waist. Leo was arranging the food on her table as she joined him.
Before the accident, they had spent many such evenings.

You're not the only one who's been lonely. She'd tried to
convey that his looks didn't matter, but little by little, he'd pulled
back until they were barely even friends, more business partners
tied by the Royale. Yet he'd come through for her last night and
braved his fear of mockery today. He considered himself a monster and expected the world to confirm his fear. It was cowardice
that kept him down in that dungeon, paying a woman to pretend
to care about him.

"Elaine will be furious," she said, perching on the edge of
the settee.

The broth smelled wonderful, light and clear. Surprise
touched her with feathery awareness; he'd remembered that she
couldn't eat a heavy meal after an emotional upset. First, something light, followed by bread. Once her stomach settled, she'd
manage more.

"Let me worry about her. And to be honest, I'm too concerned
about you to care for her pique."

He lounged on her settee, studying her through the confines
of the dark mask, and she hated not being able to see his eyes.
The black fabric contrasted with his fair hair, and she leaned
forward to whisper, "Take it off, Leo. You don't need it here. Not
with me." She'd said as much before, but not with such a heartfelt
plea.

His tone was light. "You've been through enough, Auri. I
don't want to put you off your food."

"And *I* need to see your face."

For a moment, she thought he'd refuse. His jaw pulled tight,
and he strode over to the window. She half expected him to pull
the drapes against the sunlight. Then he reached up with trembling hands to unfasten the ties. When he turned, there was an
awful vulnerability about him, as if he expected her—his best
friend—to turn away.

Yes, the scars were ugly, but it was good to see his blue eyes again. She moved to his side, stretched up on tiptoe, and kissed his poor cheek. "Do you believe me?"

He seemed incredulous at first, then grateful that she wanted to talk about her own problems rather than this rare moment. "Of course I do. You never lie."

Leo knew about her gift, and though he wasn't always honest, he offered tactful half-truths. She forgave him that for the long years of their friendship, for all the laughter. The latter had been scarce in the past six months, but he had a plateful of sorrow, and he couldn't step away.

"He'll be back . . . and I don't know—" Her voice broke, so she tried again. "The stupid thing is, when he appeared, I *knew* there was something off. I suspected him of wanting to use me."

"More than one man has tried over the years."

Leo had comforted her numerous times when a romance turned out to be largely calculation and wishful thinking. That was before she learned to focus her gift on those who courted her. These days, it was impossible to catch her unaware, provided she held a conversation with the person first. So she'd been confident she could handle Theron.

In retrospect, that was a mistake.

"What should I do?"

"Stay away from him," he answered at once. "Don't speak to him. If he approaches you, call for help. I'll escort you to and from the theater."

"That will be a lot of bother for you."

"Not if you let me stay here." His expression made her think her agreement was vital to his well-being. Then he sighed, watching her eat. "Really, Auri, what possessed you? Following a man to the Patchwork warrens, protected only by a back-alley charm?"

"Would it be better if I'd purchased the necklace in Temple?"

"No," Leo snapped. "I'm furious with you, but until today, you were too upset to withstand a scolding."

She arched a brow, smiling. "But you think I can handle one now?"

"Let's find out, shall we?"

He proceeded with the most glorious rant, impugning her common sense, intelligence, and her forethought before winding down to scowl at her. He was completely unself-conscious. No pacing to angle his scars away from her, away from the light.

They were still raised and livid, purple and red. They were no prettier, but he finally trusted her to see past them. Aurelia smiled.

His frown deepened. "Are you even *listening* to me? This isn't a negligible matter. It sounds as if this Theron sought you out for no good purpose. I fear his intentions."

"So do I."

A chill went through her when she saw it again in her mind's eye—the claws in the swirling darkness, his avid face. It had been hard to explain this part to the authorities, but he'd taken such pleasure in dispatching his enemies, a primitive, atavistic joy. He hadn't been frightened during that fight, quite the contrary; he had played with his attackers, exulting in their terror and defeat.

"You're still unsettled," he realized aloud. "Do you have anything to drink?"

"A liquid cure for what ails me?"

"Wine if you have some, enough to help you relax. Perhaps you'll sleep. You haven't rested much the past few days."

An understatement. She feared she had prevented him from doing so either. Each night, she'd jerked awake, replaying the deaths in her head. Such a reaction made her feel weak, but surely it was understandable. Nothing in her life had prepared her for such brutality, as if to Theron, those men weren't human at all.

"I'll look in the cupboard." Her flat was modest, four rooms above the club.

Shortly, she returned with two flutes and a bottle of dusty wine. "It was a gift from my father, long ago. I was supposed to drink it to celebrate something, I think. It's all I have, so I hope it's good."

"I'm sure it will be. It's the effect that matters anyway."

"Will you do the honors?"

"Of course." He took the corkscrew from her and examined the wine. "Are you sure, Auri? This is an incredibly expensive vintage."

"I'm sure. Let's live dangerously."

"Seems to me you already are."

The pop of the cork sounded like a gunshot in her quiet apartment. Her nerves jangled as he poured two glasses. Then Leo raised his in apparent toast, but his eyes were somber. "I promise I won't let anything happen to you.

So he truly does fear for my life. That wasn't any comfort at all.

CHAPTER 21

MIKANI DRAINED THE LAST OF THE BITTER COFFEE DREGS IN his cup and grimaced. His partner walked over to his desk, attaché case in hand. Ritsuko's paperwork hadn't been touched since they came back last night. That was . . . quite unlike her. He hoped she wasn't hurt too badly.

It had been a grueling three hours in that dark barn, avoiding more snares and traps. In the end, it was worthwhile. Deep drag marks indicated where the apparatus had been hauled onto a waiting cart. *There's no way it was fully assembled, however.* Mikani hated knowing there was another murder machine out there, ready to claim a third victim.

"Well," she said. "We have blueprints . . . for all that helps us."

"We already knew where the parts came from. And where they delivered them."

"Somebody took the contraption back to the city," she pointed out. "I can send word to all the companies that operate outside Dorstaad city limits—"

He slammed a fist against his desk. "He moved it himself, somehow. Someone would come forward for the reward if they'd helped him haul those damned things around the city."

"Then I don't know where else to look," she whispered.

Mikani sighed and pinched the bridge of his nose. "I know. I—I'm sorry." *And tired. Frustrated. And damned be, if I didn't almost lose you to that bastard.* "We need to stop him—before he uses that thing on another girl."

She set a hand on his arm. "We're doing everything we can."

"I know. Just wish it were enough, partner." He let out a long sigh.

"Well. It's not a direct link to locating Toombs, but . . . if you're willing, I'd like to follow up on a lead I got last week."

Mikani glanced wearily at his stack of reports. "We're expecting the initial findings on the owners of the farm. And Miss Wright's incident report looks likely to land in our laps as soon as we hear back from the morgue. So while we're waiting . . ." He stood, pushing the pile of papers to the center of his desk. "Let's go."

"When I interviewed Toombs's mother, she told me to talk to her neighbor because the woman is an inveterate snoop. From Mrs. Drusse I did learn some things about Mr. Toombs." She ticked them off on her fingers. "Toombs didn't visit his mother enough. He regularly had disreputable callers who harassed his parents. And I got the name of the man they work for."

The lift door opened as they approached, discharging a tall man in a loose-fitting tweed jacket; he had a shock of ginger hair and plenty of freckles. After a moment, Mikani placed him as someone who worked downstairs, poking at the dead bodies. *Higgins,* he remembered. *Refused to process some counterfeit Magnus whiskey when I didn't file the proper request. Bugger set us back an arrest to uphold the rules.*

Before he could ask what Higgins wanted, the man approached Ritsuko and took her hand. "I just got word downstairs. Are you well?"

She smiled up at him. "Just a few cuts."

"Have you seen a physician?" Higgins asked.

"I did, before I came in this morning."

Looking as if he were being inexpressibly forward, Higgins pressed her fingers between his. "You should've taken the day off."

Mikani observed the exchange with a growing mix of annoyance and confusion. *Higgins knows Ritsuko . . . rather well, apparently. How the hells did that happen?*

"We're too close to the end. With the pressure the Summer Clan and House Aevar are applying, we'll have Toombs soon. I can't afford to be at home."

Higgins still didn't let go of Ritsuko. "Look after yourself. I worry about you."

"Don't you have enough to fret about without adding me to it? How's your mother?" She was smiling, a friendly, open expression.

"Overall, not well. But she has good days." At that point, he seemed to notice Mikani standing at Ritsuko's shoulder. "Good afternoon, Inspector." He made as if to tip a hat and apparently realized he wasn't wearing one.

"I'll see you Sunday if not before," she said, as Higgins turned.

He watched Higgins get on the lift before turning to his partner. "You're—" He made a vague gesture, shaking his head slowly. ". . . him?" *Your eloquence is impressive, Mikani. Get a grip, man.* "You're keeping company with Mr. Higgins these days?"

Pedantic arse.

"Yes. He's a gentleman. Unexpected, dry sense of humor as well."

"For how long?" *Not your concern. She's your partner, and you'd do well to remember that.* He couldn't suppress the odd little twist somewhere deep inside, though. "I mean, I had no idea you'd started seeing anyone since Warren."

"It's only been a . . . week, I think." She didn't look sure. He understood that, as the days and nights ran together recently. "He asked me to luncheon as soon as he heard I was . . . unattached."

It's absurd that she sounds surprised. Half the men in this building would like to bed her.

He nodded once, pretending to feel sanguine about the situation, and started toward the lift. "He seems quite . . . upright? Respectable."

She grinned, following him into the cage. "He's good to his mother. The gossips say that's the way to judge how a man will treat his wife."

Mikani snorted. "Gossips are idiots. Let's chase down that lead of yours; we've a killer to catch."

His partner filled him in during the forty-five-minute drive; it wasn't the physical distance, but the city streets grew more dangerous and unpredictable by the day. Traffic snarls of blocked hansoms and irate wagon drivers clogged the lanes. A few times, Mikani considered seeing how well the cruiser was made and simply pushing his way through. But it was unlikely he could pull that off without injuring a few civilians, and despite Ritsuko's teasing, he wasn't actually a maniac.

"You never take me anywhere nice," Mikani observed, as they climbed out.

Harland Stokes, the moneylender to whom Toombs owed a substantial debt, kept offices in a nondescript building nestled between a storage facility and a shuttered shop. Mikani glanced up and down the narrow corridor of neglected businesses and semilegal operations wedged between the Rivermouth piers and the market districts closer to the center of the city. Scurrying porters and minor House nobles, conspicuous in their attempts to go unnoticed, crossed paths as they slipped among moneylenders, pawnshops, and less identifiable shop fronts and unmarked doors.

"Technically," Ritsuko said, "*you* brought me."

"You found the address. It's all you. Admit it, you're drawn to disreputable things." He grinned and made sure the security locks on the cruiser were set before heading for Stokes's door.

"It's true. Every Sunday, I drag Mr. Higgins to a different gin joint."

Mikani laughed. "I suspect Mr. Higgins would have a stroke if you tried." He rapped on the door with the handle of his walking stick, then pushed it open without waiting for an answer. "Harland Stokes? Need a minute of your time."

A squat fellow with shoulders like a brick wall answered; his coat was incongruously well tailored, and his waistcoat shone with gold thread. *Yet he has a face like a broken clock.* "Do you have an appointment?"

Mikani rolled a shrug and ambled into the room. "Inspectors Mikani and Ritsuko, CID. Consider this . . . a civic duty. We have a few questions. Mr. Stokes gives us good answers, and we all go away happy and with the satisfaction of a day well spent."

"Mr. Stokes may not be inclined to perform any civic services today. Wait here." His accent was thick as curds and whey; while they waited, Mikani tried to place it.

Apparently, Ritsuko was thinking the same thing. "Where's he from?"

"Winter. Northeast, I'd wager. But he has an odd accent, one I haven't heard much."

A few minutes later, the henchman returned. "Boss will give you five minutes. If those questions are brief, that should do it. If they're not, I'll chuck you in the street myself."

Hells. I know that accent. Don't see many Craggers this far south. Crag coasters kept to themselves, rarely venturing to the northernmost settlements of the Isles to trade. Mikani had met a few before leaving home but had never seen one in Dorstaad before.

"You're the soul of politeness, you are." Mikani gave the thug a grin and motioned for Ritsuko to lead the way to Stokes's office.

She preceded him; and for the second time in recent memory, his gaze dropped to the curve of her arse. *Focus, Mikani.* With a guilty pang, he followed her in.

The office was positively opulent, belying the seedy exterior. An expensive carpet woven of pure silk threads created a blue-and-green geometric pattern beneath their feet. The furnishings gleamed from recent polish, and the man sitting behind the ornate desk looked like a banker. Of course, appearances could be deceiving. Past the man's silver hair and spectacles, Mikani caught a glimpse of an absolutely sharkish mind.

"You have five minutes. Make it quick." Stokes wasted no time on a greeting.

"Very well. You lent Gregory Toombs a significant amount of money recently. Funds which he then used to commit capital crimes. Since men like you always keep tabs on their clients, I'll bet you have some idea of where to find Mr. Toombs."

"That's concise." Stokes smiled, then produced a humidor. "Would you like a cigar? This won't take one minute, let alone five."

Mikani inclined his head politely and took the offered cigar, sliding it into his pocket. "Most kind."

"Sir," Ritsuko prompted.

The moneylender clipped the end, then made a production of lighting his cigar. "Toombs doesn't owe me a copper. He paid his debt two weeks ago, all in old coins."

Well. That's unexpected.

"He paid in full, just like that? I take it you didn't extend him another loan."

"Certainly not. I shouldn't have done so in the first place. Actors aren't good bets for return on investment. No collateral, no job security. I must confess, I'm curious as to where he managed to get the money myself."

"So are we. You said he paid in old coins? Do you have one on you?" Some of the older coins still bore the mark of their issuing House or trading-concern pact; if nothing else, it might point them to Toombs's mystery backer.

Stokes narrowed his eyes. "On me? No. But I can procure one if you'll turn around."

Mikani looked over at Ritsuko and shrugged before turning away from the moneylender. Thumps and clangs sounded behind, probably from a hidden safe. His partner was visibly chewing on some theory; she had that thinking expression.

But before he could ask, Stokes said, "Here you are. You can keep it. And your time's up, I believe."

OUTSIDE, RITSUKO STUDIED the coin in the daylight. Stokes had been right about its being old; the silver was dull, the engraving worn. *Hard to make out what it's supposed to be.* The metal looked more like pewter, but if the moneylender had accepted these coins to clear the debt, they must be valuable. But as she traced the faint pattern, her pulse quickened in excitement.

"Mikani, come feel this!"

"That's . . . quite the offer, partner." He smirked and stepped closer.

Ignoring that, she grabbed his hand and pressed his fingers to the etching. She wondered if he would recognize the pattern. The antlers were what caught her attention, so she waited until he reached the top of the coin. He traced the shape again, his brow furrowed.

"Well?" she demanded.

"That's . . . oh. A stag's head." He frowned, hesitating. "The button?"

She bounced, then climbed into the cruiser, as the atmosphere in the narrow street wasn't such that she was inclined to linger. Inside, she didn't lean back, as the cuts still stung. Before work, it had taken the better part of an hour for the doctor to check each one to make sure no slivers of metal lingered beneath her skin to get infected.

"Exactly. So if the button belonged to Toombs, how did he end up with old coins that match the emblem on it?"

He slid into the driver's seat. "How did he get *any* coins, would be my question. If Stokes didn't lend him the money, there's someone else backing him. And I find it hard to believe that they'd be unaware of what he's doing with the money." He tapped his fingers on the wheel for a few seconds. "Or . . . he found a hidden treasure."

Ritsuko scowled as he started the vehicle. "It makes no sense that someone would pay him for this. I mean, who benefits from Miss Aevar's death? Or Miss Bihár's."

"Anarchists? I don't know. Cira's death got at least one of the Houses riled up, then Electra's murder nearly sparked a riot."

"Do you think the girls were targeted because of who they were? Wedges, if you will, to be used against social order?"

Mikani spoke carefully, seeming to weigh his words even as he dodged through traffic and makeshift blockades. "The Aevars aren't so powerful that they're unassailable. Cira had a single bodyguard, who stayed at a distance, instead of a cadre of armed guards like other Houses. Which made her an easier target than, say, a Magnus girl. And there were those who knew of Electra's family ties to the Summer Clan. Both girls were isolated from their usual support and protection."

"I was just thinking about that in Stokes's office. You couldn't discern any details about the third victim, but maybe she's . . . important but somewhat invisible, like the first two." *Did that make sense?* "A girl whose death would really rock the city in some fashion, concluding the trifecta of unthinkable chaos."

Mikani nodded. "They have the Houses scared and the Summer Clan up in arms. What would push the city over the edge? Some councilor's daughter, niece, mistress?"

"I don't know," Ritsuko said, frustrated. "But we've confirmed there's a magical connection. Mikani, you met some of the rabble-rousers. Do you think they're capable of this? Do they have the resources?"

His jaw clenched as he seemed to mull the question. "They may have the means, as far as manpower and tricks, yes. But from what I saw? I don't think they could scrounge up the coin. If they're helping Toombs, they both have a benefactor."

"Or they stole the money." Sometimes, the simplest answers also made the most sense.

"So where would you go to steal a few hundred ancient coins?"

She thought for a few seconds, then offered, "From one of the Houses? Should we check the incident reports to see if anyone's reported a missing collection?"

Mikani grinned. "A good idea. And if we can find the right records, they should tell us what House they might have belonged to. We were looking for buttons, not coins or House crests."

"To the archives first?" She slid a look at him through her lashes.

To her surprise, he was looking at her as much as the road, his gaze hooded. But his tone was light. "See? I do take you nice places."

"You were the one complaining about that, not me."

"I'm a sensitive soul."

She laughed. "Just drive, Mikani."

He actually listened. In short order, they reached the archives. The afternoon light glistened off the white stone, lending it a dazzling aspect. As usual, he ignored all posted parking regulations and left the cruiser as close as possible without actually driving up the steps. Mikani grumbled as he came along behind her, but once they were inside, he applied himself to the work with a tenacity that impressed her. Two hours later, she tapped the page, beckoning him over.

"Look," she whispered.

He came over and bent across her shoulder, presumably for a better view. *Did he always smell like cloves?* "So it's definitely Old Ferisher. Looks like . . . from one of the defunct Houses?"

"We have a name now, at least. We should head to the Academy to see if we can link them to a surviving House." She pushed to her feet.

"And that'll point us to the source of the coins. Good call."

They gathered their coats and left, pausing to button up against the evening chill. Outside, workers emerged from nearby buildings, carrying their briefcases, hats clutched to keep them from the wind. The steps were mostly empty, so Ritsuko hurried toward the cruiser. In her haste, she didn't see the nick in the step, and she stumbled, dropping her bag. With a muttered curse, she knelt to pick it up—and a bullet slammed into the ground a few feet in front of her.

She didn't panic, though she heard Mikani swearing. The crowd on the walk below reacted at first as if it were fireworks, but then someone shouted, "Gun!" and they scattered like billiard balls. Women ran, their skirts billowing to reveal ankles and the lace on their petticoats, too frightened to fret about dignity.

"More than one," a businessman called.

"Cover," she got out, scrambling on hands and knees toward a column to the right. "Can you tell where . . . ?"

"Somewhere to the left, near the underground entrance, I think. Hard to tell with the screaming." Mikani ran for the cruiser, dodging the shots that chipped the pavement just inches in front of his feet. Then he crouched against the back end of the vehicle, pistol in hand. "I—" He ducked as another couple of shots ricocheted off the cruiser and column. "Two shooters at least."

She drew her weapon and peered around the stone pillar. The people on the street made it difficult to find her targets, but they didn't prevent the gunmen from firing. A woman in a House servant's uniform went down, fleeing toward the archive, a red stain blossoming on her back. Another round slammed into the column, too close for comfort. Ritsuko couldn't even tell where to fire back.

"Ideas, partner? They don't seem to care how many they take with them."

Mikani called back, "Constables will be out in force, along with any House Guards soon. But not soon enough."

"I'm pushing toward the underground station."

"I'll cover you." He shifted his weight to the balls of his feet. "On three. Three." He rose to fire over the cruiser, the bullets striking the ground in a cascade of sparks.

Speaking her intention was easier than doing it, but she mustered her courage and rolled. It hurt tumbling down toward the cruiser, probably opening the cuts on her back. Once she made it down there, amid a smattering of fire, she caught her breath and grinned at Mikani, who seemed torn between appreciation and concern.

"Ready to do it again?" she asked.

Ritsuko waited for his signal, then, keeping low, she ran toward a bench and curled up behind it while Mikani saturated the area with rapid fire. *Twenty feet closer.* From this vantage, she saw three men, but their crouched position in the underground stairwell made it impossible for her to tell anything about them. And it would take a miracle to hit any of them from this angle. *I need to get closer.* A cacophony of whistles rang out in the distance, the signal that multiple constabulary cruisers were approaching.

At least the immediate area's clear. If we can keep them pinned—

But the gunmen apparently knew what was coming as well; they ducked down the stairs leading to the underground. Ritsuko pushed upright and went after them at a full sprint, and she heard Mikani coming at her back, but by the time they got to the bottom, the three were aboard a departing train.

She screamed, both hands clenched in pure frustration. For good measure, she kicked a rubbish bin three times. Four. Five. It didn't help. *Might as well lose my temper properly.* She hurled her attaché case at the station wall. Watched it bounce. "Not. Again."

Mikani cupped her shoulder. "Easy. We might catch them at the next station if we bully through some roadblocks." But he didn't sound convinced.

Before she could answer, a constable ran up, flushed and panting. "Inspectors . . . sirs! Gregory Toombs. At the Port Authority, they've got him!"

CHAPTER 22

THE PORT AUTHORITY TOWERED FIVE STORIES HIGH, PLUS AS many belowground. A truncated pyramid, glittering beacons transformed the building into a collage of lights. Beyond the high wall that stretched several blocks to either side, the top decks and bridges of docked ships swayed with the tide. As with so many other buildings in the city, the port was crowded and understaffed twenty-four hours a day, every day of the year.

Mikani nodded, conscious of a rush of anticipation. "I'm looking forward to this."

"I promised to keep you from killing Toombs," Ritsuko reminded him.

He cut her a look.

People trying to leave the beleaguered city for the Winter Isle stood, sat, or camped throughout the complex. In places, Mikani had to push through the throng to reach the stairwell, and it was endless flights down from there. Finally, the two arrived at the security office. The guard on duty wasn't a constable; he worked for the port, but they had saturated Dorstaad with sketches of Gregory Toombs.

It's about time we caught a break.

The officer was young, early twenties, but he seemed sharp enough. "Inspectors. Welcome to the port. The prisoner is this way."

No small talk. Good man. Mikani followed, relieved. He guessed Toombs had gotten worried as the net tightened from all quarters. With such a high reward posted and the Summer Clan blocking the roads, he must've felt the sea offered his only hope of escape. *Finally, we'll get some answers.* Ritsuko walked alongside him, still clearly aggravated by their failure at the tube station.

Never saw her lose her temper before. That was . . . interesting.

The PA officer slipped his key through the lock, then accepted their credentials as sufficient proof of their right to assume custody of the prisoner. "Have a pleasant evening, Inspectors."

As the guard disappeared around the corner, Mikani stepped into the cell. The man perched on the edge of the cot scrambled toward the wall. Toombs looked like hell. His dark eyes were ringed with bruises, sunken in a skeletal face, and his mouth seemed too large for the rest of his features. At some point he'd shaved his head and grown a beard; putty clung to his sharp nose, probably the remnants of an attempted disguise.

"Mr. Toombs." Mikani pinned him with a cold look. "Let me warn you that we've had a frustrating week. So if you lie to me, I'll break something. Every time you lie, every time you clam up, I break something else."

The actor flinched.

"I'm sure Mr. Toombs knows that his only hope of avoiding House Aevar and the Summer Clan's full reprisal rests in complete cooperation."

"True. A recommendation from us might land him on the penal farms instead." *Like hell.* This man would pay for what he'd done; and Mikani wouldn't rest until Toombs danced on the end of a rope or worse. It was too bad Ritsuko had offered a carrot instead because he wanted to use the stick.

Toombs exhaled, turning his face up as if for guidance. But Mikani suspected it was more that he didn't want to meet their gazes while he told his story. He was a shell of a man, but apparently he was still capable of shame.

"This fellow approached me . . . said he was an astronomer. He knew I used to be an engineer before the acting bug bit me." Toombs shrugged, indicating his ravaged face. "Women told me

I was so good-looking, I ought to be onstage, and I started believing them. Well. *Before*, anyway."

"Tell us the rest," Mikani growled.

"He was . . . there was something irresistible about him. I needed the work . . . it's not healthy to owe Mr. Stokes. But it was more, too. I found myself at emporiums and foundries, buying supplies without remembering the decision to go. And when I considered quitting, I couldn't . . ." He trailed off, seeming frustrated.

"Do you think he had Ferisher blood?" Ritsuko asked. She was taking notes. "Could this alleged compulsion have come as a result of a glamour?"

Right. It's not your fault at all, none of it. A wizard made you do it.

But despite himself, Mikani released some of his control to learn the man's state of mind. The room swam with his visceral terror and the ashen taste of exhaustion. Digging deeper, Mikani caught glimmers of self-loathing—*Wait. How am I . . .* He frowned, opening more of his senses. And recoiled with a gasp, disguised as a cough.

"Maybe," Toombs said miserably. "I hated him, but I obeyed him. And later, I was afraid. The things he said he'd do to me, those he *did*—"

"So you claim you were working under duress?" Mikani pinched the bridge of his nose to stem the throbbing at his temples.

"I'm a craftsman, not a killer. After the first device, I tried to run. I hid. But he always finds me. *Always*." The man's eyes darkened with terror.

"When did you construct the last machine?" Ritsuko asked.

"We finished early yesterday. I *swear* I didn't know what he intended to do with those. I thought they were strange, but it wasn't until you people found the first body—"

"That you realized what you'd gotten into," she finished.

Mikani didn't offer sympathy. "Where did you take the device?"

If they could get the site out of this pathetic waste of skin, they could set an ambush for the mystery man. *Maybe it's not too late to save her.*

"We parted ways at the city limits," Toombs said. "He didn't trust me."

"You claim you don't know where the third murder will occur."
Ritsuko made a note. Her expression looked hard, vicious even.

Mikani stood, out of patience. "Let's transfer him to Central.
We have the facilities for a lengthy interrogation."

"But I already told you everything!" Toombs protested.

Ritsuko smiled, and it was actually a little scary. "Be prepared
to spend *hours* going over your story with us. We'll also require
you to work with a CID artist to create a sketch of the man you
claim hired you to build these machines."

"On your feet," Mikani demanded.

He didn't wait for Toombs to respond, merely reached down
and jerked him upright; he wrenched the suspect around and
shackled his wrists. The actor was light for a man of his height,
all rib cage and jutting elbows. His poor physical condition supported his claim that he'd been compelled to help with the last two
machines, perhaps even held prisoner. That evidence didn't keep
Mikani from shoving Toombs toward the door. Ritsuko's steps
fell lightly behind him as they climbed toward the main level.

The crowd hadn't thinned when they emerged from the security doors. If anything, it seemed worse now that they had the
prisoner in custody. As Mikani paused to survey the area, a bullet
slammed into the actor's throat. The man tried to scream, chok-
ing on his own blood. *Hells and Winter.* It spattered Mikani as
Toombs fell against the wall, his downward slide leaving streaks.
The crowd reacted with pure panic, and soon, the area was a
disaster zone, with people running and screaming.

"Get down!" he shouted, hoping some of them had the sense
to listen. He vaulted over the fallen Toombs, pushing the nearest
bystanders to the ground and out of the line of fire.

Ritsuko dove toward the nearest man, catching the shooter
around the ankle. She landed hard, but her momentum brought
him down as well. As she rose to hands and knees, the killer
braced and twisted, kicking at her face. He connected, but she
didn't fall back. Finding her feet in a move she hadn't learned in
CID training, she feinted with her left hand and went for his eyes
with her right, finishing with a shattering kick to his left kneecap,
the one he'd fallen on the first time. Her kick connected; Mikani
heard the snap of bone as her weight followed through.

Mikani fired a few rounds at the other attackers, holding them

at bay while aiming high. *Wish these people would get the bloody
hell out of the way, already.* Passengers and staff blocked clear
lines of sight for both sides as they scrambled for the exits.

Ritsuko brought her gun up, leveling it. "If you move, I'll
shoot you."

The bastard lunged, and she fired. Her bullet plowed into his
chest, stopped him cold, but more rounds spattered the wall and
ground around them. Mikani slid behind a rubbish bin and
searched for the source. After a few seconds, he spotted them
fifteen feet or so away, now that the crowd had thinned.

"It's the gunmen from the archives," he called to Ritsuko.

"Seems logical. But are they after us or Toombs?"

"Both?" he suggested. "Let me ask them."

"I'll cover you." After rolling behind a kiosk, she laid down
fire to clear a path.

Determined the other two wouldn't get away again, he rushed
them, using columns and benches for cover. Bullets pinged the
floor, then they paused. *Reloading. Good. I have a few seconds.*
Ritsuko entertained the third man with an exchange of fire.
Mikani burst out of cover and sprinted at the second shooter; he
didn't try to slow his momentum and just slammed into the man.
The would-be assassin's pistol went flying. Mikani opened with
a ferocious right cross, followed by a left hook. The two hits put
the suspect on the ground.

He came up with the gun and cocked it. "Who sent you?"

But before Mikani could shoot him when he refused to
answer, the man's associate did. Then the third one wheeled to
run, as if he had any hope of escaping with Port Authority officers converging on him. Mikani had a clear shot, so he took it;
the gun roared, and the bullet pierced the man's spine as he
reached the foot of the stairs that led up to the street.

He holstered his weapon, moved past Ritsuko, who settled
on a bench nearby, and kicked the body none too gently in the
ribs. When the man didn't move, he turned to her, taking in her
bruised cheek.

"You look like hell. Worse, you look like *me*. But your dance
partner got the worse end of the deal." He sat next to her, staring
at the body nearby. *Getting shot at's a pain in the arse.*

"He chose to die," she said quietly. "Rather than be taken."

Mikani had no explanation. The implications were chilling. He gestured at the corpse where port security was clustered. "And *he* killed one of his own."

She looked pale, and he had the ridiculous desire to reassure her, to say everything would be fine—that there were no secrets or anarchist plots. But the truth was, the situation had just gotten even more complicated. Their only link to the mastermind was now spattered on the wall; they'd have to be clever to find Toombs's employer from what the actor had told them.

"There will be hell to pay," she mumbled. "I can't wait for the dressing-down."

"We tried to bring them in for questioning, but they wouldn't come along peacefully. I don't see how Gunwood can blame *us*."

"That's never stopped him before," she said gloomily.

"Come on, partner. There are forms to fill out and questions to answer." He flashed her a wry smile as he pushed to his feet. "And you know how I love paperwork."

RITSUKO PRESSED ICE bundled in a thin cloth to her swollen cheek. It had been an hour since the guns fell quiet and the Port Authority security detail cordoned off the area, keeping curious spectators away from the bodies. Journalists from the newssheets would be here soon, poking around, sketching the scene, and asking inconvenient questions. *Inconvenient because we don't have the answers.* It made no sense someone would've contracted such a monstrous task.

Maybe he was lying. There is *no second man.* It was the kind of thing that criminals said to lessen their sentences. *Happens all the time.* Sometimes they blamed Ferisher spirits for whispering wicked ideas into their ears as they slept. She wished she could dismiss the actor's claims, but there had been just enough proof to support his story.

More to the point, she felt shaky deep inside. Her hands lay clenched on her knees to hide the tremors. More than one constable had clapped her shoulder in the past fifty minutes, others from the Port Authority. They all thought she'd done something to be celebrated—put a bullet in a bad man, dropped him like a dog.

I killed someone today, Grandfather.

She pictured his disapproving face, his voice whispering in her ear. *The dead are with you, always, Celeste. His ghost will never let you rest.*

Mikani didn't seem to be frozen in the same way. At the moment, he was talking to the chief of security, completing the official inquiry. The Port Authority had reports to file as to exactly what had happened. Going forward, the Council would probably request armed constables on the premises. From time to time, inquiries came her way, and she just nodded at whatever Mikani said. She didn't hear the words anyway; they were blocked out by the sharp report of the gun echoing in her ears. Though she was glad she hadn't panicked, after she shot the first suspect, it was all reflex and training. Because Ritsuko had been killing the same man in her head for the last hour.

His face. His eyes.

She clamped down on the nausea and tried to stop thinking about how it looked when a person died. *You can actually see the moment when the mind slips away.* Clenching her jaw, she set the damp towel on the bench beside her.

Silently, Mikani came over, offered her a mug, steaming and sweet-smelling. She stirred, then shook her head. "No thank you. Are we finished here?"

He nodded and sipped the tea with a shrug, making a face. "Unless you want to help with the reports, we're done."

"I'd prefer to get back to Central."

To get away from this place and all those bodies.

"The sooner we talk to Gunwood, the better, probably."

He set the cup aside and led the way to the exit. Constables, the usual morbid onlookers, and journalists formed an inchoate mess right outside. Mikani shoved a path to the cruiser; and Ritsuko appreciated his willingness to do it, so she didn't have to. She followed in the channel he cleared and crawled into the passenger side after he unlocked the doors. The vehicle jerked into motion, forcing the crowd to give away. For a few seconds, Mikani was quiet, focused on getting them out of the area without running down any pedestrians.

"That was your first shooting."

"Yes." The movement of the vehicle didn't make her feel worse, at least. There was comfort in driving away.

He made a soft sound of acknowledgment. "You know it was

you or him. It had to be done. And . . . that doesn't make it any easier." He glanced over at her, briefly, then returned his attention to the road. "You can, what, hear him? See him, still?"

Startled, she asked, "Is that what it was like for you, the first time?"

I've never asked him how many . . . or when. Mikani had more time on the street than she did by far. The years she'd spent filing and working down in the Dungeon as a lab tech, he had been an inspector. *Which is a lot more opportunities to shoot people.*

"The first time. The second time. This last time." He looked uncomfortable. "I'm sorry, partner, but it doesn't get any easier. What helps me is focusing on the people that I save." He paused, chewing his bottom lip. "You've been to my cottage. You saw the religious medallions, cameos. Knickknacks."

"I did," she agreed, not understanding what he meant.

"Some belonged to victims, those I couldn't help. Their families sent things as a way of thanking me for finding their killers. Others came from the people I *did* save, as gifts. I cherish those most."

She took a deep, gulping breath, hanging together by a thread. "I really need you to pull over now."

He swerved against the curb, startling a couple of scavenging urchins. As soon as the cruiser stopped and he engaged the brake, she came up on her knees. Ritsuko felt sure he expected her to bang open the door and cast accounts into the gutter. But she needed something else entirely, and she felt too awful to care if it was appropriate. So instead she crawled over the cruiser's hand brake and into his lap.

He shifted, then wrapped his arms around her. In response, she wound hers about his neck and buried her face in his chest. She couldn't cry, but his warmth was what she needed, something to push back the cold. Shivers ran through her for long moments as she listened to his heartbeat, steady, soothing.

"Don't take this the wrong way," she eventually mumbled.

"You're no fun."

She pushed out a shaky laugh and pulled back, retreating to her seat with as much dignity as she could muster. "That never happened. I'm well enough now. We can go."

Mikani gave her a long, appraising look. As he turned his attention to getting them out of there, he said, "Larceny and thews. At least I know why you stay with me."

You have no idea at all.

Half an hour later, they entered the duty room to deafening
cheers. More boisterous yells followed and the clamor of con-
gratulations. Men toasted each other, and they raised glasses to
Ritsuko and Mikani. From the smell, it wasn't tea, either.

She cut a look at her partner, wondering aloud, "What's this?"

He looked around, ignoring the calls directed at them. "I don't
know. Let's ask Gunwood."

Ritsuko dodged around men determined to whack her on the
back, those who had never bothered to speak to her before—
except to ask for a sandwich or a hot beverage. The commander's
office was quieter, at least, but Gunwood's nose had the red shine
of someone who had been drinking, too. His eyes sparkled when
he spotted her in his doorway.

"Come in, you two. I don't remember being happier than I
am now. Well done!"

Mikani stepped in, taking his usual stance in the corner.
"While I'm glad you've finally come to appreciate our genius,
Gunwood, care to fill us in on what the hells is going on?"

"Toombs is dead. The Summer Clan are calling off the
blockades. Aevar is, of course, arguing that he needn't pay the
reward, as Toombs was killed before being formally judged and
charged." The commander reached for a document that bore his
stamp and signature, offering it to Ritsuko. "If you two will sign
this, I intend to recommend you both to the Council for
commendation."

"Gunwood . . . Commander. It's not over. Toombs wasn't
working alone." Mikani unfolded his arms and stepped forward,
looking to Ritsuko for support.

She offered, "He *said* he wasn't. But criminals will say anything. Do we have evidence to validate his claims?" She considered the button and the coins, but wasn't certain if they
constituted indisputable proof.

Mikani frowned, then closed the door. Gunwood sat up
straighter, his joy fading to the more usual *what have you done
now* expression he wore around them.

"Someone sent those men after us, and Toombs. He was trying to flee the city . . . he didn't hire his own assassins. And you
saw him, Ritsuko—there's no way he could've moved those
things on his own, disassembled or not."

She nodded at that. "True. He was in bad shape. Thin, starved even. Did you notice the ligature marks on his wrists?"

Gunwood interrupted, coming to his feet. "He probably hired the thugs to help him move the machines. They killed him when they feared he'd hand them over, too." There was doubt in his eyes, though. "Or maybe he didn't pay them, as promised."

"That doesn't explain why they chose death over incarceration," she noted.

She had a bad feeling that worsened with every inconsistency Mikani pointed out. The men in the duty room seemed to think they had cracked the case, put the maniac down in a glorious gun battle. But she feared there was more to come, between what Toombs had told them, the suicide squad, and the unexplained clues.

"Some of the penal farms are quite nice." Mikani shrugged at Gunwood's glare. "You must admit the pieces don't add up, Commander. And we still have no idea where Toombs got the money to pay for everything."

"Plus the coins that paid his debts," Ritsuko added.

Gunwood leaned on his desk, his jaw clenched. "You two can't let me have even one good day, can you?" He eased back into his seat, rubbing his jaw, and was silent for a full minute, breathing deeply. When he put his hands down, he gave them both long, searching looks. "I hope to hell you're wrong. But if you're not, well. We can't tell the Summer Clan and Houses that Toombs wasn't working alone. Or there will be more riots, or worse. Pursue this quietly. And for gods' sake, do it quickly."

Ritsuko knew that tone and headed for the door. "Yes, sir."

Mikani followed close behind, uncharacteristically quiet. She cut through the celebration in the duty room with murmured apologies, and breathed easier when she got into the lift. As soon as the cage lurched into motion, Mikani touched her shoulder.

"I couldn't tell Gunwood." He rubbed his temples, as if one of his migraines was setting in. "But when we first got to Toombs, I read him, Ritsuko." He met her worried gaze. "The man was scared, tired. And there was something more . . . that cold, dead feeling? It coiled around his mind like a snake, but . . . it wasn't *him*."

CHAPTER 23

THE BUTTON RITSUKO HAD FOUND AT THE CRIME SCENE WAS A vital clue, and Mikani figured it was time they followed up on it. A history professor might shed some light on its provenance and point them in the right direction, so they'd come to the Academy in search of an expert opinion.

Mikani hadn't been back here since his abrupt departure more than fifteen years ago. He didn't regret searching for his father, but he *did* regret not completing his studies. According to his mother, if he had, he might be a gentleman now, and not a ruffian who made his living by getting into fights with criminals.

She's not far off, some days.

Glancing around, he said, "This is more your field of expertise, partner."

"I don't know why you'd say that. I never attended here."

The buildings hadn't changed, just become more weathered. He thought he recognized a couple of professors ambling around the covered walkways. *But these kids look so bloody young. And carefree. You wouldn't think the city was on the verge of starving or burning a few days ago.*

"You have a natural affinity for academia. And you were last here a few days ago. Which way?" He turned toward her with a grin that hid his inner turmoil.

When he looked at Ritsuko, it was hard not to think about how she'd felt in his arms or the smell of camellias in her hair when she tucked her head against him. As he remembered, he got a twinge in his chest. *I liked being the one who could make things better for her.* Mikani didn't know exactly what that meant.

"The history department is over here." She held a map of the campus, indicating a shady path that wound through the quad.

Students aimed curious looks in their direction from time to time; Mikani guessed they didn't resemble the typical enrollment. It was a quick walk to the desired building: gray stone, classical architecture, multiple floors and exits. He led the way into the darkened atrium, pausing to let his eyes adjust to the gloom. Shelves full of books and sculptures crowded the walls and covered most of the windows. It felt more like the library, down to the dusty smell of old tomes. Small tables were scattered around a central space, mostly empty at this hour. It took him a few seconds to realize that the spindly figure looking in their direction wasn't part of the décor.

Seems history's not in vogue this term.

"Good morning, Professor. I wonder if we could ask a few minutes of your time."

"Certainly. I don't have class or office hours at the moment." The man shuffled toward them with steps so pained that Mikani wondered if he wasn't years past retirement.

Ritsuko moved to one of the vacant tables and set out her interview accoutrements: pen, notebook, and the research they had done at the archives related to the coins and button. This morning, her suit was immaculate, despite the fresh bruise on her cheek. He ran a hand over his own jaw, stubbled and still sore from the last few days.

I swear she has a team of house sprites to help her tidy up every morning. Probably pack her bag, too.

"I'm Inspector Ritsuko." She tilted her head. "My partner, Mikani. If you'd care to join us, we could use your expertise."

"Inspectors, are you? That's fascinating. I can't imagine what help I could be." But the professor toddled to the table nonetheless, apparently eager to be of service.

Mikani leaned against the nearest shelves while the professor leaned in close to his partner, scanned her work, then praised her research. They conversed quietly, so he looked around the room. He'd never been to the history wing before; it was across campus from his old haunts in mathematics and accounting. He wondered, idly, if his old desk still bore the marks of his wandering attention during long lectures, then glanced over when Ritsuko and the professor straightened from their task.

"Got something?"

"Professor Tarrant has translated the Old Ferisher. It's a House motto, Mikani."

He raised a brow. "What does it mean, then?"

Professor Tarrant replied, " 'Under this sign, we shall conquer.' It belonged to an old House, which lapsed, oh, four hundred years ago. There was a bloody war of succession, as I understand it, and their line never recovered. I don't believe there are any Nualls left."

Mikani pointed out, "Their coin's still around. If they're gone, who might have access to their treasury? Or their estate?"

Four hundred years is a hell of a gap to try to find paperwork.

Tarrant seemed astonished. "Their currency is back in circulation after all this time? I can't imagine where it might've come from."

A frown creased Ritsuko's brows, and Mikani knew exactly how she felt. "This doesn't make sense. Do you have any records or documents that discuss the holdings that were divided when the family name lapsed into disuse? Or who might have inherited any property left?"

Mikani suspected he knew what she was driving at. Wealth such as the Houses accrued didn't simply vanish. The challenge lay in locating whoever inherited it, found it, or stole it, though. It wasn't typical CID work.

"Yes," the professor said. "There are ledgers and historical sales records in the archive downstairs, mostly filed away for posterity. People don't tend to care how much a nobleman paid for a silk carpet three hundred years ago."

Mikani suppressed a grimace and smiled at the professor. "Oh, we live for old ledgers. Fascinated by the minutiae of people long since turned to dust, especially my partner here. Which way to the cellar?"

Lifting her hand, Ritsuko muffled a chuckle. "Thanks for your time, Professor."

After two hours of digging through old scrolls and leather tomes, Mikani paused to stretch. He glared at the rows of stacked papers and documents, trying to intimidate them into giving up any useful information that they might be hiding. *Hells and Winter, I've spent more time among books the past two weeks than in the last two years.*

"It's a valiant effort, but I don't think the documents find you frightening."

"They should. I have the power to burn them all."

"And then we'll get arrested for destroying valuable city property."

"I'd charge them with obstructing an investigation." He groaned, aiming an imploring look her way. "Tell me you found something. Anything, to get us out of here."

Her eyes twinkled at him. "I discovered a woman can be traded for two goats, a laying hen, and a wheel of cheese."

Mikani eyed her, speculative. "I'm sure I could get at least three goats for you. Think Rudo's still accepting offers?"

"Please. I'm worth at least four goats and an ox."

"I don't know. Do you cook?" He smirked.

"Not much, but I'm an immaculate housekeeper and amenable to meeting a gentleman's every other need."

Every other?

"I'm telling you, I'm a bad influence." He let out a mock sigh. *I missed the banter. But I miss the blue sky more, though.*

"I was meeting certain needs before I encountered you, Mikani. You give yourself too much credit. And perhaps it's slipped your notice, but . . . women have needs, too." The oblique words came with a teasing grin.

"My inflated sense of self-worth's part of my charm. The other part's my adamant devotion to—" He frowned, staring over her shoulder. "We need birth records, not accounting ledgers. If we can find out where the Nualls lived, we'll have a place to start."

She sighed. "I'll see what I can do." He watched as she went to the shelves and rummaged, running her fingers along the spines to find the book they needed. "Here."

The book looked enormous in her arms as Ritsuko carried it

back to the table. It appeared to be some master log of all the births recorded in noble families, going back centuries. Mikani couldn't imagine how boring that job must've been. Ritsuko flipped through, which took another fifteen minutes, and he finally sat down beside her. Eventually, she tapped a page.

"This is the strangest thing, Mikani." He stepped closer to peer over her shoulder at the faded scribbles on the yellowed paper. "The last entry I can find for the Nualls is over six hundred years old."

He shook his head. "Didn't the professor—"

"Said they died out four hundred years ago, yes. There may be records missing; but here. Look." She touched the page again, so he looked closer. *I can barely make out the writing. Would it kill them to put more lamps down here?* He was getting restless; he had hoped for a solid lead from their trip to the Academy.

He couldn't read the old tongue, but he discerned the numbers and what looked like names. "Ah. Three hundred and . . . ninety-four?"

"That's the old reckoning. Roughly the year fourteen hundred by the reformed calendar."

He arched a brow and kept reading. "Keenan . . . Keenan Nuall, Feid o'Nuall. Three hundred and sixty, Keenan Nuall and Gairdh o'Nuall." He shook his head. "I can't make out half of it, partner. What . . . ?"

"Read the last entry."

What the hells has her so excited?

He bent closer once more. "Three hundred and three, two born in the same year. Must be twins. Lorne and Theron—" He paused and met his partner's eyes. "Why does that sound familiar?"

"That's the name of the man Miss Wright followed a few nights ago. Someone who easily took out four thugs, hand to hand. Tore them to pieces."

"And who seemed to step right out of the old stories, from her description." *Damned be. We're chasing a seven-century-old bogeyman.*

She nodded and set the book back. "We have directions to Mr. Nuall's home, from Miss Wright's statement. And it happens to be in the same general area where the ledgers place the old Nuall estate."

He let out a long breath and motioned for her to lead the way back up. "Let's hunt up a ghost, partner."

THE ESTATE WAS . . . eerie. From the records they'd found, Ritsuko expected a ruin, though Miss Wright hadn't given much detail on what the place looked like. But it was beautiful, if oddly out of step with the city a couple of hours distant. They had left the main trade route half an hour before.

In a strict sense, CID cruisers weren't meant for long-distance, nor were inspectors supposed to take them so far outside the city limits, but when they were so close to figuring things out, it made no sense to cavil over trifling rules. Mikani had been confident he could find the place, between Miss Wright's account and the records they'd unearthed at the Academy—and here they were. Her nerves prickled as they slid out of the vehicle.

"What do you think?" she asked.

A frown between his brows, her partner looked around. Then he pinched the bridge of his nose before answering. "Lovely view. Can't say I care for the ambiance, though. There's something odd about this place . . . Let's take a look around?"

From his expression, she could tell something was bothering him, but he seemed unwilling to explain it just yet. It was difficult to act as if nothing had happened around him, as if she hadn't crawled into his lap and demanded comfort like a child. So far, he hadn't made a joke of her vulnerability, but she didn't know how she'd respond if he did.

Banishing such worries, she raised the knocker on the gate and slammed it down four times in quick succession. *Mr. Nuall must have money if he retained possession of the family estate. But how strange that his family's been reported defunct.* Eventually, she heard movement within.

A servant opened the gate, clad in old-fashioned livery. He raised his brows.

She stepped forward. "We have a few questions for your employer, Theron Nuall. I'm Inspector Ritsuko. This is my partner, Mikani. May we come in?"

The man looked at each of them briefly. With a nod, he stepped back, ushering them in with a gesture. Mikani tilted his head at him in what she took to be a speculative fashion, then shrugged and motioned for her to lead the way. Still no words from the man as he led them through the front gate and toward the villa, which was . . . breathtaking.

She had never seen anything so lovely or archaic. It sprawled across the land as if it had a perfect right, and the grounds were beautifully landscaped with emerald hedges and feathered fronds that nuzzled up against the stone walk. In Dorstaad, buildings were closer together, and most private gardens were bits of green-ery tucked behind high walls. The air felt warmer and softer, too, as if they'd stepped through more than a garden gate. Above, the sun shone a little brighter, dazzling compared to the city. More telling, flowers bloomed, ones for which she had no name, in colors lush and luxurious. Ritsuko didn't see the servant go. One minute she was following him; the next, she glanced away to admire the garden, and he wasn't there anymore.

Ritsuko studied Mikani, walking beside her. "I hope you have a theory."

He wore a puzzled expression. "I have several, but they all sound like fairy tales. This whole place just . . . sings."

"What does it sound like?" she asked, curious.

"It's a low hum, but there's an ebb and flow to it. Like the wind through a forest . . . only there's no wind, and no trees in here. Or a wet finger on crystal—"

Their quarry, Theron Nuall, emerged from the main house before he could finish his thought. Nuall wore a grim expression, probably more dire than their visit warranted. *It's not as if we came to arrest him. Yet.*

"What is the meaning of this . . . intrusion?" he demanded.

No invitation to enter the premises, no hospitality. It defi-nitely sets the tone.

Mikani's abstraction told her all she needed to know, so she answered for both of them. "As we told your servant, we're with the CID. We have a number of questions for you, regarding mul-tiple murders in Dorstaad."

"And I have no time for your city, Inspector. Or your ques-tions." He made a dismissive gesture with a long-fingered hand.

"Right now it's only an interview," Ritsuko said, "but if you give me reason, I'd love to haul you in for refusing to cooperate."

Theron seemed taken aback. Then he laughed. "You . . . *threaten* me?"

"She's warning you." Mikani finally spoke. He sounded strained, but he stepped up beside her, his walking stick braced under an arm. "Really, though, wouldn't you rather get rid of us quickly?"

The suspect's face darkened ominously. "I would rather plant you in my garden."

Mikani's brows rose, and he stepped closer to the other man. "And I'd rather—" He stopped, let out a long breath. "Just answer the bloody questions. We have an eyewitness report linking you to four murders and evidence tying you to a couple more. So unless you give answers, we'll call a horde of less courteous friends to trample your garden while asking you the exact same questions in much louder voices."

Mr. Nuall's face froze. Something shifted in his dark gaze— then froze. His demeanor changed in a way Ritsuko didn't like or trust. "I . . . see. Those are serious charges. It would, indeed, be best for all concerned if I cooperate. Come with me."

He wheeled abruptly and led them around the corner to a pretty park at the side of the house. There was a wrought-iron bench with matching table and chairs. The verdant plant life was an intoxicant—such a mixture of scents and colors.

Mr. Nuall gestured. "Please, make yourselves comfortable. I'll endeavor to address your concerns."

She chose the bench, facing him. Mikani sat beside her, walking stick across his knees. *There are no insects. How can a garden like this exist without them?* The whole time she had been within these walls, she hadn't seen a fly or watched a bee buzz around a flower. *I wonder if Mikani's noticed.* But it wasn't the time to ask.

"Sir, a witness placed you in the Patchwork District on the night of a disturbance. Furthermore, it has been reported that you're responsible for the death of four men." Ritsuko checked her notebook and read off the date and approximate time. "Follow-up investigation revealed that four bodies were discovered in the street, early the next morning. Urchins notified the local constabulary. It has since fallen to us to determine the facts in this matter. Where *were* you that evening, and is there anyone who can substantiate your statement?"

"I was attending some business near the Patchwork District,

yes. After concluding it, I came home. My man will vouch for that."

Mikani raised a brow. "Can anyone vouch for you who isn't in your employ?"

She stifled a smile. *That's fairly polite; a nice way to state servants can be bought.*

"I keep my dealings with outsiders to a minimum."

"So you deny that you had anything to do with those four deaths?" Ritsuko asked.

Mr. Nuall offered a thin, cold smile. "People allege many things for many reasons. Jealousy. Envy. Ambition. If you had evidence to support my involvement, you wouldn't be *questioning* me, would you, Inspectors?"

Time to wrap this up before he kicks us out.

"What can you tell us about these coins?" She produced a sketch, both front and back, that showed the stag's head and the family motto.

For the first time since they'd settled in the park, she detected genuine surprise. She peeked at Mikani to see if he'd noticed, too, but he had his eyes closed. Lines of pain framed his mouth, making her think that the hum he'd mentioned before wasn't getting easier to bear. She wanted to get up and massage his head, but he probably wouldn't thank her for it at the moment—and it was shockingly unprofessional.

"Where did you get this?" Nuall demanded.

"As I mentioned earlier, we have evidence linking your family to two other crimes. These coins are directly related. Do you have any knowledge of them?"

"Last I knew, they were in my safe," he said flatly. "If they're being used in the city, it is without my permission."

"You're saying these are stolen?" Mikani opened his eyes, fixing the other man with a look Ritsuko couldn't read. "Did you file a report?"

"How could I? I didn't know they were missing until just now. If you'll excuse me, I need to take an inventory. I'll contact your office with a list of missing articles. Perhaps you can make yourself useful and locate my stolen property." Mr. Nuall rose, a clear dismissal.

The suspect escorted them quickly, even impatiently, to the

gate, which slammed behind them as a good indicator of the
man's temper. She noticed the shift in the air again—now cool
and crisp, touched with the onset of cold weather. Along the
road, the grass had turned brown, withered. *But inside, it's eter-
nally spring.*

Ritsuko hurried toward the cruiser, anxious to return to the
city. *I don't like it here.* Though the estate was beautiful, it was
a treacherous sort of loveliness like a stormy sea dashed against
rugged cliffs with sharp rocks hidden in the churning water
below. She took the keys and opened the doors, then as usual,
she took the wheel. From Mikani's pallor, she decided his head
must be hurting, so she kept quiet until he stirred. Once they'd
put some distance behind them, color started returning to his
cheeks.

"Do you believe him?" she asked, fairly good at reading his
silent cues.

"I'm not sure. He sounded angry enough to be telling the
truth about the robbery." He shook his head. "But he evaded
every other question, and that . . . sound made it impossible for
me to get a read on him. He's hiding something. Let's figure out
what."

CHAPTER 24

Swallowing a yawn, Aurelia padded from her bedroom into her sitting room. A fine layer of dust had settled in her absence. It had taken all of her powers of persuasion to convince Leo that the danger had passed. While Inspectors Mikani and Ritsuko had been more courteous than the first two officers in hearing her out, Mikani made it clear it would come down to Theron's word against her own.

I tried to do the right thing. Time to move on.

During the days she'd spent with Leo, she hadn't shouldered her responsibility to the cast and crew of the show. Nor had she stretched or danced at all. Consequently, her body felt stiff and sore, a feeling that would get worse if she didn't address it. So she donned her leotard and went down to the conservatory, empty as usual, as per her father's request. Members who failed to obey his few edicts didn't last long at the club, and every man-about-town craved the bragging rights of membership at the Acheron. These days, few people would recognize the Architect if they shared a cigar with him, and her father exploited that powerful anonymity; he could take a man's measure with a seemingly casual conversation, then destroy his ambitions with a few strokes of the pen.

A few minutes into her warm-up, Hargrave stuck his head in the door, probably to ensure that the music sprang from her presence and not an interloper. "Would you care for refreshments, ma'am?"

Aurelia smiled, wondering how the fellow felt; over the years, he'd gotten better at guarding his reactions. When she first met him, he was a beautiful young man with golden curls and a discreet infatuation for his employer's daughter. Now, his hair was silver, and he had long since put aside those feelings, had married and raised a family. There might even be grandchildren by now.

"No thank you. Is my father well?"

"He keeps busy." He hesitated. "I think . . . he misses you."

She arched her back and bent, then lifted her leg onto the barre. "Did he say so?"

"Not in so many words, no."

"That will be all, Hargrave."

Aurelia lost herself in the movements—in the spins and flexing leaps, each one pushing her body a little more. A chill crawled over her flesh. She stumbled and whirled, scanning the conservatory. She'd felt this before, the sense of unseen eyes. It had been going on for months, long before she first met Theron. Feeling ridiculous, she searched the room, peering under the piano and behind draperies.

There's no one here.

Angry at herself for letting her imagination run away with her, Aurelia threw herself into the steps. A punishing hour later, she felt calmer. Little by little, she'd reclaim her life, return to routine. Soon she wouldn't recall the details of this tempest. Taking a newssheet from the foyer, Aurelia used back hallways to return to her upstairs apartment. Now and then, staff acknowledged her with a nod or a bobbed curtsy. This was a lonely life sometimes, but more under her control than it would have ever been otherwise.

If I'd agreed to my father's schemes, I would have him managing my affairs, as well as an interfering husband. And I'd only dance at parties.

In the safety of her flat, she ordered a meal and curled up in her favorite chair with the latest news. The front page featured a huge article on the death of the maniac Gregory Toombs. Aurelia read:

> The madman responsible for the deaths of two girls in his infamous murder machines was killed at the Port Authority last evening by unknown assailants. At the time, the CID has not responded to our inquiries regarding the victims' identities or what connection they had with Toombs. Two inspectors were on the scene; both have offered "no comment" on their involvement, though Commander Gunwood issued the following statement.
>
> "We're pleased citizens can rest easy now that we've done our jobs. Please permit the victims' families privacy and the opportunity to grieve."

A knock at the door signaled the arrival of her luncheon, so she let the maid in. "Would you mind sending someone up to tidy a bit?"

The girl, clad in a tidy black uniform, dropped a smart curtsy. "Not at all, ma'am. I'll take care of it later today if that would be convenient."

"Perfect. I'm going to the theater in a little while anyway."

Another curtsy, and the maid departed. Aurelia ate by herself, trying not to recall all the meals that had passed in just this fashion. For too short a time, she'd imagined she had found a solution in Theron, a lover who wouldn't wither before her eyes.

But that was before.

Resolved not to let him hurt her anymore, she drew some hot water and mentally ran through the numbers that needed the most work. The dancers would be rusty, too, from the unexpected shift in rehearsals; however well-intentioned, her assistant didn't have Aurelia's drive or focus. *We'll double up until we make up for lost time.* They'd complain vociferously, but when the fantastic reviews arrived, she had no doubt she would be crowned with accolades by the cast, despite being a harsh taskmistress.

After her bath, she donned her robe, then went into the kitchen and made herself a cup of tea, added milk and sugar just

the way she liked it. She carried it toward the sitting room, still
thinking about the production. A dark figure stood just inside
her window, the one that led from the balcony. The porcelain
cup slipped from her fingers to shatter on the floor, and she
opened her mouth to scream, only to find her voice silenced at
a gesture. Magic prickled over her like a noose. She couldn't
move a muscle; terror cascaded through her in overwhelming
waves, trapped in her head.

"I am most curious, Aurelia, why you felt it was your duty to
spy upon me." Theron sounded silky, but the fevered glitter of
his dark eyes revealed his utter rage. "I will return enough of
your voice to whisper, not enough to sound the alarm."

The clutch of magic eased on her throat, and she spoke in a
low, breathless gasp. "I needed to learn your agenda. To gain an
advantage in the challenge between us."

"Some games are simply too dangerous," he snarled. "Do you
have any notion what you've *done*, how badly you've complicated
my plans?"

"From what I saw, it was necessary." If he imagined she could
ignore such brutal behavior, then he had the wrong notion of her
character entirely.

"You understand nothing. You're like a child, playing at strategy when you have no idea of the consequences."

"Then explain it to me." If she could keep him talking, perhaps
she could find a way to free herself before he killed her; the memory of his fingers shifting into monstrous talons flashed bright and
sharp. Unfortunately, she had no ability to negate his magic. Aurelia only had the truth-sense, which applied to spoken words.

His features softened, touched by regret—or something else,
a complex blend of emotions she had no key with which to interpret. *No, it doesn't have to be like this. Don't do this.* "Perhaps
I might've trusted you, given time. You might have understood . . . and possibly even helped me."

Helped you kill people? I hardly think so, maniac. But she
maintained a neutral mien as she asked, "How did you know it
was me who reported you?"

Surely the inspectors didn't reveal my identity. If they had,
then she would reconcile with her father with the express purpose
of seeing them punished. *If I survive.* At that juncture, it didn't

seem like a safe assumption. Aurelia only knew she'd fight for her life. She struggled against his hold, feeling the strands loosen.

"When the CID came to my villa, Aurelia, I realized there was only one person who could have told them where to find me."

So they questioned him, and he deduced my involvement.

He went on, sounding genuinely pained, "Do you know *how long* it's been since I permitted anyone within those walls? Inside my garden?"

For a moment, doubt assailed her. She remembered the sweetness of that night, the loveliness of the plants he'd nurtured, and the way he'd cooked for her with such care. The two sides of this man seemed diametrically opposed. How could he create such beauty and kill with such savagery? It seemed impossible.

"I only wanted to know you better—to understand your sudden interest in me. Over the years, I've learned to guard my flank. There are those who seek to use me."

"Yet you betrayed *my* trust." He moved toward her, eyes dark and implacable.

Terror lent her unprecedented strength. She pulled a wave of air into her throat and produced a bloodcurdling scream that stopped him in his tracks. Already, she heard movement downstairs; the walls were thick, but not enough to block out such a sound. The magic holding her slipped away, and she scrambled for the door. When she glanced back, he was already gone, but it didn't stop her. She ran out of her apartment and down into the club. Aurelia didn't stop until she found Hargrave.

"There was a man in my room," she panted out.

The man's eyes widened, and he reached for her, before apparently realizing it would be inappropriate. He dropped his hands. "One of the club members?"

With some effort, she collected herself. Even in such circumstances, hysteria was unacceptable. "No. An intruder. Will you do two things for me?"

"Of course, miss."

"Send a message to Mr. Leonidas at the Royale. And summon a couple of sturdy men from the gardens or . . ." She gestured, indicating she didn't care where the guards came from. "I need to dress, but I don't care to go alone."

"I'll accompany you myself," Hargrave said. "Your father

would expect no less. And I shall summon security at once. If you'll wait in my office?"

It was a discreet way of getting her out of the public rooms while she was barefooted, tangle-haired, and clad in a white robe. But she didn't argue the suggestion, merely hurried along the corridors until she could hide in the masculine sanctuary Hargrave offered. *Bronze gods only know what Father will make of this. He may think it's a ploy; and that I'm trying to get him to be the first to break our silence.* It might seem extreme to an outsider, but it was consistent with games Aurelia had played with her father over the years. There was little doubt Hargrave would include this incident in his report to the Architect; it only remained to be seen what her father would do about it.

Ten minutes later, Hargrave returned with three men. By their grave demeanors and sober clothing, they were part of the team that dealt with members who became inebriated and difficult. Sometimes it took a heavy hand to convince them either to retire to a room upstairs to sleep it off or, in worst-case scenarios, that their behavior was no longer suitable for the Acheron Club and, therefore, they must surrender their memberships. Aurelia felt certain those negotiations were occasionally forceful.

The first man said, "There's no sign of how he got in, but he went out the window. There are footprints below, leading to the garden."

"Aye, I saw him running," another added. "But he was too fast. He raced right past me and went over the wall like he was hurdling a squat little hedge."

Since the wall around the club was ten feet high and covered in iron spikes, that was no small feat. Aurelia wasn't surprised. She wished they'd managed to catch him, but that was an unreasonable expectation of men who handled more mundane disturbances.

"Be careful," she warned. "This wasn't a simple intruder. He's a killer . . . and he knows I saw him in the act."

Hargrave paled. "You didn't tell me that."

"In any event, we've checked the building from top to bottom, miss." The largest guard spoke in a respectful tone, eyes on ground.

Likely because of what I'm wearing.

The factotum seemed deeply troubled, but he didn't volunteer whatever was bothering him. "I've notified the authorities, and they're on the way. If you'll come with us, we can escort you to your flat now."

"Thank you." Aurelia had no intention of staying there. She'd pack a bag.

There has to be someplace Theron can't find me. Maybe I'll take a vacation to the Winter Isle. She wanted to pretend she wasn't frightened, but the truth was, the terror still clutched in her chest, a long night of the spirit where the sun never rose. *He can get to you anywhere,* a little voice whispered, and she made a dismissive gesture as she followed the men through the club and up the stairs to her apartment.

She found it hard to focus on her appearance with the sound of four men rummaging in her flat. *Looking for clues,* she told herself, but it felt like one more violation, until she didn't have any privacy or dignity left. It had been hard enough to carve out a life for herself from the unforgiving mountain of her father's silence. He didn't care that she produced shows; what he couldn't fathom was that she wanted to escape the endless machinations and political maneuvering.

Her father *thrived* on it. Aurelia didn't.

As she straightened the white collar of her simple blouse, a commotion started in the sitting room. Fearing the worst, she stepped out of her bedroom to find Leo struggling with the guards; Hargrave, who could have identified Leo, was gone. Her friend broke free and put one of them on the ground with a ferocious overhand blow.

The other two came at him, but before they could hurt him, she said, "Stop! He's a friend. You can go, gentlemen. I'm in good hands now."

"Are you sure, miss?" By his dubious expression, the head of security thought Leo looked like a shady customer.

And with his dark mask in place, Aurelia understood why. "Yes, I'm certain. Thank you for your help. Will you notify me when the authorities arrive?"

"Of course." He helped the other guard to his feet, then the three left.

"If I didn't know better, Auri, I'd think you'd hired this villain to plague you, just to get me out of the theater." But Leo was smiling as he said it, his expression wry.

"It's working like a charm, too. I bet you didn't think about your scars the whole way here."

"I did not," he confessed. "I'm worried about you. Do you have any idea why he's so obsessed?"

She shook her head. "He appeared one night outside the club and seemed uniquely committed to courting me."

"Naturally, you suspected an ulterior motive."

"It's happened before." Her tone was more snappish than she intended.

"I know," he said gently. "Four times to date, and the *last* one broke your heart. I understand your wariness."

"What should I do, Leo? Shall I go on vacation and cancel the show?"

He sighed. "While I can scarcely afford the loss of revenue, you can't continue to direct rehearsals."

"I'll send word to my assistant . . . she can take over in my stead indefinitely. That way, the show needn't be postponed, and you won't lose the income." The girl might lack her unique flair, but she would get the job done.

"You shouldn't concern yourself with me right now."

"But if I don't, you won't be able to afford the delightful Miss Day." Aurelia managed a smile.

"I suspect that's finished. She didn't care for where she ranked in my priorities."

Before she could respond, a knock sounded at the door. Leo wheeled. "I'll get it."

To her dismay, it was the CID officers who had made light of her claims. She couldn't recall their names, but the thin one said, "Inspector Shelton. My partner, Cutler, and I are here about the attempted burglary."

"It was more of a thwarted kidnapping," Leo snapped.

Aurelia had her doubts about that. From the fury in Theron's gaze, he'd looked more as if he intended to gut her on the spot. She wished she didn't recall laughing with him, dancing with him, as it made her feel as though her instincts were suspect. But she knew the proper response in this situation.

"Please have a seat . . . I'll make some tea. I'm sure you have questions."

Half an hour later, the pair left, presumably to file a report.

Leo shook his head and sighed. "I wish I had more confidence in them."

"I don't think they know what to make of a man like Theron." In truth, Aurelia didn't either. "And they have no proof regarding the murders, other than my word."

"If the victims had been men of means, the investigation would be proceeding along different lines," he pointed out.

"You needn't protest over the inequity in the system to *me*. That's one of the reasons I stopped playing my father's games years ago." She glanced around her flat, taking in all of the things she had collected over the years, the touches that made the place feel like a home instead of an impersonal suite.

But I don't feel safe here anymore.

"Perhaps you should consider consulting your father in this matter."

Aurelia whipped around, fists clenched. She couldn't believe he would suggest it. "If I do, it's the same as admitting I can't fend for myself, that I can't function outside his sphere of influence. I'll lose all my independence, Leo, everything I worked to build."

"Better than your life," he said quietly.

She buried her face in her hands. "There must be something else we can do."

"The Royale can't hide you. He knows you work there, and I suspect the tunnels beneath the theater wouldn't prove much of a deterrent if he's determined."

"He didn't come after us there before," she said.

"From what you've told me, that was before he realized you had spied on him and informed on him to the CID."

Aurelia pushed a shaky hand through her hair. "So we were safe only because he wasn't looking."

"And if we return there, it makes things too easy for him, Auri. There's no exit down there." Leo moved to her side and wrapped a comforting arm around her shoulders.

"We'd be trapped," she realized aloud.

"The question remains—where should we go? And how can I keep you safe?"

Eventually, an idea came to her, though she wasn't certain if it was practicable. "Let's speak with Inspectors Mikani and Ritsuko down at the CID."

CHAPTER 25

MIKANI HEADED FOR HOME IN THE EARLY EVENING, FRUSTRATED and short-tempered.

Two hours arguing and cajoling for nothing. Bastard's unassailable right now even if his so-called House is only him and one creepy servant. Gunwood had finally ordered him home to cool off; Ritsuko stayed behind to make sense of the new leads once he promised to go straight home. No fighting, no looking for trouble.

Truth was, he hadn't felt like drinking for a few days now. *I owe them better than that; all of them. Cira, Electra—and Ritsuko.* Toombs was down, but there was another killer out there somewhere. And a third potential victim.

He stopped when he spotted the carriage near the corner of his street. *What in hells and Winter . . . ?* He approached cautiously until he spotted the figure by his door.

"Saskia." Dressed in gray and white, a flowing wrap and a shawl covering her head, she carried a basket in both hands, smiling as she spotted him.

"Janus. Well, it's good to know you haven't forgotten my *name*, at least."

Damned be. "Dinner. I—"

"You were headed home to change so you could come beg for my forgiveness. I know. The kind soul that I am, however, I will spare you the groveling."

Mikani snorted, finger combing his hair. "Bronze gods, Saskia, this is not—"

"What you had in mind. Yes, plans change. Now take the basket and open the door already, will you? Leaving a lady waiting outside for a half hour, your neighbors will talk. And these damned boots are killing me."

He grunted in surprise and glanced down. "You're wearing shoes."

"They hurt. Hurry up."

He took the basket and opened the door. *After two years together, I should know better than to argue with her. After two years apart, though, I shouldn't have to.*

Ten minutes later, she had tossed her boots in a corner and joined him in the kitchen.

She chopped vegetables while he added the spices and tended the sauce.

Conversation between them meandered as it had always done. Saskia gloated over the boom in business created by the temporary Summer Clan blockades. Then, as usual, she asked about his work. He'd never shared as much as she wanted him to, but tonight he wondered if a fresh perspective might help.

Can't hurt.

So as he stirred, he explained, "Toombs was under someone's influence, I could tell that much. But our other suspect was impossible to read. I've never felt anything like that damned hum." He added more pepper to the pot and watched her slice some more carrots. *Odd, how easily we fall back into old routines.*

"Not your first suspect's?"

"No. He felt different. I couldn't read him because he's blocking everyone out. Toombs, though—his mind felt like the machines. Dead. Cold. As if you could fall in . . . Those onions need to be finely chopped." He imagined Ritsuko would be amused at what a kitchen dictator he could be, given his careless nature everywhere else.

Saskia scoffed and blocked his attempt to take the knife away
from her. "Watch your sauce, it's about to boil over." He swore
and stepped away as she went on, "It takes some powerful magic
to leave that kind of psychic residue, Janus. And honestly, it had
the feel of Ferisher art, not sorcery." She was frowning, blond
hair plastered to her forehead from the heat of the stove.

"I'm not sure I follow. Magic is magic, no?"

She huffed and bounced an onion cube off his chest. "No.
What magic remains to us today is a shadow of the old ways.
We must work with rituals and patterns to call and shape the
power." She was smiling, with eyes half-closed. *I remember that
look.* "It's more like riding the waves than . . . than cooking a
meal; you need to have a feel for it, or it will drown you."

"And the Ferishers . . ." When he reached for the onions, she
slapped at his hand and poured them carefully into the pot.

"Ferishers didn't ride the waves, they *made* them. Even after
centuries of mingling with ours, their blood runs strong." She
grinned up at him. "You should know that better than most."

He snorted and flicked a gob of sauce that she barely evaded.
"I'd thank you to not remind me of my ancestors' promiscuity,
if you please."

"Oi! That'll stain like a bloody—" She covered her mouth
and glared at him.

"Ah. There's the foul-mouthed captain I used to know." She
started looking for something to throw at him. "Peace! Peace."
He held up his hands in mock surrender and turned down the
heat on the sauce. "Ferishers," he prompted.

She huffed and started cutting meat with hard, precise chops
of the knife. "You . . . you . . . infuriating . . ." He grinned at her,
and she let out a resigned sigh. *Good to know that still works.*
"Idiot. It's the blood that lets you sense things and allows me to
work my magic." She glanced up at him, briefly. "I suspect if
you would let me teach you—"

"No." *Not this again, not tonight.* All the tension that had
flowed out of him as they cooked threatened to return. "No,
Saskia. I have a hard enough time with . . . with whatever it is I
do. It lets me do some good, and that's enough."

She nodded, her eyes on the knife as she finished cutting.
"One thing bothers me, though."

Thank you.

"Is it me?"

"*Two* things bother me." She stepped aside; he took over the grilling, and she tended to the sauce. "Seriously, though. If it is a Ferisher . . . even if it went insane and was killing people, why would it need those infernal devices?"

"A boy—one of your acquaintances?—said those things were some sort of siphon. But why would a creature like that need any more power? And from girls?"

She tasted the sauce carefully. "He's working in patterns, Janus. The girls weren't chosen randomly, I can tell you that much." He swatted at her when she started eating straight from the pot. "I'm hungry!"

Mikani spooned sauce over the meat and vegetables. "There's a third machine. And a third girl, somewhere out there." *I should be out now, looking for . . . something. Anything.* He shook his head and served their plates. *But first I need a hint as to what.*

She sat. When he poured them glasses of water, she arched a pale brow and gave him a look. "No beer for you?"

He shrugged.

"I guess that partner of yours is a good influence. She'll have you combing your hair any day now."

He snorted and joined her at the table, then directed the conversation back to the case, away from Ritsuko. "Wish I could see the damned pattern."

They ate a few mouthfuls in silence, before she said, "He can't store power like that for long." He gave her a questioning look. "Well, messing with someone's mind long term and that spiritual void he leaves behind? That's all Ferisher art, sure. But the patterns, the way he's using machines? That reeks of dark magic. You can store power in charms, that's not hard. But the more you store, the more unstable it gets."

Mikani set his fork down and rubbed his temples. "So. There's someone walking around with a big . . . charm . . . thing. Full of magic."

She scrunched up her nose and stole a mushroom from his plate. "It's like one of those batteries the Academy was messing with some years ago."

"Those things had a tendency to explode when you looked at them wrong." *Hells and Winter, this just keeps getting worse.*

You can still see the scorch marks on the buildings across the street from the Academy engineering annex.

Saskia sighed. She set down her fork and reached across the table to squeeze his hand. "It *will* get worse. He has to complete his ritual soon since he can only hold on to the power for so long. And there must be a time component to his work; he's not doing anything randomly. Energy, time, pattern. It all adds to his spell."

"And if we figure out the pattern in time?"

"Then the city does not burn, the sky does not fall." She resumed her dinner. "You and your partner save the girl, get the medals, and you take me away for the weekend to celebrate." She smiled at him, lips stained with sauce.

The hells?

"I do?" He straightened in his chair, eyebrows arched.

Damned be, Saskia, you shouldn't be able to catch me off guard. Not anymore.

She gestured with her fork. "Finish your dinner, Janus. May be our last, after all."

HER HEAD ACHED. Ritsuko didn't often succumb to such ailments, but it had been a long day. With a faint sigh, she gathered up her things and packed her attaché case. It was late enough that she didn't expect to run into anyone, but she nearly collided with Cutler coming into the duty room. Shelton was never far behind, and the two spread out before her, blocking her path. The room was quiet; even Gunwood had gone. There was only Anatole mopping the hallway beyond, and she'd feel foolish calling him to help her deal with two unpleasant colleagues. This wasn't the first time they had ambushed her, though they hadn't bothered her in a while.

Seems Mikani put a stop to that. Back then, I didn't even know he noticed.

"Good evening," she said, moving to step past.

"Not so fast." Shelton snagged her arm in a painful grip.

Ritsuko stared at the five thin fingers digging into her flesh hard enough to bruise. "Don't touch me."

"Or what? You'll have Mikani clean our clocks again? He's not around, birdie."

"Business as usual," Cutler added.

Shelton nodded; he didn't let go. "I hear he can be unreliable. It would do you good to . . . make new friends."

She lashed out in a cross-body movement that broke his hold. If she'd exerted more pressure, maybe his arm as well. "You two? No thank you."

Shelton said, "Do you realize how long Gunwood ranted at us? You stole the Wright woman's statement from us, then we had to listen to the old man talk about political ramifications for an hour. I might not mind so much, if—"

"Stop right there. Whatever compensation you feel you're due, I won't be paying it. And if you lay one more finger on me, it won't be Mikani who cleans your clock. Now. Let. Me. By."

Ritsuko wasn't sure if it was her threat, her expression, or her tone that compelled their cooperation, but they did step aside. Their gazes burned her back as she strode to the lift, shoulders straight. It had been like this for years—men insinuating she owed them certain favors for the privilege of working alongside them. *Cretins.*

Down in the lobby, just before she made her escape, she recognized two people stepping in from the street. Aurelia Wright looked lovely but shaken, and Mr. Leonidas possessed his usual dark, dramatic air. The cloak and mask actually drew *more* attention than simple scars would have, but she imagined he knew that. Resigning herself to an incredibly long night, she walked toward them.

"What brings you down?" she asked.

Certainly nothing good.

The story came out in quiet bursts. Miss Wright wasn't hysterical, but in Ritsuko's estimation, she had reason to be. There could be *no doubt* that Theron Nuall, who had been so icy and so collected, so determined to admit nothing earlier in the day, had gone straight to the woman's house to terrorize her, possibly to silence her. It was fortunate he hadn't abducted or killed her, right there in the Acheron Club.

"Come upstairs with me," Ritsuko said. "I need to send a message to my superior, but I feel certain he'll wish to set a protective watch on you."

"I'm not sure that will be enough," Miss Wright replied. "The club has excellent security, and he still managed to get inside."

"We'll take you to a location unknown to the suspect. It's secrecy that will keep you safe while we hunt him down."

"He needs shooting," Leonidas muttered.

She leveled a quelling look on him. "Be that as it may, you will do me the service of leaving law enforcement in the proper hands."

Ritsuko hoped that Shelton and Cutler would be gone when she returned to the duty room, but no such luck. They were both propped at their desks, pretending to do paperwork instead of handling some of the incident reports that had piled up during the blockades. Shelton pushed to his feet when he saw them; and his smile was actually worse than his surly look.

"Is there something we can help with, Inspector?" If Cutler's false courtesy were any thicker, Ritsuko could use it to plug a leak in her ceiling.

"I won't know until I hear from Commander Gunwood." Despite their attempts, she wouldn't be drawn.

Instead, she summarized Miss Wright's situation in a note, reminded the old man of the evidence they'd collected, then asked for orders. In her mind, there was only one correct way to proceed, so if he didn't respond accordingly, she would plague him until he did. Ritsuko summoned a courier from downstairs, marked the missive urgent, then beckoned to Leonidas and Miss Wright.

"Let's wait for the reply in the lounge. I'll fix some tea."

"I'd rather have a strong drink if you have it," Miss Wright said wryly.

"I don't, but my partner might." She went over to Mikani's desk and rummaged through all the drawers, encountering reports that ought to have been filed six months ago, multiple pens, pencils, scraps of torn paper, but surprisingly, she didn't find a single hidden flask or bottle.

"No luck?" Leonidas asked.

"Apparently he's not as rakish as I suspected."

"I have some whiskey," Cutler volunteered.

It wasn't like either of those two to be helpful without a motive, but Miss Wright looked pale and rather done in, so Ritsuko went over to the inspector's desk. "I'd appreciate it. For the lady, you understand."

His cold, flat gaze met hers. "I understand perfectly."

Despite herself, she shivered as she took the bottle from him, careful not to touch his fingers. Shelton did most of the talking for the pair, but Ritsuko suspected Cutler was the truly dangerous one. He seemed never to forget a slight. She didn't doubt he meant to make her pay for the ignominy he'd suffered over the years, most of which hadn't been her fault.

In the lounge, she made a tea tray and fortified the cups with a splash of whiskey. When she added sugar and lemon, the drinks offered the bracing quality of a toddy. Miss Wright sipped hers appreciatively, some of the color returning to her cheeks. Mr. Leonidas sat beside her, an arm protectively positioned on the back of her chair.

A long friendship, there. I wonder if they have . . . odd moments, where they almost want something else. But not really, because it would change everything. Wouldn't it?

"I'm glad you were here," Miss Wright confessed with a shaky laugh. "I would've hated to try to convince those other two that I'm truly in danger."

"There's no question of it. I'm grateful you had the presence of mind to come to us." Ritsuko addressed Leonidas. "And that you were there to get her here safely."

Countless cups of tea later, though Ritsuko didn't spike her own after the first, Miss Wright seemed much more relaxed. She sat close to Leonidas, her cheeks losing some of that frightened pallor. The man touched her on the arm.

"Auri, I still think you should contact your father. He's the Architect. If he can't protect you—" Leonidas broke off, belatedly seeming to realize he'd spoken of private matters with Ritsuko still in the room.

Her breath caught. *The Architect. House Olrik.* With an abrupt click, the last piece fell into place. Nuall was hunting Miss Wright because she might be an intended victim; and she did fit the basic criteria she had just been talking about with Mikani: unseen, but from an important House, and exiled from her family. It was all she could do not to inform the woman at once that there was a reason she'd been terrorized. The only question was, what made Miss Wright different from the other victims? Ritsuko wondered why he'd courted her before killing her. There was no indication that had occurred with Miss Aevar or Miss Bihár. *But Mrs. Aevar did say her daughter had a bit of a glow, just before she vanished . . .*

Before she made up her mind what it all meant, the courier ran into the lounge with a reply from Commander Gunwood. She tipped him and broke the seal. The other two inched to the edge of their seats, and Ritsuko noticed how Leonidas covered Miss Wright's hand with his own. It took her a moment to process the best- and worst-case implications of the instructions and the enclosed document.

"What does it say?" Leonidas demanded.

"We're to make haste, as I expected." She hesitated, hating this part of her orders, even as she exulted in the rest. "Inspectors Shelton and Cutler will be escorting you to a Council-owned flat, and they will remain to guard you at all times."

"Oh." Miss Wright's disappointment and trepidation were tangible. "I'd hoped you and your partner, Mikani, would be sent with me."

"I'm sorry. These are my orders." She understood the woman's concern, but Ritsuko knew Shelton and Cutler well enough to realize they wouldn't shirk the protective detail, if only out of fear of reprisal. Cowards never wanted a light to shine on their actions, so they put their best feet forward when attention from above was likely.

Rather than drag out the farewell, she rose and briskly returned to the duty room, where she showed Shelton and Cutler their part of the letter from Gunwood. No point in enraging them. Perhaps this way, they would think she'd been removed from the case. Nothing would make these two happier, she suspected.

"Good evening," she said to Miss Wright, who had followed. "And keep safe."

This time, there was no delay to her departure. She left the CID without incident—and without her umbrella. By then, it was pouring, so she was a shivering mess when she reached the underground station. The air in the car wasn't warm enough to do much good, so she was still damp when she got off at Southie.

At least it's dry inside my attaché case.

It was still drizzling when she reached the street, just enough to set her teeth to chattering. *Wish I had that toddy right now.* But physical discomfort wouldn't keep her from Mikani. Not

when she had news like this. Oh, she could've trusted it to a
courier, summoned him to the CID, but she wanted to see his
face, watch his eyes light up.

His cottage lay ahead, down the slope. It was slick and rocky
going, but the windows were lit up and golden. Welcoming. The
rain kicked up along with the wind as she neared the edge of the
city. At this point, she was freezing, but she pressed on to rap
hard at his kitchen door.

When Mikani answered, he looked warm and tousled; his
relaxed smile squeezed at her heart in the sweetest way . . .
because she thought it was for *her*. For a mad moment, she considered walking into his arms, then she heard a woman's voice
calling from within, followed by a quiet laugh.

"What's wrong, partner?"

*Yes. Partner. And obviously there's a problem, or I wouldn't
be here. I'm the work woman, not the home-and-hearth woman.
Remember that, Ritsuko.*

She forced a triumphant smile—or what she hoped looked
like one. "You mean what's right. I have here a writ issued by
Commander Gunwood, stamped with the Council's seal, autho-
rizing us to arrest Theron Nuall." At his incredulous look, her
grin widened. "What? It's been a busy night."

CHAPTER 26

"IDIOT. ASK HER IN. SHE'S GETTING DRENCHED." MIKANI started; he hadn't heard Saskia come up behind him. "Or at least get an umbrella, if you're rushing off pell-mell. Hello," she added, while he stepped aside, "I'm Alexandra Braelan. Saskia."

"A pleasure to meet you." That was Ritsuko's neutral tone.

I've had more damned visitors in the past couple of weeks . . . maybe I should hire a housekeeper.

He watched the two women, trying to put his finger on why he felt awkward. ". . . if you'd like to have some tea and a chat, I'll go arrest this gent, shall I?"

His partner shook Saskia's proffered hand. As he took a closer look, he noticed her lips held a blue tinge, and he'd never seen her quite so wet or disheveled. "I'll pass on the tea," she said. "I'd rather get Nuall."

Saskia glared; Mikani held up a hand and smiled apologetically at Ritsuko. "Sit, dry off. I'll get my things, then we'll head out, partner." He headed for his rooms while Saskia fussed over Ritsuko, trying to convince her to drink something warm. He grabbed his coat and checked the pocket for his sidearm, got hold of his walking stick.

Hells. I still need a new hat.

He grabbed an old spare coat on his way out. When he returned to the sitting room, Ritsuko was eyeing Saskia with exaggerated patience. Most people wouldn't have been able to read her quiet annoyance, but he'd gotten used to her subtle expressions. Her mood washed over him, sharper than her mien let on.

Well. I'd rather be out in the rain chasing a killer, I think.

He slipped on his coat and offered Ritsuko the spare. "Shall we?"

After pushing a hand through her damp hair, she shrugged into the jacket without protest. Her tone was polite when she addressed Saskia. "Good evening, Miss Braelan."

"To you as well, Inspector. Be careful out there." As Mikani followed Ritsuko, Saskia gave him a smile that seemed far too amused. "I'll let myself out, shall I?"

What the hells did I miss?

"Yes . . . sorry about . . ." He made a vague gesture, meant to apologize for their interrupted dinner. *At least I cooked it, as promised.*

"Run. I'm used to it." She turned away, and Mikani hurried to catch up with his partner, who was moving at a brisk pace away from the cottage.

As he did, he said, "It'll be faster to grab a carriage, I think. There's a mirror station on the way; we can send out a call for some men to meet us there. If Nuall's strong enough to haul those machines, I'm not sure we can take him down without reinforcements."

"I've already sent word. I suspected you wouldn't want to wait until morning. I gave orders nobody's to make a move until we arrive, though."

That's my partner. Always two steps ahead.

"Excellent. We can head straight in, then; I can get us there in just over half the time if you don't mind ignoring a few traffic laws for the duration."

"Half the time . . . in the rain. And it's dark." Ritsuko sounded skeptical, then she shrugged. "Why not? I won't let this monster get away again."

With his reckless driving, it took an hour and change to reach

the villa. Over the course of that time, his partner told him what
she'd learned about Miss Wright, including the woman's family
connections. He swore. *If we'd known that sooner—*

Ah, well. We know now.

"Gunwood's making sure she's safe?" he asked, as they pulled
up to the gate.

"As houses."

It was a cloudy night, dark away from the city lights, and the
pale walls of the estate reflected the barely there moonlight. The
ground was wet and muddy beneath his feet as he moved toward
the gate, Ritsuko close behind him. Once he drew closer, he spotted a number of constables already waiting, but they were quiet
enough that they shouldn't have alerted anyone inside the walls.

"Ready?" Ritsuko whispered.

He nodded, signaling for the nearest constables to take position behind them. *I hate raids. Something always goes wrong.*
Mikani couldn't stop grinning, though, as he gave the silent order
to breach the gate. Four men rushed forward with a reinforced
ram, snapping the lock with a scream of tearing metal.

"Go!" He ran in as the bearers moved aside. "Watch the sides.
One team left, another right; looking for two male subjects." *I'm
forgetting something. Oh, right.* "CID! Official Council business!
Come out, now!"

At this point, there was usually a flurry of activity as the
suspects realized they were about to be nabbed. This time, however, the villa gave back only silence. Stillness. Foreboding
washed over him. To either side, the constables followed his
orders, but they searched all the way up to the house and reported
no signs of life.

"Perhaps he's inside," Ritsuko said. "And not trying to run."

"With any luck, he tried to move the machine, and it fell on
him. But I don't feel lucky." He looked around the garden, frowning. *He knew we were coming. As soon as he went after Wright,
he must've guessed we would come.* "Let's take a good look
around, shall we? Even if he's not here, he didn't have time to
clean everything, surely."

Ritsuko called, "You heard the man. Room-by-room search.
Set aside anything you think might be of interest."

"What are we looking for?" a young constable asked.

"Papers, correspondence, any sign of where he might have

gone to ground. There might also be a servant hiding somewhere on the premises. We need to question him. If there are no further questions, get moving!" She moved toward the house then, head down.

Something's different. Mikani braced himself and opened his senses. Underlying the eager anxiety of the constables, he could barely discern the hum. *It's moving. Maybe he's not gone after all.* He tracked the sound, ignoring the men opening drawers and cabinets, upending furniture as they pored over the villa with thorough efficiency.

As the sound got louder, he checked his sidearm and paused at an open door. "CID!" He stepped around the corner to find Ritsuko searching a massive oak desk. ". . . but, you know that already." He looked around, confused. "There's something here."

When her gaze met his, her eyes were distracted. "Many somethings. Nuall has correspondence dating back three hundred years. Just . . . casually, in his side drawer. The ink's a bit faded, but he kept the letters, as if he might reply."

He's spry for an old man. Wonder if his correspondents are still alive, too.

"Anything more recent?" He scanned the room slowly, trying to pinpoint the source of the grating reverberation in his head.

"I—" She broke off, her face pale. He'd never seen that look before.

"Ritsuko? What?" He joined her, pistol up to lay a hand on her shoulder. He tuned out the buzzing as her fear rippled against him through the contact.

"This will sound crazy, but . . . something *touched* me. On the arm. It felt like the wind, almost, but it wasn't."

"We're chasing a seven-hundred-year-old bogeyman who's killing innocent girls with dark magic. Think we're past crazy, partner." He squeezed her shoulder gently, instinctively stepping closer. The breeze she'd mentioned—that shouldn't exist in a closed house—rippled the pages of a book sitting on the edge of the desk. The sense of another presence intensified, as if something was swirling directly around them, but Mikani spun, and he saw nothing. Then it vanished—or rather moved off. Away from them until it was just a tug at the edge of his consciousness.

"Tell me I didn't imagine that," Ritsuko said. She seemed to reconsider. "Or tell me that I did. I'm ridiculously tired, so possibly—"

"I think we found his manservant. Or some part of him . . . I don't know."

Ritsuko angled her head, looking thoughtful. "When we were here last, did he ever actually speak to us?"

"Not a word. Don't think he can. I'd rather not think about the rest. Let's see if we can find anything of use." He felt the thing watching from the edges of the room.

"That reminds me. I've already rummaged through the desk, and this is the one piece of correspondence that looks new enough to help us. Care to do the honors?" With a flourish, she offered him a sealed envelope.

The disembodied servant became agitated. Mikani ignored him and cracked the seal. "I think you found something you weren't supposed to. 'I have the information. See me at once. Erebos.' Hm. Have you heard that name before?"

Ritsuko knitted her brows, obviously searching her memory. "Though I'm not certain, I believe he runs the shady end of business in the Patchwork. I don't know his whereabouts off-hand, though. Is there an address?"

"Just a marker for the transmitting mirror station. Patchwork District, east side. Let's hit up the local constabulary. They can point us at him."

"Very well. There's only one question left, then."

"What's that?" he asked.

"Do you intend for us to sleep before we follow up?" By her half smile, she already knew the answer.

RITSUKO SNATCHED A little rest despite the jouncing of the cruiser. By the time it stopped, she felt incredibly disheveled and exhausted; her eyes burned, dry as bones, and her residual head-ache from the night before had turned into a full-on pounding in her temples. Gunwood probably wouldn't approve of pushing herself so hard, but he'd made it clear getting Nuall off the streets was a top priority.

Bronze gods, I feel rotten.

She probably should've stayed awake to make sure Mikani didn't drive them into a ditch, but he woke her when they entered the Patchwork District. It was the middle of the night, a prime time to be robbed, but with their weapons and a keen eye, they should be safe enough, even here. Ritsuko slid out of the cruiser and glanced at her partner.

"Don't know who's in charge here. I'm not sure how cooperative they'll be, so let's be careful." On the other side of the vehicle, Mikani stepped out and stretched.

The constabulary for the Patchwork District was a squat, old building crammed between even-seedier-looking establishments. Even though it was past midnight, light seeped from blackened windows along the street. A nervous-looking young officer was guarding the door, ensconced in a cramped, barred booth next to the entrance. The tents, pavilions, and jury-rigged construction were in constant flux; the only permanent structures seemed to be the constabulary and the taller, scarred building that housed the mirror station. A few blocks north, the shadow of the Patchwork's looming warehouses and repurposed buildings was a dark backdrop to the tent city.

At this point, she wanted a warm bath and her bed almost as much as she'd like to lock Nuall up and throw away the key. Her clothes were still damp, clinging to her skin in the clammiest and most unpleasant way. There was a reason she always made sure she was tidy and unruffled. Men were more inclined to take her seriously if she didn't look like a wet kitten.

Nonetheless, she marched to the guardhouse and flashed her credentials. "I need an address for Erebos. It's urgent."

The young man started, his gaze darting between her credentials and the street. "Oh. I, yes. But first, I need to check with the officer of the shift, ma'am, and he's out at the moment. Maybe if you would care to wait . . . or return in the morning?" He gave a hopeful smile. His eyes had a hard time focusing on her; they kept twitching away.

"Kid's on something," Mikani whispered. "Thorn, maybe."

Ritsuko searched her memory for what she'd heard about the stuff. There were lots of chemicals with fanciful names; House scions preferred the expensive ones, but the poor had their own habits and vices, too. Thorn was a hallucinogen—cheap, dirty and quite addictive. Unlike Dreamers, she'd never heard of anyone successfully shaking Thorn, once it dug in. *Hence the name*.

At this point, Ritsuko was in *no mood* to be polite. So she leaned both arms on the counter, got up in the constable's face, and said, "You can get me that address right now, or I'll wait until the shift officer returns. Then we'll chat about why you smell like you've been smoking blackthorn all night."

The gate officer blanched, then shook his head vehemently. "You don't know what you're asking, you're not—"

"You heard the inspector, boy. Move." Mikani tapped the bar with the handle of his walking stick, calling the kid's focus. "You don't want to make her mad. Trust me."

The panicked constable looked at Ritsuko, then scribbled something on a piece of paper. "Fine, just get out of here, please." He offered the address with trembling fingers.

"Excellent. Thanks for your cooperation." She took it, scanned the locale, and headed east. "Looks like he's fairly brazen, operating a scant six blocks from here. They must be on his payroll."

"He'd use the locals to keep rivals in check. The district's fairly quiet since there are no gang conflicts." She was conscious of him close behind her, his walking stick tapping on the rough cobblestones. "Pragmatic, if not entirely what the Council intended, I'm sure."

Ritsuko set a bruising pace, a near run; and it took only moments to cross the necessary streets and make the turns. She surveyed the run-down structure, noting the number of stories and how many windows. From this vantage, she couldn't spot all the exits, and a man like Erebos probably had bolt-holes all over the place.

Like a rat.

"He'll have to forgive us for calling after business hours. How should we play this?"

Presuming he's even here.

Mikani looked up and down the street and shrugged. "We were spotted as soon as we arrived at the constabulary. So let's knock?" With a grin, he struck at the door. "Mr. Erebos! Need a word!"

After some muffled sounds, the door opened wide, answered by a large man with colorful tattoos up and down his arms. He tapped a lead pipe into his palm in silent expectation. Ritsuko took that to mean they'd better have a good reason for showing up.

Three men sat behind him at a table, cards strewn before them. From the combined stink of hard liquor and smoke, a gaming session must've been in full swing. Or maybe that was how all thugs smelled at this hour; she didn't have the practical experience to be sure. She nudged Mikani, a silent signal telling him he should do the talking. These eyes didn't look friendly, and anything she said might cause a fight.

"Gentlemen." Her partner stepped forward, planting his walking stick firmly between his feet. "Frightfully sorry to intrude on your revels. But we've the need to speak to your boss. A friendly chat would be much easier than going through official channels, so what do you say one of you goes and rousts him?"

The nearest man stood slowly while the rest rumbled and shifted, exchanging dark looks. The tattooed doorman slowly circled behind them.

Mikani smiled. "Well." He whirled, thrusting the tip of his walking stick into the throat of the man behind them. As the doorman staggered in pain, Mikani cracked the stick across the nearest man's cheek, kicking him back into his stumbling friends.

Before they had the chance to swarm him, Ritsuko drew her weapon. "I'm truly not in the mood for this. I bet I could shoot at least three of you before anyone could get to me. Or you could go get your boss. On my word, we just want to talk. He's *not* a person of interest."

Mikani leaned closer to the men. "I'd wager on all four, actually. She's fast."

With a huffed sigh and a muttered word that sounded like *bitch*, the tattooed one broke from the pack and loped toward some shadowed stairs. Ritsuko didn't lower her sidearm until she heard footsteps returning. From the sound of them, it was more than one man. *Good.*

She couldn't make out much of the boss's features, but he summoned them with a gesture. "We'll speak upstairs. Don't mind their diligence. I pay them for precisely that."

Her partner bowed to the men and motioned for her to keep her gun ready. Erebos turned and led the way up the rickety steps to an office perched above the main warehouse space. Mikani stayed by the door, keeping an eye on the men below. She passed him to step into a surprisingly opulent office with silken carpets and expensive crystal touches. None of it was tasteful, though, or matched in any particular design scheme. In that regard, it suited the man settling behind his desk with that desperate clutch at refinement, where none of the pieces lined up quite right.

"I'll be brief," she said. "I have a note here from you to Theron Nuall. It's of the utmost importance that you tell me what information you meant."

Erebos scowled, leaning back in his creaking chair. "That'd be Mr. Nuall's and my business, now wouldn't it, Inspector? It seems outright illegal to be inquiring into it just like that."

"It's also illegal to murder young girls. I said you weren't a suspect, but if you protect a killer voluntarily, I have no choice but to assume you're a willing accomplice." Her voice was hard, so there could be no mistaking her intent.

That's not a threat; it's a promise.

The man hesitated, drumming thick fingers on his desk. "Murder is . . . bad for business. If he's involved in that, you'd put him away, aye? Maybe even the noose?"

"I can't guarantee what his sentence will be. That's up to the judge. But he certainly won't be around to demand your time." She thought that was what he was driving at. "Or take you away from more lucrative pursuits."

"The right bastard's been a thorn in my side since he showed up." He shook his head, digging through his desk. "Very well. I want it clear, I'm merely an information broker here. I had no idea what he was planning to do with this."

"So noted. What do you have?" Ritsuko held out a hand, for she'd found it was best to assume people would give her what she wanted.

Erebos held out a folded piece of paper. "He won't come looking for this, will he?" He looked nervous, his fingers trembling slightly.

Ritsuko glanced at Mikani, wondering if he had the same idea. "If he does, give it to him. I'll just write a copy of it. But *if* he comes to see you, try to find out where he's heading next. Then send word to us immediately."

Mikani stepped forward. "Don't try to stop him, don't let him know we're looking for him. The farther away you keep from him—"

"The happier I'll be," the criminal muttered.

Ritsuko took the sheet from Erebos and unfolded it. She skimmed it, and her breath caught. "Names. Five of them."

It's a death list. Her fingers trembled when she showed the page to Mikani, because she didn't trust herself to reveal the rest out loud. *Do I sound as frightened as I feel?* She scrawled them in her notebook while trying to calm down. But she couldn't forget Mikani's vision, or his sense there would be a third victim.

Her partner swore quietly and turned for the door. "Cira Aevar's on here. Electra. And Miss Wright, along with two others. We need to send constables to check on them. Nuall might be heading for one of them even now."

Ritsuko handed the paper back to Erebos. "Thanks for your time."

The men in the warehouse watched her leave, Mikani at her side, but they didn't interfere. Their card game continued, and Ritsuko was relieved when the night air hit her, even cold and wet as it felt.

She rubbed her eyes. "If we have more yet to do, I need coffee. Or . . . something illegal. I'm on my last legs."

Her partner chuckled wryly. "Let's get our people moving, then get some rest. I don't think either of us will be of much use tonight. And I'd rather not corrupt you further, partner. You're already dressing like me."

For once, she was too tired to argue.

CHAPTER 27

"You're a little late," Mikani observed, as Ritsuko strode into the duty room the next morning. It was nearly noon, and he'd been at work for over an hour already.

Actually, I was about to go check on you.

"I had some errands." Her brow was a bit damp, as if she'd been running up and down flights of stairs. "They took longer than I expected."

"Problem?" He was a bit surprised to hear she'd managed to do anything but sleep, but that was Ritsuko. She hadn't risen to inspector by failing to exceed expectation.

"Just personal business. What do you have there?"

Mikani had found a report waiting in his bin; he scanned it while Ritsuko checked her messages. "Two of these girls aren't in House holdings . . . but it seems they're keeping better track of their errant daughters these days. One of them's renting a studio not far from here. Shall we check on her?"

"Certainly. I have some questions."

He glanced at her. A night's rest had done them both a world of good; they no longer looked like they'd just crawled out of a weeklong bender. *Well, she doesn't, anyway. But then, Ritsuko's always cleaned up well.*

"I've a shortage of answers, but shoot."

Ritsuko laughed, a rueful tone to it. "I meant for the girl."

"Very well. I'll drive, you question them."

Nodding, she fetched her jacket from the coatroom. Mikani sometimes slung his over the back of his chair, but not Ritsuko. She was tidier than that. *It was hardly worth it to hang it up, no longer than she's staying.* As she shrugged into it, he caught sight of five purple marks on her arm.

"That looks . . . Did one of those thugs grab you?"

He stepped closer. *I wasn't paying attention, damn it. Should've gotten some reinforcements before we rushed in.*

Ritsuko rubbed her arm, seeming surprised. "No, that was Shelton, actually. We tangled last night before I received the writ from Gunwood."

Mikani made a sound deep in his throat. *That bastard's gone too far.* "I'll just have a word with him, then we can head on out." He grabbed his walking stick, fist clenched tight around the metal handle as he started toward the lounge, where that pair could often be found dawdling.

"He's not in. Gunwood has Cutler and him on protective duty with Miss Wright."

He stopped and turned to her. "He did *what*? Those two?"

"And he gave us the arrest." She shifted, her expression quietly imploring. "I appreciate the concern, but . . . let's get to work."

Mikani hesitated, rubbing his thumb along the carved handle of his walking stick. "Very well. Let's see to these girls, then. Shelton can wait."

This is not over.

Just before they arrived at the building where the first girl kept a flat, Ritsuko said, "I didn't realize you'd reconciled with Saskia."

Mikani started and turned toward her. *What the hells?* Then he swerved as they nearly ran over a cycle messenger; the rider spat a few choice words as he sped past.

"How in Winter's name—" He paused. "We haven't. Reconciled, that is."

"She isn't as I pictured from the way you used to describe her."

He chuckled wryly. "It was around that time that we started talking about our lives outside HQ, yes. I was angry back then."

I was furious. And not ready to deal with what happened.

"Yes, your confidences did possess a rather . . . rantish quality." Her eyes laughed, though her lips didn't so much as twitch. Ritsuko's voice carried a throaty edge, too, as if from suppressed amusement.

He snorted. "I tried to get her arrested, you know."

"Oh, Mikani. Your women should be offered a manual and a waiver to sign before they get involved with you."

He turned at the corner and pulled the brake hard. "Would that have helped *you*?"

"I'm your partner, not your woman."

"True. You're paid to put up with me." He smirked and slid out of the cruiser.

"Not nearly enough," Ritsuko muttered as she headed for the building.

The apartments had a carefully cultivated artistic air. Shutters and doors were distressed, but the locks and fittings were new. The light sconces were antiquated but clean. Even the threadbare carpeting of the aisles was obviously expensive. Mikani pushed the door open and went up to the second floor, where the Reinert girl believed she was hiding from her interfering parents.

A muffled thump and a choked shriek drove him forward; he shouldered the door once, twice, and the jamb split. He tumbled in to see the girl half-dressed and cowering in the corner nearest the doorway. A man lay on the floor in the middle of the room, his features rendered indistinguishable by swelling, and blood smeared the wood beneath his head. There was only one person moving in the room; after a lightning glance between the prone victims, the attacker sprinted toward the window. Not even gunfire slowed him down; Mikani emptied his revolver, and one of the bullets struck the suspect's calf as he crashed through the glass. Mikani ran after him while Ritsuko checked on the other two, but by the time he got to the sill, the assailant had vanished from sight.

Impossible.

"Did you get a good look at him?" Ritsuko asked, kneeling. "Was it Nuall?"

"Tall, dark-haired, and fast. I didn't get a look at his face, but I did wing him."

There was a spatter of blood on the window ledge, and he

could distinguish a trail on the ground below. "He can't keep running for long. How's she?"

Ritsuko shook her head. "She hasn't said a word. I don't see any physical injury, so she must be frightened out of her mind. We need to summon a physician."

Mikani knelt by the man and shook his head. "I don't think her companion's breathing. I'll get the landlord to send couriers to HQ and to her House."

That was too close. A few more minutes, and we'd have missed him and lost her.

"Track him down," Ritsuko said. "If you hit him, he can't get far. I'll stay with her until her family arrives."

He stood, hesitating. *She can take care of herself.* "All right . . . be careful, partner."

"If he comes back, I'll shoot him in the face."

Hell and Winter, at this point, I don't even know if that would be enough.

Mikani loped off down the stairs and around the corner, reloading as he moved. Before he left the building, he ordered the landlord to notify HQ. *Hopefully it won't take long.* The delay might have cost him the chance to capture the attacker, but there should be officers swarming all over this building soon.

That accomplished, he ran outside. As soon as he spotted the shattered glass and bloodstains on the cobbled street, he slowed and looked around while he tracked the attacker into an alley. He glanced into the shadows and paused, trying to sense him. *There's that familiar reek. It's him.* He proceeded carefully, senses open and gun at the ready. The detritus cast long shadows and offered too many hiding spots; crates, sacks of litter, and unidentifiable piles of refuse made for slow going.

A dark figure lay slumped by the wall.

"Identify yourself." Gun in hand, Mikani crept toward the body. He didn't think he'd hit the assailant in a vital artery. *But maybe I got lucky.* He braced for a trick, but when he shook the person's shoulder, he tumbled forward.

Damned be.

It was a scrounger, his throat torn away. The trail Mikani had been following mingled with the growing pool of fresh blood under the body. He looked around with growing frustration, but could spot no other exits. Just sheer brick walls on three sides.

The lowest window was at least four stories up on the right and looked undisturbed. But on closer examination, he noticed narrow runnels scraped into the bricks; they were staggered, almost like . . .

Claw marks. As if the killer dug his nails into the walls and hauled himself up. Mikani remembered Miss Wright claiming that Nuall's hands had turned into talons the night she saw him kill four men. *Now I have another body with the throat torn open and no plausible explanation for how the suspect got away.* Cursing beneath his breath, he headed back to the apartment. *Hope Ritsuko got something from the girl, at least. I can't follow a blood trail up the wall and on the rooftops.*

When he stepped into the flat, he spotted Ritsuko still on the floor, but she had the sobbing girl in her arms. There were constables on the scene, mostly looking bewildered. Mikani understood their confusion; it was improbable that a normal man could jump through a glass pane, down a full story, and land strong enough to run away. He didn't look forward to writing this report.

"There's another body in the alley down the block, heading east. Two of you get over there, secure it for transport. Get this poor chap covered, at least." He nodded to the young man in the middle of the room as the uniformed constables sprang into action. "Statements from the landlord and neighbors. Move, men, move!" *Gunwood'll be so impressed at how quiet we've kept this.* He came up to Ritsuko, lowering his voice. "Is she better? Bastard got away."

She whispered, "Crying instead of rocking. I'm not sure. I can't leave her until—" At that moment, a woman burst into the room; she was overdressed for the flat, but she paid attention only to the young woman clinging to his partner's neck. When the girl saw, she stumbled toward the newcomer with a broken, "Mama!"

"It looks like I'm dismissed." Ritsuko pulled to her feet. "There's another girl you need to secure." Without explaining why, she snagged two constables and wrote down the information. "Make sure she's safe, then notify Commander Gunwood."

"But, ma'am—"

"No questions. Just do it." Then she strode out the door, and it felt more like flight to him than a purposeful exit.

Mikani could tell she was thinking hard as she ran down the

stairs and pushed out of the building onto the street. "I know that look. Tell me."

"It seems this maniac has every advantage. You shot him . . . he didn't stop. He's faster, stronger, and presumably more powerful. How are we supposed to *fight* that?"

He caught up to her and wrapped an arm around her shoulders as they got to the cruiser. "Ritsuko—" *Hells and Winters, she's right.* "I don't know. But I'm sure you'll figure something out, then I'll improvise, and we'll stop him. Because we have to."

"Actually," she said grimly, as if she expected him to argue, "I have an idea."

RITSUKO DIDN'T SPEAK after Mikani handed over the keys. She drove in silence, mentally mapping the address she recalled from Aurelia Wright's statement. After this errand, it would be prudent to check on her, ensure that Shelton and Cutler were doing their jobs. *It should be safe enough, though. He has no way of locating her.* That was the one comfort in this situation.

Hansoms and carriages clogged the road, and parking was difficult here. Pedestrians crowded the walks, fighting for space with the vendors. Muttering, she slammed the brake on and turned off the cruiser, some three blocks from her destination.

"It'll be faster to walk from here," she said, climbing out.

Mikani looked up and down the street, rubbing his temples. "Where to?"

"Just . . . come on. It's bad enough that I'm *doing* this. I refuse to discuss it."

She set a rapid pace, weaving in and out of the shoppers. This was the lower-class version of the park's lake promenade with cheap wares and copious bargains all spread out over raw wooden tables. Farther on, the shops had walls and ceilings, too. She passed all the goods and swung into an alley that had Chen the tattooist on one side and Sad Sue's pharmaceutical emporium on the other. Sandwiched between them was a nondescript doorway—unmarked, just as Aurelia had said. Ritsuko knew she had the right place by the crescent moon etched into the door. Though it was Sunday, the stores didn't close up, as it was the only free day many citizens had to do their marketing.

She entered without knocking.

The room was dimly lit, two gaslights flickering on the back wall. Though some shops had bright windows as a showcase, in this one, they had been blacked out, probably to discourage prying eyes. It looked like a jewelry store with various necklaces and amulets laid out on blue cloth. None of the items were marked with description or price.

She felt Mikani's gaze on her, and Ritsuko turned with a quiet sigh. "Do you know what this place is?"

He nodded, his voice low. "The question is, why are we here? We've a suspect on the run, and we nearly had a third victim. I'm not sure how much a luck charm will help."

"If there's anything here that can give us an edge, then we need it. And you have *no* idea how stupid I feel saying that."

The curtain leading to the back room stirred, then parted. A man stepped out; Ritsuko placed him in late middle age. He had a crop of salt-and-pepper hair and a well-groomed mustache; he didn't look as seedy as his shop did from the outside. Possibly that was the point.

"May I help you?"

Ritsuko felt ridiculous. Though she had no extra senses like Mikani, she felt keenly that her partner thought she was wasting time better spent elsewhere. She was aware that time was ticking away; by this point, it was late afternoon, and they had neither the means to catch the monster nor any method of defeating him should they happen to stumble on him.

Sadly, she didn't even know what to *ask*, but that didn't stop her from trying. "I . . ." she started. Then she tried again. "Do you have anything to help win a fight, when the odds are stacked against us?"

"That's . . . a rather unusual request." The arched brow told her the charm merchant suspected she was mentally unstable.

Lovely. Even in a place like this, the gentleman thinks that proper young ladies don't engage in behavior such as I'm describing.

"We need something quiet and fast. Can't spend five minutes focusing, and nothing flashy." Mikani stepped up beside her; he still looked dubious, rubbing at his temple as he examined the displayed items. He held his open hand an inch above them, as if searching for one in particular.

The proprietor watched him with a furrowed brow. "I deal in subtlety. So if you're looking for . . . stronger items, I wouldn't know anything about that."

Mikani scoffed. "Of course you would—" He paused, tilting his head. "This one, I think."

"Ah." The amulet vendor hesitated a second before picking up the charm. It looked like a misshapen man, cast in pewter and roughly finished. "You're not fooling around, I see. This could be dangerous, if misused." He wrapped the figurine in a small square of silk. "You realize I can't be held responsible for any malfunctions or if harm befalls you—or anyone else—as a result of its purchase."

Her partner looked over at her, brow arched as if to ask, *Are you sure?*

Not even slightly.

But Ritsuko nodded. "That's what we're looking for. How does it work, exactly?"

The man waited until Mikani handed over a handful of coins. Then he smiled, handing her the wrapped charm. "Quite simple. First, you attune it to your target. An image, his name on a piece of paper. A strand of hair . . . blood, if you have it, or tears. Those would be best, dripped over the charm. And when you face your enemy, touch him with it. That triggers the hex."

"What kind? Like a curse? What does it actually *do*? Or are we supposed to . . ." She trailed off, unable to ask the question in a way that didn't sound ridiculous.

If I have to shape a spell with the power of my mind, then Mikani just wasted those coins, and I threw away our valuable time.

"I can't answer that. Generally speaking, these are purchased by people who know precisely what to do with them. In the hands of an amateur, the results can be . . . unpredictable." The salesman offered a cool smile. "Hence the warning."

Nothing I can say to that, is there?

Ritsuko actually laughed as she shoved open the shop door. Outside, she said to Mikani, "I'm sorry about that. I thought . . ." She shrugged, feeling foolish. "That it might help. But it was probably pointless, and now we have . . . this thing. Which might blow up in our hands."

Mikani offered a bemused look. "You thought of something. Now, I improvise. Told you that's how it always works, partner . . . but we need to get back to the Reinert girl's flat. Fast."

It took her a moment, but she worked out the why of it, then threw him the keys. "What happens if the blood's dry? Or mixed with other things, like dirt?" Then she added, "I bet Miss Braelan would know."

"I'm sure she *would* know. She promised me something like this after I threatened *her* with that stay on the penal farms." He smirked. "Let's get to the apartment, then we'll worry about the details, shall we?"

His relationships always sounded so colorful. Ritsuko had only ever been with Warren, who wasn't dramatic about anything. It was probably best, however, that she remembered one thing about Mikani—his women always went away in the end. As his partner, she had the better end of the deal. So she couldn't afford to mind if she turned up at his cottage and found a woman there unexpectedly. The absurd part was that she'd actually been surprised.

No more of that, please. You have work to do. It was just the case, she told herself. The past few weeks had been intense, creating intimacy where none had existed before; and once they apprehended Nuall, life would return to normal. Gunwood had said they were both getting commendations, but she wasn't sure if he still meant for that to happen since Toombs hadn't been working alone.

She climbed into the cruiser after Mikani unlocked it. "I can't help worrying. I suspect it might be part of my job."

"You're probably right. I never read my job description. It just seemed like a good way to get paid for getting in trouble." He kicked the boiler's throttle into high heat, and the cruiser leapt forward, startling a vendor who had set up near the front wheels.

"Is that why you joined the CID?" Ritsuko couldn't recall if she'd ever asked.

He was silent for a few seconds. "No. I joined to try to right some wrongs."

"A knight fighting for justice?" She grinned and pressed a hand to her heart, wondering if he'd hear the sincerity beneath the teasing. "You're my hero, Mikani."

He'd be unbearable if he realized that it's true.

"If that were so, you'd do all my paperwork so I could get on with the fighting."

Ritsuko didn't answer. She was too conscious of the weight in her palm, even through the layers of paper. The thing felt heavy and cold, and she fancied she could feel it burning clear through to her skin. Her momentary good humor fell away. This was a desperate gambit, provoked by an intimidating foe.

But if we don't finish this, who will?

They got to the flat in time to use the still tacky blood, but there was only one way to find out if it would work—and perhaps neither she nor her partner would survive it.

CHAPTER 28

AURELIA HAD BEEN COOPED UP WITH THESE INSPECTORS FOR nearly twenty-four hours, and she already regretted reporting the intrusion at the club. They refused to let her leave, and the food they brought back when one of them ventured out was always fried. She was starting to feel nauseous, both from the stale air and the monotony of her diet. There was no space for her to dance; when she stretched, she received such *attentive* looks from both Shelton and Cutler that she felt as if she were offering a lascivious performance.

The flat was institutional, with plain gray plaster walls and a floor that wouldn't look out of place in a hospital ward. *I do have the bedroom for privacy, at least.* But that left the two men camped out in the sitting room; she hoped the CID would send replacements soon, as they were growing testy. Yet perhaps their superior was concerned about multiple officers knowing her location. Her father would approve, as the fewer people who knew a secret, the fewer who could reveal it via incompetence or bribery.

Still, it didn't ease the discomfort of being trapped. Her dislike of being forced into particular behavior was part of the reason she had fled the luxurious cage the Architect had designed for her. *But this is temporary, just until they catch him.* Unable to focus, Aurelia paged through the novel she was reading, impatient with the travails of a heroine who seemed altogether self-indulgent.

She went to the doorway. "Do you know how long we'll be here?"

"As long as it takes," Shelton told her with what was probably meant as a reassuring smile.

"Don't you have wives or families to mind that you're gone?" As she asked, Aurelia realized it was a mistake.

The two exchanged a look, apparently flattered by her personal interest. Then Cutler said, "We're free as birds, miss. Care to play cards with us?"

"You're not gaming, are you? What are the stakes?"

"It's a friendly wager," Shelton assured her. "Copper a point."

Even on a careful budget, she could afford that. *It's better than reading that book for the third time.* So she came into the room and joined them at the table, where the cards had already been dealt. Cutler cut her in, and she examined her hand, though she didn't give anything away about it. *Good thing they don't know about my truth-sense.* It was an unfair advantage in a game where bluffing played a role, as she always knew when someone was pretending to have a better hand.

Four games later, Shelton threw his cards in disgust. Hiding a smile, Aurelia raked the pile of coppers toward her side of the table. "Is there a problem?"

"You're a bloody sharp," Cutler accused.

"Then it's a good thing the stakes were low, isn't it?"

To her surprise, Shelton laughed. "Indeed, miss. I'm off to fetch some food. Do you want anything special?"

Aurelia decided her skill at cards had won her some respect from the thin one. So she asked, "Could you get something fresh? Fruit and vegetables perhaps?"

"Tired of fry-ups? I don't blame you. I'll see what I can do."

The inspector made a point of checking the hall before he opened the door fully. Then he cautioned, "Secure it behind me and don't open it until you're certain it's me."

His partner revealed a trace of annoyance when he said, "I know what I'm doing, Shel. She'll be safe as houses with me."

"I'm sorry about that," Cutler said when Shelton had gone.

"He thinks he's the clever one, and mostly, I let him. It's easier than setting him straight."

Aurelia laughed. She'd noticed that Shelton did most of the talking even when that wasn't the best idea. "So he thinks he's in charge?"

"Indeed," Cutler said wryly.

But there was a darkness in his gaze that made Aurelia uncomfortable. While he looked harmless, and his mouth said all the right things, there was an undercurrent to this inspector that made her feel it would be unwise to cross him. While his partner blustered, this man would quietly do terrible things. She didn't think he was evil, but she suspected few things would stop him from attaining his goals, whatever they might be.

And it was not knowing that unsettled her.

She made polite conversation with Cutler until Shelton returned, knocking a complicated pattern on the door. His partner opened up to find the other man juggling multiple bags. Aurelia hurried over to take a few off his hands. Though Shelton was sallow-faced and rather unattractive, he was still capable of looking sheepish and eager to please. When she took the bags, he said, "I didn't know what you wanted. I'm not much of a shopper, but I hope you can make a salad or . . . something."

He'd gotten an incredibly random assortment of vegetables, not the sort that were suitable for eating raw. "I can do soup."

Years past, she wouldn't have been that self-sufficient, but since she'd taken up residence above the club, sometimes she didn't feel like sending downstairs for a meal. So she'd learned to fend for herself—to boil water—and prepare simple meals, like soup and toast. Ignoring the two inspectors, she took the bags to the kitchen and got to work.

The cupboards revealed some seasonings, which made the task easier. And an hour later, she had a nice veggie soup simmering on the stove. Shelton and Cutler sat at the table behind her, looking rather awed. Given so many factors about them, she suspected neither had ever convinced a woman, apart from their mothers, to cook for them. At that point, she decided she felt sorry for the pair.

I should be nicer to them. It's not their fault they didn't take me seriously at first. I imagine most of the CID would've reacted the same way.

She dished up three bowls and offered them along with slices of toasted bread. When added to the cheese and butter Shelton had brought, it created quite a nice meal. Once she sat and took up her spoon, they dug in with flattering alacrity. Shelton's eyes actually closed when he tasted the soup.

"This is amazing, miss. I thought you House ladies knew only how to order people about. I've never heard of any who could do for themselves."

Aurelia remembered what it had been like in the Olrik compound; her days had been spent complying with her father's agenda. There was no opportunity for real personal growth or achievement. She'd tolerated it for years, until she couldn't anymore. Her throat tightened as she recalled the moment where she sat toying with a vial of poison, wondering if death would be preferable to such endless machinations.

Leo stopped me.

He'd said, "Auri, no. If you can't bear it here, then come away with me. I'll help you get started on your own."

And he had. She wished he was here, but the CID had made it clear they couldn't permit a civilian to remain with her. *We can't assume responsibility for someone who isn't in danger. It would complicate our protective regimen,* Cutler had said. At first she'd feared they had inappropriate intentions—and that was why they wanted her alone—but so far, they had been professional.

Belatedly, she realized they were still waiting for her reply. "I learned after I left the compound. So yes, that's partly true."

"How long have you been in exile?" Cutler asked.

"Forty years or so, I suppose."

The two exchanged a look, a silent judgment on her Ferisher blood, she supposed. And their friendliness waned accordingly. After the meal, relations became silent and brisk. Aurelia retreated to the bedroom to hide. There was little to do, however, which made her pick up the only bit of entertainment she'd brought with her. The first line read, *You will never understand me, or what's driven me to this end, but I pray as you read these lines, you may find some compassion in your heart.* That set the tone for the rest, as the heroine seemed convinced nobody had ever loved as fiercely or suffered so much anguish.

"Rubbish," Aurelia muttered.

It was late now, and she tried to sleep. Though she'd lost track of time, it must be past midnight. Behind the closed door, she stretched a little, but there was no space to dance, which would've exhausted her enough to rest. Nerves frayed, she lay down to try again, and she must have dozed.

The sharp crack of repeated gunfire startled her from a fitful dream; Aurelia ran to the bedroom window, but it had bars across it to keep criminals out. It also effectively trapped her in the apartment. From the faint glimmer in the east, it must be right before dawn, what poets called the darkest hour.

There's only one way out.

Terror clogged her throat as she dropped to her knees, crawling through the doorway into the sitting room. She expected to find Theron murdering her two guards, but in fact, she couldn't focus on the intruder; glamour swirled around him so heavily that there was no way to glimpse his face. He was a swathe of pure night, staining the room. Shelton flew back in response to a blur of a blow, smashed into the wall. His gun was on the floor, the smell of cordite in the air like a pepper sauce overlaying the stink of blood. Shelton's face was a map of agony: swollen mouth, smashed nose, cheeks spattered with blood. When he slid down, his arm hung at a ruined angle.

The table was smashed, shards of crockery all around. Amid the wreckage, Cutler staggered to his feet and grabbed a lamp. Aurelia had correctly reckoned him the clever, cautious one, so he wasn't as badly injured. Yet. Cutler still didn't rush; instead he hurled the lamp, and the maniac knocked it away in a casual gesture, so that it exploded into glass shards, sprinkling all over Aurelia. With more determination than sense, Shelton hauled to his feet despite his injured arm and dove for his gun. Cutler was a little smarter, keeping furniture between him and the intruder while he searched for a weapon strong enough to hurt the creature. *Man. Whatever it is.*

"*Shoot* it!" she called.

"I'm out of ammunition," Cutler replied. "Run, Miss Wright! I'll hold it—" Before he completed the thought, the dark form flew at him, faster than her eyes could track.

If I'm fast, I can get away while they're fighting. Broken shards sliced her palms when she shoved to her feet and ran for the door. She fumbled with the locks, terror keeping time with her heartbeat, hammering in her ears. Incredibly violent sounds erupted behind her, but she didn't look back, didn't check to see if the inspectors were dying to buy her a few precious moments to flee. Aurelia couldn't breathe until she flung the door open. She took two steps, then blackness dropped over her head; at first, she thought it was a charm, but then she felt the coarse fabric on her cheeks.

She lashed out with blind but ferocious swings. One of them connected, and she screamed at the top of her lungs. *Someone will come. Someone—*

An arm went around her neck, and her air was choked off. Not enough to kill her—just to incapacitate her. Her panicked flailing weakened despite her best efforts. She kicked out, and was rewarded with a grunt, but it wasn't enough. His strength washed over her, making her realize he could kill her with a casual touch. The only reason he hadn't was because he needed her alive. For now. The man threw her over his shoulder as if she weighed nothing. Dizzily, she tried to kick, but a band went around her ankles, lashing them together. She felt like an animal bound for slaughter. *And to him, that's precisely what you are,* an awful voice whispered.

She gouged her nails into his back, but if it hurt, he didn't let on. Instead he yanked her wrists together and snapped restraints on them as well. *Surely someone will see him taking me away. They'll try to stop him.* But if they did, given how the inspectors had fared, they'd probably die. Aurelia choked a terrified sob.

The bouncing movement told her they were running down stairs, and she tried to count, but she lost track when he slammed her head into a wall. It wasn't intentional cruelty, she thought, more the way one handles luggage that couldn't object to such treatment. *I'm a thing to him. I'll be used and discarded.*

"I'm sorry." Those were the first words he spoke, and she should've been able to identify him then. But like his features, his voice was thick and distorted, as if it came through water or a layer of muffling earth. *Truth.* Whoever had taken her did regret the necessity. Yet he wouldn't stop. This, too, she knew—and that was all, for afterward, a sharp pain blasted through her temple, dragging her down into silence.

When Aurelia roused, she had no way of knowing how much time had passed. She wasn't being carried anymore. The ground beneath her felt hard and rocky, stones digging into her side. It smelled damp; and the air was cool against her ankles where her skirt had ridden up. Fighting nausea, she took stock of her physical condition. No soreness between the thighs. *Good. At least he didn't rape me.* Her head ached, along with her limbs. They had been bound long enough for circulation to be impaired. If it continued, she risked losing use of her extremities, but she didn't imagine that was a concern for the monster who had stolen her. The hood was still in place, bound firmly at her throat. Breathable fabric permitted air to reach her lungs.

When she squinted, she could make out movement through the tight weave of the cloth, but that was all. More telling, she heard clanking and banging, as if something was being assembled. Her blood ran cold. Like everyone else in Dorstaad, she'd read the speculative accounts in the newssheets. One story had been written from Cira Aevar's point of view, an attempt to re-create the terror of her last moments.

Is this what it was like for her? Lying on the ground, bound and helpless, so she could only wait to die?

"Hello," she called. Her voice didn't come out bold as she intended. Thirst and strain turned it into a croak, pitiful as it echoed.

So we're in a large space. Aurelia didn't know how that helped her, but she was determined to collect as much information as possible. *I won't be another victim. I refuse.* Her captor's strength, however, had been truly terrifying; he'd made her resistance feel childlike, and she wasn't a weak creature.

"So you're awake. I wondered if you would rouse before the finale." The reply sounded nearby, still laced with that maddening distortion.

Time to find out the truth.

"Theron?" she asked softly.

"Does it matter?" The question came with enough amusement that she heard it.

And most awfully, her senses remained quiet—or rather, they swirled with confusion. It might be the blow on the head or the glamour she'd glimpsed around him. Whatever the reason, she might die without being certain who'd killed her.

"Why are you doing this?" she asked without an expectation of an answer.

But he did reply. "To fix that which was broken long ago."

"And why me?"

"You're the last piece of an intricate puzzle. Your sacrifice will be remembered."

Somehow, it was no comfort to imagine her death being immortalized by this madman. *Ask him something else. Anything.* But as it turned out, she didn't have to. He was eager to confide, eager to be understood, and there was no risk because, soon, she would join the first two girls in his collection.

"I'm going to change the world. I'm going to bring back strength and brightness, no more death. No more frailty. The Ferishers are out there, starving in tree and stone, and they want to come back. They want to come home. This was *their* world first. I am doing no wrong in liberating it from the invaders."

For a moment, she considered trying to manipulate him, but she discarded the notion. Her head ached too fiercely for Aurelia to imagine she had the mental acuity for such a complex game. "Those girls didn't do anything to you. Nor have I harmed you. So spare me your excuses."

Aurelia figured she had nothing to lose with the truth. She was already helpless. If he wanted to kill her, it would be like swatting a fly. But then, he wouldn't, would he? Not until he finished the machine, and it sounded like it was immense, so without Toombs, the accomplice she'd read about in the scandal sheets, it would be slow.

Of course, that means it will take longer for me to face my fate, longer on the hard ground, longer in the darkness. But every moment she survived, that was another opportunity for someone to track them down. *Leo will be crazed. He's probably tearing apart the CID offices right now.*

"Really?" He was whispering, leaning close enough for her to smell the blood trickling from some wound she couldn't see. *He's injured.* That gave her hope because if he could bleed, then he could be killed, regardless of how powerful he was. "In truth, they were small sacrifices for me to regain what's rightfully mine."

"And that is?"

She heard him pacing nearby, and as Aurelia listened, she heard a faint difference in the drag of his footsteps. *He's hurt his leg.* He ignored her question; for long moments, Aurelia knew only the sound of his feet crunching over earth and stone. The air smelled odd, even through her hood.

We're underground, she realized. Then despair crashed down on her like a poorly mortared wall. There was no chance anyone would stumble upon them. He had all the time in the world to complete his murder machine and strap her into it. According to the newssheets, Miss Aevar had burned to death while Miss Bihár drowned. *What does that leave for me?* Pure dread wrapped her in a stranglehold until she barely controlled the urge to scream until her throat gave way.

The killer growled, "After all this time, I will have vengeance. He'll pay for what he's done. He thought to sit in judgment of *me*?"

"Who?" she gasped. "My father? Do you have some vendetta against him?"

"Enough questions. You distract me."

Something crashed into her skull, and the world dissolved.

CHAPTER 29

THAT MORNING, MIKANI SENT WORD TO RITSUKO TO MEET HIM at the Council flat. They'd intended to check on Miss Wright the day before, but Shelton and Cutler would've sent word if there had been a problem, and there was a great deal to do after the attack on the Reinert girl. Still, it was good to follow up.

"Were you followed?" he asked Ritsuko.

There was a reason they hadn't come together or directly from HQ. He'd spent an extra half hour taking an extracircuitous route to make sure he wasn't followed. Mikani trusted that Ritsuko had done the same.

"No. I made sure of it."

He nodded. "Then let's go up."

The building seemed secure though his senses prickled, the closer they got to the flat. The apartment door was ajar; Mikani frowned when he caught the distinctive smell of gunfire. He signaled to Ritsuko and drew his pistol. As he tensed, he sensed it. *He was here.* Leading with a foot, he pushed the door open all the way and stepped through, turning to scan the room. Broken furniture and shards of glass littered the room; he spotted one body—*no, he's alive, he just groaned*—slumped against the far wall.

Can't stop yet, two people unaccounted for. Then he saw Cutler, blood pooling around him where he lay facedown on the other side of the overturned table and chairs. The inspector stirred slightly, and Mikani heard the gurgle of his labored breathing. "Found Cutler, no sign of Wright or Nuall."

Ritsuko went into the other room, caution in every motion. When she emerged, her head hung low. "No sign of Miss Wright. It looks like he got her."

Mikani put away his gun and knelt next to Cutler. The man flinched at the first touch. "Easy, man. We'll get you help." Mikani felt his pain, the grate of broken ribs and the lingering taste of fear. He'd been in enough bar fights to know Cutler'd likely be fine, if worse for the wear. "Don't try and move. I'll be back." He straightened and headed for Shelton, stepping over the debris scattered throughout the room. "How's he look?"

"Like he was run over by a hansom. We need a physician up here. The arm looks like a compound fracture, and I can't rouse him." Ritsuko opened Shelton's eyes, but the man didn't respond. "See what you can find here. I'll run to the nearest mirror station."

She went out the door in a sprint, her heels clicking against the tiles until he couldn't hear them anymore. *Bastards did not deserve this.* He left Shelton alone rather than risk making it worse, and half closed his eyes to better concentrate on the room. The tang of violence was sharp, if expected; he could tell that Shelton and Cutler had put up a good fight against Nuall.

Mikani walked slowly toward the door, head cocked and temples starting the familiar pounding. The dark reek of decay cut through the air in a line from door to bedroom, blurring the edges of the rest of his impressions of the room. His outstretched hands slid along the cold spots, where they'd managed to slow him down. *There's more here.* Something was twisting his perceptions, jabbing at his senses. *Damned be, what—more magic?* It was slippery, achingly cold but different from the void.

Like the first murder scene. He's hiding. If Saskia was right about the nature of the ritual, the killer's time was running out. He couldn't permit interference. *And that makes our job twice as hard.* Shelton was completely unresponsive, but when Mikani walked past, Cutler stirred, throwing out a hand. His bloody fingers flexed against the floor, and a shiver went through him. *He looks like he's dying.*

An unintelligible whisper fluttered like breath from the inspector at his feet. Mikani crouched to hear what the man had to say. "What? I didn't catch that."

Cutler tried again, his throat bruised. ". . . grave."

Mikani started. "What about . . ." *How does he know about the killer's aura?* "What do you mean, 'grave'? Stay with me, Cutler."

The answer came as if on the inspector's last breath. ". . . smelled like dirt. Of the grave."

Then the full weight of Cutler's pain hit Mikani like a brick wall. The other man was swimming in a red sea, cuts and bruises, and possibly internal bleeding. He couldn't answer further questions for reasons Mikani totally understood, as he was flooded by the backlash. In response, nausea swept over him. His nose was bleeding, and his eyes burned, so he stumbled to the door to catch his breath and wait for Ritsuko.

Twenty minutes later, she bolted up the stairs. Judging from the flush in her cheeks, she hadn't paused before or after she contacted Dispatch. "They're sending help right away."

He managed a nod. "Let's see if we can get them comfortable at least, then."

Ritsuko's sharp gaze skimmed him from head to toe. "If I didn't have more pressing business, I'd lecture you. Or rub your head. Or both."

He chuckled, wiping at his bloody nose. "You can lecture me while we work."

She didn't, though. Once she headed into the sitting room, she went over to Shelton. Mikani located the pump in the kitchen and brought a bowl of water; then he hunted up some supplies, including clean cloths. Between the two of them, they patched the worst of the men's cuts and stemmed Shelton's bleeding; Ritsuko handled most of the treatment. *She's better at the delicate stuff. And her hands are not shaking like an addict's. But, then, I'm the one with the firsthand experience of most of these injuries.*

As Ritsuko finished with Cutler, Mikani heard a heavy tread on the stairs. *Multiple feet, coming fast.* He was relieved when two teams of inspectors entered the flat with Dr. Byfeld in tow. He endured countless moments of questions from his colleagues before Ritsuko broke away from her discussion with the physician.

"We need to go."

"Agreed. He has enough of a lead as is." He led the way down the stairs, rubbing at the back of his neck. The headache had receded to a dull grating at the edge of his senses. "How the hells did he track her down here?"

"I was wondering that myself. It's possible . . ." Ritsuko hesitated, looking faintly ill in the morning light. "That we have an internal leak."

Damned be. "Hells and Winter, who, though? You knew, Cutler and Shelton knew. Gunwood has to sign off to check the safe-house log." He let out a frustrated sigh, slamming his fist on the roof of the cruiser. "He might have been tailing her all this time."

That'd explain the need to hide.

"We know he hasn't been back to the villa, which means he's in the city somewhere."

"He felt . . . different this time. Maybe he was using a charm, I don't know. But it wasn't the same as before."

She frowned, looking thoughtful. "Are you sure it was the same person? If it turns out we still have multiple suspects, I may resign."

He shook his head. "No. It's difficult to explain, but . . . it's like an aroma. You, say. You always carry the faint scent of camellias and vanilla. Even after we've been running around all day and we've smoke, sweat, and gods know what else clinging to us, I can still tell it's you from the way your hair smells . . ." He trailed off and looked at her to see if he was making any sense.

Her mouth was half-open, as if she couldn't decide how to respond. Finally, she seemed to focus on the pressing question. "So the killer has that base odor, but with something added to it. The foundation hasn't changed. It's just gained layers. Do I understand correctly?"

"Exactly. He's splashing perfume—" He paused. "No. It was like that first machine. I think he wrapped himself in a glamour or charm that makes you not *want* to see him."

"Before . . . or now?"

"Now. Something's changed. He's becoming stronger. We're running out of time, partner."

"Then we should get going. We have the worst interview of our lives ahead of us." She climbed into the cruiser, looking positively pale with dread.

He frowned as he got the engine running. "What, Leonidas again? I've seen worse. Hells, *I'm* worse. Not sure what he'd have to tell us, though."

"Her birth name was Aurelia Olrik," she reminded him. "And she's the Architect's daughter. How long do you suppose we'll work for the CID if we don't inform him immediately?"

"Hells and Winters." He rested his head on the wheel for a second. "Wish we had the reward for Toombs. An early retirement sounds perfect about now."

Mikani eased the cruiser into traffic as Ritsuko murmured, "When I studied Olrik, my history instructor said the Architect is actually the most dangerous of House patriarchs. Because you don't see him coming until it's too late."

THE OLRIK HOLDING lay on the easternmost edge of Dorstaad. Ritsuko noted the Academy as Mikani drove past, then simple row houses that offered affordable student accommodations. In the next block, the street grew tonier in an understated fashion. Unlike some Houses, the Olriks didn't hole up in a fortress. Their interests were interconnected through walkways and covered porticos, joining a host of different buildings and architectural styles into a whole.

Ritsuko shivered as she slid out of the cruiser. Maybe the structure wasn't imposing like the Aevar stronghold, but she dreaded this encounter with every fiber of her being. She hadn't heard of anyone who had successfully gotten a meeting with the Architect in the last ten years. *Of course, it's possible I just wouldn't know. I don't exactly travel in these circles.*

Briskly, she moved up the walk toward the main building and used the massive knocker. It was early but not indecently so. *Hopefully they're up.* The door opened promptly to reveal a liveried retainer, the epitome of a man who had aged in a distinguished fashion, from the fine lines on his face to his silver hair.

He executed a correct half bow and inquired, "What is your business?"

"Inspectors Ritsuko and Mikani, CID. We have grave news regarding Lord Olrik's daughter." Her partner sounded subdued, as uncomfortable as she felt.

"The young miss? I'll notify him at once. Please step inside and take a seat in the antechamber, just there." The servant hurried inside with an absent gesture toward a small room past the front hallway.

Ritsuko did as he invited, astonished by the casual opulence. The seats were upholstered in cream silken damask with a fine golden stripe, echoed in the gilt around the edges of the elegant frescoes in the ceiling. It probably took two servants half a day to polish the floor to its current shine, and the antechamber was half the size of her new flat.

"Why do you suppose Miss Wright turned her back on all this?" she asked.

Mikani looked around before answering. "Boredom? She looked the type to get antsy sitting around for more than a few minutes." He shrugged and lowered his voice. "Maybe she wanted to get out of the family's shadow. Or perhaps it wasn't her idea . . . ?"

Before she could reply, the efficient click of shoes against the floor heralded the servant's return. "Mr. Olrik will see you in his study. Follow me, please."

Ritsuko followed her partner out of the room. Maybe he was used to such surroundings—or possibly just better at covering his awe—but every step she took made her conscious of scuffs she might be leaving on the gleaming floor. Impressive artwork by old masters lined the hall, and in various niches sat complex clockwork devices the purpose of which she couldn't guess. They might be prototypes of items available for purchase or projects that never came to fruition. Whatever the case, it was amazing.

Try not to look so dazzled, she scolded herself. *You need this man to take you seriously, and that won't happen if you come into his office all starry-eyed.*

Andrew Olrik, the Architect of Dorstaad, stood by the window of his cluttered office. He was tall and solidly built, especially for a reputed scholar. Thick waves of salt-and-pepper hair framed sea-green eyes. He frowned and motioned for them to sit though he was still in his dressing gown. "You have news of Aurelia. Tell me."

She saw a resemblance between father and daughter though his features were bolder and more masculine. Despite the dire circumstances, a giddy refrain ran through her head: *I can't believe I'm in his office.* She locked down the juvenile excitement and incredulity as she perched on the chair across from his massive cherry desk. Gears and bolts lay scattered over it, fighting for space with the papers, but she ignored the urge to surreptitiously inspect his work, see if she could puzzle out what he was designing.

How many people can say they've been this close?

"I'm sorry," she said. "This is difficult, but your daughter has had some trouble with a man named Theron Nuall . . . to the point that she entered protective custody yesterday. Today, she was abducted, two of our officers seriously injured in her defense." She added the last part so Olrik wouldn't imagine the kidnapping had occurred easily or due to negligence.

Not that it will help.

He narrowed his eyes and loomed over them as he leaned on the desk. "Theron did what?" His voice filled the room, a tic in his jaw hinting at barely repressed fury. "Why in the Veil's name would he do that?"

Mikani shifted, extending his arm as if to shield her. He sat back, looking sheepish, when he seemed to realize what he'd done. "Sir . . . you know Theron Nuall?"

"Yes. For a long time." Olrik turned to the window, presumably to regain his composure.

"I'm not certain what his ultimate agenda is, but we believe him to be responsible for the deaths of two girls in magically charged rituals and guilty of more murders of opportunity." Ritsuko outlined the investigation as succinctly as she could.

The Architect listened. As Ritsuko spoke, he sat, hands folded before him. When she was done, he nodded. "You say he's using rituals and devices to help him. He's following a design of some sort?"

"I wish I knew more. We've pieced some of it together through a consultant friend of Mikani's." Ritsuko tilted her head at her partner. "The reason we're here, in addition to providing information, is to inquire whether you have any resources or knowledge that could be helpful in locating your daughter."

Before it's too late. But there was no need to say it aloud. *Surely he knows.*

"He came to see me a few weeks ago, claiming to have sensed something strange, but . . ." He made a vague gesture with one hand. "I suppose it's possible he was lying to me, which would be *most* regrettable."

"Is there any chance he's descended into . . ." Ritsuko couldn't think of a politic way to phrase the question. "I believe some people call it age madness."

"He seemed agitated when I saw him but not devoid of his faculties."

"That doesn't really answer the question," Mikani put in.

"Pardon me?" The Architect faced her partner with an imperiously arched brow.

"The one she asked before . . . as to whether you have any insights that can help us. If you're acquainted with the suspect, then you might remember something about him. His habits, his tendencies. Anything."

"I only care about finding my daughter," the man bit out.

A chill washed over Ritsuko at the icy glitter of his eyes. She sympathized with his perspective. Answering speculative questions must seem like a waste of time better spent elsewhere. But she had to convince him to cooperate, somehow.

So she said quietly, "I want to find your daughter, unharmed, more than anything. But that requires full disclosure on both sides. I've told you everything I know. If you can say the same, then I'll thank you for your time and join the manhunt that's already in progress."

She held his gaze for two beats, then rose. Mr. Olrik held up a hand. "It doesn't matter who has her, does it? I know machines, and I know rituals. And I understand what you can do when you combine them."

"Go on," Mikani prompted.

Olrik swept an arm over the desk, clearing it with a clatter of metal and breaking glass. Grabbing a letter opener, he carved lines on the surface. "If you're focusing a ritual, you must adhere to the rules. More important, however, you seek the patterns.

The more of them that make up the ritual, the stronger it is. When is he killing? *Whom* is he killing?"

"Have we checked whether there was any rhyme to the dates?" she asked Mikani.

Her partner shook his head. "Two killings. What, a week apart?"

For a few seconds, she couldn't hear over the thump in her ears, as she did the arithmetic in her head. *Mikani wasn't kidding when he said we're running out of time.* After a few seconds, she forced the trepidation away, so she could continue the questions. The implication of the schedule had to wait until she and Mikani were alone. Ritsuko schooled her features to calm composure.

"Yes," she said softly. "As to whom, the girls both belonged to powerful families . . ."

But neither of them was precisely well protected *at the time they were taken.* She didn't say that aloud, either, as it didn't reflect well on Mr. Olrik or the CID. Best not to enrage him, as he hadn't blamed them yet.

"You have the when and the how. There's at least a third component to his goal. Patterns come in all types. Sometimes they're personal. There are meanings in various symbols, for example, geometric shapes have long been associated with ritual."

Ritsuko frowned. "So he could be making a cross or a dragon or—"

"No." Mikani paced a few steps, his expression hinting at deep contemplation. "Saskia said there's a limit to how long energy can be stored. For the time to align with the ceremony, he must be near the end, and that limits his scope." He cast a familiar look at her, which she understood to mean *let's go.*

"Thanks for your time," she said to Mr. Olrik.

CHAPTER 30

"MIKANI," RITSUKO SAID, AS THEY ENTERED THE MOSTLY deserted duty room.

He glanced around; most of their colleagues were out combing the city, searching for any sign of Miss Wright. As a measure of the situation's severity, Commander Gunwood was out in the field, too. *How long's it been since he left his office?* They'd stopped at HQ to report the new cooperation with House Olrik, but it appeared Gunwood wasn't around to reprimand or commend their behavior. *Whichever it would be.*

"What?" he asked.

"I've been thinking about what Mr. Olrik said . . . about the when and why. You said it was about a week between the first two, right?" She paused as if he'd know what she meant.

He nodded, looking around the room. "That's about right, yes. Go on." He started pulling maps from the racks on the walls, looking for one that gave them a good overview of the city.

"So how long has it been since Miss Bihár was killed?"

He paused as he lay out a map and frowned up at her. "It was . . . Monday, right? So a week?"

I think today's Monday. Damned be, if I've not lost track of time.

"That means we're really under the gun."

"Hells and Winter." He slapped down the map and secured the edges, then started locating the sites. "He's going to kill her today . . ." He glanced out the window. The journey from the Olrik holding had taken longer than he'd wished, with all the traffic clogging the streets—new supplies arriving from the lifted blockades—so it was near noon. *Hope we're not too late.* ". . . help me with this. Where was the first body found?"

Ritsuko ran a finger down the wrinkled paper, peering at streets, then she tapped a spot. "Here. Miss Aevar was discovered on a rooftop in Iron Cross. Mark it."

Mikani pressed a pin into the map. "Electra was found . . . here. Landing Point. Down by the river." He put down a second pin, and sketched a rough line in red ink between them. "He's in a hurry now. He's running out of time, and we made him change his plans . . ."

"We kept him from taking the other girl, you mean?"

"Right. So. If he was going for a pattern . . ." He glared down at the map.

"In Olrik's office, you said he was limited in scope by the number of victims he's chosen. It can't be an intricate design. So what are the options with three points?"

"Line. Triangle. Even a circle would touch the points of a triangle, right? So if he's bound to a pattern, and he had three girls . . ." He drew a line out from either end. "I don't think it's a line. That's not a pattern, that's just a sketch. And one end of this line ends up in the arse end of nowhere in the foothills, the other end in the middle of the plains south of the city. Triangle?"

"The circle is too big . . . it goes out into the water, here." She frowned at the map. "Let's say you're right. There are only two possible points, east and west, equidistant to the first two locations."

He nodded, tracing a rough line east. ". . . this one's in the middle of nowhere. I think it's a weekend inn. If he could finish this elsewhere, surely he would? There must be a reason he's doing this inside city limits."

"Yes, because it's far more complicated here than it would be in the territories."

Mikani measured the line between the bodies they had,

tracing arcs west. "There's an underground station here." He thought for a moment, then remembered aloud, "They shut it down for repairs a couple of years ago. I don't think it ever reopened. Most of the shops around it shut down after that. So he has plenty of places to choose from."

She nodded. "Let's get a squad to help with the search. We've narrowed it down, but there's no telling precisely where we'll find him. The more bodies, the better for Miss Wright."

Ritsuko collected her belongings and filled her coat pockets with extra ammunition from the box on her desk. Then she took a special protective jacket from the closet, reserved for emergency use. Mikani imagined this qualified . . . because if they were right, they'd find Nuall trying to finish his grisly business up in the Heights.

"We'll send word downstairs; see who they can get to meet us there." He checked his pistol, then grabbed his walking stick on the way out the door. "Let's go catch this bastard, partner."

Two hours later, Mikani was conscious of time ticking away. He had twenty fresh-faced constables standing before him, all awaiting invaluable instructions on how to apprehend a killer who ran away, even with bullets in him. *If any one of you finds him, shoot and pray.* A grim thought, but it had been that kind of week. Ritsuko always let him take the lead in such circumstances, not because she wasn't capable but because the men listened to him better. They shifted, then quieted beneath his watchful eye.

"Listen up. We're after a dangerous subject. Six-foot-four, dark hair, brown eyes. Appears to be mid-forties, but spry as the devil. He may have a hostage with him, so keep your heads straight." He met their eyes, briefly. "He's a killer. If you spot him, and he tries to run, shoot him. If he comes at you, shoot him until he drops. Don't take any chances. Break into teams of four, stay together. Collins, Jasper, John . . . and . . . you, and you. You have lead. Get your teams and hit the nearest buildings. Go."

I really hope I'm not sending these kids out to die.

After offering sharply earnest salutes, they hustled like he was Commander Gunwood. For a few seconds, he stared at their uniformed backs, then turned to Ritsuko with a sigh. She wore a faint half smile; he knew that it amused her when he stepped in as an authority figure, considering his own inclinations.

She said, "That was good, just the right amount of tyrannical nonsense. Where should we start?"

Mikani pointed at a nearby building, the tallest on the block, with his walking stick. "There. If he is going for a rooftop, my money's on that one."

It took less than five minutes to run straight up, and he was disappointed to find the area clear. He and Ritsuko cleared the building floor by floor, but it was just empty offices. On the third story, he surprised a squatter who had set up a cozy nest, but Mikani didn't care about such minor infractions. With every minute they spent on the wrong places, Nuall had more time to complete his agenda. Saskia's words echoed in his ears, adding to Olrik's warnings. Whatever happened as a result of this stolen power, it wouldn't be good.

Moving at top speed, they cleared two more structures while his temper rose. The afternoon faded toward evening. Ritsuko seemed calm enough until he studied her eyes; they held a fierce spark. He slipped enough control to touch her mood, and her determination, laced with fear and anger, washed over him. Mikani left his mind open, hoping he might catch a flicker of the killer, but with so much feedback—all the constables, plus those who still lived in this part of the city, it was too much, and he had to draw up tight again, or he'd end up useless.

"I'm so worried we won't get to her in time," Ritsuko said finally. "She came to us. She *trusted* us."

"We'll find her." He gestured at the buildings around them. "If we have to tear this place down brick by bloody brick, we'll save her."

She nodded; and he couldn't tell whether she believed him. "We checked most of the buildings immediately nearby. Let's head over to the underground station."

"The others can finish canvassing here," he agreed.

Long shadows fell across the pocked and empty streets. The boarded-up shops gave the emptiness a sinister air, as if the bustle of the rest of the city couldn't touch this place. It felt separate somehow. *A good place for doing bad things.* He led the way toward the closed underground station, with Ritsuko close behind.

From half a block away, he spotted movement, a dark figure heading for the derelict stop. He called out, "Halt! CID! We need to talk to you."

"He's not interested in being a good citizen," she muttered.

Beside him, Ritsuko quickened her step. As they drew closer, he identified Nuall, who, instead of stopping, vaulted down the stairs, his pace increasing. "It's him!"

Ritsuko drew her weapon and they ran.

SHE KEPT HER head low in case Nuall launched a spell at them, but he showed no signs of slowing. Her footsteps pounded down the stairs. It was dark, dank, and it smelled like urine, along with earthier scents. The platform looked like nature had started to reclaim it in just a few years, edged by moss and mushrooms that crawled up from the ground. Ritsuko dropped onto the rail line and listened for a second.

"This way. Did you notice he was alone? Is that a good sign or a bad one?" she asked, pushing to a full sprint.

Nuall's fast. If I couldn't hear him on the rocks, we'd have already lost him. Shouldn't he be limping, at least a bit? Damned inhuman bastard.

"It's a sign we can shoot him. Let's take what we can get." Mikani loped alongside her, pistol in one hand and cane in the other. "Can't see a damned thing down here."

The few gas lamps that were not broken along the disused tunnel cast a flickering, fading glow that did more to create shadows than dispel the dark. That intensified the other senses, though, making it easier to follow with the ears. Nuall took no care to lose his pursuers. *Which means he's insane . . . or he's utterly confident in his ability to deal with us once we catch up to him.* Ritsuko had to admit that his record to date made the latter a reasonable theory.

"He has to stop sometime, provided we don't miss a turn."

"Ideally, he'll lead us back to Miss Wright."

"And then we put a bullet in him," she said grimly.

"Or ten. And then drop him down a shaft, for good measure." They came to a crossing where she paused to listen. Echoing footsteps rang out from the right, downward path. "Hope he's winded at least. How far down do these go?"

"This isn't part of the Council construction," she said.

Beneath her feet, the imported stones gave way to regular earth, and the walls weren't cut or lined with stones. Instead, they were veined bedrock, and the lamps didn't extend so far in, so even the uncertain light died away. She fought the temptation to close her eyes, for then if she ran in the dark, at least it would be of her own choosing. But that might lead her to miss something, so she pushed forward in the dreadful gloom.

Mikani grabbed her arm, slowing their pace. "Hold up, we won't help anyone if we break an ankle." He sounded strained. "And . . . I hear something. It's strange, though; I can't pin down a direction. Like the walls themselves are muttering."

A chill ran down her spine. *I don't hear it.* "Can you make out any words? And more important, do you have a light?"

"Not in any language I know. Hold on."

She heard him digging through his pockets before he struck a match. The flare of red light summoned a darting motion in her peripheral vision for a split second, then it was gone. The wavering flame didn't help beyond a few feet; Mikani had to blow the match out before it singed his fingers. His soft curse told her he hadn't done so quite soon enough. In the fresh darkness, her skin crawled.

She whispered, "There's an old man who watches me out his window when I go to the market. Even when I can't see him, just the flicker of his curtain, I know he's there. And that's exactly how I feel now."

"If your old man steps out of the shadows, I'll kiss him. I feel a breeze, though. And I think I hear voices, down to our right . . . Can you hear anything?"

More voices? Ritsuko took a step forward, wondering if his imagination was getting the best of him. This time, however, her ears detected the tones of people trying to be quiet. *So we're not alone down here.*

"Do you think these are conspirators? We've known all along that Nuall must've had help, more than just Toombs."

"It would mean we're on the right track, at least." He touched her shoulder, then took her free hand. "Quiet, steady. Let's see if we can get the jump on them."

Ritsuko hated how much steadier she felt with his fingers laced through hers. Since he had better night vision, she let him lead, following the length of his arm. She tried to keep her steps quiet, but as they approached, the voices stilled. *Which means they've probably heard us.*

She stepped boldly around the corner into the dim lantern-light, weapon in hand. Ritsuko was surprised enough that she stilled, eyeing the four shabbily dressed men, each armed with a weapon. Smugglers, she guessed. One stood atop a handcar beside a stack of crates while the others were planted in front of him. From their scruffy faces to their dark hats pulled low, they didn't look friendly . . . or pleased to see her.

"Did a dark-haired man run past you?" she asked, as if they were law-abiding citizens who would be glad to assist. It took all her composure not to raise her gun.

"We didn't see nothin', and you shouldn't be 'ere." The nearest man set down the crate he was unloading to draw a long knife from his belt. The others stirred, spreading out. "So why don't you come 'ere, nice and slow-like?"

Mikani stepped up next to her, stick resting on his shoulder and pistol against his thigh. "We don't give a damn about the goods you're moving. We're chasing a killer, and don't have time for this. So answer her question, then let us pass. Otherwise, the dog who just ran by you will murder more innocent girls."

The one perched on the car said, "Kill them. Dump the bodies."

Below, the one with the blue eyes shook his head. "They're CID, you daft git. You want coppers rolling through these tunnels like a plague?"

She felt tempted to shoot them while they argued, but two to one offered a challenging scenario close-up, and they couldn't afford further delay. Which a fight certainly offered. She asked Mikani with her eyes, *Thoughts?*

He shook his head slightly, signaling her to wait as the smugglers argued. She could see his finger sliding around the trigger to his pistol, but he held still for the moment.

"We need to move these fast. They won't stay fresh for long down here, yeah?" The man who had spoken, short and nervous, glanced at them, then back at his companions. He shuffled his feet, as if ready to run.

The blue-eyed one asked, "If we help you, you walk away? No reports, no constables dogging our steps?"

"We've other things to worry about. Which way did he go?" Mikani asked.

"I promise," she added. "You have my word we won't interfere with your operation."

"She looks a trustworthy mort," one of them decided. "We need to get a move on, like he said."

"That way." The man standing on the handcar aimed his lantern down opposite the way they'd come. "Now get out of here before I change my mind."

It was quiet; Nuall's footfalls had died away during the argument. *I hope he hasn't gone too far.* If there were excess twists and turns, they had no hope of finding him. *Unless . . .*

Ritsuko pulled Mikani past the smugglers, onward into the tunnel. As they left the circle of lanterns, the shadows crept in again. After she put some distance between them and the men, she whispered, "Do you think you could . . . look for him?" *Up on the surface, probably not. Too much interference.* "You did it under the Royale when we were searching for Leonidas."

He hesitated for a second. "Yes. I can try, at least." He closed his eyes and tilted his head, turning slowly. He reached for her hand, as he took a few steps along the tunnel. "Don't let me trip, this place is . . . noisy. I won't be paying much attention."

"I won't," she said. "Just tell me left or right, if you know. I'll take care of the rest."

He squeezed her hand in response. "Straight ahead. I can taste the decay. It's faint, there's something . . . it's Nuall. The same buzzing as in his villa, somewhere up ahead."

Her pulse fluttered. She suppressed the urge to be impulsive— and kiss Mikani—because facing Theron Nuall might be the last thing she ever did. Instead, she pushed into a run, Mikani's warm fingers wrapped around hers. The weight of her gun in her other hand was reassuring, if not a guarantee of success.

We can do this. We must *do this.*

"To the right, coming up ahead, I think." She spotted an opening in the rock wall, and the passage sloped down. Mikani pressed her hand. "Here."

Ritsuko led him through; the way was narrower than it had been, a side channel connecting it to a different section. Her feet rasped over the stone, and in the darkness, she heard only her breathing, Mikani's, no sign anybody else had come this way. But she trusted him, so she pressed on until they emerged in a bigger tunnel.

"Is he close?" she asked.

"I believe so."

She took two steps, then glimpsed an ethereal light up ahead, raying out into the darkness; and in that eerie half-light echoed the terrifying sound of embattled giants.

CHAPTER 31

M ikani staggered. He held fast to Ritsuko, a dark wave washing over his vision. His temples throbbed, and the familiar warmth of blood rolled in a thick trickle off his upper lip. *I'll bleed at him if he gets too close.* He straightened as best he could. His breath rattled in his chest, and the pistol felt far too heavy in his hand. She drew him forward as the tunnel widened into a natural cavern.

Two figures were locked in battle, fifty feet away. Their growls echoed off the cavern walls illuminated fitfully by torches crammed into cracks in the rock. As Miss Wright had reported, massive talons sprouted from Nuall's hands, but . . . they did on his opponent, too. *Who the hell is that?* The blows they exchanged were quick and ferocious, slammed and blocked almost before he could see where the strike would've landed. Beneath the throbbing of his head, he was tempted to shoot them and sort it out later. *But if they're both prone to ignoring bullets, I'll have them both on me.*

Mikani moved a bit closer. He recognized Nuall, but the other man, the one determinedly trying to kill him, looked familiar, too. He crouched, watching them until he realized, *What*

the . . . ? That's Mr. Gideon from the Royale. Then Nuall landed
a blow that rocked his opponent; he pressed the advantage into
a ferocious choke. The other man stumbled back as something
pinged on the ground; and his whole appearance . . . shifted.
He'd never seen anything like it, but the man looked nothing like
Mr. Gideon, and quite a bit like Theron Nuall.

Two bogeymen, no wonder we couldn't catch him.

Deeper in, he glimpsed the low brass gleam of the machine.
It had extra components around it, unlike any of the others; an
array of gears and chains hummed in constant movement around
a gleaming cylinder that shone with its own light. The smaller
device was connected with pipes and wires to a slim, vertical
tube with a faint seam that revealed where it opened. Since Miss
Wright was nowhere to be found, she must already be inside it.
He didn't feel steady enough to run in just yet, so he said to
Ritsuko, "See if you can get her out of there. I'll cover you if
they turn your way."

She nodded and slipped along the edges of the room, keeping
well away from the fight. His partner was smart; if there was a
way to liberate Miss Wright without alerting the juggernauts
currently locked in combat, she'd find it. Once his head settled,
he moved forward, too, but he used the rock face and the bulk
of the machine to keep the two from spotting him. He wanted
to be close enough to help if Ritsuko needed him.

A low snarl of pain indicated one of them had struck a powerful blow. Mikani heard the snap of bone as Ritsuko inched forward. She twisted the latch and pulled the door open. A mountain
of dirt nearly crushed her; she tumbled back, and Mikani pulled
her out of harm's way. *That's why I'm here.*

"I've got you," he whispered, hands on her shoulders.

She was breathing fast. Silently, she nodded as she slid forward, boots sinking into the loose earth. *The grave smell.* He
remembered the other inspector's choked words. *This is what
Cutler was trying to tell me.* With her hands, she dug into the
remaining dirt, freeing Miss Wright's upper body. Mikani leaned
close to see if the woman was breathing, and then he heard it, a
shallow gasp, so faint as to be almost imperceptible. The woman
was pale as death but not there yet.

"She's cuffed." Ritsuko's voice was a low thread of sound.
"Help me."

Mikani knelt next to her, checking the iron restraints around Miss Wright's wrists and ankles. "Larcenous skills. See?" The cuffs were of good quality, an older design. "Keep an eye on them. I'll be a minute. He set aside his cane and pocketed his sidearm to free his hands to work on the lock.

After Ritsuko edged to the side, presumably for a better view, he took his picklock kit from an inside pocket and set to work on the cuffs. Miss Wright's trembling, his shaky hands, and the dancing lights made the process far harder than it should have been. It was almost a full minute before the first cuff clicked open, but it was faster going for the other three. The woman tumbled out of the restraints and into his arms; it was all Mikani could do to catch her. Ritsuko hurried over to him, adding her strength to the mix.

"We have to get her out of here," she murmured.

Nodding, he shrugged out of his coat and wrapped it around Miss Wright's shoulders. With Ritsuko's help, he carried her toward the arch leading into the tunnels. But it was impossible for three people—one of them largely unconscious—to be as quiet as they had been coming in. He didn't look back though he heard a murderous exclamation.

"We can't carry her fast enough to outrun them," Ritsuko said.

"Lay her down. Make sure she's breathing well enough. I'll cover us." He spun.

The Nuall look-alike ran toward him with an expression of pure rage distorting his features. Mikani brought up his gun, braced, and fired twice, aiming for the man's chest. The bullets slammed into him. Unfortunately, they didn't slow him down. *Well. This might be a problem.* Theron Nuall hit the other man from behind. Mikani swore and did his best to cover the women with his body as they barreled past them.

On the ground, Miss Wright choked and spat mouthfuls of dirt. She rocked onto her side, her whole body wracked with coughing. Ritsuko patted her back, looking terrified in the low light. The other woman grasped his partner's hand.

"Theron . . ." Miss Wright gasped. "Came later. Tried to help. The other one . . . Mr. Gideon! He said he's tracked me for months . . . I'm *not* mad. But I never had a chance."

"I understand," Ritsuko said. "We'll take him down." She

stepped up beside Mikani, her weapon in hand, so that they formed a barrier in front of Miss Wright.

"I hope you have a plan."

Like the other sites, there were herbs scattered around the perimeter. Mikani wondered at their purpose, but perhaps it had to do with a summoning ritual. He watched the two struggle, Gideon—or whoever he was—slamming Nuall against the rock hard enough to rain debris on them. *They're blocking the way out . . . and it's unlikely they'll let us take the girl and go.* Beside him, Ritsuko took a deep breath, then nodded.

Before she could elaborate, Nuall stumbled back, the other man's claws sinking six inches into his stomach. Then the look-alike spoke for the first time, his tone mocking. "It feels better than I expected. You've had this coming for centuries. Brother."

Hells and Winter. I hope no other family shows up to this reunion.

Blood and breath trickled out from Nuall's lips before he pushed out the words. "I never wanted to hurt you, Lorne. Only to . . . stop you. Even after what you did to . . . Galene."

As Nuall dropped to his knees, Miss Wright pulled her trembling body up and wrapped an arm around him. She whispered, "I'll get us out of here. I'll call for help."

Five minutes ago, Mikani wouldn't have guessed she had the strength to stand, let alone crawl, but somehow, she was pulling Nuall to his feet, his arm sealed across his stomach to hold his guts in. The man was disfigured with bruises, but like Miss Wright, he moved when the alternative was dying. They were a formidable pair.

At the same time, Ritsuko backed into the cavern—and Mikani saw how the killer's attention was split; he apparently couldn't decide whether to finish the two creeping away or go after those heading for the cavern. His face was a mask of spattered blood, thwarted ambition, and madness. Dark, glittering eyes cut between his intended victim, his brother, and the two of them. Mikani could imagine the killer's thought process: *Those two won't get far. They're too badly hurt. And I can finish these others quickly.*

Then Ritsuko raised the stakes.

She called, "Mikani, if I disable this machine, he won't be

able to do whatever he intended. I'm not an expert, but pulling out these pipes and wires should do some damage, right?"

Ritsuko, you beautiful genius.

Beneath Lorne's roar of rage, Mikani heard Nuall and Miss Wright stumbling in retreat. He ran into the cavern, with Lorne coming behind him like a railcar; he used rocky outcroppings to keep the monster off him. He'd seen enough of the fight between Nuall and his brother to know that he and Ritsuko didn't have a chance in straight hand to hand, and bullets hardly seemed to bother Lorne at all.

That's it. Going forward, I'm having cold iron bullets fashioned for my gun. And silver bullets: better safe than sorry. Wonder if that would help. But until the upgrade, we have to fight smart.

A thunderous blow slammed into the stone between them, and it crumbled as if it were made of spun sugar. Mikani didn't wait to see how that would work out. He hoped the bastard's hand hurt like hell. He kept moving though he was already tired, running toward the murder machine, where Ritsuko was pulling at the parts with all her might.

"Need some help, partner?"

Her smile was weak, halfhearted, and worried. But she had bravado to spare. "I thought you'd never ask."

RITSUKO DIDN'T EXPECT to come out of this alive. She had a number of regrets, but if they could buy Miss Wright and Mr. Nuall enough time to get to safety, then it would be worthwhile. The maniac charged, his hands lengthened into monstrous claws, his face twisted and smeared with blood. At the last possible moment, she threw herself to the side and his claws sliced into the device.

"I will enjoy gutting the pair of you," he snarled, as she scrambled to her feet.

Keep moving. Even with him hurt, all it'll take is one hit, possibly two, and you're dead.

"Why don't you use your magic on us?" Mikani taunted him from the other side of the machine. "There's a reason you're stealing from these girls. Can't do it like you used to? You're

probably getting old." Her partner grabbed a handful of wires
and yanked, kicking the side of the cylinder to rip them loose
with the screech of tearing metal.

Lorne spun and swiped at Mikani, the claws slicing the air
near her partner's face as he dropped back. The killer chased
him, shaking the ground as Mikani dove and rolled. Uneven
footing helped; Lorne's taloned feet slid with the rasp of claws
on stone.

Her partner laughed as he scrabbled on the ground, heading
away from her and the machine. *He's crazy.* Ritsuko wasn't sure
if she meant Mikani or the other one. Gun at the ready, she
scanned her target from head to toe. *Mikani shot him in the calf.
Is he limping at all? And then he took two more rounds earlier.
He should be bleeding more.*

No matter how strong an opponent was, a bullet in the brain
had to slow it down. Taking a deep breath, she braced the revolver
on her forearm, sighted, and fired. Between the flickering lights
and Lorne's movement, she nailed him in the neck. He rocked
back, blood bubbling from the hole. *No exit wound. It's like he
has reinforced skin.*

"What the hell are you?" she muttered.

The shot drew him away from Mikani, so she ran. For a few
seconds, she considered continuing into the tunnels, but he would
probably double back, and she couldn't leave her partner to deal
with the maniac alone. Her feet slid in the loose stones and she
ran up a rock formation close to the ceiling; it formed a half
ledge around the room. Spinning, she fired four more times as
Lorne came up the slope, this time aiming for his kneecaps.

*If I can't kill him, I can slow him down. We just need to buy
some time.*

Two of the shots struck; the others pinged off the stones.
Lucky they didn't ricochet and kill me. Dark patches bloomed
on his left leg; before he could reach her, she leapt down and
darted away, putting more distance between them. Mikani was
pounding the hell out of the device. At this point, it would probably take days, not hours, to repair the thing. When the killer
seemed to realize as much, he screamed, more in rage than pain,
she suspected.

One shot left. Doubt he'll give me time to reload.

Lorne dropped from the ledge with a groan. Apparently multiple bullets in the knees hurt, at least a little bit. *But it's not nearly enough.* He paused, rotated his leg, and then bent; she couldn't tell what he was doing, but she used the moment to dig into her coat pocket. *Five more shots. Which I can use to further annoy him.* With efficient motions, she fed the bullets into the cylinder, then rolled it.

The killer pressed his palm to the seeping wound on his throat, blood slipping through his fingers like butchered meat, and he was smiling. Then a soft light gathered beneath his palm; she'd rarely seen magic done, but Ritsuko had no doubt she was witnessing it now. Without Mikani's extra senses, her impression was of an imminent lightning strike, raising the hair on her arms and the nape of her neck. Shivering, she took a step back.

"Do you see how futile this is?" he snarled. "You're wasting my time."

Primitive dread washed over her; for a moment, she truly wanted to drop to her knees, like the force of his will could force her to obey. Despair followed, so that her knees trembled. A whimper escaped her; she tightened her fingers on the gun, but it was pointless—

"I agree. So surrender, before you make me angry. The commander hates it when I drag creepy old corpses back to HQ." Mikani's voice disrupted the frozen feeling.

She pushed out a shaky breath, unsure whether she was steady enough to shoot, but there was no choice. The chances were excellent they'd die in a few seconds. Lorne was healing himself and regaining some strength, whereas she had no ideas left. There were a few things she wanted to say to Mikani first, but overall, it was probably best to go quietly. Well, in the sense that she wouldn't get emotional first, anyway. Ritsuko didn't plan on dying without making the monster pay for every wound she took.

"What now?" she asked her partner.

Mikani bent to retrieve his walking stick, still propped against the open cylinder. He was breathing hard, with blood, dust, and sweat smeared over his face. And he was grinning. "Well, hell. You heard me. Now we kill him. Maybe we can beat him to death with the glowing cylinder. Looks like it's about to fall off."

"What is that thing anyway?"

"If I had to guess? The battery Saskia mentioned. Looks like the ones that the Academy tried to build."

"Then maybe I have an idea," she said. "It's suicidal, and we'll probably all die. But the important word there is *all*. Are you in?"

"Your last idea was to get the monster to chase us. How much worse could it be?" Mikani tossed his pistol down to grab his walking stick in both hands.

She dug into her jacket pocket and handed Mikani the silk-wrapped charm. "You're better with this sort of thing I am. Do your best."

"What're you—"

She cut off his question with an adamant shake of her head. *No time. But there are so many things I wish you knew.* Ritsuko skimmed her partner head to toe with a wistful glance, then moved into position, drawing the knife from her boot. The light was dying from beneath the killer's palm; he looked strong. Invincible, even. When Lorne dropped his hand, the wound was gone, just a bloody swathe of skin. He bared red-smeared teeth and rushed, talons extended to gut them both.

Closer. Closer.

"Now!" she shouted.

Mikani hurled the charm straight at the madman's chest; it hit him with an actinic flare and a dull shriek. Lorne seized for a moment, unable to strike while he clawed at the metal charm stuck to his chest and burning with acrid smoke. She took the opportunity to drive her knife into the glowing cylinder. The stored power sailed up the blade like lightning, pulsing through her body and exploding out the top of her head. Three walls cracked; the ceiling gave way, rocks and dust tumbling down from above. The whole cavern trembled, and Ritsuko flew back in a cascade of sparks.

Her vision swam, stones spinning amid black and white flecks. Her whole body burned as if she had been set on fire, roulade instead of a human being. The tumble of stones continued, landing all around her; and she couldn't crawl away. Nearby, her partner was on the ground, too, but she couldn't go to him. None of her limbs would respond, and her eyes teared, filling with dust. She blinked them ferociously as Mikani staggered to his feet. *Not dead. He made it.* Gladness and relief poured through her.

He took a step toward her. *No, don't worry about me. Finish this.* But she couldn't speak. Then Lorne stirred. With a growl, her partner unsheathed the slender blade hidden in his walking stick. A brutal kick spun the killer to his back, then Mikani slammed a booted foot into his shoulder. Slow blink, leaving the cavern fuzzy. Dirt clung to her lashes. The world went distant as the monster lunged, swiping at Mikani's leg. Sound of pain. Then her partner sliced downward in a fierce stroke, cutting clean through the thing's neck. The head rolled away in a spray of blood.

Hurts to breathe. But at least I watched the bastard die.

CHAPTER 32

AURELIA FELT AS IF SHE WERE DYING—WEAK, SHAKY, AND
beyond horror.

Her lungs burned with grit, and her throat was sore from the
screaming. Endless hours; and Lorne had let her wail until he
apparently couldn't bear it anymore. Then he'd lashed out with
fist or boot to silence her. With each blow, she yielded a little
more hope that anyone would ever hear her.

The last time, she'd thought, *I'll die alone.*

But being buried alive had been the worst part of that infinite
hell, feeling the earth trickle down, chained up, and unable to
save herself. Heart hammering, she tasted dirt on the tip of her
tongue, deeper still, as if no water could wash her clean. It would
make her feel better if she'd killed the bastard, but she hadn't
possessed the coordination to fight after Inspector Ritsuko
opened the machine. It had been all she could manage to help
Theron to his feet; now she could barely keep sliding her feet in
the forbidding darkness. Each movement nearly made her feel
that her knees would buckle, and her muscles wobbled like
blancmange.

"I can't," she gasped.

"You have to. You're saving me."

"Did I promise that?"

"You implied it."

Needles pricked her skin all over as circulation returned. She rubbed her forearms, trying not to yield to the panic threatening to swamp her. *I almost died. I don't know the way out.* Her feet were still numb, no sensation at all in her toes. Strange, just the sense of weight.

Conversation will surely help.

"What do you think that noise was?" she asked, referring to the explosion that had rocked the tunnel a few moments ago.

His voice rasped with pain, but he was already moving better. Only cold iron could do him permanent harm. "If I had to guess, the inspectors found a way to detonate my brother's machine."

"Your brother," she repeated, numb.

It wasn't a question, but he seemed to take it as such. "My goal has always been to keep Lorne from hurting people. He wasn't always like this . . ." He trailed off, probably guessing she didn't want to hear excuses.

But she was curious, and answers would take her mind off this crushing weakness. Her limbs felt as if they weighed half a ton; each step was a miracle. "Who was Galene?"

"Our sister," Theron said softly. "Lorne killed her when she took a mostly human husband. He felt she should seek to strengthen our line, not dilute it."

Bronze gods.

"I'm sorry for your loss.

And other things.

Theron went on, "We fought. And I . . . crippled him. Quelled his magic so he would be limited in the harm he could wreak. For a long time, he was in exile."

"Where? The Winter Isle?"

"No. In the world beyond the dreaming sea."

Aurelia sucked in a sharp breath. Unlike most, she knew the truth of the place; she realized it was more than legend. Once she knew of her father's role in closing the door, it was impossible for her to pretend it didn't exist.

"He returned in the last crossing?" she asked.

His hand sought hers in the darkness, lacing through. It was better than an arm around her shoulders. "I don't know. I presume so. I felt flickers of him from time to time, but it was only when he activated the first machine that I felt his old magic."

"You said you hurt him. Is that why he killed those girls? To get his power back? And what did he plan after he had it?"

"I don't know. Nothing good."

A thought occurred to her. "But . . . he saved me. I knew him as Mr. Gideon. Worked with him at the theater. The night I was running away from you, I nearly stepped out in front of a coach, and there he was, pulling me to safety. Why would he do that when he meant to kill me later?"

Theron sighed. "It sounds perverse, but that's precisely why. He had plans for you. Therefore, you were only permitted to die on his schedule."

"That's . . ." Words failed her. "I did sense him, following me. It made me worry I was going mad."

"If I'm sane, then I suspect you have a few good years left."

"If," she murmured. But it was good to know she hadn't imagined the feeling, and that she could banish the fear of losing her faculties.

Their footsteps rasped in the dark, every inch taking them farther into the labyrinth of the natural caverns aligned to the underground. It would be a miracle if she could find an exit. At least Theron wasn't leaning on her so heavily; in fact, he was lending *her* more support, which meant his wound was closing.

It occurred to her to ask then, "Why did you leave? In a few moments, you'd have been strong enough to fight again."

He hesitated, then said, "To get you away from there."

She actually stopped for a few seconds. "You wanted to protect me that much?"

"Yes." An unadorned answer that lacerated her with guilt.

"I owe you an apology," she said quietly.

"For spying on me, trying to have me arrested, and eventually making me a wanted man, so it was nearly impossible to find my brother in time?" His tone was grim.

Oh, how she wished she could see his face, but the darkness made her bold. "Obviously. But also because I misjudged you badly. I couldn't conceive why you seemed interested in me. I was sure you had shady, secret motives."

"Everyone has secrets, Aurelia. Mine was this—after so

many years of tranquillity, my brother's power spiked high enough for me to sense what he might be doing. So I went to see your father because—"

"He has a hand in all emerging technologies, all innovations," she finished. "You wondered if he might be running an experiment?"

"I hoped so. Hearing that would've been a relief . . . I *wanted* to be mistaken. We met at the club, and afterward, I was pacing in the maze, trying to calculate how to stop Lorne before he did irreparable harm. And that was when I met you." With gentle fingers, he tilted her chin up. "There *was* no calculation in that, Aurelia. I liked you. That's all."

"And I made a complex game of something so simple." She closed her eyes with a weighted sigh, feeling both chagrined and stupid. "I am too much my father's daughter."

"At first, I didn't mind. Your determination to unearth my secrets was amusing. But after a while, it became . . . inconvenient."

"I'm so sorry," she said again, as she resumed progress along the tunnel. "But you must admit, the pieces aligned too well. It wasn't all my wariness and tendency to think the worst. I saw you kill four men!"

"Four men who were hired to murder me by a criminal who didn't care to honor the compact his predecessor had made."

"You could've disarmed them and turned them over to the CID. So don't tell me you didn't enjoy it. I *saw* you. And before that, you made yourself so mysterious, so enigmatic—"

"To *tease* you, not to terrify you." Theron sighed. "It was private family business . . . and I didn't know you well. You treated our courtship like a game, and it's been years since I cared enough to play."

Immediately, Aurelia cast back over their interactions and saw that he was right. There hadn't been a moment where it made sense for him to lay everything out for her. "I never gave you the chance. I was too afraid of letting you matter because so many men have pursued me for my father's favor."

He growled, "When I saw what he'd done to you, I wanted to *kill* my brother. Before, I'd only ever thought about stopping him."

"I don't think I deserve that."

"Don't you understand? It's not as though I could help it. It was instinct. And it's been *so* very long since I felt territorial about anything other than my garden."

The stress he placed made her ask, "How many years? Don't tell me you're a lost full-blood Ferisher prince."

"Half." He took a deep breath. "Do you have any notion how many years I've guarded this secret? In prior ages, I was hunted like a dog."

Before she could reply, she heard footsteps behind them. Aurelia tightened her fingers on Theron's, whispering, "Is it—"

"No. He's gone." His tone was stark, awful because he probably mourned the monster who had shared his blood. His memory was likely long enough to recall the sweet moments before the madness.

"Then they killed him," she whispered in amazement.

"Miss Wright? Mr. Nuall?" Inspector Mikani called quietly.

She nodded, then realized he couldn't see her. "Yes. Are you well?"

"Bit knocked about, and my ears are humming, but my partner's worse." Fear and tension laced his words, perceptible despite his attempt to sound collected. "There should be one turn, then a passage leading up."

"If you know the way, lead on," Theron invited.

Inspector Mikani pressed ahead; and as he passed, Aurelia made out the woman cradled in his arms. She followed as quickly as she could, for the inspector set a grueling pace. Some distance on, she spied the glimmer of multiple lanterns.

Mikani muttered, "If it's those damned smugglers again, I'm killing all of them."

She had no doubt they all looked like survivors of a particularly brutal war, but that awareness didn't stop her from breaking into a stumbling run, for the men holding the lamps were Olrik Guards, led by her father himself.

"I must apologize for not arriving earlier," he said in his dry tone. "But it took me some time to acquire the information I needed to locate you." Then he jerked his head at two of his men. "Secure the site. Recover all artifacts and components—we can't allow scavengers to carry off any of the detritus. And you, collect the body. Mr. Nuall will want to inter him."

Though it had been years since they'd spoken, he had neither changed, nor aged. In the glimmering lamplight, he looked the same, dark hair just touched with silver at the temples. His face was immutable. It spoke to her state of mind that she felt happy to see him. She went into her father's arms like a child, fully prepared to endure any lecture.

He caught her to his chest and hugged her fiercely. "You're unharmed?"

"I'd be lying if I said I wasn't frightened. And weak. But I hope there was no permanent damage. I'll . . . survive."

"You'd better. Your mother would never let me hear the end of it, otherwise. She's quite annoying enough as is, about our little disagreement." The Architect held her, released a long breath, and stroked her hair as he spoke. "I do wish you'd told me. I could have done . . . any number of things. You think I don't respect your wishes, but I never want you to feel as if asking me for help is a fate worse than death."

"I'm glad you're here. Thank you." She dropped her gaze, unable to face Theron, who had, in fact, been trying to protect her.
I misunderstood everything.

"I hate to break up this reunion," the inspector said, "but I need to get my partner to a hospital. Either help me do that or get the hell out of my way."

Her father gestured. "This way. I know a shortcut. We'll take a private car directly to the stop closest to St. Freya's."

"That's more like it," Mikani muttered.

It didn't take long for her father to escort them back the way he'd come, considerably shorter and less painful than being dragged over the rocky ground. Her back was a mass of bruises, not to mention the blows to the head she'd taken. And she felt so shaky, as if she hadn't eaten in days. Theron took hold of her hand again as they stepped onto the car waiting beyond the access door.

One of the guards touched the rare, privately owned mirror, and sacrificed a breath to activate it. *Of course Father has all the expensive conveniences.* He used the bound air elemental to notify station authorities to clear the track. Passengers on other platforms wouldn't understand why this sleek car went zooming by, throwing off their schedules, but it was a House perk.

Aurelia sank onto a seat, grateful for the respite. Across the way, Mikani reeled onto a bench, looking filthy, battered, and exhausted, but he didn't lay his partner beside him, as he could have. His arms were like bands around her slim form. The guards remained standing, while Theron settled to one side of Aurelia, and her father, the other.

To them, she murmured, "I made a number of mistaken assumptions, for which I apologize again. But I'm surprised the two of you are old associates."

"Not in the way you suspect," her father said. "Perhaps I should have taken the matter more seriously when Theron came to me. If you must know, I thought age madness had driven him out of seclusion, making him imagine improbable threats and conspiracies where none existed."

Her truth-sense should've kicked in, but . . . it didn't. Likely because of whatever Lorne had done to her in that hellish machine, she could judge only by the remorse and self-recrimination on her father's face. *How . . . odd.* But she didn't doubt he wished he'd focused his resources on the danger before it yanked her out of CID custody, before the bruises and the terror. Remembered impotence boiled up inside her like a sickness.

"I made mistakes, too," she said quietly.

He kissed her lightly on the temple, then stared hard at Theron over her head. "If I see any signs that you have . . . ambitions like your brother, I'll come, you understand." He scowled and added, "For that matter, stay away from my daughter."

Aurelia coughed, partly because it was so typical and partly because she had earth in her lungs. To her surprise, Theron made eye contact with the Architect. "Aurelia can make up her own mind, I think."

She liked that fearlessness about him. So few men could stand up to her father's ire or walk away from the prestige and power he could bestow. Curiosity rebounded; before, she had taken Theron's interest for a game, one he hoped would end in some boon from the Architect. *But I got it* so *incredibly wrong.*

"Yes," her father said wearily. "She can."

It was more than he'd have granted before. In his eyes, there was a sharp awareness that he might've lost her for good—that their estrangement might have become permanent before he could mend fences—and the realization that even the long-lived didn't possess infinite quantities of time. Aurelia smiled at him.

Theron shifted, taking her hands in his. He was still darkly fascinating, powerful, and ancient. *His brother tried to kill you,* a warning voice said. There were no guarantees that this would end well. *And that's what makes it so exciting.* But she couldn't assume he was interested in taking up where they had left off, after the night in his garden.

"I have to let my family fuss over me at the hospital and have a physician look at my injuries. Perhaps you'll call on me later?"

"Are you asking to begin our courtship anew?" His tone gave her no hint as to his reaction to that suggestion.

"Is that what it was?"

His eyes were grave. "Yes. It's an old-fashioned concept, I expect. But I understand if you wish to see the last of me, as I can only remind you—"

"No," she interrupted. Just that.

Let him make the next move.

And he smiled. "I'll come with you to the hospital."

In the public wards, it was pure confusion, with physicians, surgeons, and nurses dashing everywhere. House Olrik could expect a better standard of treatment. Her father escorted her off to the pricey private wing before she could protest that she wanted to thank the inspectors who had saved her life. But she'd underestimated her father. As her mother rushed down the hall toward them, he was making arrangements to foot the bill for the best possible care for the CID employees, Mikani and Ritsuko. That permitted her to sink into the wheeled chair with a relieved sigh.

Aurelia's mother was a tall, slim woman with autumnal hair and hazel eyes. Kneeling, she hugged Aurelia despite the dirt, eyes damp with tears. "I was so worried I'd never see you again. Come home, darling. I promise I won't nag or complain about your ties to the theater. Leo's here, and—"

As if she'd summoned him, he came down the hall at a run. Leo wasn't wearing his mask, like it was the least important thing in the world, and he wrapped his arms around her. "Auri. I'm so sorry. I thought you'd be safe with the CID. If I'd had any notion they wouldn't be able to protect you, I'd have—"

"Stop. Nobody could've predicted what happened. We believed we were doing the best thing at the time."

"If someone had bothered to give me a hint before it all blew up, *I* could have predicted it," her father muttered.

Then Leo kissed her full on the lips with both her parents looking on, something he had *never* done. Behind her, Theron made a sound in his throat; and she drew back.

Bronze gods, not this. Not now. She was too exhausted and sore to deal with territorial males at the moment.

The nurse said softly, "I need to get the patient into the exam room. The doctor will be along presently to assess her condition and recommend treatment."

Aurelia gazed up at her father. "We have to tell them exactly what happened . . . or they won't be able to help me."

She glimpsed ambivalence in the green eyes so like her own. He didn't want to discuss magic or murder machines with the medical staff, but they would be well compensated for their discretion. And this weakness wasn't going away. She'd expected a little rest to help, but so far, it hadn't.

"You may be right," her father said. "And we need more than a physician. I'll bring in a specialist."

Someone who knows about magical illnesses, I hope. The ritual had stolen something from her—*and my truth-sense doesn't work any longer.* Aurelia said as much, though obliquely since she didn't know the nurse well enough to be open about her former gift. For the first time, the fear dawned that this malaise might linger forever, a result of whatever Lorne had done. Aurelia knew of people who sustained permanent injuries and never recovered. *Look at Leo.* She had a friend who had been caught in a fire, breathed in too much smoke, so she was broken thereafter, unable to catch her breath.

Aurelia refused to spend the rest of her life as an invalid, reliant on a strong man's arm to keep her upright. She had never heard of an ailment like this one, but surely there must be something they could do—some innovative treatment—to restore the strength to her watery limbs—

Oh, bronze gods, no. I might never dance again. And if that's true, she thought in despair, *better if I had died in that infernal device.*

CHAPTER 33

SHE LOOKS SO SMALL.

Mikani shifted away from the windowsill. The bandages on his back were itchy, and his entire right side throbbed through the pain medication. He limped over to the bed, leaning on what came to hand to keep weight off his injured leg. Though it took all his combined obstinacy and charm, he'd refused to let the doctors banish him to a separate room, barely allowing them to stitch the long gash Lorne had cut from knee to ankle.

I should send someone to look for my stick. When he'd feared the cave would collapse, he'd abandoned it to save Ritsuko. *Sorry, Dad.* It took all his strength to hobble out of the cavern, stumbling down the dark tunnel until they'd caught up to Wright and Nuall. *Half feared the bastard would get up, pick up his head, and come after us.*

He glanced down at his partner, running a fingertip along the line of her jaw. *Still, I'm up, hurting but here. And they can't bloody tell me if she'll wake up.* Her eyes were closed, her lashes dark against her pale skin. *Hells, they can't even tell if she'll live.* He clenched his fist around the metal rail of her bed to stop the trembling of his fingers.

I should have been the one to blow the device. Then she wouldn't be in that bed.

Mikani sighed and cupped her cheek. "Stubborn woman. I'm supposed to be the reckless one. And there's no way in hells that you're sticking me with explaining all of this" He leaned in, pressing his lips to her forehead. "Don't you *dare* die on me, or I'll find a way to hunt you down and bring you back. I . . . need you, Celeste."

He straightened when he heard footsteps at the door, and wiped at his face with a bandaged hand. "Come in," he said, as someone knocked softly at the door. "But you bloody better have good news, or some whiskey if you don't."

Gunwood stepped in, his face tired. "How are you, Mikani?"

The old man's probably been up all night, dealing with the details.

"You know me, can't get rid of me . . ." He stopped, the other man's mood drifting to him. *Hells. He's concerned, too.* "I'm worried as hell, Commander." He glanced over at Ritsuko. "She won't wake up. We don't know if she's going to make it."

"I came by to tell you two that commendation is going through as we speak. But I hope they don't have to award it to her posthumously. What've the doctors said?"

"She suffered some cuts and bruises, nothing major. They can't figure out why she's still sleeping; they found no sign of a head injury." He made a vague gesture to a low copper tub in the corner. "They even tried the chalice. Olrik paid for the elementals. All her cuts and scratches are gone . . . but she still won't open her eyes."

"Damn. Take as much time as you need. I've got things in hand down at HQ. Though . . ." Gunwood hesitated as if he felt like an arse for what he was about to say. "I could use a firsthand account of what happened."

Mikani nodded absently. *It will be something to do other than stare and try and remember how to pray, anyway.* "Very well."

He gave a brief rundown of the last couple of days; from the time they'd gone to arrest Theron Nuall to the death of his brother, Lorne, in the cavern. "Olrik's men arrived . . . and we came here. He gave orders to secure everything. If you have more questions, you'll have to take it up with the Architect."

"That's some first-rate investigation," Gunwood said.

He actually sounds . . . approving? Mikani couldn't be sure, as he'd never heard quite that tone from the old man before.

The commander went on, "If you need anything, either of you, let me know."

"We will. And . . . thanks for stopping in, Commander."

I hope this doesn't become customary. I couldn't deal with a pleasant Gunwood, day in and day out. Now he has me waiting for the other shoe to drop.

Visitors trickled in throughout the day. A woman from filing stopped by, two more people who had worked in the clerical pool with Ritsuko, years past. None of them stayed long, but they mentioned being fond of her and brought small gifts—a tin of sweets or a potted plant. Mikani found dealing with them a test to his patience. *Ritsuko would want me to play nice. Hells.* He greeted them, promised to relay their best wishes, and tried not to ignore them too pointedly until they hurried out.

He was standing at her side, holding her hand, when the door opened again. ". . . leave the flowers, come on in." He did not look up until he heard the familiar voice.

"You look like hell. Or, more to the point, more like hell than usual. Like you really *tried*, this time." Saskia padded in, carrying a small box. Her hair was tied back, and she looked genuinely concerned as she came up to lay a hand on his shoulder.

He glanced down. "You're wearing slippers."

"Idiot. Don't get used to it. They wouldn't let me in without them." She studied Ritsuko, setting the box down on the bedside table. "I won't stay long. I wanted to bring you that . . ." She nodded at the parcel. "It might help. It won't hurt, anyway; it's just a little charm for attracting good health."

I've had enough magic for a few lifetimes . . . "I—"

"I promise, it's nothing strange." She squeezed his shoulder. "Have faith, Janus. For her, if not me." She pressed a kiss to his cheek, before heading for the door. ". . . and shave, man. Get some rest and find clean clothes. For *all* our sakes." She flashed him a smile before stepping out.

It was the longest night of his life. He ate Ritsuko's dinner, as she didn't stir to touch it, and at one point somewhere between midnight and three, her breathing went soft and shallow. *Don't die, don't die.* Mikani jerked to his feet, ready to get the physician, but . . . she rallied. Exhausted, he sank back into the chair, head against the leather. Nurses tiptoed in and out, checking on her regularly, but they seemed baffled as to what treatment might help.

This just hurts too much.

In his darkest moment, he delved into his jacket and found his last two Dreamers. Right now he needed to be numb. Needed not to feel *this way*. Mikani didn't mean to sleep, but days of snatched naps and long hours caught up with him.

THE LAND BLEEDS.

Summer and Winter are broken in the iron of the invader's blades, but their numbers are dwindling, too. When magic and immortal clash against might and ferocity, everyone dies. The world dies.

"No," says the Summer Lady. "There is a way to save us."

A procession of ragged survivors meet in a green vale. Princes and princesses from both courts are offered to the invaders. Only a union of two disparate warring peoples can save them from extinction. Days pass; the arguments rage, but in the end, the Winter Lord agrees.

The Iron War ends in sacred vows and a mingling of blood. Music and revels abound where there had only been death and destruction.

"There will be peace," says the Summer Lady.

"But at what cost?" the harlequin asks.

NEXT THING MIKANI knew, it was daybreak, the sun creeping over the windowsill to paint shadows on the floor. His eyes felt gummy; he pushed out of the chair to stretch. *Hells and Winter, what a dream.* For the first time, he realized the visions came strongest after he'd taken Dreamers. Maybe he ought to have made the connection sooner. *An interesting reaction to an unpredictable drug.*

As so many times before, his gaze cut to the slender figure in the bed. Who was watching him.

"Good morning." Her voice was a raw rasp.

The distance between them disappeared. He didn't notice he was hugging her until she exhaled against his chest. Easing back, he left one hand on her arm, the other sifting through her hair in reflexive strokes.

"I . . . About time you stirred. We've paperwork piling up, you know." He cleared his throat as a knot threatened to form.

"I'm a . . . little surprised to be waking up at all." Her eyes didn't hold a teasing light.

She felt bird-light in his arms and fragile; he'd never thought of her that way. Ritsuko had such force of personality that you didn't look at her and see a small woman. *Seems she's always been at my side. Never realized she could be taken from me.*

"You had me worried sick."

"I *did* warn you it was a suicidal plan. It worked, didn't it?" She seemed anxious. "You killed him?"

"You knocked him out long enough for me to finish him."

He wondered if she knew what she was doing when she rubbed her head against his palm, eyes half-shut. Her head probably hurt, though he wasn't certain why she had been unconscious for a day and a half.

Damn Lorne and his murder machines.

"The Reinert girl . . . and the other one on the list. Are they both safe?"

It was so like her to ask that, first thing. Mikani nodded. "Lorne never got to the last one, and we saved Miss Reinert. She's recovered and home with her family."

She pushed out a soft breath. "Good. Then it's worth it. But . . . bronze gods, I've never felt this bad. Could you get me some water?"

In response, Mikani slid off the bed and poured a glass from the pitcher nearby. "Here. Should I order you something to eat?"

"I don't think I could just yet." She sipped, her lips cracked and pale. Even now, she looked like a ghost to him; it was hard to believe she was awake and talking. When she looked up at him, her eyes were vulnerable. "This will sound stupid, but it's like I was set alight inside my skin. Was that . . . magic?"

He sat at the foot of her bed. "I've no idea. The whole cave felt wrong to me, but when you destroyed the device, the world burned with cold fire."

"I expected to earn a hero's funeral. Now . . . I just don't know. And I'm afraid—" Her voice broke. She took a breath, then continued, "Is there any precedent for what we've done? Any way to predict the consequences?"

"Right now, I don't give a damn about the consequences. You're alive, that's what matters." Mikani slid up and wrapped his arms around her, pulling her close.

I won't lose you.

TWO DOCTORS EXAMINED her; they took the better part of three hours, checking various vital signs and murmuring to each other. If Ritsuko hadn't felt so shaky and nauseated, she would've protested more. Before they got started, she'd sent Mikani home to bathe and sleep though she had no confidence he would do the latter. Then the nurses insisted she eat a bowl of broth, which was more exhausting than it sounded. She wasn't ready to go back to sleep, but her body insisted.

Callers continued to pour in, Miss Wright and Mr. Nuall among them. Ritsuko found the chat with the latter particularly enlightening. To her surprise, she also entertained the patriarch of House Aevar. The Architect stopped personally in to give her a formal marque of appreciation. They all expressed gratitude for her courage. Though she wasn't sure if she deserved the accolades, she took pride in them. *Not bad for a woman they promoted under extreme duress.* The staff had a hard time keeping journalists away, though. More than once, a nurse marched someone out of Ritsuko's room in response to her bell.

Later, Mr. Higgins visited, his freckled face drawn. "I brought pastries from your favorite shop if you feel up to eating them."

"Possibly tomorrow. It's been a rough day."

"So I understand. You and Inspector Mikani are in all the newssheets though some versions of the story seem rather . . . outlandish."

"What are they saying?" she asked, amused.

"In the seedy one, they claim you stopped an invasion of underground dwellers."

Ritsuko laughed. "Not exactly."

They chatted awhile longer, but she guessed Mr. Higgins could tell she was tiring, as he stood with a smile. "I won't keep you from your rest."

As he went to the door, it opened and her partner pushed

inside. His shoulders squared when he saw Higgins. The two men exchanged a few words and did an awkward dance so that Mr. Higgins could depart, then Mikani came over to the bed.

"What're you doing here? I thought I told you to get some sleep."

Even his smile looked tired, but at least he'd cleaned up. "You tell me many things. If I started listening, you might worry."

There was no point in arguing with Mikani, so she didn't even try.

"True. I hate hospitals." She closed her eyes, shutting out the sight of him.

He'd gained a hungry edge to his wolfish look, new lines about his eyes. They had always been an odd shade of blue, too dark for her to name the hue. Now they seemed layered, as if he no longer saw the world as she did, as if the magic she feared had changed him, too.

"Is the last time—"

"Yes. When my grandfather died." Others might find their verbal shorthand confusing, but it was reassuring they could still *do* that, when so much else had changed.

"I've been thinking," she said.

"That never ends well."

"I'm serious. Remember where we got the lead to investigate Gregory Toombs?"

Mikani looked puzzled, then the answer came to him. "Mr. Gideon . . . Lorne came down to HQ with a tip, as I recall."

"Doesn't that seem odd? Why would he report his own accomplice?"

He thought for a few seconds. "Possibly the city was getting too hot to maneuver, and he thought offering us a suspect to chase would grant the time he needed to finish his grisly work."

Ritsuko nodded. "As good a guess as any. I suppose we'll never know."

Mikani spent the night in her room—and he was there every time she woke up. Once, from a bad dream, another just because she'd been sleeping so much that her mind thought it was beyond time to get moving again. In the small hours, they talked. He tried to make her laugh. And with only periodic absences for food or hygiene, he stayed until she convinced the doctors to release her, two days later.

Ritsuko was relieved to see the hospital doors close behind her. No matter how luxurious—and it was good care with Olrik paying for a private room—it still smelled of antiseptic and the masked odor of illness. Mikani opened the car door for her and helped her in; if she wasn't still a little shaky, she'd have grumbled.

It wasn't until he turned the cruiser toward the Mountain District that she realized he didn't have her new address. "No. I'm closer to Central now, just outside of Temple."

He angled a look her way. "Since when?"

"I told you I was moving." She remembered that night well; Mikani had teased her two or three times about them setting up housekeeping in his cottage. Usually she enjoyed his sense of humor, but that memory carried a bit of a sting, as she sometimes imagined coming home to him for real.

"I thought you were joking," he said.

"No, turn here."

He followed her directions, then parked at the curb before the rooming house where she'd rented a suite. It was warmer than the flat she'd left behind, with a building full of people with whom she shared a bath and regular meals. Though her hours meant she didn't always get to eat with them, she enjoyed having the option when her schedule allowed. People fussed as Mikani escorted her up the stairs, and the woman who owned the house wouldn't go away until her partner leveled a dark look on her.

"Don't frighten my neighbors," she chided. "I have to live here."

"It's . . . not what I'd have pictured for you."

"I like it. And it's closer to work." She'd managed to move that last morning before everything exploded, the day he commented she had arrived late.

"Cozy." He wandered through her flat, touching knickknacks here and there, probably because she'd never had any before.

It's . . . nice, having him here. I shouldn't get used to it.

"Thank you. I'd offer tea, but I've been ordered to rest."

"I'll make it. I know my way around a kitchen better than you do anyway." He went into the kitchen, and the cheerful sound of clinking china reached her ears.

Ritsuko laughed, as it seemed unlikely, but after visiting his place, she knew it was true. "So how long do we have before we resume the madness?"

"Gunwood's giving us a full week, provided the rumor of an underground invasion continues to prove untrue."

"You read that, too?"

"It's the most entertaining of the theories." A few moments later, he emerged with a tray, tea and sandwiches.

"But I haven't been to the market in . . ." She trailed off, unable to remember.

"Seems your landlady likes you . . . and stocked your larder."

"I'll have to thank her." Ritsuko bit into a cheese-and-cucumber sandwich and decided it was the best thing she'd ever tasted.

Across the sitting room, Mikani settled into a new armchair. *I bought that because I imagined he'd like it.* The strange feeling persisted, growing into an ache. She wished he reached for her now as easily as he'd done when she was in the hospital.

But no. Things must return to normal. And I'm the work woman.

But she remembered, then, the other errand from that morning before. "Hold on. I have something for you." Mikani protested, but she was strong enough to go into the bedroom and bring back a black box. "Open it."

"Ritsuko . . . ?" But he did as she asked, and his expression was appropriately delighted when he drew out a smart bowler hat, a fair replacement for the one he'd lost. "I can't believe you remembered."

"You're not the same without it," she said, easing into her chair.

"Thank you." Then he went on, "I'm glad this business is over, and we can put it behind us," he said, fixing her a cuppa.

Oh, Mikani. I do so wish that were true. The moment was so peaceful, she hated to bring up all the inconsistencies she'd considered in the hospital. But in time, she was sure they would occur to him as well—and he wouldn't thank her for being reticent. *Not where the job's concerned anyway. He gave me such a stern lecture over Toombs's model, I can't withhold this.*

"Not just yet, I'm afraid," she said.

Mikani raised a brow. "Why not?"

"It takes someone with a lot of resources to operate in Dorstaad with CID and House blockades in place. *How* did Lorne manage to move his machine after the Summer Clan shut the city down? He had to bring it in from that farm, outside the city limits." She shook her head at the impossibility of it. "There's only one way he managed."

"Which means one of the Houses. You're saying Nuall's brother had a patron."

"I've been over it and over it in my head. Nothing else makes sense."

Her partner jumped from his chair and paced a tight little circuit to the window and back. "Why? What's the point?"

"I talked with Theron Nuall one afternoon while you were gone. His brother was stealing Ferisher power by killing those girls, trying to heal a wound. Lorne had more power once, I gather. I'm not clear on the details, but Lorne thought once he was whole again, he could call back the fey spirits who have faded and reshape the world."

"So he was trying to open a doorway of some kind?"

"Perhaps. But I believe someone *wanted* him to make that happen, or he wouldn't have gotten as far as he did." Saying the words aloud sent a chill through her.

This makes it real.

Mikani's blue gaze met hers, so very grave. "Someone powerful."

"Yes. And that person is every bit as responsible for the murders."

"Who stands to benefit?" he asked. "I doubt it's one of the four principal Houses, as they like the world the way it is."

She set down her sandwich, not hungry anymore. "Those are questions we'll have to answer. The person responsible must know we won't stop coming until we do. If I'm right, we'll face strong opposition from the highest levels. Beyond the Council, though we might be able to count on some support from Mr. Olrik. If we pursue the matter, it may mean our careers. Are you with me on this?"

He took a step toward her, his expression enigmatic yet beautifully familiar. "Always, partner."

About the Authors

A. A. Aguirre is the pseudonym for Ann and Andres Aguirre, a husband-wife writing team. She specializes in compelling characters; he excels at meticulous world-building. By day, she's a *USA Today* bestselling novelist, and he is a pharmaceuticals tycoon.

Born in Mexico, Andres spent his early years traveling and getting in trouble everywhere else. Along the way, he got a degree from Pepperdine in economics and international business. Ann was born in the Midwest and has a degree in English literature from Ball State. She's traveled less than Andres and gotten into less trouble, but scaling Machu Picchu should count for something, right? Now settled, if not fully domesticated, Andres lives with his love, Ann, their fantastic kids, and various pets.

Together, they form Megatron. Or not. Actually, they write books.

From *USA Today* Bestselling Author
ANN AGUIRRE

The Sirantha Jax Series

GRIMSPACE

WANDERLUST

DOUBLEBLIND

KILLBOX

AFTERMATH

ENDGAME

Praise for the Sirantha Jax series

annaguirre.com
facebook.com/Ann.Aguirre
facebook.com/AceRocBooks
penguin.com

M1208AS1112

From *USA Today* bestselling author
ANN AGUIRRE

The Corine Solomon Series

Corine Solomon is a handler. When she touches an
object, she instantly knows its history and sometimes
its future. Using her ability, she can find the missing,
which is why people never stop trying to find her....

Blue Diablo
Hell Fire
Shady Lady
Devil's Punch
Agave Kiss

annaguirre.com • facebook.com/Ann.Aguirre
facebook.com/AceRocBooks • penguin.com